THE
WOBBLE
CLUB

SIMON RUMLEY

First published in Great Britain in 2023 by
Simon Rumley, in partnership with whitefox publishing

www.wearewhitefox.com

Copyright © Simon Rumley, 2023

ISBN 978-1-915635-54-9
Also available as an eBook
ISBN 978-1-915635-55-6

Simon Rumley asserts the moral right to be identified as
the author of this work.

While every effort has been made to trace the owners
of copyright material reproduced herein, the author
would like to apologise for any omissions and will be
pleased to incorporate missing acknowledgements in
any future editions.

Designed and typeset by Typo•glyphix
Cover design by Dan Mogford
Project management by whitefox
Printed and bound by CPI Group (UK) Ltd, Croydon CR0 4YY

Dedicated to anyone who's ever tried to lose weight . . .

CHAPTER 1

The day started like every working weekday; at the shrill behest of Brolly's 7.45 a.m. alarm. The noise pecked his skull and drilled into his consciousness. He itched his nose on the KitKat pillowcase and wiped his eye mucus onto the Freddo duvet. He scratched his cheek, dragged his left arm above his head and dug his right arm under his belly. With capillary-bursting effort and an extended elephantine grunt, he pushed into the heavy-gauge bedsprings and leveraged his body onto its left side. He dropped onto his back and used his weight's momentum to roll onto the other side of the super-king-size bed, which, with its reinforced and melded mesh base, was designed, like everything in Brolly's life, for the obese.

He rested on his right flank as he wheezed and caught his breath. He stretched for the phone and stopped the alarm. Its intrusive digital piercing was replaced by the seamless fade of aeroplanes' secret greetings. He swivelled his cracked, swollen feet, his ankles barely discernible, to the edge of the bed, ripped back the duvet and pushed against the mattress with guttural wrenching. His frame extended in a diagonal line from shoulders to legs as his stomach engulfed his thighs and dropped halfway to the floor. He didn't like the uncontrollable pull of flesh and groaned, rubbed the soles of his feet against the solace of the shagpile carpet, offered a message of consolation to the rest of his suffering body.

Upright, he punched his right thigh and kneaded its subcutaneous knots. His heart pounded and his lungs flapped. He squeezed his legs together and, like an oversized testicle, cupped his stomach from below, moved it onto his lap. He opened his legs and leaned forward as he let it slip, inch by inch, to the floor. He released his hands, inhaled a deep breath and heaved upwards so that he stood, finally, fully erect, his head woozy from the effort.

In his self-designed British Racing Green dressing gown, he hobbled onto the landing and made a beeline for the filing cabinet that nestled in the corner diagonally opposite. A six-slice family toaster stood on top of the cabinet and on top of that rested an oat-coloured plate, two dirty knives and a half-consumed bag of sliced white bread. Next to the toaster, on the right, lay butter and jars of Marmite, marmalade, raspberry jam and peanut butter. Brolly grabbed two slices of bread, crumpled one into a ball, shoved it into his mouth and spread the other with butter and marmalade. After he devoured the second slice, he grabbed six more and dropped them into the toaster before sidestepping to his right.

He knocked gently on the door like always. He waited courteously for a response, which he never received. He wiped a marmalade globule from his lower lip and entered. Gill always slept on her back, mouth wide open, her snoring interminable, pulmonary rumble in, apocalyptic road drill out. Not that this was the reason they no longer slept together (that was because no bed was sufficiently large or strong enough to support them both), but Brolly was glad he didn't have to endure the disturbance on a nightly basis – an ungodly noise that would surely top the CIA's annual torture playlist at Guantanamo Bay.

Brolly took Gill's hand and watched her with love: her plucked eyebrows, her ski-jump nose, all her chins. She muttered unintelligibly and stopped snoring. Stopped everything. Brolly's wheezing, a wild animal sleeping deeply, filled the silence before schoolchildren gurgled outside. 'Gill . . .' he whispered. 'Gill?' She didn't answer. He froze. Assessed her danger. No rapid eye movement, no heaving of mountainous chest, no random twitching. Time trampolined in front of him. Did a somersault. And then a double flip. He grabbed her shoulder and shook it gently. 'Gill!' He concentrated on the lack of movement in her upper torso. He gripped her upper arm and shook it harder. 'GILL!??' With a panicked start and a sword's slash of air, her body wobbled. Brolly jumped. The toast popped. She coughed. He involuntarily sucked in a small kangaroo pouch of her musty bedroom smell. She greeted him with a winning smile.

'Hiya . . .' she croaked with a languorous, deep-sea trawl.

'You OK?'

'Bit tired but yeah, why?' The fillings in her teeth shone as she yawned.

'I really think you should see the doctors.'

'What for?'

'Your breathing.'

'Oh, for God's sake! I've just woken up.'

'Yeah, I know, but, you know . . . breathing is quite important.'

'Best way to go, in your sleep . . .'

'Not when you're thirty-four.'

Gill shook her head, snarled like an Elvis impersonator without a building to leave.

'I'm hungry. Let's talk about this another time.' Gill's indifference kneecapped Brolly's worry. He knew he was fighting a losing battle, that he'd never persuade her to do anything she didn't want to do. Her nose twitched, sniffed in staccato bursts. 'Smells good.'

'Come on then, let's get on with it.' Brolly staggered to the bottom of Gill's bed, also designed for the obese. She closed her doughy legs but even with her thighs squashed together, her two feet remained two feet apart. She kicked them from underneath the duvet, groaned and panted as she pushed her arms into the mattress and struggled to sit up. Brolly grabbed her legs, lifted them into the air and swivelled her to the side of the bed nearest the toaster. He let go of her legs and grabbed her hands. She focused, inhaled confidently, and after a mutual glance, a balletic nod, pushed as he pulled. Pain strangled her intestines, stabbed at her shins, ground her hip bones and, with noises befitting a zoo, she stood up.

After he buttered the first two slices of toast, she layered them with jam on peanut butter and munched both with unassailable vigour. The third she spread for him, also jam on peanut butter, and fed him as he prepared the remaining slices. She lacquered the next two with marmalade on Marmite and ate one herself as Brolly snatched the other from her clutches. Although she had every intention of giving him the final slice, an every-woman-for-herself fog clouded her generosity and she devoured it aggressively.

Brolly slipped another six slices into the toaster as Gill hobbled to their specially installed bariatric bathroom, which both agreed had been a worthwhile investment; getting stuck in showers and baths and falling off toilets was no fun for anyone. It hadn't come cheap, but after Gill's Aunt Violet's unexpected death almost a decade ago and her equally unexpected will, which designated Gill as sole beneficiary, not only could Gill afford it but she could also afford to eat whatever she wanted, whenever she wanted it. The almost 2,500-square-foot Victorian terraced house off the Walworth Road, on the Kennington side towards Camberwell Green, had five bedrooms, of which Gill and Brolly only ever properly used three, so the conversion had been an easy decision on every level.

The extractor fan rumbled as Gill clung onto one of the room's many grab rails next to what had become, by default, a decorative loo roll (they'd been using the same one for almost three months

4

now) and lowered herself onto the toilet. She took a deep breath and pushed until her face turned cherry-tomato red. Guttural snatches of concentration punctuated her effort, along with a large gush of urine.

'Any luck?' Brolly shouted.

'Not so far . . .' she muttered.

'When's the last time you went?' He sauntered in and handed her three slices of dripping toast.

'Monday, I think.'

'This Monday just gone?'

'Monday before that.'

'That's almost two weeks!'

'Yeah. What about you?'

'Tuesday.'

'This Tuesday?'

'Yeah.'

'Not bad!' It was Friday; only three days ago. Gill hid her jealousy well.

'Yeah, I was pretty chuffed. You gonna try again? Third time lucky?'

'Nah, it's hurting a bit. Think I'll just have a shower.'

'Maybe we should get you some more of those laxatives?'

'I'll be fine.'

Brolly had had enough problems down there to know that irregular bowel movement was not fine. Not for anyone or anything, least of all for Gill and her anus.

The shower's downpour momentarily deafened Gill. She looked like an amateur disco dancer practising bad moves as she kept repositioning herself to keep warm under the spray. Brolly squeezed an antifungal shower gel into an exfoliating mitten and lathered it. She closed her eyes and splashed her face as he followed in small circular motions with the mitten. He cleaned her skin, all of it. No pound left unturned, no intimacy unexplored, no fold insanitary. Her chins, her bulging neck, her bony shoulders, her sticky armpits, her pendulous breasts, deep into the layers of her tummy and below to just under the knees. 'All done?' Gill asked after he'd washed and rinsed front and back.

'Almost.' Rogue suds slipped under a nipple-less breast-like hanging, below the back of her ribs. He tried to lift the hanging. It slipped out of his grasp. He grabbed it more assertively. His grip tickled. She shivered.

'What you doing?'

'Hang on . . .' He aimed the nozzle and sent most of the suds packing, but a few slithered down the crack between her buttocks. He grabbed Gill's left cheek, squeezed it as if testing the fullness of a football and moved it to one side. Her haunch contracted involuntarily and she giggled.

'Brolly! What're you doing!?'

'Just getting rid of all the soap.'

He paid similar attention to drying and moisturising Gill and to cooking their daily breakfast, which was always a variation on a theme: the Full English. Six rashers of bacon, four sausages, four medium eggs (scrambled or fried), four slices of toast, a tin of baked beans, a tin of tomatoes, a tin of mushrooms and deep-fried chips. Each. Sometimes more.

After waving Gill off to work and cleaning up the kitchen, he hunched over the confectionery cupboard. Stocks were depleted, but they were always depleted on a Friday. He grabbed a packet of Haribo Tangfastics, a tube of Pringles Originals, a five-pack of Curly Wurlys, a solitary Twirl and a packet of Starburst chews. He bent his left arm across his belly and entrusted the confectionery into its nook.

He wobbled along the hallway and salivated as he debated which to eat first: chocolate, he decided quickly, but a Curly Wurly or the Twirl? There were five Curly Wurlys but they were wrapped within wrappers wrapped within a wrapper and fiddly to open on the move. The Twirl was an easier proposition and always burst like a pure adrenaline rush in the mouth. But there was only one, and eating it first was like a band opening a set with their most popular song: not a good idea. Brolly squeezed into the stairlift, which they'd installed at the same time as the bathroom. He strapped the safety belt underneath his belly, twisted the dial to minimum speed and pressed the start button. He opened the Curly Wurly five-pack and pulled out the first bar. He tore that open, stuffed the bar into his mouth and tasted his childhood. He finished it halfway up the stairs and started on the second Curly Wurly.

He ate the third while dressing and started on the Pringles immediately after. He loved Pringles. Admired the uniformity of their curve, their USP that elevated them above other crisps, which were shoddily made, crinkled or overly geometric, unequal in size, calloused in comparison.

As he brushed his teeth, he saw a human football with squashed, stray-puppy eyes in the mirror. He wasn't sure what had happened to his chin, how many he now had. He attempted a smile but looked like a neurotic pufferfish without the stubble. It wasn't a good look. He opened the Tangfastics, fed the different shapes into his mouth like coins into a slot machine. He watched himself with morbid fascination; more and more coins, a game he'd never win, a game he'd always lose.

The second flight of stairs to his office at the top of the house was too small to justify another stairlift and as his stomach had expanded over the years, so his breath had shortened. He crashed into his bariatric office chair and was overcome with lashings of disappointment, stabs of self-disgust. How long did a packet of Tangfastics last normal people, he wondered? An hour? A day? A week? His packet had lasted under four minutes. He hadn't even appreciated the subtle flavours, the different textures, the fizzy tang. Couldn't remember discerning the sweets' individual and carefully thought-out identities. His life felt meaningless. He glared at the remaining confectionery as if trying to incinerate it with disapproval. He picked up the Twirl and tried to throw it in the wastebin, but it stuck to his hand. He did love the semi-metallic midnight-blue wrapper and all that it teased. He ripped it apart, stuffed the first finger into his mouth; demolished it before regretting his boldness. Without further ado, he threw the rest of the packet and the remaining confectionery into the bin.

'Ha!' Self-control was great, self-flagellation productive, self-denial to be encouraged. A halo hovered above his head like a large Polo mint. He opened his computer and started on his work emails. Inspired by a three-piece suit, part Scarface, part Savile Row, which his best friend Tiny Tim had brought back almost eight years ago from a trip to Thailand, he'd contacted the tailor, Bangkok Dave (real name Bhumibol Sripariyattiweti) and ended up commissioning a one-button two-piece for himself. After a glut of compliments, he had a 'Eureka!' moment and decided to set up Suits You, Sir!, a bespoke business offering tailored solutions to the paunchy fop. No size was too big, no design too fantastic. Through word of mouth and expert customer services, a sustainable, web-based business was born and boasted clients from all over the world.

Less than a minute and a half after he opened the first email, his self-control jumped off a cliff. He picked up the bin and rummaged through it. The Curly Wurlys were easy to rescue, as was the Twirl, which he ate immediately. Waves of compressed chocolate unravelled in his mouth, sent bursts of ebullience, telegrams of cheer to his furthest reaches. He devastated the Curly Wurlys with similar vigour. Sticky dregs of phlegm desecrated the Starburst packet, which had fallen to the bottom of the bin, but he didn't care; he ripped that open, poured the chews onto the desk and counted them. He arranged them in a straight line, colour-coding his least favourites first: three orange, two lime, three strawberry, two blackcurrant. He unwrapped the first orange sweet and ate it as he unwrapped the second one and ate that as he unwrapped the third. He did this meticulously until he finished the packet, which took under a minute. He clasped his hands together, rotated his thumbs around each other, knew he had no control over what he was going to do, hated himself for what he was about to do, encouraged himself to do what he was about to do.

Back downstairs by the confectionery cupboard, with eyes shut, he raised his arm as if it was a machine claw. He dropped it gently and lucky-dipped a Crunchie bar. 'Yeah, baby!' But as he jerked upright, he started to suck his cheeks and chew his lips. He admired the Crunchie's geometry, marvelled at its elegance, salivated over its honeycomb sweetness, but swallowed a shot of his own saliva and threw the bar back into the cupboard. He guffawed. Abstinence felt good. Abstinence felt like a million dollars. He left the kitchen.

But returned.

He gnawed on his thumb; it tasted of washing-up liquid and badly cooked human sacrifice. It started to crack, to bleed. He sucked the blood, drowned it in spit, opened the confectionery cupboard again, grabbed the Crunchie and devoured it. It wasn't good, it was great. It was all-conquering. It overpowered the tang of his blood. He rummaged around for another Crunchie, grabbed that, a four-pack of Picnics, a large sharing pack of Chilli Heatwave Doritos, some Fruit Pastilles, a Toffee Crisp, a Bounty and, from the fridge, a bottle of Lilt. He puffed his way back to his office and finally settled down to work.

CHAPTER 2

Butterflies scratched metallic wings against Brolly's stomach for reasons he subconsciously knew but had yet to admit to himself. The night tightened around him like a trench coat's belt. The street lights and traffic headlights attacked him with kaleidoscopic jarring. Raindrops meandered vertically along the outside of his mobility scooter's vinyl weather canopy, which had steamed up way before the Elephant and Castle roundabout. Now, as his journey approached its end, his vision became doubly impaired by the weather's torrential battering. He wiped the canopy's side as he pulled onto Southwark Street. A raging speed horn blasted to his right. Brolly's heart tried to escape its cage. Four tyres screeched to a slippery, sliding halt, a few spare ribs away from his flank.

'Watch yer arse, ya fucking Muppet!'

'Sorry, mate!' Brolly shouted as he rolled across the road and through the opposing, stationary traffic, into the relative safety of Borough Market. He'd heard worse. Much worse. He liked the Muppets, didn't mind being called one at all, and his critic hadn't cast aspersions on his weight, which made a refreshing change from the norm.

He pulled up next to Gill's mobility scooter. They looked like drenched baby mice huddled together for warmth and comfort. His legs felt more leaden than ever, his body less his own, his nerves more fractured for reasons he still couldn't pinpoint. The rain had turned a gaggle of high heels and lurid dresses into shimmering matchsticks. With heads bowed low, the iridescent tarmac was their mercurial guide for the night. He decided he didn't like being called a Muppet after all, wanted to avoid further jibes and furtive giggles, so remained static in his makeshift cocoon. Only after the matchsticks flickered by, after their high-pitched honks dulled, did he unzip his misted weather canopy.

He was hit by the benign one-two of human sogginess and alcoholic yattering as he pushed open the door to the Southwark Tavern. 'Alright, mate, wondering if we'd see you. Just on the way out!' It was Gay Keith, one of Gill's colleagues. A glazed grin flattered his weathered face, his omelette crewcut.

'Oh, 'ello! You off now?'

'Just heading into town.'

'Yeah, an' I'm his fag-hag for the night!' chimed Dagmara, a Polish colleague with a humorous post-office-red mullet. 'Gill's in the corner with Potatohead.'

'Where else?'

'Right!?'

Like a bomb-disposal expert edging through a field of landmines, Brolly navigated his way through the clamouring office workers and the wide-eyed tourists, their evening's receptacles and their weekend's plans.

'YAAAAAY!' Gill shouted as she spotted him through the crowd. She clapped and Potatohead, also a colleague, punched the air.

'Brolly! Brolly! Brolly!' He and Gill were on their way to tipsy and Gill had started to slide down the same corner she slid down every Friday evening. The table grouched in a mysterious shade, an antisocial gloom, at the opposite end of the pub, and was distanced from the other tables.

11

'Hello, lover!'

'Alright, lover? Alright, Potatohead?'

'Alright, Broll?' Potatohead flashed his crooked teeth, shook hands with Brolly. Gill held hers out and Brolly squeezed it.

'You drinking pints?' he asked her with a shot of wariness, a dash of surprise.

'It's alright.'

'You sure?'

'Potatohead's meeting his uncle at eight o'clock, up in Kilburn, so yeah, I'll be fine.'

'Yeah, can't stay too long,' Potatohead confirmed.

'Alright, well . . . if you're sure.'

'Fancy a drink, mate?' Potatohead asked.

'Didn't come here just for the craic! Get 'em for us, will ya? Take my card.'

'That alright?'

'Yeah, of course.'

'Start a tab?'

'You know it; double round all round.'

Potatohead took Brolly's debit card and bounced off to the bar. Brolly pulled together two wooden chairs and sat with one buttock on each. They'd been frequenting the pub for so long and on such a regular basis that, without having to ask, management reserved the same table for them every Friday, so it was worth the arse-splitting discomfort.

'Good day?' Gill asked.

'Yeah. Not bad. Nothing special. Picked up some packages from Bangkok Dave, sent them out, a couple up north, one to Malmo and one to Barcelona, so that was kind of exciting, and then, er . . . Yeah, just sent some fabric samples to a couple of new customers – well, potential ones, and, er . . . So yeah, not bad actually. How about you?'

'Well . . . Mr Carmichael bought me two burgers and two sticky toffee puddings for lunch. I think I had four pints an' we also shared half a bottle of wine, so that was a result!'

'Why'd Mr Carmichael buy you two of everything?'

'He wanted my advice about Harry's; he's thinking of selling it.'

'Oh no! Should you be worried?'

'Don't think so. He wants to pass it on to his kids and retire down the Costa del Sol, but they're not interested. His nephew was up for it but 'e got arrested for big-time possession, apparently.'

'What about his brother?'

'Stroke.'

'That's shit.'

Potatohead plonked the tray with six pints on the table and guzzled his in half an hour. Before he left, he paid for another round and some tequila shots and downed both in under five minutes. By then, most of the casual drinkers, the lightweights and family-friendlies, had also left. 'Think I gotta piss,' Gill said as Potatohead vanished from sight.

'Oh God. What? Now?'

'Yeah, if you don't mind. Had five pints already and been holding it in for the last ten minutes or so.' As if it were a mixing bowl, Gill stirred her hand around her courier bag. 'Fucking Tardis in here!' she exclaimed before extracting a vulva-coloured plastic receiver, a tissue and a shopping bag.

Brolly clenched his teeth as he laboured to stand up. He shuffled to his right and blocked as much of Gill as he could. He moved his pint glass, picked his stomach up, rested it on the table and leaned in to engage in a pretend conversation as she pulled her leggings over her thighs. In her right hand, she picked up the plastic receiver and fluffed its bag. She manoeuvred her left hand under her tummy's drooping folds and loosened her pants' gusset. Her eyes darted around with furtive angst, criminal intent; hoped not to be caught red-handed. She jammed the receiver against her privates, contracted her stomach and pressured her bladder. Her urine gushed and she shuddered with relief.

Brolly looked everywhere but at Gill, tapped his fingers against the table, slugged down the remainder of his pint, looked shiftily over his shoulders. 'Almost done,' she confirmed some seconds later as he ventured a glance and offered an English nod, embarrassed and half-hearted. She returned it with the hint of a smile, an acknowledgement about necessity being the mother of all invention and disposable urine bags being the mother of all necessities. She pulled the receiver away from her groin, inspected the contents and squeezed the bag, which had already hardened into a barely flexible gel. She hid it in the shopping bag, wiped the dribbles with a tissue and dropped that in the bag, too. She pulled up her leggings and thanked Brolly as she handed the bag to him.

He disposed of it in the men's under an orchestra of crumpled hand towels. Gill ordered eight pints, four honey and mustard crisps, two spicy Bombay mixes, two continental sharing boards, two pulled pork sandwiches, two bangers and mash, half a chicken, two chocolate brownies with salted caramel ice cream and, because they'd been so fresh and gooey that afternoon, two more sticky toffee puddings. And moments before the kitchen closed, she ordered a cheese board for each of them and a bottle of red wine.

On the way home, they hummed past solitary postboxes and lonesome trees, neglected cars and anonymous buildings, followed backstreet bike paths through Dickensian back alleys and became curious obstacles for late-night cyclists. They avoided the Elephant and Castle roundabout but passed its shopping centre on their left as Gill led Brolly down the uncharismatic ashtray of Walworth Road. Just after midnight, they pulled up outside King Kebab, the premises for which had never changed and looked like every other kebab shop in London. It was run by an older man with an eye patch and his various sons, nephews, cousins and compatriots. The old man didn't know Gill's or Brolly's name and they didn't know his, but their exchange had become a ritual over the years that all were fond of.

'I'll have two medium doners, please,' Gill would always say.

'We don't do medium doners, just small, large and extra-large,' the old man always responded.

'If you've got three, isn't the large one the medium one?'

'No, we don't do medium doners, the large one is a large one.'

'Alright, in that case I'll have two extra-large doners, please.'

'I think I'll just have a large one,' Brolly would contradict.

'I think that's a medium one.'

'No, they don't do medium ones. They only do small, large and extra-large!'

Gill and Brolly always studied the backlit menu that shone above the dripping, revolving double spit, but for all their outward show of contemplation, neither actually read it. They were like teachers trying to disguise favouritism for a pupil before picking him anyway. They knew exactly what they were going to order.

Or Gill did.

Or she thought she did.

Brolly snuck a glance at her, trying to gauge her mood, which thus far had been like a child's dinghy bobbing happily on a clear blue sea. He questioned his own resolve, his own bravery, poked his stomach, squeezed it with both hands. He glanced at a slumped City worker who kept trying to eke the last drops of beer from her bottle. She groaned. The groan conjured up unrealised potential and distracted Gill, who also stared at her. The woman looked offended by her kebab. Gill returned to the menu but changed her mind and returned to Brolly, who looked to the floor for inspiration, for courage, for truth. The truth was faded mustard in colour, scuffed, dirty, with cracks. Gill searched for the old man. Opened her lips. Gave birth to a noise that never matured into a word.

'I don't think I want anything, actually,' Brolly said in a tone not dissimilar to a young Oliver when asking for more.

'What d'you mean?' Gill asked.

The old man and his son cocked their ears.

'I think I'm . . . I'm a bit full.'

'What d'you mean?'

Brolly had never uttered anything so shockingly slimline in his life.

'I just . . . I think I've had enough for the day.'

'I don't know what you mean?'

'I just . . . I don't want any more.'

In the time it took Gill to process Brolly's words, a combative twinkle glimmered in her eyes and she turned to the old man. He stared at her, felt guilty for staring at her, wanted to avert his stare but also wanted to support her in her hour of need. For the first time in his life, he wondered if he shouldn't offer his loyal and trusted customers a medium-sized kebab.

'I'll have two extra-large doners, please,' Gill said confidently. The old man's jaw dropped a little. His son guffawed silently. Brolly tensed, bit his lip, pinched his stomach again, started to resemble an uprooted beetroot. He knew he had to man up quickly, to own the situation. He didn't like confrontation, least of all with the one he loved, but he'd just been slapped in the face by a wet kipper. And a large one at that; if the smell was unpleasant, the aftertaste would be worse.

'Gill! I said I don't want one!'

'Yeah, I know – they're both for me!' Gill flashed her teeth. The old man tried to stifle a titter but failed. His son accidentally spat gum into the tzatziki. The City worker stopped mumbling to herself. Two boiled-potato road workers at the end of the counter turned to ogle at Gill and for the second time, Brolly did his best to come up with a manly put-down.

For the second time, he failed.

Gill tried not to gloat, twisted her head towards the boiled potatoes, fluttered her eyelashes as one grinned at her with chilli sauce, winked at her with pickled-pepper salaciousness. She shone her teeth but returned to Brolly. 'You sure you don't want one?'

'I'm sure,' he mumbled, taking a sudden interest in his phone, which hadn't rung since Gill last called him two days ago.

'You OK?'

'Yeah, I'm fine. Just not hungry, that's all.'

The moon peeked from behind a curtain of cloud. It made their front door, which hung ajar, glow with an uncanny and deceptive luminance. As Brolly drove up the walkway to the front door, the kitchen light shone through the hallway's pitch blackness, not so much like an inviting beacon of conciliation but a blast of glaring defiance – come in if you dare. After finishing both kebabs, without exchanging a further word, Gill had rushed ahead on the road while he'd remained on the pavement and adhered to the slower 4mph speed limit. As he drove up the ramp into the house, the moon vanished and he felt like he was being sucked into a foreboding and unavoidable black hole.

The first thing he noticed was an opened tub of Ben & Jerry's Cookie Dough. It sat on the kitchen table, emptied and discarded. The second thing he noticed was Gill. Quiet, concentrated, scooping, licking, tucking into her second tub of Ben & Jerry's. They locked eyes. His subconscious emerged like a seven-headed zombie bursting from a dank cave. It growled, challenged him to be true to himself. To utter the thought he hadn't dared articulate to himself, let alone to Gill. It dared him to accept it. To share it with his love. To say it out loud. Those nine words that could change their life forever.

CHAPTER 3

'**G**ill, I think we should go on a diet.'

CHAPTER 4

L ike a rabbit caught in pinprick headlights, Gill went as frozen as the Phish Food she was digging into. Her hand resisted a lifetime's habit by not feeding the spoon into her mouth. Her jaw gaped in disbelief and caused her triple chin to collaborate with a hitherto rarely seen fourth. Her eyes darted erratically. She looked everywhere but at Brolly and did the only thing she could think of: pretended not to have heard him and carried on demolishing the ice cream.

Almost seductively, she felt, she slipped the holy marshmallow, caramel and chocolate trinity into her mouth and masticated, slowly, joyously, allowing an erotic dribble to highlight her lips and trickle suggestively down her chin. She didn't watch porn but she knew what porn stars did, albeit with other substances. She stuck her tongue out and swished it lasciviously around her lips. It left an insalubrious trail, which she wiped with her forefinger as if to convey a lurid proposition, a naughty position.

'Gill, did you hear what I just said?'

'Do you want some?'

'Did you hear what I just said?'

'There's a tub of Sofa So Good Together if you prefer that?'

'Why aren't you answering me?'

'Are you drunk?'

'No, I'm not drunk. Why? Are you?'

Gill pounced on Brolly's tactical blunder. 'A little bit,' she lied. 'And I'm tired, as well.' She peeked into the Phish Food; a smattering of caramel and marshmallow barely hid the tub's bottom. She corralled its remains and took one final mouthful. 'Think I'm going to bed now.'

Brolly tried to penetrate her soul, bored his eyes into hers, but she leaned forward and tangled his boring with a flourish of hair. He stepped back. She pushed in further. Their tummies caressed each other, two innocent children unaware of their parents' disruption. 'Night, night,' she said before kissing him. He felt like biting her tongue but bit his instead. Did he really mean it? Yes. Did he think they could go on a diet? Well, of course. Did he think they would go on a diet? Difficult question. If they didn't, would he go on a diet alone? Even more difficult. Possibly. Probably. Maybe. Perhaps. The idea seemed outlandish. Outrageous. Out of this world. It made him guffaw.

He ambled into the kitchen, turned towards the freezer. Opened it. Gill was right; there was an unopened tub of Sofa So Good Together. He ripped apart the circular plastic seal, tore off the lid, but hesitated, agonised over what it would be like to exercise more self-control. *Not very easy* was his conclusion as he sank his canines into the Ben & Jerry's. If there was any possibility of going on a diet in the near future, the chocolate brownie and cookie caramel ice cream, enhanced with salted caramel swirls, would surely make no difference at all.

The next morning, each listened to their separate, lonely breathing and the otherwise Saturday quiet. Brolly stared at his ceiling. Gill stared at her curtains. He mauled his lips. She picked her fingernails. A figure of eight wriggled in his stomach, a reef knot in hers. Neither had slept well. Both had woken early. Both had surfed on their phones, tried to go back to sleep but failed. A ringtone disturbed Brolly's fugue.

'Alright?' he asked.

'Bit of a throbbing head, what about you?' she replied.

'Yeah, something like that . . .'

'Just thought I'd see how you were . . .'

'Yeah, I'm fine, how are you?'

'I'm alright . . .'

'That's good.'

'Yeah . . . We should get up soon.'

'Yeah, I was just about to . . .'

'I was gonna bring you some toast but just woke up,' she lied.

'Oh . . . That would've been nice.'

'Yeah. Thought I'd surprise you.'

'But you didn't . . .'

'No . . .'

Uncomfortable pause.

'We should get up really.'

'Yeah, don't worry about helping me out of bed, I'll do it myself given time's on the short side.'

'Fair enough.'

'See you soon, then.'

'See you soon.'

A familiar vaudeville punchline rapped at the front door as Brolly puffed down the stairs. 'GIIIIIIIIIIIIIIIIIILL!?' She didn't respond so he called out her name more forcefully, more staccato. 'GILL!'

'Coming!' she screamed as he pulled the front door open.

'Alright, Rob?' he asked dispassionately.

CHAPTER 5

t was the late 1980s, Halloween, a Saturday night. Ghouls jived, wounds festered, fake blood and cheap alcohol did the twist. Wrapped in bandages, little Rob's mummy was a mummy. She wagged her finger at a green man. Draped in a black cape and with fangs, his dad leaned against a wall as a witch chewed his ear off. His uncle sported big fluffy sideburns and a furry face, flicked madly through a pile of vinyl stacked against a battered record cabinet. The living room hyperventilated as guitars escaped crackly speakers and a singer with a sandpaper voice screamed about unrequited love.

A stained white sheet with jagged holes for eyes flopped over Rob's body. Underneath, his face and hands glowed in the half dark with ghostly make-up. All spindly legs, buck teeth and inquisitive disposition, he teetered on a kitchen chair in the corner of the living room when the needle scratched the tailspin of the song and the dance floor ground to a halt. Friendly jeers and slurred cries tumbled off the walls as his uncle rushed to rescue the party. The needle jumped but the music kicked in and the room hyperventilated once again, shone with malodorous sweat. The new song seemed less tuneful than before, more jagged flick-knife. He slipped off the chair and extended his hands like extraterrestrial feelers as he weaved through the crowd and avoided a clutch of gyrating crotches.

In the dining room, a large man with silver skin and black Y-fronts leered at Rob as a Frankenstein creature wrapped his arms around two nurses and a housemaid beat a gorilla's chest. It was when a wizened old man with tangled grey hair and a rat on his shoulder brandished a bottle at Rob that his heart suddenly pulsated like a frog on a dissecting table. He snatched some peanuts and scurried out of the room.

He slammed shut his allocated bedroom door. He floated over to the TV, which was plonked on the dressing table by the window, and switched it on. It flickered before a speeding American police car blurred the screen. He tapped through the channels and stopped when confronted by a man who resembled his dad, or had similar fangs and cloak. The man walked elegantly, defiantly, down a narrow and deserted street. Everything was black and white. The man's heels clicked loudly on cobbled stones. His cloak slipped through the air, hovered above the ground. Rob turned off the light and retreated to his bed, grabbed one of the two pillows and stretched himself out, face down, along the crimson blanket. The blanket was cosy. Rob pulled it over his whole body.

His breathing calmed, his demeanour relaxed, his eyes drooped. He rested his chin on his knuckles and his head started to tilt. Just as he was drifting into a spectral state of semi-consciousness, the door opened and nearby braying, donkeys treading on broken glass, jolted him out of it. Sarah, his twelve-year-old cousin, a woman in his eyes, barged in. She'd replaced her Halloween costume with a pink nightgown that complemented her strawberry-blonde hair.

'What are you doing?' she asked, her nose stuck in the air.

'Watching TV.'

'I want to watch too.'

'OK.'

'I want to lie on the bed, you sit on the floor.'

'No, I'm on the bed.'

'It's my house, I can do what I want.'

'No, it's my bed and I'm lying on it.'

'No, it isn't.'

'Yes, it is.'

'Move.'

'No.'

'Yes.'

'No.'

Sarah sighed. Rob watched with quizzical gaze. She shut the door and stepped towards him. Her nightgown bulged in places it hadn't bulged until recently. The top few buttons exposed her slight but curving breasts. Rob didn't understand his fascination with them but was transfixed nonetheless. He swivelled onto his side and swooned onto his back. She towered over him like an Amazon. She lifted one knee onto the bed and straddled him with the other. His instinct was to cry for his mum but something deep inside, something primeval, disabled his tongue and all he managed was a whimper as she dropped onto him, flopped all over him. Their bodies bounced in unison, their hips ground together. Her right nipple poked his left eye, but she quickly jiggled her shoulders to nestle her breasts either side of his face. Rob fought his urge to protest again, to struggle, to scream, to slap. He waited for Sarah's next move, but none was forthcoming; her body traced his, hid it, remained static, on top of his. Dracula's victim pierced the air with second-rate screams as Rob rested breathless, flabbergasted, triumphant, confused, muffled, smothered by his cousin's femininity, her flesh's silky warmth.

A sense of belonging and connectedness overcame him, unlike anything he'd experienced in his previous nine years. Her weight was a sensual elixir from which he always wanted to drink, always get high on, always pass out from. Her breathing was a sedative he always wanted to ingest. The unpredictable nature of her slight twisting, her breathy turning, was a pressure he never wanted to let go of. He stretched his arms around her waist, clasped his fingers together and hoped his parents didn't burst in.

CHAPTER 6

'Alright, mate?' The years hadn't been so kind to Taxi Rob; he looked like a crack addict with an expensive hygiene habit.

'Hello, Rob!' Gill shouted more enthusiastically as she strapped herself into the stairlift at the top of the stairs. Taxi Rob bent to one side, crouched down, raised himself up on tiptoe, all to no avail; Brolly filled up the whole door frame and blocked his view.

'Hello, lovely! How are you today!?' he shouted over Brolly's shoulders.

'Ready to rumble!'

'That's what I like to hear!' Taxi Rob guffawed. 'Know what you're gonna have?'

'I think I do, but I'm not gonna tell!'

'Little tease!' he said knowingly as he smirked at Brolly, who forced back a grin. Many years ago, if Brolly's biology teacher had told him that, one day, he'd have his very own symbiotic relationship with a 35-stone woman and a 5-foot-4 taxi driver, he would've burst into tears. He really didn't want to have a symbiotic relationship with Taxi Rob.

'What about you, mate? Know what you're gonna have?' Taxi Rob asked with genuine interest.

'Not yet, not yet, haven't thought about it. You?'

'Probably just my usual.'

'Well . . . it is your usual.'

'Don't fix it if it's not broken.'

'Don't eat it if you don't like it.'

'Wise words,' Taxi Rob added charitably as Brolly decided the conversation had floundered sufficiently to step outside.

Trees lined the Camberwell Green back street. The sun shone like a con artist pulling off a convincing scam. A hippie cyclist with loudspeakers and a baby box at the front shot by. Taxi Rob's Viano pulled up on the pavement. The queue outside Bellybusters – the frivolous fry-uppery, the ball-breaking, tummy-teasing greasy spoon meets eccentric eatery – was too small to be shambolic but too hungover to be orderly.

After helping Brolly and Gill out of the Viano, Taxi Rob drove off in search of a parking space. Gill and Brolly were lurching, not towards the back of the queue but to its front, when a familiar movement, a clandestine pointing, caught Gill's eye. 'Oi, mate! You takin' photos of us?' The queue, which had been eyeing her and Brolly with a morning-after-the-night-before incredulity, froze. The guilty millennial, his skull a few centimetres short of Tefalhead status but decorated with an anomalous chin curtain, stuck his phone down his drainpipes.

'No,' he squeaked in a voice higher than he would have liked.

'Show me your phone,' Gill demanded as she waddled towards him, and Brolly shook his head, uncertain in that split second if his disdain was directed at Gill or the almost Tefalhead.

'No.'

'So you were.'

'No.'

'Did you take a photo of me?'

'No!'

'Can you ever say anything apart from "No"?'

27

'Is that a trick question?'

'Do you feel tricked?'

He did, actually, and Gill saw his pallid, freckled mask crack as his mates, a bunch of adders, glistened with delight at his imminent humiliation. Gill suddenly realised the power she held over him, the kind sociopaths spend weeks and months cultivating. She couldn't deny it felt good, practically godlike. 'So you weren't trying to take a photo of me?'

'No.'

'Why not?'

'Sorry?'

'Why not?'

'What d'you mean?'

'Why weren't you trying to take a photo of me?'

'Erm . . .'

'You think I'm embarrassed by the way I look?' Gill demanded.

'No.'

'Exactly; I'm not, I love the way I look. An' I like to be noticed when I go out and, in fact, I get quite upset if people don't notice me. I mean, I know they do notice me, so I get even more upset when they pretend they don't. Like yeah, right! You blind or what? D'you see what I mean?'

'Erm . . . I think so . . .'

'So basically, if you weren't taking a photo of me, I'd ask that you do. And if you were, I'd ask that you take some more where you're actually looking properly at the composition.'

Like a teenage delinquent who'd narrowly escaped the attention of a priapic master, the almost Tefalhead did exactly as he was told. Brolly shuffled out of the frame and scoured the road for Taxi Rob, who was taking longer than usual to park. With trembling hands, the almost Tefalhead pulled his phone out of his drainpipes. He snapped away as Gill pouted. The queue watched with a finger-twitching, memento-making curiosity, which slowly morphed into a tea-spilling fear of missing out.

'Can I take a selfie with you?' the almost Tefalhead asked, his freak back on, his forehead possibly growing. Brolly reacted with a smirk, a sigh, a shake of his head, a slanting of his eyelids.

'Course ya can, mate!'

The almost Tefalhead leaned into Gill as she weighed her hand around his scrawny shoulders. He shrunk the best he could but failed to fit both of them in frame, so asked a mate to oblige. The mate did so without irony and asked the same question. As did the rest of the mates and half the queue until Brolly finally stepped in, her celebrity minder, and ushered her towards the main event.

Inside Bellybusters, a sibilant coffee machine spurted out syrupy cappuccino. Waitresses glided in and out of tables like ice-skaters. A cloud of Saturday-morning leisure dawdled in the air and everything smelled fried, even the furniture. 'Be with you in a minute, mateys!' shouted Steve the owner, as he segued from dining area to counter to kitchen in one easy slink. He sported a quiff that looked like it had been ravaged by an infestation of moths. Gill and Brolly looked at each other. Their eyes locked. He offered a mawkish grin. She, a conciliatory smile. He fumbled for her hand. Her heart skipped a beat.

'I'm sorry . . .' he said.

'What for?' she asked.

'Oh, you know, last night.'

'What're you talking about?' she asked disingenuously.

'You know . . . the kebab . . . And, you know . . . what I said afterwards . . .'

'Oh . . . yeah . . .' Gill hoped the ground didn't swallow either of them up.

'I didn't mean to upset you and . . . I dunno . . . I guess I was just tired . . .'

'It was a bit of a shock . . . But . . . hey, we were both tired and drunk and we're both here now, so let's forget about it.

I already did,' she lied, and kissed Brolly's hand.

'Can we just try an' have a nice weekend, please?' Brolly asked as he reciprocated the gesture.

'I'd like that.'

'Me too.'

'That's good, cos I was thinking maybe we should finally try the Quadruple Full English?'

'You serious!?'

'Deadly!'

'Bloody 'ell!'

The first part of Bellybusters' tabloid-baiting, common-sense-defying Quadruple Full English was a traditional Full English. Exactly what Gill and Brolly ate every weekday morning, without such generous portions but with black pudding.

The second part was a Vegetarian Full English, which included all the non-meat products from the Full English but replaced the pork sausages with vegetarian ones, the bacon with halloumi and the black pudding with avocado.

The third part was the Full English Pizza, which was exactly as it sounded: the Full English but served on home-made 12-inch pizza dough with mozzarella.

For professional eaters like Gill and Brolly, the first three parts offered no real challenge, but the reason they'd never tried the Quadruple before was because of the fourth part. The Full English Smoothie. Which was also exactly as it sounded; two sausages, two rashers of bacon, two slices of toast, scrambled egg, baked beans, mushrooms, tomatoes, chips, black pudding. And a cup of tea. All blended together.

The café erupted into a carbuncle of phones as Steve carried four pints of sludge towards Gill and Brolly's table and sported a demonic smile that looked like it had been tattooed by the Devil himself.

'Sure you wanna do this?' Brolly asked.

'What are we? Mice or men!?'

Brolly wasn't sure they were either, but said nothing as Steve lifted the Full English Smoothies onto their table.

'Good luck, Gill!' the almost Tefalhead shouted from the other side of the café. His sidekicks wolf-whistled and cheered. Gill looked over and raised both thumbs.

'Got any spirits, Steve? Vodka? Tequila?' she asked.

'Course I don't. No liquor on the premises, luv. Lose my licence if I did.'

Brolly dipped his finger into the sludge, dipped his finger into his mouth, threw a lasso around his face as his features tried to stampede.

'Anyone ever finish this?' Brolly asked.

'Couple of Northern nutters on a stag-do once, but that's about it . . .'

'Can you get us some toast, maybe?'

'There's some in the smoothie.'

'Yeah, but, you know, not mushed up, just, like, real toast.'

'How many slices?'

'Four each, I reckon. With butter.'

'OI! JANET!'

'Oh, and a couple of pints of tap water,' Brolly added.

'OI, JANET! BRING US EIGHT SLICES OF TOAST, WILL YA? WITH BUTTER. AN' TWO PINTS OF TAP WATER. SOON AS YOU CAN, LUV!'

Customers cheated on their own breakfast and stared disbelievingly at Gill and Brolly's. The kitchen staff gathered behind the till and even the queue outside, having heard the commotion, turned to investigate. Someone dropped a pin; everyone heard it. Taxi Rob's heart beat with pride. Janet rushed across the café and unloaded her tray. Brolly cut his toast into soldiers; Gill grunted at his technique, didn't follow his lead.

'For those who care too much, and those who don't care enough,'

31

Steve projected. 'For epicurean adventurers and frontier-breaking bellybusters. Two full pints of Full English Smoothie. Only two other nutters've ever finished the Bellybusters' Quadruple Full English, so you might well be witnessing history here. Are you ready to witness history?!' The café screamed it was ready; cameras started to point. 'Alright, if you don't know 'em already, these are my good friends Gill and Brolly. Gill and Brolly, are you ready to make history?'

'We're ready!' they said in unison.

'Alright! I'm gonna do a countdown and then the game's on. Ready? Five . . . Four . . . Three . . . Two . . . One . . . Go!'

Gill and Brolly picked up their glasses, clinked and tipped them upwards. The café burst into caterwauls of delight, whoops of disgust, whistles of solidarity. The slop stuck to its guns, barely moved. Almost at right angles to the table, it started to relent, to ooze. Like it was a grease ball of jelly from the wrong side of the kitchen tracks. It had no real beginning and no real end, just an indeterminate middle. Brolly copped some first. Used a tablespoon to sweep a dollop into his mouth, to taste the full extent of their recklessness. He gagged. Coughed. Tried to force it down. Couldn't budge the sludge from his mouth. Slammed the glass back on the table. Tried not to vomit as it coaxed his oesophagus. Splashed some water down his throat as Gill chickened out, placed her glass back on the table.

'How is it?' she asked, already knowing the answer.

'Worse than I thought,' he replied. The response didn't surprise her. She stared at the two pints. Strategised. Wiped her face of any lingering doubt. Picked up a pint glass. Poured a quarter of it over a slice of toast and with blanket confidence, as if she'd cracked the code, levelled out the sludge. She knew she had to be strong. Follow through with her hunch. She risked a bite, quashed her face's rebellion, nodded confidently like she was in control, like she was a genius, a Nobel Peace Prize winner.

'Get me four more pieces of toast, Steve, mate,' she said.

'Brolly?' Steve asked.

'Not yet.'

'JANET! GET US FOUR MORE PIECES OF TOAST!' Cheers, claps perforated the air. Brolly took the plunge as Gill munched on her first slice. He dipped his soldiers into the goo, transported them to his mouth. The toast, its double texture, its external jaggedness, its internal softness, pilloried the sludge. Gill and Brolly maintained their stiff upper lips, ate stoically and with dedication. Janet brought four more slices. The crowd sat spellbound. Its clapping grew louder, slower, found a rhythm, became metronomic, only stopped when Brolly slammed his first glass on the table, empty; erupted into individual claps, cautious but congratulatory.

Throughout, diners dashed up to the table to take selfies. Some made peace signs, others the devil's horn, some pulled shocked faces, others couldn't contain their laughter. Taxi Rob stroked his manhood twice as he watched the sludge dribble down Gill's chins. Soldiers collapsed. Soldiers were rescued. Soldiers were swallowed. New soldiers were dispatched. Same with the slices.

Halfway through the second pint, Gill almost choked on a slither of unblended bacon. Her flesh wobbled as she coughed and spluttered and Steve smacked her back. She emergency-gulped a glass of water, but to no effect. She stuck her forefinger down her throat, almost regurgitated the whole breakfast as she plucked out the fat, fleshy slither, threw it on the table with a flick of disdain. She and Brolly had been neck and neck, but he overtook her. His heart catapulted around his chest as he scraped his nails against the bottom of the second glass, scooped out the last globules and smeared them over his face like a chimpanzee at a tea party, a commando on a night raid. 'Finished!' he cried as the premises burst into spontaneous combustion.

'Amazing!' Steve said, clapping his hands violently. 'Fucking amazing!' Gill slammed her glass on the table not long after. 'Stand up! Come on. Show your fans what you're made of!' Steve encouraged.

With Cheshire-cat grins camouflaging their sickly complexions, Gill and Brolly extricated themselves from the table and shuffled to either side of Steve. He grabbed their hands, lifted their arms. Gill and Brolly struggled against anti-peristaltic waves of sludge but stood firm and proud as the other diners stood up; cheering burst into euphoria and good humour ribbed the air.

CHAPTER 7

'WHAT DO WE WANT!?' Brolly shouted triumphantly as they headed north on the Old Kent Road.

'ASDA!' Gill returned.

'WHEN DO WE WANT IT!?'

'NOW!'

'WHAT DO WE WANT!?'

'ASDA!'

'WHEN DO WE WANT IT!?'

'NOW!'

'TAXI ROB! WHAT DO WE WANT?'

'ASDA!' Taxi Rob shouted.

'WHEN DO WE WANT IT!?'

'NOW!' both replied.

Gill and Brolly loved those four nonsensical letters that dominated the exterior building on the Old Kent Road like a jolly green giant surveying his concrete fiefdom. They loved how the word combined two infantile and almost meaningless monosyllables into something far greater than the sum of its parts. Asda wasn't just a word, it was a way of life. It was your mother, father, brother and sister all rolled into one, likewise your birthday and Christmas. It was the rolling meadow at the end of every rainbow, filled with pots of shining gold and a sea of beautiful stars twinkling and signalling that, yes, maybe there was life on another planet and no, life on this one really wasn't so bad. It also had an endless supply of mobility scooters for its customers, unlike most of the other supermarkets in the area.

Young Mike sat crossed-legged in his usual spot, in front of the brick column opposite the plants. He wore a long green army coat, which in the soft sunlight made him look like a streetwise model who'd been in an altercation the night before. As Gill and Brolly drove past, he grabbed the handful of coins from his begging cap and slipped them into his front trouser pocket. He spat in his hands and brushed his hair back.

'Alright, Mike!? How's your week been?' It was one of those insensitive questions he never knew how to answer. Truthfully, and say it had been shit? Or gloss over the truth and say it had been OK? He could never bring himself to say it had been great.

'It'th been alright,' he lisped.

'Good to hear. You got any special requests today, mate?'

He liked Gill and Brolly because they always bought him a sandwich, a fizzy drink, a chocolate bar and a packet of crisps, which was more than anyone else ever did.

'Well acthually, I know beggarth can't be chootherth but, well, I woke up with a craving for a banana, which ith weird coth I can't remember the lath time I had one. Tho I wath wondering if you might get me one? It'th fine if not coth I know you're alwayth nithe to me, but I wath wondering if you could get me a banana inthtead of thome chocolate?'

'Why don't we get you a Chunky Monkey? Best of both worlds.'

'Gill!'

'What?'

'He wants a banana, not Ben and bloody Jerry's.'

'Why would you want a banana when you can get banana ice cream with chocolate and walnuts!?'

'Because that's not what he asked for!'

'Mike, d'ya want a banana or a Chunky Monkey?'

'Er . . .' Mike didn't want to appear ungrateful, but wasn't entirely sure what a Chunky Monkey was.

'No need to put the poor bloke on the spot. We can get both.'

'Fine, but do it yourself. I'm not going down the fruit and vegetable aisle. Gives me the creeps, it does.'

Gill and Brolly clambered onto Asda's mobility scooters, inferior to their own, cheap plastic, one gear only, maximum speed a contradictory 2mph. Taxi Rob followed Gill into the shop with a trolley and they immediately sloped off to the left, past the newspaper and National Lottery section, as Brolly continued ahead.

Neither he nor Gill ate fruit or vegetables (except with their Full English), but Young Mike's request had piqued his curiosity and he wondered if it was time to eat them again, like he had as a child. His staccato laughter vocalised an exclamation mark. The array of colour was breath-taking, the textures and potential tastes, all portals into a brave new world, a gallant new life. Lemons stacked on limes below oranges next to melons across from onions above potatoes, lots of different potatoes, to the left of cauliflowers, next to cabbages, next to lettuces, next to parsnips. He stumbled off his machine and grabbed a pomegranate. He rubbed its smooth core against his lips. He fondled a ripe melon and felt like he was cheating on Gill with another man's wife. He smelled strawberries and the hint of childhood summers; satsumas and long-gone Christmases. He played with a coconut, chafed its itchy beard over his cheeks, and soon found himself in front of the bananas.

Brolly caressed geometric curves, scratched calloused tips, rubbed off-kilter necks. He spotted a bunch that would make Andy Warhol proud, was about to flip it over to inspect its undercarriage when he froze. A pretty little fella, dark ruby, a minuscule but delicate crocodile replica, poked its head from behind a neighbouring bunch. 'Hello, there!' Brolly whispered as he withdrew his grip and shakily moved his veiny invitation, a strange vantage point for a strange landscape, closer to the little lizard. He expected it to dash away, but snickered as it flicked its forked tongue before darting onto his hand. The little beauty's body was no more than a couple of inches long, its tail the same. Brolly raised his forefinger and lowered it slowly down the back of the creature's head, stroked its intricate scales, all the way down to the tip of its tail. He did it again and again and the lizard started to change colour. Effortlessly. Magically. From Aperol sunset to chipotle campfire, to heartfelt emerald, to a more naturalistic lime.

Waves rolled gently behind Brolly. He turned around to behold a crystal-clear ocean that ebbed across a beach and blasted sun rays off its shimmering surface. The crescent bay took his breath away. Distant kettle drums danced off a warm breeze and a nearby BBQ charmed his nostrils. Not a boat bobbed. Not a person pouted. Not a camera clicked.

The lizard scurried up Brolly's arm and vanished over his shoulder.

Brolly turned around, hoped to see it scarper across the sand, but was drawn to something altogether more alluring. A topless woman with a tight figure and a swarthy tan. She lay face down on a lounger, just a small stone's throw away. Her hair hid her shoulders and although Brolly didn't recognise her, he knew she was his and he, hers. His gaze languished on her peachy backside, each handful of which was accentuated by a white thong. His pupils dilated and he licked his salty lips, but a crackling to her side distracted him. Fresh catch of the day sizzled over a hazy clay pit and, next to that, a stately wooden table offered island fruit and greenery. An ice bucket with chilled champagne guarded the feast with officious diligence. The woman brushed her thigh, lifted her backside and twisted onto her flank. Brolly averted his gaze and looked down. His mouth dropped open, practically burned on the sand. He couldn't believe his eyes. They couldn't believe themselves either. The sand reflected its brilliance but couldn't hide the fact that, for the first time since he was a teenager, he could see his toes.

CHAPTER 8

Brolly didn't mind the upstairs session, thought it was quite funny. He trusted Gill and, actually, he trusted Taxi Rob. The agreement was a quid pro quo one where Rob drove them around every Saturday, in return for which Gill offered her services for half an hour. Everyone was a winner, baby, especially him; he got to relax with a few beers and the Saturday papers.

'That's it, then,' Taxi Rob confirmed as he lifted the final Asda bag onto the kitchen table.

'Thanks, mate,' Brolly returned.

'I'll slope off, then.'

'Yeah, have a good one.'

'Yeah, cheers, mate.'

Taxi Rob felt his heart speed up, the blood in his body surge. Like always, he felt self-conscious as he snuck down the corridor, wary that Brolly might be watching, judging his every move. As he U-turned onto the stairs, free from any prying gaze, his teeth peeked out of his lips and his mouth snuggled up to his nose. One day he'd take the stairlift, but the time never seemed right and his urge to progress with the afternoon's pleasure was too strong. He undid the buttons on his white polo shirt and just before he stepped onto the landing, pulled it off. He shivered. The cold ribbed his skin. He didn't mind though; Gill would warm him up soon enough. He tweaked his nipples, slipped out of his trainers, stuck his socks in his trainers and held the footwear in one hand as he unfastened his jeans with the other. They dropped down his thin, shapeless thighs and he stepped out of them. He took a deep breath as the house enveloped him in a quiescence of calming cotton wool. The stillness caressed his pores. He caressed his manhood but didn't want to harden himself too much; that would happen soon enough. Gill's bedroom door gaped open. It held him in its grip, hypnotised him, beckoned him, but he knew Gill would still be preparing herself. He knocked on the bathroom door to his right.

'Be with you in a minute!' she projected as she peeled off her polo neck and dropped it onto the floor. She unzipped her skirt and pushed it and her leggings down until they reached her knees. She poked them with her grab-and-grip device and stepped out of the messy pool of fabric. She kicked the clothes next to her polo neck. Her arm sockets twinged and her skin chafed as she pulled her bra strap to the front of her chest. She unclipped it with ease but pulled it off with a struggle. Her breasts tumbled to just above where a slim person's belly button would sit. She grabbed the pink nightie that Taxi Rob had bought for her, having first made sure it wouldn't offend her or Brolly. She smelled it. It smelled of mothballs and stale Wotsits. She made a mental note to wash it for the following weekend. She stuck her arms in the air and pulled the nightgown over her head. A low-pitched rent ranted. 'Oh, for fuck's sake!' The tear looked like an imitation Silk Cut advert, cheap and badly colour graded. Her skin brooded through the tear, looked like it was pregnant with angst, ready to burst. She squeezed the fabric together but it split apart as soon as she released her grip. She squeezed the flesh. It didn't do anything except redden and throb.

Taxi Rob folded his clothes in half and placed them next to the hairbrush on Gill's dresser. He grabbed the brush, stroked it through the greying hairs on his chest. Her bedroom was another world for him, his fantasy, his truth, his life, his happy place, his everything. He jumped onto the bed, away from the headboard, yelped as the bathroom door announced Gill's imminent arrival. Her thighs scraped together. Flakes of gold sprinkled magically through the air. His breathing sounded like water lapping against a secret cave. Her rasping sounded like a fishing boat in the distance. The bedroom trembled with her every step. He rolled over. His eyes grew too big for their sockets. She was still growing, her body was still expanding. He loved her body. It spilled gloriously out of her nightgown. Gill laid her phone on her bedside table and smirked at Taxi Rob.

The beginning was a ritual.

Always the same.

At his behest.

Gill goaded one knee onto the mattress, close to his hip. Her flesh tweaked his. The bed cried chicken as she placed one hand on either side of his shoulders. Her breasts tickled his cheekbones. She groaned like she was giving birth. Grazed his testicles as she lifted her other leg across him. He groaned like he was trying to impregnate her. She recalibrated her breath, straightened herself, squared her shoulders. She stared deep into his flying saucers. Her breasts heaved in unison with his. His tongue dripped. She raised her hands high. He marvelled at her hairy armpits, panted and moaned. Her smile brightened the whole room as she surrendered to gravity. He barked. She fell honestly and without restraint. Her flesh smacked against his, with a firework's thunder and a summer storm's lightning. The bed shook, its headboard smashed against the wall. Her flesh flattened over his face, smothered his nose and mouth. Its warmth pressed over him as the rest of her body squeezed the air out of his lungs.

Gill lay as still as she could but still twitched from time to time. Her twitches felt like jolts of electricity and Taxi Rob finally felt liberated from his shackles, from his life's mediocrity. He was an eagle soaring high above the Amazon forest. He was a snowflake melting in the ocean's magnanimity. He was a dirty football smashing against a goal's net. He was himself again, aged nine, the only thing he ever wanted to be when he grew up, after years of self-hatred and denial, of not being able to share his fetish.

Gill's arms flopped over the end of the bed, her nose grazed the duvet, her toes dented her pillows. She took his groin's poke as a compliment, liked to wriggle her tummy against it sometimes, tease him. Given he was a grown man, he was surprisingly comfortable to lie on. A trance-like calm, an overwhelming lassitude crept up on Gill; her heartbeat calmed and her muscles relaxed. She felt electricity, too, but in a slightly different way to Taxi Rob. Lying there was like plugging into an electrical pulse. The longer his skin touched hers, the more she felt reconnected, to the human race, the world, the universe, to everyone and everything.

There was only so long Taxi Rob could lie under Gill without breathing and he gave her the sign. He tapped her. On the side of her right thigh. But she didn't respond, didn't register, didn't budge. He tapped again, the same rhythm but more forcefully, as if thinking that, somehow, she just hadn't felt him before. She still didn't move. His mouth was superglued to her flab, but his lungs fluctuated like bellows, burned from the inside. He smacked again, harder, quicker, more forceful. Still no response. He started to hit her. His chest imploded, his brain frazzled, his heart floundered but he didn't stop.

The slaps jolted Gill from her semi-consciousness. Her thighs stung. It took a second for her to remember she was lying on top of Taxi Rob. He was smacking her with open palms for maximum flesh interaction. He was panicking. He was suffocating. He was always suffocating. Suffocation was part of the thrill, he'd once told her. Death by mammary gland. Asphyxiation by bosom. Brain tumour by tits. Her breasts were deadly weapons but they jittered with a beautiful life-force as she heaved them off him momentarily, extended him the hint of a lifeline. She giggled, exercised her mastery, retracted the lifeline. He managed a desperate gasp before she fell back on him. A pigeon smashed its beak against the window. Communicated demonically. Flapped its wings. It was the universe cooing. She let Rob stew, percolate, panic, self-immolate, destruct. He started flapping wilder than the pigeon outside.

His slaps sounded like whip cracks, firework snaps. They reverberated fiercely through the room, started to hurt Gill. The pigeon flew away. She heaved herself off him, rolled onto her back. He hyperventilated, sounded like a racing car accelerating down a long straight as he gasped for air. His jaw stretched open as if about to consume itself. The veins in his neck poked out of his windpipe. His erection poked out of his Y-fronts. Gill concentrated on standing up, exorcising the pain from her extremities as he squeezed himself and stuck his erection back in his pants, watched her ample flesh, more flesh than he'd ever seen in his life, flap, flop, finally drop as she stood up.

Her weight arched her back, rounded her shoulders. She hobbled to the foot of the bed, trod on something that stuck to her foot. She dared not inspect it, for fear of falling over; a good monopod she was not. She scraped her foot on the carpet. It was a crusty Fruit Pastille. Strawberry. Her favourite. She wished she could bend down to pick it up. To eat it. She wondered about eating Taxi Rob. His pale skin glistened with a thin layer of their conjoined sweat. The hairs on his body lay flat, defeated and lifeless. His Y-fronts looked like a tent that had fallen in the wind. He basked in a kind of postcoital glaze and arched his neck backwards to stare at her. His look was loving. Their silence was golden but the wind communicated for them, whistled tunelessly outside. A plane emulated the wind. Gill stepped back. Taxi Rob's neck clicked as he followed her. Her nostrils flared; he wiggled

44

further down the bed, scratched the inside of his thigh as she toyed with what her next position would be. Which part of him to squash with which part of her? There was a vague science to the madness. To punish or reward? To tease or to suffocate? Gill wondered if she continued to put weight on, if one day she'd break the poor bloke in half, snap his spinal column, paralyse him. She mumbled incoherently, cleared her throat, hobbled back against the wall.

'Oh God!' he whispered as she started towards him, not at a run but a waddle slightly less languorous than was her custom. She couldn't exactly jump onto him but launched herself, dropped with momentum, with determination, with integrity. The bed lurched, banged against the wall. Her breasts bounced, slipped over his face, halted his enforced exhalation, as his upper torso disappeared and her stomach flattened out to its natural extreme. She grabbed hold of his feet and pulled on them, used them like sturdy pickaxes to drag herself, inch by inch, up the bed, up his body. He was practically in tears of ecstasy as her flesh melted over him.

She circumnavigated his erection and rested her cheek on his left thigh as his head burst through her legs like a newborn baby and his delirium turned into a cough. His cough pawed her bottom. Her bottom spread out in front of his gawping eyes. In the negative space where her thighs stopped touching, the inverse droplets of cellulite, puddles some of them, welcomed him. He nuzzled her flesh not romantically but practically; tried to scratch his nose. His body tingled. He flexed his manhood. Under all that, he could still feel its power, could still feel it twitch. He rippled his stomach, stared at Gill's magnificence, her glory, just a few inches from his face. He wanted to grab her buttocks and eat her out but that was a line he couldn't cross. His fantasies had grown more sexual over the years, but in reality there was nothing he'd prefer to be doing on a Saturday afternoon than a 'dry 69' with Gill.

CHAPTER 9

'Don't look now, but that girl's starting to freak me out.'

'Which one?'

'In the corner.'

'Why?'

'She keeps staring at me.'

'Tell me something I haven't heard before.'

'Yeah, but there's something weird about her. Can't quite put my finger on it . . . Oh. You can look now; I stared her down. Don't think she likes eye contact.'

Outside, the Sunday sky's duvet lingered above Peckham Rye's periphery, threatened snow. Scarves strangled pedestrians and woolly hats made them look like walking teapots. Inside the Carpenter's Arms, the radiators scalded, tinny speakers' Northern Soul snorted amphetamine and the teapots played fancy dress with beer goggles.

'What? The sexy Satsuma?'

'No, the other one.'

The girl cajoled her eyes back towards Gill but they strayed to Brolly. Gill was right. For a nanosecond, he thought he noticed a mushroom of psychological warfare. But that softened into a cry for help. Or for attention, at least. And not just a cry to anyone; to them in particular.

'Almost looks like she knows us and wants to say hello. D'you think she's a contestant?' Brolly asked.

'Doesn't look like she eats enough.'

'Yeah, but you can never tell these days . . .'

'True, but even so. Maybe she's a fan. Seen us eat before,' Gill conjectured.

'Maybe.'

'Can the All You Can Eat Carvery competitors make their way to the lounge, please!?' shouted Landlady Kim – all Botox, bones and pneumatic breasts – in a native London accent from the edge of the saloon.

The competition rules were simple:

The entry fee was £15 and had to be paid at the bar by 1.30 p.m. Anyone could enter but there were only ten competitive slots (excluding Gill's and Brolly's) and these were filled on a 'first come first served' basis.

At 2 p.m., each contestant was called to sit down at the competition table, after which they were given a plate consisting of two slices of beef, five roast potatoes, three carrots, two scoops of mashed potato, one serving of kale, one parsnip, one Yorkshire pudding, one tablespoon of horseradish sauce and a ladleful of gravy.

Each plate had to be completely finished before the contestant could start the next plate, which consisted of exactly the same.

Drink, alcoholic or otherwise, could be consumed, but any contestant leaving the dining room during the competition would be immediately disqualified.

The competition lasted thirty minutes.

Whoever ate the most plates was the winner.

The Master of Ceremony's decision was final and if anyone beat Gill or Brolly, the in-house champions, they would receive £25 prize money.

If they beat Gill *and* Brolly, they would receive £50 and be immortalised on the Carpenter's Arms All You Can Eat Carvery Wall of Fame.

The waft of Yorkshire puddings imbued the mock-Tudor pub's function room with a divine aroma, like a cherished afternoon spent in the bosom of loved family. Plaid mixed with denim and sweatshirts with Sunday blouses as those gathered listened to Landlady Kim recite the rules. Gill scoured the room for the girl with the eyes. She didn't see her but did see the sexy Satsuma, who crouched in the corner opposite the entrance, rummaging through her bag. She stuck her upper lip inside her lower lip and sucked on it. She needed to win but felt threatened and queasy, like a cheese dip about to be invaded by an army of nachos.

"'Ladies first!" Isn't that what they say?' Landlady Kim projected. 'Well, today we have a remarkable lady. Some of you will know 'er by name, some by sight, almost all by reputation. Personally, I know 'er by all three and I promise you, she is ALL lady. Put your hands together, please, and make some noise for the first of our two in-house champions and Wall of Fame legends, Gill "Don't Give a Fork!" Monteith!' Gill waved regally as she shuffled over to take top billing on the two rustic oakwood tables.

With similar schtick, Brolly 'The Bear' was introduced. He roared loudly but with more of a pantomime campness than the call from the wild he'd intended. The crowd lapped it up nonetheless. He lurched to the opposite end of the table and heartily slapped the sides of his stomach, as if warning the kids not to do this at home. The other competitors were a motley bunch of teapots, beer bottles, wine glasses and spirit chasers and Gill and Brolly welcomed them like lesser dignitaries to their own state banquet. The girl from the bar was still nowhere to be seen and Gill started to drip time, relax like a Dalí clock. She sharpened her nails against the table's underside, was desperate to tuck in, to lay waste to the competition, to the Sunday roasts that simmered in the mobile buffet next to her.

'Last but not least, maybe a superstar in the making with a name like this!? "The Garbageman!"' Gill and Brolly stole an eye-wobbling glance at each other. They'd never been challenged by a noun before. Outlandish nicknames and fantastical descriptions were the domain of the professionals. Nicknames had to be earned. And bestowed. You couldn't just pluck one out of thin air and force it upon an audience because you thought it might be a laugh. Gill and Brolly scanned the crowd. The crowd scanned the room. The Garbageman was nowhere to be seen. The polite applause died quickly and a querulous hush settled. '"The Garbageman!" Is "The Garbageman" here!?' Gill whistled through her teeth and homed in on the Satsuma, who was crouched down again. 'It's three strikes an' you're out, here. I had an inkling it was gonna get messy but it looks like I was wrong. I will not ask again and the contestant will be disqualified! For the last time . . . is "The Garbageman" in the house?!'

A truck started its engine in a tunnel. The crowd turned towards the noise. The Satsuma's phone was plugged into her portable speaker. A psychobilly song spat vitriol. The door exploded. A fireball of energy burned brightly. Wearing a black polythene bin bag, black DMs, black executioner's mask, and a mouth very much open for business, The Garbageman swaggered, dazzled, high-fived her way down the room, past Landlady Kim, who gamely pumped her fist in the air, towards the competition table. The Garbageman pointed a vituperative finger at Brolly and screamed 'HISTORY!' She prowled past him and up the table. 'LOSERS!' she accused the other contestants. Gill waited for her turn with an ice-cool stare. The Garbageman didn't dare catch her eye but snatched Gill's fork and bent it in half, discarded it like worthless rubbish over her shoulder before grabbing her knife too. Gill tried to stop her but was too slow. The Garbageman jammed the knife against the table, bent it into an L-shape and pointed at Gill. 'HISTORY! HISTORY! HISTORY!'

The table trembled as Don't Give a Fork stood up, a living colossus. The Garbageman's eyes drowned in fear, flailed for rescue. Don't Give a Fork grabbed her water, threw it in The

Garbageman's face, ripped a leaf out of The Bear's book and roared. Not with pantomime theatrics but with legendary, grizzly inferno; mad, bad and terminally dangerous to know. The crowd burst their Sunday-afternoon chains, rained epithets of approval, grabbed their phones. The Garbageman swivelled towards the buffet, squashed a Yorkshire pudding into her mouth and strutted back to Landlady Kim like a punk singer dancing on broken glass. The Satsuma turned off The Cramps and The Garbageman spat the undigested clumps of Yorkshire pudding onto the carpet. She ringed Landlady Kim's waist with one spindly arm and pumped the other into the air.

'I AM THE GARBAGEMAN!' She could eat a hundred and seventy chicken wings in ten minutes, eighty Jaffa Cakes in eight minutes.

'I AM THE GARBAGEMAN!' She could eat forty-four hard-boiled eggs in five minutes, two hundred and three oysters in three minutes.

'I AM THE GARBAGEMAN!' She could eat three quarter-pounders in one minute and a 12-inch margherita pizza in fifty-two seconds.

Landlady Kim took centre stage as The Garbageman took her seat. The room fell silent and all eyes focused on the Master of Ceremonies. She wasn't sure what to say but the more she thought about it, the more her silence seemed to say it all. The silence revered her. She revered the silence. Silence equalled tension. Tension equalled drama. She looked at Don't Give a Fork, who clenched the new cutlery in her hands, flashed her gritted teeth. Landlady Kim looked over to The Bear. He snarled. Landlady Kim smirked. She lifted her right arm into the air. Hovered her thumb over the start button on her stopwatch. Continued silence equalled continued tension. Time stood still. Hearts shredded, became dog meat. Landlady Kim thrashed her hand downwards like a dominatrix cracking her whip. The crowd tore into the air with abandon. Metal scraped on china. Lips slurped and sloshed.

The Bear was first to finish his sixth plate, roughly halfway through the competition. With a punch of the air and a rumbling, rip-roaring rollick of a belch. Stale garlic and foetid lamb from the previous evening's Indian molested nostrils closest to him, irritated some further away.

'Go on, Bear!' Hands slapped against hands and vocal cords exercised exuberantly.

'You can do it, Bear!' The Bear saluted his fans as a server swapped his old plate for a new one. A carrot fell onto the table. Steam rose off the gravy. He wanted to give himself a Caesarean, rip out the baby cow that lay comatose at the bottom of his stomach. Instead, he took a deep breath and dug in as Don't Give a Fork repeated his earlier word. 'Finished!'

'Finished!' The Garbageman shouted, seconds after Gill; despite her bluster, she was a talent. The room erupted. News spread around the pub. The competition record, held by competitive food-eating legend The Urban Turban, might be broken. Everyone held their place, everyone held their bladder, some held their breath. More and more people slipped in, no one left; the room started to burst at the seams.

'Twenty minutes!' the Satsuma bellowed. Their sign. For The Garbageman to sprint into overdrive, destroy her opponents. The Garbageman laughed, practically spat her parsnips out. She was feeling good. She was feeling omnipotent. All-conquering. These suckers didn't know what was about to hit them. She had them. In the clutches of her little hand. With a smile, she swivelled towards Don't Give a Fork, whose hamster cheeks wriggled, whose red polka-dot skin shuffled, whose drug addict's eyes darted, whose farm noises . . . Whose farm noises . . . Whose farm noises sounded obscene. The smile on The Garbageman's face uncurled. She twisted her head in the opposite direction.

The Bear was an animal but his weight was crushing his soul, every mouthful was dulling his will to survive, contributing to his body's pained demise.

The Garbageman's killer instinct withered, waned, died as she rested her cutlery on her plate. She no longer wanted to destroy her rivals but to hug them. She wanted to weigh them both, measure their BMI, their blood pressure, their heart rate, do blood tests, take their cholesterol. To sit them down and offer free expert physical and nutritional advice on how to shed their weight. She was studying for a BSc in nutrition, after all. She wanted to tell them competitive food-eating really wasn't a sensible lifestyle choice. Not for them, at any rate. She didn't want them to die, she wanted them to live and skip and hop and jump, like lambs over the moon, athletes over a high jump. She wanted to take them prisoner and spruce up their jail sentence with the warmth of her human kindness. But The Garbageman surely took no prisoners!? How could she become an international competitive eating star with such empathy, such maternity, such hypersensitivity? It was a sham. She wasn't The Garbageman at all. She was Jane Elliot, twenty-one, from Leeds, who didn't have a boyfriend, lived just under a mile from her parents and was currently wearing an executioner's mask over her head and a dustbin bag over her chest. She stood up. 'Mum, what's The Garbageman doing?' a little boy asked his mum. Jane's heart leaped. The little boy knew her nom de guerre. Her legend was already growing, like her flatmate and business manager Karen promised it would. The mum didn't answer. No one answered. Jane turned around and was confronted by Karen.

'You alright, lass?' Karen trembled. A couple of hundred eyes asked the same question. She waved her hand weakly. The crowd stepped aside. Their eyes followed her. She walked deliberately to the door. The Sunday roast infiltrated her olfactory senses. Wrapped itself around her breathing apparatus. The walk seemed to take forever. Jane gripped the door handle. It cooled her hand. Steadied her nerves. She pulled. The door sang as if welcoming her to the Pearly Gates. One small step, that was all it took. Disqualification would be hers, her old life reinstated. Lazy morning lie-ins whenever she wanted, no vomit-inducing squash balls for breakfast to strengthen her mandibles, no gallons of water to stretch her stomach twice a week. One small step, that's all it required. She wavered as if she stood high above the ground on a tightrope. She tried to coordinate her brain with her feet.

'Be a woman! Do it, ya coward!' It was Don't Give a Fork. She was leaning back precariously on her chair, sneaking an angle through the buffet's glistening golden structure. Her barbed-wire smile taunted Jane, who returned her gaze to the Pearly Gates, saw her future; she was an animal nutritionist. She saved cuddly little fluff balls, no longer ate them for pointless and arguably pathological fun. 'Do it, coward!'

'Jane!?' Karen called out. The name sounded strange. She stroked her mask. Rustled her bin bag. Her garbage bin bag. She wasn't Jane. She was The Garbageman. And The Garbageman took no prisoners! And did eat baby cows for fun! She was wearing her armour. Her armour made her invincible. She slammed the door in front of her. Applause thundered, caterwauls rained and the little boy tugged excitedly at his mother's skirt. 'She's coming back, Mummy!'

At the table, she practised a Mexican wave of one, thrust her hips in circles, teased an invisible hula hoop, wiggled her breasts, go-go danced like a Maori haka, expounded exorcist groans. She grabbed her cutlery, stood on her chair, turned round to the crowd. She bent the fork in half and threw it on the floor. The crowd jumped up the walls, clawed at the ceiling, threw beer over each other. She leaped off the chair, deformed the knife into another L-shape and handed it to the little boy, who stamped his feet with glee.

The Garbageman ripped a strip of beef from her plate and stuffed it into her mouth. The Satsuma whistled like a pot of contagious tea. Landlady Kim confounded her Botox. Don't Give a Fork stood up. Eyeballs flew to her. She stuck her fork in her mouth and chewed. A jolt of electricity sparked Gill's fillings. Enamel chipped off her front molars. A prong bloodied her roof. She tasted metal but her smile tickled her nostrils. No pain, no gain, that's what real athletes told each other. And actually, it did bloody well hurt. She threw the mangled fork into oblivion and stuffed the knife into her mouth but immediately realised the error of her ways, that a fractured jawbone and savaged dentures weren't the way forward. She gurned like a vigilante stitching up his own wound and roared as if the skies were opening and Hell was sucking Heaven through its anus. She threw the knife behind her and picked up her plate, smashed it against her forehead. Gravy splattered all over her. Potatoes, parsnips and a chunk of beef dropped onto her. Tiny birds twittered above her head. She scooped the food off the table, stuffed it into her mouth. 'FINISHED!'

Six minutes.

The three remaining contestants stuffed their faces like escaped convicts at a feast; scooped up the food, crammed it in their mouths, burned their roofs, crashed their jaws, inflated their cheeks, gulped with abandon, chewed improperly, smeared their faces, soiled their attire, hurled their water, wet their chins, picked up their plates, slurped final trickles, smashed their plates back on the table, raised their arms high and screamed.

'Finished!'

Five minutes.

On plate nine, The Garbageman's throat itched. She poured water down it. Half of it splashed off her bin bag. She was trailing, still third. So much for her bluster. So much for her talk of annihilation. This was a tough gig. Death by firing squad. Burial by committee. There was no denying it, her opponents were formidable. Terminators. Indestructible siphons. Something had to change. If not, all would be lost and she'd return home with her tail between her legs. She'd already pulled out a few stops but wondered if common sense would be her downfall. She hoped her diaphragm didn't rupture. She hoped she didn't end up in hospital. But she was a winner and winners never quit (unless they had ruptured diaphragms). But she wasn't a winner, she was currently a loser. She had to strategise. Again. And quickly.

Four minutes.

The mashed potatoes were easy. You just swallowed them down. The kale was the same, pretty much; you eased its descent with gulps of water. The carrots and parsnips, you snapped in half and swallowed, similar to the Solomon Method with hot dogs. The roast potatoes you chewed until you could swallow and same with the Yorkshire pudding. The beef was the tough one; properly chewy, stringy, hard to ingest. But if you squashed the roast potatoes while swallowing the other vegetables, that would save a few seconds. And if you dipped the Yorkshire pudding in water before you stuffed it into your mouth, it would disintegrate and be easier to ingest. But the beef ... What to do with the beef!? It needed the most chewing but if you left it till last, stuffed both strips into your mouth as you announced your plate's completion, four or five seconds at least would free up during which the old plate was exchanged for the new.

Everything together might save her twenty seconds per plate. It was a superb strategy and good for future practice, but she'd left it too late, surely!?

'Finished!' Gill shouted to her right.

Three minutes.

The server threw down Don't Give a Fork's eleventh plate.

'Finished!' The Garbageman struggled for air as she slammed down her tenth.

'Finished!' The Bear shouted jubilantly as he finished his

eleventh. He'd smashed his own record. Time to smash The Urban Turban's. He felt stuffed, like a turkey on Christmas Day. Didn't look dissimilar to one either. His eyes shone like cracked marbles and a guard-dog drool glazed his bloated face. The server gripped his twelfth plate. He was on a roll and snatched it, grabbed a strip of beef, dropped it into his mouth. His voice suddenly rattled. His epiglottis warbled. His whole body convulsed.

Two minutes.

He forced himself up. Grabbed his throat. Tried to strangle himself. The crowd dropped its stadium act. Landlady Kim shouted for a doctor. None replied. Landlady Kim pulled out her phone, intended to dial 999, but was transfixed. One of the other contestants, a slim public-school girl, a Goldilocks type, sprang out of her seat. She smashed The Bear's back with her childlike palms. In between his lungs. On his spine and either side of it, until she started to tire. Just as she was about to give up, a caterwaul defenestrated the room. A morsel of beef catapulted out of The Bear's mouth and landed on the little boy's face. The little boy burst into tears. The Bear coughed uncontrollably, grabbed a jug of water, threw it down his throat.

'Finished!' Don't Give a Fork bellowed. She was oblivious to what had happened. Her war cry fell on deaf ears. Only The Garbageman's slurping and The Bear's gasping filled the room. She looked up. Brolly was standing when he should have been sitting. He looked desperate. Confused. Concerned. Tired. Out of breath. She crinkled her forehead, looked towards the crowd. It had just witnessed its own infallibility, immortality, immorality. It looked pale, like it had eaten too much chalk. Brolly looked at Gill. He was beat, he was out, but like a circus freak who knew the troupe was in trouble, he had to get the show back on the road. Don't Give a Fork's twelfth plate crashed onto the table in front of her.

'COME ON, DON'T GIVE A FORK! YOU CAN DO IT!!!!!' The crowd jingled, jangled, jumped with delight.

'Finished!' The Garbageman shouted. She sawed at the beef with her teeth. Swabbed it with her tongue. It slithered down her throat like a disintegrating snake. This was lunacy. Sweat greased the inside of her mask. Her twelfth plate smashed onto the table. She grabbed the potatoes and stuffed snowball portions into her mouth. The crowd had become a fire hazard. The crowd had closed in. Its exhortations tickled her neck and damaged her eardrums.

One minute.

'THIRTY SECONDS TO GO!' shouted Landlady Kim as Don't Give a Fork stole a glance at the monster beside her, the monster who seemed to be catching up with her. Don't Give a Fork ripped her plate off the table, shoved it against her face and hoovered up the food. Industrially. With industry. More dribs and drabs dropped onto the table, onto her trousers. She sucked and swallowed, licked and lapped. Her tongue gyrated, her lungs inflated, her stomach commiserated. For a twelfth time, she punched the air. 'FINISHED!' Her twelfth plate was replaced with her thirteenth. She bent over the table and shoved her face back against the bone china, turned the hoover back on.

'FINISHED!' screamed The Garbageman in full-on panic mode.

'STOP!' Landlady Kim belted out. The Garbageman slumped against the back of her chair, over the moon at not having to eat more but under it for having lost. Don't Give a Fork ignored the command to stop and hoovered up her thirteenth plate. The crowd's jaw bristled against the carpet as its eyebrows cleaned the cobwebbed ceiling and it listened to a noise like water gurgling down a drain. When she finished, Don't Give a Fork quietly laid her plate, clean as a whistle, back on the table. She struggled awkwardly to her feet. She clenched her fists together and threw them into the air. 'FINISHED!' she roared as the crowd spontaneously combusted and the other contestants honoured her with a standing ovation.

After the crowd emptied and the little boy had secured Gill's autograph on the back of a Carpenter's Arms menu, Gill waddled down the table to The Garbageman, who sat splattered, comatose, eagle-starred in her seat. Her showmanship had fled her sunken ship. Her stomach rumbled like a foghorn, too late to warn the rest of her body of the danger ahead. She wiped her hands against the tablecloth. Her sweat was dirty and yellow. She dared not turn to her side as the hulk stopped next to her.

'You're brilliant!' said Don't Give a Fork. 'That was amazing! Completely amazing.' The Garbageman's eyes twinkled. She took off her executioner's mask.

'That's so kind of you. That's amazing! You're amazing! Thank you so much!' she said as she stood up and extended her clammy hand. Don't Give a Fork took it in hers, also clammy, and they shook. 'I'm Jane . . .'

'I'm Gill, an' I can put my hand on my heart and say that, without a doubt, you're the most formidable contestant we've ever had here.'

'Really? Wowza! Thank you! That means a lot to me.'

'Are you a professional?'

'In training. Planning on it but not yet.'

'You should be. You got the talent for it, no question.'

'Are you?'

'Me? Nah. Just having a laugh.'

'You should be too. You could make some good money, I reckon. Both of you. I've got a few more competitions lined up in the next few months – you should come along, would be fun.'

'Like what?'

'Well, erm, next stop's in Wakey, near me – the Abergavenny Arms' Yorkshire Pudding Contest – and then after that I got the Herne Bay Oyster Eating Competition and after that the Down a Doner Tournament in Glasgow.'

'Travelling's a bit hard for us, to be honest, but, you know, I'd like to see you back here, give us another run for our money, see if you can make it onto the Wall of Fame.'

'Oh, I'd fucking love that. That's, like, one of my ambitions!'

'It's settled then. I'll look forward to your return.'

Brolly didn't sleep well that night and as he helped Gill with her ablutions the next morning, his heart splintered. Little shards, here and there, pierced his chest, irritated his mind, disturbed his soul. Breakfast was no different from usual but after he waved Gill goodbye, he did something he'd never done before. Never dreamed of doing. It contravened every instinct he possessed but he was stubborn when he wanted to be. He hobbled upstairs to the bathroom, deliberated over the sink and stuck his hand down his throat. He vomited all the bacon and all the sausages and all the eggs and all the mushrooms and all the baked beans and all the tomatoes and all the chips and all the toast he'd just eaten. It was harder and more painful than he'd imagined, and it took ten torturous minutes, but he successfully vomited it all up and was perversely proud of himself for doing so.

He brushed his teeth, splashed water on his face, brushed the remainder of his hair. He returned downstairs, made himself a coffee and sat at the kitchen table, where he stared into the abyss and remembered his best friend.

CHAPTER 10

The gravel in the blender of Tiny Tim's phone call, the dash of desperation in his tremor, the zest of urgency, the hint of self-pity, convinced Brolly to convince Gill to do something they rarely did. Venture out on a Saturday evening. The roads were alive, Christianity was dead, but a friend in need was a friend indeed.

'Alright?' Tiny Tim asked, not wanting much of a response after he opened the door to his second-floor council flat just down the road from the Oval.

'Evening,' Gill and Brolly replied in unison.

'Good timing. Pizza's just arrived.'

The pizza hid the room's dirty-Y-front smell. It blossomed out of a cramped coffee table in the equally cramped living room. Gill and Brolly crouched as best they could on the edge of a drooling sofa. Tiny Tim squashed a less slobbering armchair opposite. Conversation was stilted and Tiny Tim acted like he'd recently watched an Italian gangster film where business is always conducted after the meal, not during it. Little more than ten seconds subsequent to Gill suffocating the last potato wedge, Tiny Tim cleaned his face with a lemon wipe. 'So, er . . . thanks for coming . . .' He lit a cigarette, inhaled deeply, picked up the bottle of wine and swigged from it as if he were alone. 'I wanted to show you something . . .'

He shoved the pizza boxes onto the floor and, with a sense of showmanship that belied a nervous dread, picked up a long, dark shoehorn and slipped it under his left sock. He made a quiet dinosaur noise as he lifted his leg onto the coffee table. He pointed his foot in his friends' direction and studied their reaction. Drill music from the flat above knifed the silence. A ground beef and pepperoni transmogrification tickled Gill's tonsils. Brolly simultaneously snacked on his own flesh and massaged the animal hibernating at the back of his neck.

'H-h-h-how long's it been like that?' Brolly finally stuttered.

'Is it that bad?' Tiny Tim's voice wavered. The husk of the man had withered to its kernel. He knew the answer to his own question.

'How long's it been like that?' Brolly repeated.

'No idea. Doesn't hurt or anything,' Tiny Tim added with completely unfounded confidence. 'Don't usually see my feet or wear socks. But pretty sure it wasn't like this last time I saw you.' That was at the Carpenter's Arms the previous weekend. The drill music started stamping on the silence's face.

'I think . . .' Gill coughed, hoped she was hallucinating. 'I think there's a drawing pin in the middle . . .'

'Of my foot!?' Tiny Tim honked.

'Where?' Brolly demanded. Gill picked up a nearby biro and pointed as close to the foot as she dared.

'Oh fuckin' 'ell, there is!'

'A drawing pin!? Seriously?' The goose sounded less angry, like it had been given a last-minute reprieve from a good stuffing. It seemed like good news.

'Literally in the middle. Doesn't it hurt?'

'Can't feel a thing.' Tiny Tim wiggled his toes, hoping to prove he possessed full control of his body, which he obviously didn't. His foot looked like it'd been marked on by an overzealous make-up artist for a muddy-trench-set horror film. Underneath, an elevated and purulent fleshy circle surrounded the drawing pin, a golden ring in an oil spill, not a mysterious and beautiful by-product of the disaster but its cause. Two big toes oozed with pond-like glee, two shrivelled like battered and bruised piglets and his little toe, jet black and withered, looked like it was about to devour itself out of sheer malevolence. On the front of the foot up to the ankle, the darkness gave way to a muddle of bloody discharge.

The nurse who saw Tiny Tim at St Thomas's Hospital, next to Westminster Bridge, experienced a similarly visceral reaction to that of Gill and Brolly, but was better trained at hiding it. So was the senior registrar, who asked Tiny Tim if he had diabetes. He did; diabetes type 2. And if he smoked. He did; two or three packs a day. And if he drank. Who didn't? Beer and vodka mainly, every day, but wine too and Guinness and cider and, actually, pretty much everything really.

Tiny Tim had wet gangrene, caused by diabetes. High blood sugar had most likely damaged his nerves and caused loss of feeling. Simultaneously, less blood was being circulated to the feet, which meant there were fewer infection-fighting cells so that abrasions were much likelier to become infected.

Tiny Tim's foot would have to be amputated.

His lower leg might have to be amputated too.

Wet gangrene was life-threatening, so he'd have to be operated on as soon as possible. Tomorrow. The next day. He should quit smoking and drinking and start losing weight with immediate effect.

After the diagnosis, the first thing Tiny Tim did was to find fresh air. It was still night, but Sunday morning had trounced Saturday evening. The hospital buildings clustered around him. Towered above him. Closed in on him. The orange lights blinded him. The white lights goaded him. The yellow lights taunted him. The sky did its best to piss on him. The cold bit him. Gill and Brolly internalised their own demons. Held each other's hands. Tiny Tim filched through his pockets. Pulled out a pack of cigarettes. Lit and smoked two simultaneously.

'That's a bit of a fucker, isn't it!?' he said stoically, with true British reserve.

'I'm so sorry, mate,' Brolly empathised.

'D'you think we should get a second opinion?' Gill asked. But Tiny Tim didn't answer, just shook his head and smoked his remaining three cigarettes. It was the moment he officially considered himself an old, if not moribund, man; fifty-two, fat and fucked. If he hadn't smoked so much or drunk so much or eaten so much, he probably wouldn't be in hospital, about to become an amputee. Time used to be his friend. Now, he realised, it was his two-faced enemy. It had just stabbed him in the back. His dance with the Devil was over. The fat lady had sung, the curtain had fallen and there would be no encore. If only he'd been ten years younger. Or a year younger. Or a month younger. He could've done something about it. Or a week younger. He could've opted out of the Carpenter's Arms All You Can Eat Carvery Competition. If only he'd known what damage he was causing himself . . . But of course he fucking knew. He knew exactly what he was doing and he did nothing about it. He was his own man, who'd lived the life he wanted and now he had to pay the price.

The surgeon was blonde, Swedish, looked under twenty-five and was probably born in a magazine. With a purple marker pen, she drew a horizontal line halfway down Tiny Tim's shin with an arrow pointing to his foot.

'Have you ever cut the wrong leg off?' asked Tiny Tim with flirtatious sardonicism, seeking reassurance without asking for any.

'Not so far, but I'm still young . . .' she replied, too drily to refute the misinformed belief that Swedes don't have a sense of humour.

'Just as long as you don't chop my bollocks off . . .' He forgot to smile. And was finding it hard to carry on flirting while talking about his own castration before his own amputation. It sounded creepy and toneless and flat, but Brolly laughed. Out of solidarity. Which made him sound creepy, toneless and flat too. For a fraction of a second, Tiny Tim looked like a cat having its stomach caressed. Sure, it wasn't that funny, but it was funny enough. And what man hadn't cringed at mistaken testicular removal hospital horror stories? He was glad Brolly had laughed. It reaffirmed something that had been lost over the previous day and a half; that he wasn't about to die.

'Don't worry, I won't touch your bollocks . . .' the surgeon responded, wondering if she didn't touch them, then who would? Tiny Tim was about to contend he didn't mind when she pulled a sudden handbrake on their levity. 'And did your anaesthetist tell you?'

'Tell me what?'

'Ah . . .' The surgeon contemplated how to break the news kindly but knew that sugar-coating a cyanide pill never helped anyone, least of all the person taking it.

'Well, due to complications with your weight, we can't give you a general anaesthetic.'

'What the fuck!?' Brolly wondered to himself, alarmed.

'Which means?' asked Tiny Tim, also alarmed.

'The anaesthetic will be regional . . .'

'Which means?' asked Tiny Tim again, hoping it didn't mean what he thought it meant, praying it didn't mean what he thought it meant, pretty sure it meant exactly what he thought it meant.

'Which means the anaesthetic will go through your spine.'

'OK . . .' Tiny Tim extended his response, raised his tone a pitch towards its end, sounded more and more like an Australian.

'You won't feel anything below your waist, but you'll still be awake . . .'

Oh Jesus Christ. The surgeon nodded sympathetically as Brolly's head fell off.

'What do you use to cut it?'

'A reciprocating power saw, if you mean the bone. I usually advise people to close their eyes and think of something nice. It's not as loud as you might imagine, and it'll be over before you know it.'

'But I'm going to be awake?'

'You're going to be awake.' The surgeon nodded again and smiled a smile that conveyed there was nothing to smile about.

Tiny Tim held on to his dignity for as long as it took the surgeon to turn her back and start shimmying towards the ward's exit. His face collapsed and his body shrivelled. He looked like a baby bird thrown out of its nest. Tears greased his cheeks. Brolly tried to take his hand, but Tiny Tim snatched it away.

The pubs weren't open so Brolly found the nearest off-licence, one near Lambeth North Tube, and felt like a complete alky as he bought six tins of their strongest lager, a medium bottle of vodka and a red wine with a screw top.

He chose a bench diagonally opposite Parliament, overlooking the Thames, which was choppy and at high tide. A couple of seagulls squawked as he drank. The politicians opposite probably did the same. He wanted to explain to every tourist and every office worker who passed by that he wasn't a complete loser but doubted anyone would believe him. In the end, a Croatian traveller stopped to chat, so Brolly told him, but the Croatian was an alcoholic himself and was disappointed his new friend wasn't.

A crisp white sheet hid the Swede's handiwork as the United Nations nurses pulled Tiny Tim back into the ward. Tiny Tim stared vacantly at Brolly, more like a lobotomy victim than an amputee. Brolly averted his gaze. It was only after a pale and flimsy curtain had been drawn around them that Tiny Tim found strength to stare into his eyes again. 'Who's going to drive you home?' Tiny Tim asked, the concern for his friend's welfare strangely touching.

'I came on my mobility scooter. With Gill. Do you remember? Taxi Rob brought you cos some kids vandalised yours.'

'Who's going to drive you home?'

'Well ... er ... Well, I am ...' The drugs had worked well.

'No, who's gonna drive you home? You know, that song by The Cars. Drive. They was playing music. And that's what was playing as they ... That's what they were playing when they ... When she ... Looks all sweet and cuddly but a mean bitch, she is ... When she cut it off ...'

'It's a good song, I suppose ...'

'Bit gay, but it's alright ... Pointed ...'

'Pointed?' Brolly wasn't sure what a pointed song sounded like.

'Yeah, you know ... Fitting the occasion ...'

'Poignant, you mean?'

'Oh yeah, poignant ...'

'Ironic if you're in the mood ...'

'Ironic if you're not ...' Tiny Tim seemed to be firing on a constantly changing number of cylinders. Brolly smiled. So did Tiny Tim.

'So ... could you see them actually ... you know ... cutting it off ...'

'There was a curtain in front of me, but I could hear every word and every fucking instrument. Wish I'd known; would've at least listened to some music on my phone or watched a film.'

Only one way to cope with this, Brolly thought. He pulled out the red wine and took a massive glug. He handed the bottle to Tiny Tim, who downed half and spilt some over his gown. Its bloodiness was a febrile reminder of what had just happened, as if they needed one.

'I'm sorry, mate ...'

'Yeah ... Thanks.' Tiny Tim handed back the wine dregs to Brolly, who finished them with aplomb. He stretched out his hand to Tiny Tim, who, this time, took it. Tiny Tim's fingers were cold. Together, the consoled and the consoling, hand in hand, passed out.

Tiny Tim remained in hospital for another twenty days, a full ten days longer than he should have due to forgetting about his amputation and falling over one morning as he got out of bed. He damaged not only the folds of skin around his stump, ripping the stitches apart, but the stump itself, necessitating a further operation. During this time, he became a recognised character in the hospital pond life and interacted with his surgeon, his rehabilitation consultant, his nurses, his physios, his occupational therapist, his prosthetist, his counsellor, his nutritionist, his social manager, the canteen staff and the two Indian brothers who ran the gift shop.

He often awoke at night screaming from pain, as if his amputated limb was being electrocuted by a cattle prod while he drowned in a bath. Phantom limb syndrome was, his various carers assured him, a common affliction among amputees and he was offered various techniques to alleviate it, but none helped. On the positive side, he was awarded a private room, since the other patients on his ward complained about him. His prosthetist discussed the possibility of an artificial limb but decided against it, due to Tiny Tim's size. After he lost weight, which his nutritionist would help him with, and after his stub had shrunk, the prosthetist would reconsider. Tiny Tim left hospital with a redundant shoe and a crusty sock and spent another two weeks in Lambeth Community Care Centre, which was a fifteen-minute drive between his home and St Thomas's.

Gill and Brolly kept in constant contact and visited him as often as they could. He handed over his flat keys so they could spruce the place up prior to his return. They were surprised to discover ripped-out door frames littering the living room and worried there'd been a burglary, but it turned out a council employee had been sent to adjust the door widths to allow easier wheelchair access. The result was a botch job but domestic aesthetics seemed of trifling concern, so Brolly disposed of the timber and Gill hoovered up the dust. She bought 'Welcome Home' bunting and balloons and he bought a chocolate cake but immediately regretted the purchase because of Tiny Tim's rampant diabetes, so ate it all himself.

They were hoping to celebrate his dismissal with a Chinese takeaway fit for royalty, but Tiny Tim had lost weight and learned a great deal about a great many things, nutrition being one of them. It hadn't been easy, but he'd given up cigarettes and alcohol too, and wanted nothing more than a chicken salad and some finely tuned ginger in a glass of cool water.

Brolly's phone cachinnated like a Chihuahua. It was meant to be a novelty ringtone, but Brolly had forgotten to change it and it was now a grating one. 'Alright, mate?'

'Alright?'

'What's up?'

'What's uuuuuppp? I was just thinking about the Carpenter's Arms tomorrow and, er, well, I think I'm done. I'm liking the new me an' I haven't drunk anything this week. Or smoked. Or snacked. But being in a pub kinda scares me cos I gotta be sensible these days so I don't think I'm gonna come tomorrow . . .'

Technically, Tiny Tim was still the Carpenter's Arms in-house champion as Landlady Kim knew nothing about the amputation, working under the false understanding that Tiny Tim was on an extended holiday in Scotland. Gill and Brolly were filling in as the de facto in-house champions and enjoying the perks and minor adulation that the title entailed.

'Oh . . . well . . . We was looking forward to seeing you but you know what? I applaud your decision. I think that's . . . I'm proud of ya . . . I think that's the right thing, to be honest . . .'

Sunday morning was stumbling towards Sunday lunch. Gill and Brolly were stretching their stomach muscles, enjoying free beer and crisps on what had been Tiny Tim's regular table by the entrance. ''Ello, 'ello! Thought 'e said 'e'd retired?' Gill said as Tiny Tim barged through the double doors with an ungodly kerfuffle.

'He did.' Brolly stood up to help.

'Fuckin' get health an' safety down 'ere for these things. What a nightmare. Wonder if Kim's even aware this doesn't work for wheelchairs . . .' Tiny Tim's T-shirt looked like it had been washed but not dried.

'You alright?'

'Just fuckin' wheeled here all the way from home.'

'That's like four miles or something?'

'Yeah, I know. I'm back!'

'You coming to cheer us on?' Gill asked naively.

'Nah, I'm back! *Rocky II*, innit? *Return of the Jedi*!'

'What about your diet?'

'You know what, luv? I think I've done pretty well since I've been out and, well, I got to thinking last night that maybe just once a week I can let my hair down, have a bit of fun. Gotta have something to look forward to, otherwise I'll die of boredom!'

Gill and Brolly nodded politely but it was Landlady Kim who brought their collective denial plummeting to the ground. She didn't even look at Tiny Tim as he wheeled into the room, registered only a bulky blur out of the corner of her eye. When she snuck a better glance at the wheelchair, she didn't react immediately. Looked away. But did a double-take. Her chin stroked her breasts as her mouth momentarily gaped open. Confusion tickled her wrinkles and pity tried to hide them. She hid her true feelings, ignored Tiny Tim's glaring omission, smiled as if she meant it and asked about his holiday in Scotland.

To the gathered crowd, she welcomed him back professionally and introduced him as the reigning in-house champion, but the afternoon was uncharacteristically mute. There was no cheering or applause or whistling like usual and many left before the competition's end. Of those who remained, questions about mortality, morality, responsibility and voyeurism flitted through their consciousness. What was supposed to be frothy and lightweight had become existential and gruesome. As she watched proceedings, Landlady Kim could only think a diabetic amputee fronting an All You Can Eat Carvery Competition was as suitable as a convicted paedophile judging a little girls' beauty pageant, and asked to see him in her office afterwards.

Gill picked her fingernails. Brolly finished the bottle of wine. Gill looked at her phone. 'Twenty-three minutes. I could sneak outside her office? Have a listen? Maybe he's not even there any more?' Before Brolly had time to answer, a tray of glasses smashed on a hardwood floor. So did a posh yelp.

'Get the fuck outta my way!' Tiny Tim sped into the saloon and smacked into a waitress, who swore in German as she dropped the three-bowl mess of chilli con carne she was carrying.

'Tiny?' He ignored his friends, struggled with the exit. People stole glances. People muttered under their breath. People secretly thanked God they weren't him. His wheelchair blocked the door, the door knocked against his machine. He described his inability to stand erect and kick a fucking hole through the fucking thing. 'Tim?'

'Just open the fucking thing!'

Brolly did as he was told, then followed outside, where Tiny Tim ranted. He was a 44-stone freak show. He had a disability. He was an invalid with one leg. He had a wheelchair. He scared people. He was bad for business. He hated everything and everyone. He hated the pub. He hated the food. He hated the customers. He hated the alcohol. He hated the furniture. He hated the staff. He hated the All You Can Eat Carvery Competition. He hated Landlady Kim and most of all he hated himself. He fled the pub, but not his own sense of worthlessness.

'Tiny!?' Brolly cried out, but he was summarily ignored. After his third effort, he gave up and watched a lonely and isolated figure struggle up the gentle incline, head bowed, elbows flapping like an injured chicken, the only indication of life in an otherwise stilted, seemingly headless body.

Ten months after Tiny Tim had ghosted his friends, Brolly was cutting up pinstripe samples, about to send them to Bangor. It was close to 10.30 in the morning when his phone rang. Tiny Tim was in a pub in Camberwell, wanted to meet.

The Falcon was a Wetherspoons-type space full of men bludgeoned by life's club, their eyes shot by its pain, bloodied by its remedy. Tiny Tim fitted in well. His stomach spilt over his wheelchair arm rests and where his face had been blotchy, it was now a uniform vulva red offset only by burst capillaries, which ran down his face like miniature tributaries searching for lost parent lakes. Both grinned happily. Tiny Tim held out his hand. 'You won't mind if I don't stand up . . .'

'No worries, mate; reckon we'll both be a bit legless by the end of the day.' Brolly momentarily worried he'd pushed the boat of familiarity out too far as he noticed Tiny Tim's fingers, which had advanced from insipid nicotine to calming earthenware clay.

'Ha! I've missed you, mate!'

'I've missed you too!'

'That's good to hear . . .'

'Yeah. Probably not a big surprise . . .'

'Don't presume anything any more, I don't.'

'Well, I presume you want a drink?'

'Well, yeah, you can assume that. But on me.'

'If you insist. I'll get the next round.'

'Nah, all day or for however long you stick around. I've been a bit of an arsehole and wanted to apologise.'

Brolly couldn't deny it and didn't try to. 'Alright.'

71

'Didn't think you'd agree so readily!?'

'Well, it's true . . .'

Male muscles flexed. Stubble bristled.

'So it's settled, then. We both agree: I've been an arsehole and I'll buy the drinks. Only catch is, you have to get them. Here's my bar tab thing.'

After their third round, when Brolly started to spin through the air and wonder if there'd been a point to the reunion beyond the cursory apology, Tiny Tim stuttered backwards. His rubber wheel stuck to the heavy, carpeted floor. His teeth exuded a depressed chamois-yellow grimace. He flexed his upper torso, twisted to the left and then the right, sweated sour beads, retreated a couple of metres. For a second Brolly feared he might be leaving, although he couldn't think why. But it suddenly struck him.

'What the fuck!?' Tiny Tim had had a further amputation due to infection. This time a transfemoral alignment above the knee, in the upper thigh area. 'You should've let us know!'

'Naaah . . . You an' Gill already did enough the first time round. Didn't wanna impose again. And it wasn't so bad, to be honest.'

'Not a discussion. You should've let us know. That's what friends are for,' Brolly asserted angrily. 'Gill'll be really pissed off.'

'How d'you think I feel?!' That shut Brolly up. 'Whatever; it's my leg, my life. It wasn't such a big deal, to be honest. I knew the score, even knew half the staff. Had my wheelchair, paid one of the nurses to smuggle vodka in. Hasn't made much of a difference, really. I mean . . . You know, obviously I'd prefer to still have my leg but . . . I dunno . . . Everyone remembered me, which was nice, and I even had the same surgeon.'

'Ask her out on a date yet?'

'Half my age, a fifth of my weight, twice as many legs – didn't think it was a starter.'

'Probably not. Same regional anaesthetic?'

'Yeah. This time I watched the new Eddie Murphy film, but

they said I was laughing too much so I just listened to Spotify. I asked to see what they cut off. Felt like the Log Lady from *Twin Peaks*. Didn't wanna let it go but they took it from me anyway. They burn them, you know . . . all the amputated parts . . .' Tiny Tim trailed off. Cat guts scraped violin strings.

'Well . . . I'm glad it's over and done with. Least you can get on with the rest of your life.'

'Yeah, well . . . That's what I wanted to talk to you about . . . I won't bore you with all the details but my other leg's infected now an' they have to amputate that too . . .'

'Jesus Christ.' Brolly wished he'd stayed at home. Never picked up the phone. Left his friend as a memory, angry, passionate but mobile and with one leg and the promise of some future.

'Yeah, but fuck that! I'm done. Two's enough. Two fucking amputations is more than e-fucking-nough. My doctor said I'll die if I don't have it but I'm gonna die anyway, so fuck it.'

'Have you spoken to your counsellor or anyone?'

'Yeah, plus a session with my doctor an' my occupational therapist. Told 'em all the same thing. Fuck off. Not gonna do it.'

'So what you gonna do, just die?'

'Yep.'

Brolly felt limp, lame, helpless, powerless, impotent and unimportant. He studied the men's toilet sign to his left. He studied the secret universe of the swirls in the carpet below. He sucked in his cheeks. Puffed out his chest. Wanted to beat it like a hysterical baby monkey watching its father ripped from its grip. He spied on Tiny Tim's vodka eyes. There was a splash of water in the mix. He tried to turn off his own waterworks. Managed to squeeze the supply dry except for a small trickle. Barely noticeable. Except Tiny Tim noticed. Tiny Tim threw out his pudgy lifebelt of a hand. Brolly took it. Tried not to sink, although it was really Tiny Tim who was sinking.

'I know you're a stubborn bastard when you want to be but . . . is there nothing I can do to persuade you otherwise?'

'It's bin a long process coming to this decision but no, but thanks . . . But look, it's not all doom an' gloom. Could've been worse; I could've had a stroke, could've had motor neuron disease, could've been born a paraplegic . . . I mean . . . You know, I can't say my life's been remarkable, but I've enjoyed it and at the moment, well, I'm still mobile, just about, I've got some savings in the bank and I can still enjoy 'em, you know? Want to enjoy 'em. I mean, all that stuff with the amputation: don't drink, don't smoke, don't eat this, don't eat that. It's bollocks. It's like being locked in a cell with only water and raw vegetables but seeing tons of pubs an' takeaways right outside the window. Some people rise to the challenge, I suppose, but, honestly, can you see me losing 33 stone and running a fuckin' marathon without any legs?'

'Not really.'

'Nor can I. So fuck all the doctors. Fuck all the marathon runners. Fuck the pricks who find self-realisation in adversity. Fuck both my legs. Fuck my diabetes. Fuck Landlady Kim and fuck everyone and fuck everything. I'm gonna do what I do best. I'm gonna drink as much as I want and I'm gonna smoke as much as I want and I'm gonna eat as much as I want and I'm gonna do it all until it kills me. And I want you to do it too . . . I mean, not until it kills you but, just . . . I'd like to share the experience with you and Gill. You're my family and I want you to come on this final journey with me. And when I say that, I mean I'll pay for everything, so you don't have to worry about money. As I said, I got enough savings an' I want it to be full of joy for as long as it lasts . . . And . . . you know . . . hopefully one day I'll just have a heart attack and drop dead . . .'

Gill's reaction was similar to Brolly's. Sad but practical. He was their best friend and if he wanted to go that way, then that's the way he should go. A pint of euthanasia with a packet of hedonism. A plate of the old palliative with a dollop of rock 'n' roll. The hours blended into the days, which blurred into the weeks. It was almost a month after their odyssey had begun when the Falcon's manager, a cheery sort who'd fictionalised the factuality of his receding hairline by turning his mane into a lion's mullet, commandeered Brolly as he was sidesaddling off his mobility scooter.

'Excuse me, sir, I wondered if I might have a word?' The manager sounded more like he'd shoot a lion than cultivate one on his head.

'Something the matter?'

'Well, it's Mr Milligan . . .'

Brolly had never heard Tiny Tim called that before. 'What about him?'

'Well . . . Erm . . . He's no longer welcome here . . .'

'What!? Why?'

'Well, the thing is . . . I mean, you know . . . You spend a lot of time with him but, erm . . . Basically, he's drinking two bottles of vodka a day. And twenty-five-odd pints. And . . . well . . . I know we're a pub, but that's not even alcoholism . . . That's like . . . he's got a death wish . . .' Brolly didn't confirm the observation. 'I saw him passed out in his wheelchair on the way to the Tube last week and Lucy saw him screaming at the pedestrian crossing a few days ago . . . And I should add there were no cars or anyone to scream at. One day he shat himself and another he pissed himself. Godawful smell. The space around him, where you sit, it's become a no-man's land and the staff are frightened of him and . . . Well, just to clarify, it's nothing he's said. When he's sober, he's an absolute gentleman and he's always paid his bills and left generous tips, but his presence is disturbing and . . . and he's a car crash none of us wants to watch any more.'

'What d'you want me to do about it?'

'I wanted to let you know because even when you're drunk, you're more sober than he is and . . . Well, it upsets me to see someone have such . . . issues . . . And I know it's not my business to say so, but I think he needs help . . .'

Brolly nodded, didn't disagree with anything the manager said. 'Does he know about this?'

'Not yet. I thought it might be easier if I spoke to you first.'

Tiny Tim was surprisingly understanding and that evening he left his five favourite members of staff, including the manager, a tip of £100 each. Soon after that, he visited a lawyer to draw up his will. He made Brolly his estate's executor and left whatever remained to Gill and Brolly equally. He visited a funeral director to plan his interment, which, due to his size, proved complicated. Not that he cared, but he couldn't be embalmed and had to purchase two burial plots and pay two burial fees in advance. The closest cemetery to accept the 'outsized' was in Beckenham, a suburb Tiny Tim had never visited in his life and was momentarily aggrieved at for having to spend the entirety of his death. The funeral director pointed out he wouldn't fit into even the largest ready-made coffin so introduced him to a bespoke coffin-maker in Streatham, where, on a whim, Tiny Tim asked if his casket could be covered in leopard-skin fabric.

Brolly accompanied his friend to each and every increasingly depressing meeting but kept his melancholia to himself. He wondered if his business associate, Bangkok Dave, could make a matching leopard-skin suit for the burial, the idea of which pleased Tiny Tim no end. Bangkok Dave said he could, but it would take a while to find the correct fabric. Brolly felt guilty about haggling over the price, believing – correctly as it turned out – that he could save money by making the suit one-legged.

Tiny Tim had Brolly make ten copies of his flat keys. He gave one set to Brolly for 'emergencies', one to his next-door neighbour, who promised to supply his alcohol, and the remainder to the delivery staff from his favourite takeaways. Above the sofa, he pinned a hand-written note, which told the reader to contact Brolly in case of death or any other emergency. And if he wasn't contactable, then Gill. Barely able to move, the sofa became his knotty terrain. He became its putrid mountain. His facial features sank as the flab around them continued to swell. His neck consumed his jawline. The dimension of his arms became equidistant, and flesh hung from them like inbred sucklings. What remained of his legs, he hid under a blanket like an inverse, malignant picnic.

As well as the incessant eating and drinking, Tiny Tim entertained Gill and Brolly with a smorgasbord of his life's cultural highlights, which veered from high art to the lowest common denominators of popular (and sometimes unpopular) culture. They watched Jodorowsky's first four films, Roeg's first six, the gangster films of Scorsese plus *The Wolf of Wall Street*. They watched most of Waters, Rohmer, Meyer and some of Chaplin as well as the *Rocky* series, all available *Star Wars*, all the Halloweens and Hellraisers as well as *Saturday Night Fever*, *Staying Alive* and *Dirty Dancing* as a triple bill. They binge-watched *Breaking Bad*, *Stranger Things* and the first season of *True Detective*. They watched *The Office* twice, including the Christmas Special, and they watched *The Inbetweeners* TV series and films. They listened to every Bowie studio album in chronological order, they listened to *Sandinista!* by The Clash all the way through, they tried to listen to *Lulu* by Lou Reed and Metallica but failed, they spent a day listening to Krautrock and another day listening to all volumes of the psychobilly compilation *Stomping at the Klub Foot* and then *Nuggets I* and *II*: *Original Artyfacts*. They listened to ABBA *Gold* followed by The Beatles' *1* and had a lively discussion as to which was better; and they listened to Tiny Tim's five favourite Motörhead albums. Tiny Tim read passages from his favourite novelists, including Alistair MacLean, Frederick Forsyth, John le Carré, J.R.R. Tolkien, Richard Price, Terry Southern and Clive Barker, and they played board games too, mainly Risk and Cluedo but also Scrabble, which Tiny Tim never lost, and Battling Tops, backgammon and draughts.

Outside Kennington Underground, a white marker board with invisible writing distracted Brolly and made him run a red light.

Jeers and curses swerved around him as he tried to shrink in size. He started whistling, because that's what he did in panic mode. The tune started randomly but ended up as the James Bond theme. He'd just about calmed down when his phone rang. He'd recently changed his ringtone so didn't recognise the chirpy gambol as his own. It rang twice before Brolly remembered the notes were his, but he refrained from answering, didn't want to suffer more road rage. But then remembered the Grim Reaper had his phone number. It was Giovanni from Paolini's Pizza.

Tiny Tim's belly looked like it had escaped from a zoo. His hands looked bored. His nose pointed upwards as if trying to gauge Heaven's culinary competence. Brolly wondered if it wasn't a practical joke, Tiny Tim's gallows humour soldiering on to the bitter end. 'Oi, mate . . .' Brolly ejected. Hardly poetic or worthy of life's greatest mystery but it was, he decided, succinct and to the point. Leaning closer to Tiny Tim and testing his death mettle was out of the question. So was kicking him. Brolly didn't want to aggravate the gangrene. Then remembered he'd had no feeling in his gangrenous foot, so kicked it. He half expected it to fall off. It didn't. He half expected Tiny Tim to burst into laughter. He didn't.

All of a sudden, Brolly needed a drink. Tiny Tim was molesting a svelte tin of exotic lager in his right hand. It could be a low point, nicking a drink off a dead man, but could also be the wake-up call Tiny needed – he loved his lager, wouldn't let it go easily. The tin was lukewarm. Most of it still remained. His friend didn't budge when Brolly grabbed it or guzzled it. He threw the tin at Tiny Tim, who still didn't budge. 'Wanker! Fucking arsehole wanker!'

Gill burst into tears upon seeing her dead friend but didn't throw anything at him. Even though she abhorred religion, she recited the Lord's Prayer, which she remembered from school. She wanted to kiss him on the forehead but dared not lean in that far, so picked up his right hand and kissed that. She thanked him for inviting her on his final journey and tearfully asserted it had been a privilege. She went to the fridge and helped herself to a bottle of wine and various foods.

The ambulance arrived first. Then the police. Then the fire brigade. Then Tiny Tim's funeral director. Then a locum, who certified his death. No one had ever seen a body as large as his and it took almost an hour to work out how to proceed. There was no way anyone was going to lift him, let alone carry him out of the front door, so the firemen chipped away at the bricks around the window and removed them. A mobile crane operator advised a larger crane was needed, so everyone made themselves scarce until the larger crane arrived. A tabloid journalist started snooping around, asking questions and taking photographs. Gill tried to hit him but the police intervened and calmed the situation. She and Brolly sat with their friend and continued to do in his death what they'd done in his life: eat all his food and drink all his alcohol.

When the crane finally lifted Tiny Tim out of the flat, Brolly had the inspired idea to blast out one of his friend's pre-selected funeral choices, 'If I Can Dream' by Elvis Presley. The tempestuous and brooding clouds were enthralled. The moment felt like a gritty, depressing British film with a nod to the opening of Fellini's 8½, which Tiny Tim had shown Brolly a few months earlier. Covered in four red ambulance blankets, Tiny Tim was fastened, like an aspiring Gulliver in an oversized land of Lilliput, under a handful of ratchet straps and driven to Greenwich Mortuary on a flatbed truck.

The suit didn't arrive for the funeral but everything else went smoothly. Eight coffin-bearers pushed the double-sized leopard-skin coffin into the church, which was overflowing with mourners. The Elvis medley soothed the atmosphere and heightened the heartbreak: 'Love Me Tender', 'Always on My Mind' and 'If I Can Dream'. Brolly delivered a eulogy. A chaplain offered divine thoughts. Eyes glistened. Handkerchiefs did their duty. Hymns were sung. Monty Python's 'Every Sperm Is Sacred' played as the coffin was pushed back outside and, rather than roses or dirt, those gathered threw chocolate bars, sweet packets, bags of crisps onto Tiny Tim's coffin.

The evening ended in the same insalubrious pub basement near Liverpool Street where Tiny Tim had first put on the Wobble Club, a safe space for plus-sized people, their friends and their admirers to dance the night away. Tiny had compiled the playlist himself and his set ended with a reworking of Toni Basil's 'Mickey', which he'd re-recorded in his living room, replacing the word 'Mickey' with 'Fatty.' The song became a tribute to his life and to all the men and women who chose to do with their bodies what they wanted, not what society dictated. It was a classic ending to a classic day and the dance floor didn't thin for almost twenty minutes after the lights came on. The club honoured its dearly departed friend and chanted, 'There's only one Tiny Tim . . . one Tiny Tim . . . There's only one Tiny Tim . . .' to the tune of the Cuban protest song 'Guantanamera'.

Brolly remembered when he and Tiny Tim drank nothing but Black Velvet all afternoon and stuffed themselves with Chinese. They'd just watched a double bill of *Pretty in Pink* and *The Breakfast Club* and were waiting for Gill to arrive before progressing to another, as yet undecided double bill. Tiny Tim was reminiscing about the first time he'd seen the John Hughes films in his local cinema. A maudlin disposition oozed over him as the seismic gap between the promise of his youth and the reality of his adulthood sprawled in front of his blurry eyes. 'You know what?' he asked.

'What?' Brolly grabbed a prawn dumpling.

'I've been putting a brave face on this whole thing but . . . And I don't regret my decision, what we're doing but . . . It's a fuck-up. It's a complete fuck-up. I mean . . . when d'you actually feel old? I don't feel old now. Never have done, don't suppose I ever will do. But fifty-fucking-two. I could've had another thirty years if I was fitter. Maybe more. It's too young, innit? I mean . . . I'm not saying this cos I want your sympathy. I don't. Don't want your tears either.

Definitely don't want your pity. Don't want your fucking anything except your company, but . . .' Tiny Tim grabbed the nearby bottle of champagne and downed it. Brolly felt the maudlin disposition ooze over him too. 'I suppose what I want to say is . . . if I could go back and change everything, I would. Wouldn't drink so much, wouldn't eat so much, would've even done some exercise, you know? But all that . . . I can only call it greed, really . . . all that greed, gluttony, I loved it, I really did, still do, as you know . . . But it's so . . . I mean, what was the point? Really? I've always been proud of my weight, really fucking proud, defined myself by it and most people don't know . . . I mean, you do, obviously, but most people don't know how fucking hard it is to live like this. Not amputated, just bloody big . . . But . . . you know, just fucking climbing stairs, sitting down, getting out of bed, going for a shit, doing what most people take for granted . . . I'm not one to preach, but you and Gill – you're still young, still got your life ahead of you and it's not too late to change. It's never too late to . . . Well, it's never too late to change until it is, I suppose . . . So I just hope you don't make the same mistakes I've made and I hope once all this is over, you can look back on the experience and . . .' Tiny Tim filled his lungs as if for dramatic effect. Brolly preferred Tiny Tim when he was the lairy alcohol guzzler rather than the sentimental philosopher.

'When all this is over, I'd like you and Gill . . . I want you and Gill to think of me as a cautionary tale and I want you to lose some weight. I really think you should both lose some weight. Trust me, you don't want to end up like me. You don't wanna get diabetes. You don't wanna lose a foot or a leg. Certainly don't want to lose two. And who knows, maybe you want kids? Maybe you want to travel? To fly. To ski. To scuba dive. Fuck. To skydive! So stop it, alright? Lose some weight. You won't regret it, I promise you. One day, when I'm not here, when I'm fuckin' caning it with Lemmy, looking down over you both, I want you to think about your life and make me proud.'

CHAPTER 11

Brolly let his tears tickle and trickle until they ran dry or reached the corners of his lips, whereupon he snagged them and savoured their intricate saltiness. Like raindrops running down the windowpane of his soul, they glimmered and were cathartic. They crystallised his resolve.

He stood up and shuffled over to the sink, turned on the tap and splashed his face with water. He grabbed a strip of kitchen roll and blew his nose. He grabbed another strip and dried his face. He threw both balls into the bin and walked over to the fridge, which he opened and scrutinised. It was like looking at a police line-up of trusted friends and confidants who'd recently been revealed as seasoned con artists. The sausages, the bacon, the fizzy drinks, the ketchup, the mayonnaise? Guilty. Miscreants, all of them. Over decades, they'd inveigled their way into his life and stolen his best days, but the truth had finally been outed. Things had to change. He slammed the fridge door and pulled open the confectionery cupboard below. Similar feelings of love, loss, betrayal and deceit ravaged his heart.

At his desk, he googled 'how to proceed with a diet'. The breadth of results corralled his taste buds, chastised his appetite, made him giddy with the prospect of change. The search's conflicting nature confused him. The similar photographs intimidated him, devices all, for the terminally gullible, the narcissistically driven, the constantly hungry. Raw this, raw that, raw everything. Roar, roar, roar. In various states of undress, avocados popped up everywhere, like an army of benign jack-in-the-boxes. Tape measures tumbled down flat abdomens like self-righteous cinctures constricting religious robes. Healthy glows prepared healthier salads with slender fingers, toned stomachs, bleached teeth. He read about Atkins and Ketogenic, Paleolithic and Zone, Vegan, Dukan, HCG, South Beach, Mediterranean, Dash, Flexitarian and F-Factor. He read about Mayo and Nordic, Ornish and Volumetric, Vegetarian and Pescatarian, the Whole30 and the 5:2, the Alkaline and the Jenny Craig. He read about injections and fasting and milkshakes and probiotic supplements and decided someone, somewhere was making a lot of money out of a lot of people's insecurities and miseries.

He started taking notes on everything but finished taking notes on nothing. After a few hours, a migraine beat against his skull, coded secret emissions for pints and burgers. How he craved them, pints and burgers, five of each, please. With cheese. And bacon. And chilli con carne on the fries. He closed his computer as a little worm, orange and throbbing, with deep-set eyes and grinning fangs, taunted his peripheral vision and wiggled into his fraying cortex.

It didn't take a genius to work out that if you stopped eating pizza and ice cream and takeaways and sweets, especially stupid-sized portions thereof, and replaced them with fruit and vegetables and chicken and some exercise, you'd lose weight. Or maybe it did, judging from the cornucopic esoterica and gastronomic philandering he'd just been privy to. It was all about willpower, self-discipline and single-mindedness, he decided, similar to a heroin addict going cold turkey but without the execrable fashion sense. He'd successfully given up smoking on his thirtieth birthday without taking even a puff again, so why shouldn't his new resolve be just as successful?

Behind him, Auntie Violet's cupboard stood like a grieving soldier, ponderous, uncertain of what it was or why. From it, he used his grab-and-grip device to pick up a box wrapped in brown Kraft paper and prettified with exotic stamps. On his desk, he unwrapped the box and turned it upside down; a package, protected by diaphanous tissue, fell out. Brolly forced a smile as he held up a leopard-skin Teddy Boy jacket. Black lapels sunk in a deep V to navel level, where one self-covered button joined the sides together. The cuffs pulled back on themselves, matched the black decorative trimmed pockets. He couldn't resist temptation, struggled out of his chair, stood up and tried on Tiny Tim's burial suit.

The jacket was way too big, of course, which made a refreshing change and, Brolly hoped, was a talisman for his future. He unravelled the one-legged trouser and held it to the light. A black band ran around the trouser waist, accentuating the leopard-skin loops under which a belt would slide. The absent leg stopped just below the groin, like a short-cut swimming trunk; it made the trousers look like a one-legged dress, a Ziggy Stardust *Rumble in the Jungle* curiosity. Brolly grabbed his mannequin. It wasn't ideal – it was female – but had come cheaply for a fiver at a car boot sale and if it had tennis-ball-sized breasts, so what? So did most of his customers. He slipped it into the trousers, fastened safety pins around the back, halved the waist and did the same with the jacket so that its button kept the sides together. He stepped back to admire his design. He forced another smile, grunted with maudlin sentimentality, regretted Tiny Tim hadn't been able to take the outfit with him but was pleased it now presided over his working day like a cross-dressing cautionary tale about the sins of the flesh. Or the stomach, at least.

He opened his desk's second-to-bottom drawer on the left and rummaged through it, grabbed a tabloid, THE tabloid, and flicked through the faded, yellowed pages until he found the double-page spread. His emotions spun around in his own noisy blender. His tears, his anger, his love, his hate, his regret, his occasional self-blame. Four pictures of Tiny Tim rationalised the national infamy. Three were anonymous and taken outside his flat; one pointing up at him being hauled out of his home, the second a close-up of him being strapped into the flatbed and the third from the council block, looking down on the circus below. In the fourth, it was night-time. Tiny Tim was younger and slimmer but still no waif. His hairy breasts and hairless shoulders glowed almost healthily on a beach littered with fellow farangs. A Red Bull bandana was pulled tight around his sweating forehead. His arms were wrapped around two giggling Thai women, one of whom was wearing glowing green horns, the other, yellow. From each hand dangled a vodka bucket with a cluster of straws. His smile was so acute, it practically forced his eyes closed.

Headlined 'Obesity Epidemic Shows No Sign of Slowing Down', the piece used Tiny Tim's 'rescue' by the emergency services to report on the epidemic that was spreading across the nation like wildfire. More people had diabetes and were using more insulin and visiting more hospitals than ever before. Absolutely no one saw this trend being reversed. Ever, it seemed. By 2050, obesity and its related issues would cost the NHS £10 billion a year and affect half the nation. There was a quote from one of the firemen about having to winch an increasing number of obese people from their homes and there was another quote from a fat activist. He blamed the government for this surge and bemoaned the lack of sugar tax, without which its strategy for tackling the crisis had a fat chance of success. Boom boom. Along the right side of the article, a slender and pretty blonde wore panties and a bra and practically molested herself into persuading the readers, if they didn't already know, that slim girls had all the fun.

Brolly Blu-tacked the double spread, mid-chest level, on the wall to his left. He hobbled back to his computer, googled 'diabetes', clicked 'Images', found nothing too repulsive, mundanities for the afflicted: test kits, pricked fingers, goody-goody foodstuffs. But then he google-imaged 'amputation'. 'Oh Jesus Christ . . .' A severed hand; the flesh at the wrist, minced meat. A foot; rough and curved like an apprentice had done a bad job filing down its missing toes, the skin, if it could be called that, all bananas and oranges. A woman, her amputated stump awkwardly spouting from her lap like an unwanted bastard child. Bandages and stumps and limbs and prosthetics and one-legged athletes and doctors and diagrams and saws and survivors. All encouraged evil words to escape his mouth and his brow to crease. It made him sick and it made him upset. It made him want to cry and it made him want to hug each and every person he saw.

He google-imaged 'gangrene'. More swear words followed, louder, more disbelieving. The amputations suggested survival and some quality of life, but the gangrenous images suggested the opposite. Hellfire and death. They looked like every body's satanic apocalypse, skin devoured by nightmares of black, disfigured and disgusted, slimy reminders of what was once human, gnarly horror shows dipped in hellish pits of sulphur and tar. Someone, somewhere, something, monsters or men, God or the Devil, infinity or the space beyond, had a bitter and twisted retribution for the human psyche, the human condition. Swollen hands resembled psychedelic amphibians, withered coal-coloured feet resembled goats' hooves, whole stomachs looked like they'd been nibbled and defecated on by legions of rats.

Brolly took fifteen screen grabs in all, but opted against taking one of the baby that had lost its left arm and lower leg, or one of the decayed penis, which was hollow, pustular and hardly looked like a penis at all. He repositioned his desk under the printouts. He stood back and inspected his work; it made him want to vomit again, retch and cleanse his soul with soap-water and detergent. But most of all, it made him want to lose weight and not lose any part of his own precious body, which was, of course, the whole point.

Outside the Tesco Express on the Walworth Road, a red Ferrari canoodled with double yellow lines and two rough beanpoles with poor balance circled each other shoddily. Brolly ignored his pain as he wobbled off his scooter and, with a sense of breathless pomp, practically slipped through the sliding doors. A worker mopped up a smashed red-wine bottle. Brolly picked up a wire basket, walked around the corner and was greeted by an intoxicating scent: the American dream he'd never lived. Pecan nuts and maple syrup, almond paste and cinnamon. He gobbled up the air, shuffled past the bread but lingered around the crisps, eulogised the sweets and the chocolate bars. Nostalgia teased him but he turned his back as resolve congratulated him.

Much like Asda, the store was chilly. More so next to the long, refrigerated aisle that shivered from the entrance to halfway down the left side of the store. Brolly zipped up his jacket as he threw his eyes over the contents, stumbled across his new nirvana. Chicken thighs and chicken drumsticks, chicken breasts and chicken slices, chicken chunks and chicken pieces, plain and flavoured, sweet chilli, BBQ, mango, lime and coconut. Chicken, chicken, chicken. His lunch jumped out at him like a flasher from a park bench. A pack of dogs barked in his stomach and saliva fondled his taste buds. He slipped open the misted glass door and pulled out a ready-to-eat whole roast chicken. He pulled out another for the following day. He grabbed a bag of spinach, his random vegetable of choice, and two loose avocados, the special guest star from his online research.

'Honey, I'm home!' he shouted as he opened his front door, even though he knew Gill was at work. Overcome by baser instincts and uncontrollable urges, he ripped the cellophane wrapping off a chicken as he hobbled to the kitchen and stuffed a wing into his mouth. Without sauces and spices and crunchy coatings, it tasted pure. Natural. Like something from his childhood, like, well . . . chicken. He tore open the spinach bag, plucked out a small bush of leaves and stuffed them into his mouth; grit, earth and metal. They were inoffensive enough and he'd do some research as to how better to serve them in the coming days. The avocado was a trickier beast altogether. He stopped himself from eating one like an apple. The skin was too tough, too calloused. He sunk his finger into it like he would a satsuma, tried to tear a piece off, but that didn't work. He grabbed a knife and cut the fruit in half, gouged out the stone with his teeth and spat it onto the table. It crashed to the floor. He tried peeling the skin but that was too fiddly. He cut a half in half and tried to eat it like a pomegranate, but the skin was too sharp and obstructive. He finally came up with a brainwave: he'd use a spoon. It melted in his mouth, tasted like guacamole.

He threw his meal's remains into the wheelie bin and carried his next day's lunch upstairs so that Gill didn't spot the chicken and smell a rat. Online, he bought a medium-sized fridge for his office and some warehouse packing scales (the only ones that guaranteed a maximum load of up to 45 stone) to measure his progress. He was about to slump back in his chair when a word leaped out of his subconscious, clawed his breast, ripped at his throat. The word was anathema to him and Gill; the disease by which they measured the decline of Western civilisation. Exercise. They scorned it on a regular basis, made jokes about it, derided gyms as Temples of the Insane and ridiculed body-hugging-Lycra-clad lunatics as if they were lemmings running over a cliff. But enough was enough. If he was going to do this thing, he was going to do it correctly. Excuses would no longer cut the mustard. As he trekked back down the stairs and struggled into his parka, he wondered for the first time if he'd ever become one of those Lycra-clad lunatics himself. Crazier things had happened, but at that particular moment, he couldn't think what.

Outside, the street lights were psyching themselves up for another glowing appearance. The temperature matched Tesco's. A lonesome newspaper page pranced across the tarmac. Brolly wished he had more hair to swish around his face and wondered how far to walk. Fifteen metres was about the limit without completely killing himself but for the last few months, with what now seemed like uncanny prescience, he'd eschewed his home's stairlift and tackled the stairs on foot. It didn't sound much, but to begin with he'd almost died on a daily basis, so it must count for something, he reasoned. He scanned the landmark destinations; at about 100 metres, Portman Square to his left was way too far. At about 5 metres, the nearest lamp post was way too near. There was a black chunk of a motorbike 10 metres away and a red hulk of a Jeep about 20. Beyond them was a turning to Charterhouse Road on the left, and a spindly wooden totem pole in someone's front yard, about 10 metres in front of the square.

Brolly rummaged through his jacket, plucked out his phone and failed to fit his whole face into his portrait mode. It was for this exact reason he never took selfies, but this was a momentous occasion and he wanted to capture it for posterity. He turned his phone to landscape and grinned. He looked at the picture and a moment's clarity punched him in the face. His heart sank, his pride plummeted, his shame soared. He suddenly saw what everyone else saw and realised the joke he always thought funny was at his expense.

But nothing could dampen his spirits; he was exercising! He was going to be thin. Or thinnish. Or even a bit overweight, a bit of a bulger, a chubster, a Pudgemeister General. But not really fat. Not totally overweight. Not completely obese. Certainly not morbidly obese. No, sirree. He'd walk to the shops, catch buses, wave down black cabs, hop on the Tube. He might even run. For fun. Or jog. Or cycle. Whenever he wanted. Wherever he wanted. Just for the hell of it. It was going to be great! He fantasised about showing the portrait to slim friends, as yet unknown, or casual acquaintances in public houses. Maybe in the Lake District or the Peak District. After an all-day ramble through glorious rolling fields and trickling rivers. They'd giggle incredulously, guffaw disbelievingly. That wasn't him, was it!? The image was fake, surely? Manipulated through some faddish body-distorting app? But he'd assure them it was, absolutely, him and it was, absolutely, real. He'd explain his theory on weight loss and regale them with his experience of it (although he'd leave out the vomiting). After further protestation, their reluctance would waver, whip to acceptance and snap to admiration. They'd high-five him or punch him affectionately on the shoulder, ask if he fancied a pint. He wouldn't; alcohol, beer especially, piles on the weight, but . . . well . . . maybe . . . just . . . He had walked 15 miles, after all, burned off God knows how many calories and only eaten half an apple so . . . Go on then, just the one, but definitely no crisps.

A delivery man with delusional but optimistic shorts and a pessimistic haircut powered into a UPS van across the road and snapped on the engine. It lurched forward, then leaped as a grey plume of smoke disintegrated in its wake. Brolly shuffled onto the pavement and took the first step towards the rest of his life.

The 5 metres to the lamp post were beans on toast. The following 5 metres to the motorbike were coq au vin. If the distance wasn't exactly comfortable, it was still one he was accustomed to. His heart belted. His lungs wheezed. His breath deepened and his steps, quarter-circle gyrations, shallowed, slowed and diminished in size the further he walked. But that was all par for the course. He ground to a halt at the bike. It had a flat tyre. He rested his hand on the leather saddle. His stomach was being stitched by a surgeon. He clamped it with his cool fingers. The surgeon didn't notice, carried on needling. He considered his options. The journey from bike to Jeep would be a chilled lemon soufflé. He contemplated returning to the house, but it was only another 8 metres or so. He took a deep breath and wended his way forward.

The pavement stuck to his soles, his legs started to fatten. His chest pounded. His eyebrows scissor-jumped, his brow backflipped. A lonesome bead of sweat escaped down his forehead. He didn't have a walking stick to rest on. A banister to lean on. His face started to colour like the rosy apple in his rambling fantasy. If he wasn't up shit creek, he was certainly close. And without a paddle. Quite possibly without a canoe, even. As another trickle of sweat abseiled down his brow, stung his left eye, he started to think he'd made a big mistake. Halfway there, it was just as easy to carry on as to turn back but he couldn't turn back, not now, not without losing any of the little self-respect he retained.

His feet tugged the concrete pavement. His heart battered his ribcage. He no longer breathed but balled. Industrial moaning interspersed the balling. His thighs cramped. His lower arms tingled. Pins and needles jabbed his hands. His inner organs railed against his lungs. He smashed his hands against his chest like a failed Tarzan, king of the urban jungle. No animals rushed to his side. He attacked his thigh like he did in the morning. A stroke wasn't what he wanted. Or a heart attack. Especially when he was doing this to avoid God's cruel humour. Just his luck to suffer both at the same time. He didn't want to be paralysed. Or die. Not on that pavement. In that jacket. At that weight. In that weather. He didn't want Gill to go through what he'd been through with Tiny Tim. The snarky solicitor, the self-righteous funeral director, the blasé coffin-maker, the terribly nice vicar; he knew exactly what they were all thinking. Not *would* Brolly be next, but *when*? He was sure fewer people would turn up to his funeral than Tiny Tim's, which would be embarrassing. And what about his mum? He hadn't seen her for such a long time. He didn't care so much about his dad, but his mum? And his brother? He should really contact them again. He should do many things before it was too late. He was barely in control of his limbs as he reached for his phone, which practically flew out of his hand when he pulled it from his jacket. What should he do? Phone 999 and demand an ambulance? Tell them he was stuck 15 metres from his home but was too fat to walk back? They'd laugh him off the line. He could call Taxi Rob and arrange a pick-up, but Gill would surely find out. Either way, what would he do in the meantime?

A yellow football suddenly flabbergasted his face. Its drag ruffled the air in front of him. Brolly rippled. The ball missed him, smacked a nearby wall and rebounded into the gutter. Brolly's instinct forced him around. The effort was more than he cared to admit. His body continued to panic. Two white overalls smoked outside a house that was halfway through changing shades of grey. They were suspiciously placid, as if one had bet the other to take aim at Brolly and were now feigning complete ignorance. He wished he could knock the ball back in a gesture of shared masculinity but worried about collapsing. The potential mishap distracted Brolly and perversely calmed him, made him grin, reacquainted him with his senses. He wiped sweat off his head, from under his chins. He flexed his stubby fingers. The pins and needles dropped out. He rubbed a hand in an armpit. It comforted him, smelled like his life, his trials, his tribulations. He expanded his lungs. The air no longer bit but licked and lapped.

He could do this.

His premature death symptoms collapsed to the ground, died before he did. He nodded at the universe, winked at God, smiled at a crumpled tampon box next to his feet, took those last treacherous steps towards the Jeep with pride and gutsiness. Once there, he turned around, smacked his backside against the grille and dented the refreshingly cool bonnet with his heavy hands and heavier backside. The Jeep sunk and its registration plate dug into the road, but he didn't care; he'd done it, achieved his goal. This was it. This really was the beginning. He was going to conquer this thing.

CHAPTER 12

I t was raining cats and dogs when Gill left the next morning, so Brolly didn't follow her outside like usual, but stayed in the warm, dry hallway. He felt like Judas, betraying his love with a kiss, as he bade her farewell. She bounced off the pavement, traversed the road. He watched her scooter's back wheels kick up small arcs of water, toyed with using the sink or the shower for his purging but dismissed both as he shut the door.

He stared into the abyss of the toilet's porcelain ventricle, looked like a man who had no choice but to commit an atrocity. He brushed his hand over his thinning hair, felt like he was in a stand-off between himself and the toilet. The toilet was intractable. Had the patience of a saint. Wasn't going anywhere quickly. Brolly knew he had to make the first move. He would always have to make the first move. He snivelled. Molested time. Puffed his way to the sink, twisted the tap, bent over, swallowed untidy mouthfuls of water as it thundered outside. A storm was closing in. He turned the water off, dried his face and picked up his toothbrush, which looked like an inverse mohican. He contemplated tickling his epiglottis with it. Contemplated whether it would be easier than sticking his fingers down his throat. Dropping the toothbrush down his oesophagus and choking to death felt like a sufficient deterrent. He put it back down and shifted back to the toilet. He locked and unlocked his jaw as if he was an alligator practising for supper. He snatched lungfuls of centrally heated air and held them for as long as he could. His body started to sway, his blood massaged his brain.

And then he did it.

In his body's brief civil war, his body fought uncivilly. Three fingers jammed into his mouth and forced themselves downwards. They smashed his uvula and rammed the soft nodular flesh at the back of his throat. His teeth fought valiantly, clamped his digits and pressured bones to breaking point. Inner demons gurgled. His psyche grappled his instinct. His resolve bludgeoned his common sense. Nature triumphed. So did he. So did his breakfast. An arc of a gush. Baked-bean colour. Small chunks of bacon. Glistening gristle of sausage. Stomach acid and weak tea burned his nostrils and his pharynx. His body convulsed. His stomach revulsed. Larger splashes of vomit decorated the toilet seat, smaller ones, the floor. And just as the gush ran out, he did the right thing, the wrong thing, the brave thing, the foolish thing, the diet thing, the same thing. He stuck his fingers back down his throat. Three more times. The dedication to his cause was unerring and brutal. Towards the end, it felt like safety pins ripping through sandpaper. It was only when the retching became dry and was replaced by seismic coughing that he knew his job was complete and he could rest, traumatised but fulfilled.

With a sense of achievement, he treated himself to the stairlift on his return to the kitchen. He was hungry. And thirsty. And dizzy. He drank chlorinated tap water. Opened a tin of baked beans and heated it. He poured them on three slices of toast and devoured them unapologetically and unashamedly. He figured he'd already lost weight that morning and had earned it. He eschewed the sausage or bacon, which, if he was being honest, would have been his preference. The baked-bean flavour reminded him of the vomit and the pain of the vomit, but he was hungry. The toast's crisp rigidity felt like more sandpaper, and he wondered about not toasting the bread the next morning. Nothing felt like the safety pins.

He enjoyed the breakfast but towards its end noticed the skin on his middle and index fingers was scuffed with blood. He hadn't felt his teeth rip into his flesh, but his body had been in such a state of shock and repulsion that the abrasions didn't surprise him. He giggled as he licked his fingers. They tasted of metal. The metal tasted better than the chlorinated tap water. At least he knew where it came from. He wondered if his fingers would bleed the next day and the day after. He wondered how much of his own blood he could drink before collapsing. He wondered if the blood would become an integral part of his weight loss and his regurgitation's tang. 'Move over teenage waifs and dysmorphic housewives, there's a new kid on the block: the bulimic fat fucker!' he thought with a chuckle.

The fridge arrived on the Wednesday and the scales two days later. He hid them in the corner opposite his office's entrance. Rectangular and aluminium, they looked like a futuristic skateboard for the hard of balancing. White and clunky, the fridge looked like a fridge. Brolly weighed 42 stone 1lb. He was glad to have a figure to wage his clandestine war against and was relieved the scales didn't buckle under his weight. Rather than torture himself on a daily basis, he opted to do so on a weekly one and to tabulate the results in a notebook.

The following Friday, after purging and going to the toilet, Brolly listened to an electric machine drill into brick near his office. It sounded like an unemployed dentist trying to expand his horizon. Or someone else's horizon. It frayed his nerves. Grated his carrots. He unknotted his dressing gown and encouraged it to the floor. He retained his Santa-Claus-themed red-and-green Y-fronts and blue-striped Paul Smith socks (the only item of regular clothing he could still purchase and wear) and stood like a dazed ape in front of the scales. He chewed his lips and tried not to dribble. He scratched his underarms. Could feel his heart message the rest of his body but wasn't sure what the message was. He squeezed his testicles, suddenly felt self-conscious and drew the curtains. The electric drill stopped. He expanded his lungs, took a step in what he hoped was the right direction. He couldn't hide from the truth any longer, didn't want to be an ape for ever. He shuffled onto the scales. The aluminium chilled his soles, admonished his soul. He closed his eyes, bowed his head, swooshed his tongue around his gums, squeezed his tummy, started to waver but finally did what he had to do, opened what he'd just closed.

'YES! YES! YES!' His hands shot in the air. His eyes shone with triumph. His optimism glimmered with self-congratulation. 'YEEEEEEEESSSSSSSSSSS!' Brolly lapped his study victoriously. He stepped back on the scales to relive his moment of glory, to rule out mistakes, visual impairments and foul play. Nope. He'd actually, bloody well gone and done it! He'd actually bloody well lost weight! He'd never lost weight in his whole life. Just added and added and added it on. But no longer. He could hold his head high, stare in the mirror and formally describe himself as a slimmer. Someone who slims. Someone who loses weight. Someone who has lost weight. Someone who weighed less than he weighed the last time he weighed himself. The sides of his mouth tickled his earlobes. It was his first step towards re-ingratiating himself with the human race. He'd lost 4lbs. He was down to 41 stone 11lbs. Brolly stuck to his regime with military precision and resolve. He downgraded from one chicken a day to two chickens every three days and replaced the chicken twice a week with salmon. He reversed a habit of a lifetime by tightening rather than loosening his braces and his dressing-gown belt eventually lengthened. Despite everything, though, he felt like a sequoia crashing in a forest without anyone to see it or even hear it. And if that was the case, he wondered, had the crash really happened?

The All You Can Eat Christmas Carvery took place on the three Sundays preceding Christmas Day. The beef was replaced with turkey, the horseradish sauce with cranberry, the Yorkshire pudding with stuffing and the kale with Brussels sprouts. The competition started with contestants pulling crackers. Once they'd crowned their heads with the colourful paper hats from inside, eating could begin. On the first Sunday, Brolly managed a relatively unimpressive six plates.

'And the winner is Don't Give a Fork! With a massive ten plates of turkey with all the trimmings! Let's hear it, ladies and gentlemen, for Don't Give a Fork!' Gill made devil's horns out of her fingers and thumbs and gurned at the audience as her eyeballs grappled her eyebrows. She momentarily resembled the Grinch, but didn't look as seasick. Brolly slapped his hands together as she struggled to her feet. Brolly was embarrassed to watch her. So was most of the audience. The pain distended her triumph but she hid it well. Enthusiasts snapped photos and youngsters bagged selfies, but the audience soon dwindled.

'I remember when we first started you wouldn't even do the Christmas Carveries 'cos of the Brussels . . .' Brolly said as their last fan left the room. Gill laughed.

'Yeah. I must be maturing.'

'Or going senile.'

'Or my mouth's getting bigger.'

Brolly wanted to say, 'Or your stomach.' But didn't.

Gill continued. 'As long as I don't chew 'em, don't really taste 'em.'

'Don't you chew 'em?'

'Nah.'

'Swallow them whole?'

'Yeah.'

'Wow. Sign of a pro! The turkey kills me every time. Too dry. Way too dry. Can't get it down my throat. Can't wait until we get back to the beef,' Brolly lied.

'Gravy. That's all you need to know. Cranberry sauce and the horseradish help too. Lubricate, lubricate, lubricate!'

'Yeah, I think I need to work on my technique,' Brolly said disingenuously.

He purged himself five times before he eliminated the Christmas Carvery from his system. Over the last few months, he'd become more adept at aiming his vomit, but lumps and bumps still violated the toilet's porcelain rim with a cranberry aesthetic. He ripped some toilet roll and wiped and flushed away the evidence. He washed his hands, pulled two extra-strong mints from his jacket, chomped on them as he rippled his wattle and imagined himself to be a turkey and what it would be like if someone ate him. With a ghostly image of a large, inhuman creature sawing the flesh off his thigh, he exited. Gales of high-pitched hysteria oscillated down the corridor. Opposite, Landlady Kim balanced expertly on a randomly placed dining chair.

'You alright?' Her coarse voice, barbed and grating at times, sounded caring, concerned. The change confused Brolly. He was expecting the worst, somehow. Though what that entailed, he wasn't sure.

'Yeah . . .' He tried not to twitch like a guilty schoolboy. She scrutinised him. Assessed his monosyllable.

'You sure?'

'Yeah, I'm fine . . .'

'It sounded like you were vomiting.'

'Oh . . . Well . . . Yeah, I was . . . Think it was something I ate . . .'

'In the carvery?'

'No, I think it might've been breakfast. Or last night. Felt a bit sick this morning, to be honest.'

'Is Gill alright?'

With Landlady Kim's questions being almost too forensic for a passing conversation, a casual interest, Brolly sensed he had to tread carefully. 'Yeah, I think so.'

'I can ask her if you want?'

Brolly smudged an eyebrow. 'No, I don't think you need do that.'

''Cos I've got some Pepto-Bismol in my office. Can't be very pleasant throwing up all that carvery . . . What was it? Six plates?'

'Well . . . Six an' a half. Yeah, it's not, but . . . I'll be fine, thanks, and I'll let Gill know in case she's feeling the same . . .'

'Will you come with me, please?' Landlady Kim didn't even look at Brolly as she stood up and walked down the corridor towards her office.

Stacks of paperwork made her wooden desk look not so much erudite as beleaguered and an old-fashioned record player promised to fall off a chunky filing cabinet behind. There wasn't a record in sight, but a signed photo of Amy Winehouse punctuated a barren wall, her only company Mr December, a fireman who was so hot he'd taken off all his clothes. The room lacked ventilation and was contaminated by chain-smoke and festering catarrh.

'Close the door and take a seat, please . . .'

Brolly did as he was told and Landlady Kim sat down. She made it look easy, like she'd been doing it her whole life. Brolly's seat was armless and skeletal and he prayed it didn't make a mockery of him. He tried not to drop himself onto it but rather ease himself into it. He held his breath as he did so. The chair creaked, wobbled, swayed and squeaked. He refrained from further physical activity as he gripped its underneath.

'Are you sure you're OK?' Landlady Kim repeated.

'Yeah, I'm fine, thank you . . .'

'You know you can talk to me if there's anything wrong. I know we don't exactly . . . talk a lot, but . . . we have known each other a long time and . . .' She trailed off. Gazed deep into Brolly's eyes. He practised his fifth amendment, even though he wasn't in America.

He'd seen it in crime thrillers and the ploy invariably served the accused well. She leaned across the desk. Brolly thought it rude to stare down her cleavage but couldn't help himself; her proud breasts demanded it. She stretched her arms out.

'Give me your hands . . .' The gesture was intimate, the intimation almost sexual. All of a sudden, Brolly wondered if Landlady Kim had a fetish for larger men. Some men had fetishes for big women, so why not? BBM. Big Beautiful Men. Mr December suggested otherwise but Brolly was pretty sure no calendar offered a yearly fix of excessively large male pin-ups. The idea might work well for his company, Suits You, Sir! All the men could be completely naked except for one of Bangkok Dave's strategically placed creations. He made a mental note to explore the option later as he stared at Landlady Kim's talon-like hands.

'Are you sure this is appropriate!?' Brolly was flummoxed, wondered why it had taken Landlady Kim almost a decade to declare her attraction to him. And why now?

'Just give me your hands, please.' Brolly locked eyes with her, confronted her kink. Her pencilled eyebrows shaved his conscience. Her surgically enhanced lips fluffed his guilt. Her pointed nipples massaged his impending panic. His forced smile deceived his karma. He did as he was told. Again. Held out his hands. Palms up. Docked them in hers. An electric eel wriggled through his body. Brolly couldn't remember the last time he'd been so intimate with a woman who wasn't Gill. A butterfly fluttered across his face. Her hands felt soft, not dry. They felt warm and comforting. The butterfly fluttered across her face too. She turned his hands over and investigated them. She confirmed something to herself and lifted her eyes back to his. 'I'm so sorry . . .' The butterfly died.

'Sorry?'

'How long?'

'How long what?' This wasn't the romantic segue Brolly had started to fantasise about.

'You can talk to me, you know. I understand . . . I really do.'

'I don't know what you're talking about . . .'

'How long have you been doing it?'

Brolly shook his head; he really didn't know what she was talking about.

'As I said, I know we're not, like, mates, but honestly, I have a great deal of affection for you . . .' Brolly wondered if the romance was back on. '. . . And Gill . . .' Obviously not. Unless she was bisexual. Which now he came to think about it, she might be. For a second, he imagined her squashed in between him and Gill and looked back at Mr December to distract him but imagined Mr December and Landlady Kim squashed between them both and subconsciously threw a glass of water over himself.

'I don't think I follow . . .'

Landlady Kim pulled her hands from his and spat on their back. She rubbed them vigorously, clenched her fists and presented them to Brolly.

CHAPTER 13

'Don't go!' a street mouse begged. She wanted to smack her mouth for being so whiny. She hated her weakness. The bloke twisted around and pulled a *Zoolander* face. She'd been asleep but he'd woken her. He wasn't really her type but then again, she'd slept with so many blokes in the last year, she'd forgotten who her type was. Not Cornish pasties, though. Definitely not Cornish pasties.

'I told you I couldn't stay,' he said without judgement. She couldn't remember. Couldn't remember his name either. Could she ever? She wondered if he could remember hers but opted not to venture down that potholed road to the twin towers of Humiliation and Consternation.

'Why don't you stay?' There it was again. She needed to buy a cat to prey upon the mouse.

'I told you. It's Mother's Day. I'm visiting my mum.'

This threw Kim. Most of the blokes she slept with didn't have mums.

'Just for a while.'

'I can't. I gotta be in Tunbridge Wells in about six hours but I've gotta go home first and . . .'

Suspicion tugged her ears. Too nice to be true. Definitely not a real man.

'You got a girlfriend?'

'What? No!' Quite a few of Kim's pulls did.

'Wife!?'

'Of course not!'

'Divorced?'

'Kim! We had this conversation last night. I went through all this before I came back. I guess you were . . .' He trailed off. Didn't want to announce his complicity in her recklessness. In her blind drunkenness. In his taking advantage of her. It wasn't like he'd forced himself upon her though. Quite the opposite. He couldn't stop her. Usually, he liked to get to know girls better. Didn't subscribe to the school of casual sex and one-night stands. Never cultivated the killer instinct that some of his mates had. But he'd been chaste for close on two years, and this was the wet patch to end his dry spell. A one-off evening class on irrigation. The lesson had practically thrown itself into his arms. But he liked her. Thought he might want to see her again.

'I'll suck your cock.'

The Cornish pasty's meat tensed.

'You don't have to say that . . .'

'I like sucking cock.'

He buttoned his high-street shirt and pretended he hadn't heard the second fellatio comment. They were normal people in a normal situation, not a stud and a slut in a porn video.

'You can fuck me up the arse if you want.' Kim was laying her cards on the table. Even the DJ who thought he was going to miss his plane threw caution to the wind with that offer. So did the boxer whose girlfriend kept calling him. And the supposed jewellery thief who had to go to work. Their caution was windy.

'Kim. Really . . .' His awkwardness spilt over his belt as he fastened his shoelaces.

'I can suck it hard and then you can fuck me up the arse and we can film it if you want . . . I don't mind filming it. I quite like it,

103

actually.' She grabbed him from behind. He hadn't realised she'd snuck out of bed. He cringed. Disassociated his meat and veg from her knife and fork.

'Don't you like me?' He did. Or had. But his confidence in his judgement was melting like an ice cone in a BBQ pit. He barged past her. Kim interpreted his silent brusqueness as a double negative that might still make a positive. 'Is my bum too big? Is that it?'

'What!?'

'Is it!?'

'What are you talking about?' The pasty grabbed his jacket from the TV room.

'Is it my bum? My thighs. I fucking hate my thighs. It's OK if you hate them too. I don't blame you. And my arms. Am I too fat? Is that what it is? They hang down like fucking water balloons. I know I'm too fat. At least I can admit it. Not everyone can. You gotta gimme credit for that, at least. I'll go on a diet for next time we meet. If you want to meet . . . ?'

'Yeah, sure, I'll call you . . .' he lied, sad that in under five minutes she'd convinced him not to call her but to get out of her flat as quickly as possible. She grabbed his arm. He shrugged off her grip, ripped open the front door, disappeared forever.

'Wanker! YOU FUCKING WANKER!' Kim knew better than to scream at a prospective boyfriend she'd only just met. She also knew better than to punch the door. She slapped it with her palm instead. The thud sounded inconsequential compared to the distress that sawed through her bone and the despair that flooded her body. She strode into the kitchen. The table was full of alcohol and crisps for a small gathering that evening. She remembered it was her birthday. It was the first one without her dad. She wished it wasn't her birthday and that he was there. She felt like crying but instead threw a bottle of wine against the wall, next to the cooker. A jagged red crown decorated it. She tore open the fridge and pulled out a bottle of champagne. And a birthday cake. She popped the cork, washed her face, refreshed her gullet. She ripped open the cake and was about to gorge, but hesitated. Spun around and searched the floor. The great thing about living alone was she could put scales in every room without anyone thinking she was a complete nutcase. She pounced on the scales. The gesture calmed her but confirmed her suspicions. She was overweight.

She gorged on the cake and the crisps. Couldn't stand their flippant colours and mixed messages. Purged herself in the bathroom as their tastes lingered. Puked her guts out. Down the sink, which she did sometimes for a change. Wasn't so grotesque as doing it down the toilet. She grabbed the box under the sink where the laxatives relaxed. The instructions said to take two. The instructions were patronising shit. She took four.

She lived in the two-bedroom flat at the top of the Carpenter's Arms. Never liked walking through the pub so early in the morning, always imagined a drunk psycho waking up from under a bench in a corner she and the staff had overlooked at closing time. Was relieved to step outside but the night was no longer jubilant. It had grown drowsy and self-conscious. The blackness above the city was still fierce, though, its infinity still oppressive. It gave Kim some solace as she started to pound the pavement, as taxis sped furtively past her, and stray clubbers staggered or floated by, depending on what they'd ingested. They didn't know if she was a devil in disguise or an angel in distress as her pistons pumped on sinewy cylinders, her breath punctuated the crisp air and her dayglow colours shamed the depressive street lamps.

She ran down East Dulwich Road and down Lordship Lane to Forest Hill. She ran up Stansted Road to Catford. She ran up Lewisham High Street to Adelaide Avenue where she turned right to Brockley and then left to return home. It was a long way, punishment fit for the crime.

In her flat, the first thing she did was to rip off her clothes and weigh herself. 'Fuck!' The numbers didn't lie. The numbers never lied. That's why she respected the numbers so much. She staggered into the bathroom to grab a towel but couldn't resist a purge. It might help. It was more aggressive this time. Hurt more because there was less to throw up. Sounded like a distressed goose giving birth to an unexpected duck. The results were bilious but minimal. The pain, welcome. She grabbed a box of sleeping pills. The instructions had been written by the same copywriter as the laxatives so she ignored them, too, and swallowed four. She squatted over the toilet to see if the laxatives had yet run amok. They hadn't. She forced a few squirts of urine. Weighed herself again. 'Yay!' Things were looking up. She'd lost 1lb.

She tied the towel above her breasts and returned to the kitchen. She popped another champagne bottle and opened her laptop. She was cancelling her birthday. Thirty was shit. She'd celebrate next year, assuming she made it that far. She wrote a cursory group email, which she signed with three kisses, and hit send. She played a video of her dad telling a joke behind the bar. She really wished she could talk to him; laughed and burst into tears simultaneously.

Thunder crashed nearby. A few times. With a sense of urgency. Kim moaned as if she was still being penetrated. Rubbed her eyes. She'd passed out on her bed, wrapped herself around her duvet. The sky shimmered against the edges of the wonky blinds. It looked sunny outside, but it was hard to tell for sure. She hoped it wasn't sunny; it didn't suit her mood. The urgency continued from down the hallway. 'Kim! Kim!?' She unravelled herself from the duvet, flopped onto her belly, scoured the floor for her phone. It looked like the floor from Tracey Emin's bed. She wondered if she'd ever grow up, ever be tidy. The phone lay on top of a toy bunny. Thirty-two missed calls, of which half were from her message service. It was her birthday. It was almost five in the afternoon. She stood shakily and shambled towards the noise.

'Kim!?'

'Nita!?'

'You OK!?'

'What you doing here?'

'Just open the bloody door!'

Kim's ovaries felt like prunes. Her stomach like a punchbag. Her mouth like an ashtray. Her head span like a ride at a fair. She flicked the lock, pulled the door open. Nita stretched her jaw and contracted her brow.

'You alright?' Kim asked.

'What's that smell?' It wasn't a smell. It was a stink. A farmyard shit-bomb. Kim's dignity jumped into the nearest hedge. Her pride followed but she had nothing to hide from her best friend. She had a sense of what the smell was and undid her towel. Her legs bent the truth, suggested she'd been frolicking in a sea of mud. 'Fuckin' 'ell, Kim!'

'Don't rub it in, mate. Rough night. I'll 'ave a quick shower.'

'No, I mean, fuckin' 'ell . . .' Nita was staring at her body, not so much a temple as a dilapidated outhouse.

'Oh. Yeah. Don't start on that, neither. I know I need to lose weight.'

'What you talking about!? You look like a fucking concentration-camp survivor!'

'Don't take the piss.'

Nita's sympathetic chestnut eyes wrangled their way into Kim's psyche, jimmied their way into her soul.

'Kim . . . I'm really worried about you. I think you need help.'

CHAPTER 14

'Takes one to know one, right?' The tooth scars on the back of Landlady Kim's hands jostled like a patchwork quilt of self-loathing and regret.

'I'm so sorry...' Brolly said as she shrugged. 'How long've you been doing it?' he continued, blushing at the turn of events and his inept reading of them.

'Since I was fourteen or so. I mean... I don't really do it any more... I mean, I suppose I do but only on special occasions, which sounds a bit sick, dunnit? And when I overindulge. Which I try not to now, for obvious reasons, but... Christmas is a tough one. All that drinking an' eating but, you know, still wanting to look nice... and slim... Same with me birthdays. They're still tough. Haven't done it for a while – not since my fortieth, which I'm proud of, but... I dunno... I'm not sure the urge ever completely goes...' Landlady Kim stared at a dried coffee stain on her desk, chewed her thumb, tried to puncture the skin to distract her welling tears until she remembered she had company and wasn't the focus of her own self-pity for a change. 'Or it hasn't with me anyway... I can suppress it much better than I used to but... When you least expect it, there it is... I went to self-help groups and did cognitive behavioural therapy and that helped a lot but . . . I dunno . . . Sometimes I think if I had a husband or even a boyfriend, like a proper boyfriend who doesn't just fuck me around, that might make a difference, but then again . . . Story of my life . . . Maybe that'd just make it worse. Always worrying what he was thinking. If I was too . . .' Landlady Kim stopped herself.

'You can say it, you know . . .'

'Didn't meant to offend you . . .'

'You haven't said anything . . .'

'Well . . . I think we both know what I was gonna say.'

'There's nothing offensive about the truth . . .' Brolly shrugged. 'Go on. Say it. Might make you feel a bit better.'

'Alright then . . . Fat . . .'

'Come on. Bit more enthusiasm. You can do better than that. Fat!'

'Fat!'

'And again. FAT!'

'FAT!'

'That's better. One more time with feeling. FAATTT!!!'

'FAATTT!!!' Landlady Kim's laughter muddled her tears but didn't hide them. Brolly wanted to take her in his arms and try not to squash her. He looked to Amy Winehouse for advice. She said no, no, no. He wanted to ask Landlady Kim about the autograph. A hollow heart flourished above the 'A'. Dead space from a dead icon; it seemed like everyone could do with a little love now and then. 'So what about you? How long you been doing it?'

'Not long . . . A few months . . .'

'I can introduce you to some groups if you want. You'd be surprised; there's more blokes doing it than you think. Therapists, too, I could introduce you to a couple . . . If you want.'

Brolly's eyes flitted uncontrollably around his skull like a whirling dervish. He didn't want. Didn't need. Therapy or self-help groups. They were for the staves, stamens, throat-fuckers and bog-sprayers. The ones who couldn't control themselves. They were for the swimmers sinking in their own sea of distortion. The archaeologists excavating their own fucked-up bones. He didn't have body dysmorphia. Didn't have a brain disorder. Didn't require any knots untied. Didn't need a lifeline. He needed to lose weight, that was all. He was fat. For real. For sure. Hundred per cent. He knew it. She knew it. The whole world knew it. It wasn't a secret; his bones didn't poke through his skin like a cannibal's worst nightmare. His purging was doing him the world of good. His scales said so. So did his braces. So did his bathrobe. One day he wouldn't, but for the time being, he liked purging. He'd go on prime-time TV and sing it out to the world. Bulimia was a happy holiday destination. Its sea sparkled and its sand practically shone. He was a Bulimic devotee, a Bulimic jingoist.

'It's not how it seems . . . I mean, it probably is, but I'm not gonna do it forever.'

'That's what everyone says but an eating disorder's an eating disorder, innit?'

'Well, yeah . . . I suppose so . . . Unless it isn't . . .'

With bonhomie and good nature, they discussed denialism before unintentionally segueing into Tiny Tim. She felt bad about how she'd treated him. And felt uncomfortable at his funeral. Like a hypocrite. They chatted about Gill. How did Brolly feel about her? Did she know about the purging? They wondered about the Carvery competition. It really wasn't such a healthy option for a pub to be showcasing. Not in the twenty-first century. Especially when two of its six Hall of Fame inductees, her dad and Tiny Tim, had died of the very thing they were promoting. What did Brolly think? Should Landlady Kim close it down? Should she sack him to lessen his pain? She didn't know how he did it. Eat seven or eight roasts and then vomit them up. With all the trimmings. It was a disgusting habit. One of the worst. More about low self-esteem than anything, but she didn't want to get into that. Maybe she should just sack him and Gill? It would be good for Gill, too, surely? But then that might well open up Brolly's can of worms?

Maybe she should inject new blood? Someone for whom it might not be so dangerous? Someone younger. Someone thinner. *Someone more beautiful*, Brolly questioned sardonically. What about the girl with the rubbish bag over her head?

The conversation felt like an autumnal walk in the park with a new lover. But one that, like all good things, had to come to an end. Not least because the current girlfriend was innocently waiting next door.

'How did you know?' Brolly asked, not exactly fishing for a compliment but wondering, more accurately, if a compliment might be there to be fished.

'I thought you'd lost weight and . . .'

'What!!?' Brolly's mood, which already tingled pleasantly with sticky subterfuge and sloppy complications, suddenly burst through his trousers.

'Yeah . . .'

'Really!?'

'Yeah, really!'

'How can you tell?'

'Well . . . You look . . . healthier to be honest, innit? Not so ghostlike, not so . . . I can see your cheekbones for the first time and your posture's better and your clothes fit better and your tummy's not so big and . . . Well, quite a lot of stuff, to be honest.'

'Bloody hell!!' The momentous occasion tickled Brolly's ribs, slapped his back, shook his hand, lifted his arms high in the air, pushed him onto life's podium. He didn't know how to show his gratitude. Wanted to kiss Landlady Kim. Hug her. Buy her a drink. Magic up a bunch of flowers. This was one for his personal archive of lifetime milestones, along with losing his virginity and going to the Wobble Club for the first time; no one had ever told him he'd lost weight before.

As he headed back to Gill, the carpet he trod on felt like water, and for the first time in living memory he had the distinct impression that he was actually walking. Not hobbling. Not shuffling. Not struggling. Not wobbling. But actually walking. He liked the feeling very much and wondered if Gill might comment. But she didn't. Not that afternoon and not the following Saturday morning after he flopped next to her in the Viano. If she'd made a three-course meal of her entry, his was a light starter. He recalibrated himself on the seat and searched for the seat belt under his buttocks. Seat belts had for a long time been off the menu, a legal jibe, an authoritarian piss-take, but Brolly felt confident enough to court failure. He tried to join the safety tongue with the buckle. It felt like artificial insemination. He strained, stroked, jiggled, squeezed. He huffed and puffed and, finally, he clunked and actually clicked. As the belt strangled his belly and he silently congratulated himself, Taxi Rob, who'd just slammed the driver's door, looked around.

'You lost some weight, mate?' His question was rhetorical but demanded an answer. Brolly shivered pleasantly. Tried not to reveal his soul's blossom. Wondered why Gill hadn't noticed his shrinking. Or hadn't commented on it. He snuck a glance at her. She continued to stare out of the window as if deaf. As if she hated him. Or herself. Or them both.

'Me? Nah. Think my clothes got a bit bigger!'

'Ha! You could make a lotta money with an answer like that.'

'If only it was so easy.'

'Tell me about it. We'd all be millionaires.'

Gill pretended to be transfixed by two little girls playing hopscotch on the pavement opposite. They giggled uproariously, reminded Gill of herself when she was younger. When life was simpler. When the world was simpler. She had, of course, heard Taxi Rob's comment. Had, of course, noticed a difference in Brolly. Had done for a while.

But she was in a dilemma.

A position.

A moral quandary.

She knew what she should do, what she should say and how she should act but was still uncertain as to what she would do, what she would say and how she would act.

CHAPTER 15

'Alright, luv?' Blue-Eyed Pete's voice rasped as if it had been mined backwards through a rocky South London estuary.

'Alright, mate? What you got there?' she responded professionally and dispassionately, but with a quicker-than-usual pulsing of blood through her veins.

'Just some primer an' masonry.'

'Nice.'

He deposited four tins on Gill's counter as she tried not to swim in his azure gaze for fear of drowning in it. Instead, she studiously scanned the tins' barcodes.

'That's £101.32, please, mate.'

He pulled out his Visa and stuck it into the card machine. Dagmara and Gay Keith impinged on her vision's periphery. They were gravitating towards the till. Towards him. They usually did when he visited. She shifted her periphery as Blue-Eyed Pete tapped his digits, looked up and caressed her face with his stare. She blinked and their eyes locked for a few seconds. He smiled. She tried not to. Returned to the machine. It was still trying to connect. She wished Mr Carmichael would invest in a slicker, more expensive system so she could avoid moments like this. Not that there were many moments like this. Blue-Eyed Pete's gaze didn't waver. It dehydrated her. Exhausted her. Made her want to take up macramé. She sighed. Wiped her brow. Stared at the machine. Willed it to do its job.

'You like whispers, don't ya?'

'Sorry?'

'Whispers. You like a good whisper, don't ya?'

It was a strange question. She liked a good giggle. A good laugh. A good time. A good joke. A good night out. A good natter. Even a good fiddle sometimes. But she wasn't sure about a good whisper.

'Erm . . .' He pulled the Cadbury's mainstay from his denim jacket as if it was their conversation's punctuation mark.

'Oh . . .' Gill suddenly understood. 'Yeah, of course I like a good Wispa!'

'There was a two-for-one offer at Shell. Sucker for those things, I am. Thought of you when I saw it 'cos I was on me way here. Bought one for meself, thought you might like the other.'

Dagmara's green-eyed monster flounced. Gay Keith's one-eyed snake shrivelled.

'Oh. Yeah, cheers. Cheers, mate. Thanks very much!' Gill took the Wispa, ripped off the wrapper and deep-throated it. The card machine connected and accepted the payment. Gill tore off the receipt and handed it back with the card.

'Enjoy that, did ya?' he asked with a sparkle.

'Yeah, I did, thanks.'

'Well, no, thank you, luv. See you again, soon.'

'See you again soon.' Gill blushed. Blue-Eyed Pete strutted towards the exit. Dagmara fanned herself. Gay Keith straightened his trousers. The silence giggled. Blue-Eyed Pete palmed off the door. The door swooned.

'What's that behind you, Gill?' Gay Keith asked.

'What?' Gill wasn't very good at turning around. She marginally twisted her head to acknowledge the question she knew she wouldn't be able to answer.

'I think it's Cupid!' Gay Keith teased in an excitable teapot way.

'Fuck off!'

''E likes you, Gill, 'e likes you!' Dagmara joined the tea party.

The Wispa turned into an Aero Sharing Block which turned into a Minstrels three-pack which turned into a five-by-two Milky Way Crispy Roll pack which turned into a large Toblerone which turned into the masterstroke of romantic insinuation: a box of Black Magic. Gill wished she'd been able to keep that gift for herself, but she wasn't a soulless beast, and although her larger part railed against her smaller altruism, she shared the gift with her colleagues on condition that they left her the bottom tray. They happily squabbled over the top tray and speculated over Blue-Eyed Pete's next move and how he might up his ante. Gay Keith suggested 8 inches of dark-chocolate cock filled with fondant cream would definitely up his ante, but thereafter the group's enthusiasm for innocent tittle-tattle waned and the gang returned to work with a bitter saltiness in their mouths.

Mille-feuilles and Black Forest Gateaux, Strawberry Tarts and Double Chocolate Slices, Caramel Eclairs and Coffee Kisses followed. Sublime, all of them, and what they lacked in size, they made up for in sensory overload. Blue-Eyed Pete was working on a construction site near a patisserie on the South Bank and thought of Gill every time he passed. He always bought two of everything – his and hers, if you will.

Gill loved Brolly and would never do anything to hurt him but, at work, Blue-Eyed Pete became her default dream, her idle moments' think piece. She speculated as to when he'd next surprise her. With which combination of winking words and salacious snacks. In what sullied overalls and scuffed boots. With which coloured paint his fine physiognomy would be flecked and in what detritus his golden mop would be adorned. It was an idle indulgence and one she never considered more than harmless fun, the schoolgirl crush of a grown-up woman, but one that put wine in her water and bubbles in her wine.

It was during the no-man's land between autumnal cheer and festive abandon when people were too busy to cheer and too sober to abandon, on a Thursday lunchtime when absolutely no one seemed to be lunching, that Blue-Eyed Pete approached the till. He'd already spent every day that week loitering for no discernible reason, picking up product and inspecting it with a surgeon's eye for detail. Sometimes he'd step towards the till and swerve away before another customer unexpectedly beat him to it. He never bought anything and the few words he exchanged were perfunctory and disappointed. None were the magnetic missives they'd once been. And more tellingly, he hadn't lavished Gill with any gifts.

'Alright, luv?' Gill's colleagues were fully engaged with all the customers; no one was rushing to the till to buy anything.

'Alright, mate? Looking for something special?'

'I am actually. Bin looking for a while. Lemon Zest in the Antonin range. Can't seem to find it. Hoping you'd have it?'

'Yeah, we got that. It's in the storeroom.'

'Ah . . . There ya go . . .'

'Yeah. We only display the most popular paints out the front. Which is white or magnolia. Should be a sign that says that somewhere.'

'Didn't see one.'

'I'll get someone to get it for you.'

'Great.'

Gill scanned the shop, but her colleagues were still busy.

After the chains and the ropes and the scraggly strings that no one ever bought, Gill wheezed as she pushed the green door to the storeroom; she didn't usually walk that far but this was an exception. Her hand was sweaty, her walking stick's handle greasy.

'D'you want me to wait out here?' A sign indicated that the door was for staff only.

'Nah, you're alright. Might need you to help me find it. Come on.'

She held the door open as he walked in. His fingers touched hers. A shock of electricity. Flesh on flesh on fingernails. It might have been a mistake. His mistake on hers. But it might have been deliberate, a Hannibal Lecter linger. Her hand jolted. She ripped it away and entered the storeroom. Rows and rows of homogeneous paint tins froze on shelves opposite, from floor to ceiling, from one end of the room to the other, small strips of frontal colour their only defining differentiation.

'It's here somewhere. Just gotta look.'

Her eyes flitted, unable to focus; too many options, too many thoughts. He stepped closer to her than was necessary. A small step. She could hear his breath, feel it on her neck, him so close to her she could sup in his sweet exhalation, kiss the air that kissed him. Her wheezing distracted the moment, so she started breathing through her nose. It made her dizzy. All she had to do was step back to feel his whole body against hers. She was wondering what his bones felt like when the tin jumped out at her. 'There it is!' Two rows from the top. A metre to her left. The Lemon Zest. Too high to reach.

'Oh yeah, well done!'

Gill couldn't remember the last time she'd climbed a ladder. Asking Blue-Eyed Pete to do it felt wrong. Not to mention open to legal recourse should he tumble and injure himself. She lifted her foot lackadaisically, trepidatiously, onto the first step and heaved herself upwards. It wasn't made of wood but she wanted a drum roll, wanted to share valedictory words. She prepared for disaster, but none was forthcoming. Instead, she discovered courage and confidence, gripped the curved handrail and rose another step. And then a third. She reached for the paint tin, but something reached for her first.

Gentle initially, a tickle on her calf. An itch that needed to be scratched but then an insect that needed to be quarantined. It scurried up her leg, crawled past the back of her knee and spread over her thigh, pressured her flesh, clamped itself around her right buttock. She twisted more than she could remember twisting for an age, was confronted by Blue-Eyed Pete grinning like he was James Bond moments before his martini but moments after he'd just saved the world. His arm stood erect and thick and expertly kneaded her bottom. He was a baker and she was his dough. She waited for an explanation but knew she would wait an eternity. Men like Blue-Eyed Pete never had to explain. His perfect teeth challenged her to smash his silence. To cry wolf. To shout sexual assault. But she didn't and his silence became her silence and their silence. She wanted to scream. First in panic. Second in fear. And third and finally in ecstasy, the longing she most dreaded, the longing she no longer had to long for.

Blue-Eyed Pete's hand trawled the fabric on Gill's leggings. Her moan, high-pitched and shimmering under moonlight, affirmed the trawl. His hand was a slow but experienced captain. Her sea was thick as oil, smooth as silk. His hand followed the uneven contour of her buttock, slipped through her squashed thighs, found the area of her clitoris through layers of fabric and rubbed it. Back and forth. Expertly.

Gill admonished herself for allowing him to touch her there and hoped he'd never stop touching her there. But he did. As quickly as he started. As if it was all a ploy. A harbinger of what secrets they could share with deceit and duplicity. His forefinger traced her vagina, tickled her perineum and sunk for a moment into her anus before cleaning the crack between her buttocks and consigning the touch to history.

'Glad we found what we was looking for. I'll see you at the till.'

'Yeah, alright, mate.'

An emptiness wrapped itself around Gill like overzealous poison ivy around a decaying statue. She wanted to smash the tin around Blue-Eyed Pete's pretty head. Pour it down his throat and turn him into a Blue-Eyed Lemon Cocktail. Shake him. Stir him. Sparkle him with zest, smash him on the rocks. But she also wanted to lock him in her arms, throw away the key and smother him in her breasts forever, her little plaything, her doting Chihuahua.

She retreated to the microwave and opened the fridge below. Its light shone like a beacon for the perennially hard of eating. Its noise hummed like a toneless anthem for the forever undernourished. Its contents mocked all of the above. A solitary Pot Noodle shivered in social isolation. A refugee from who knew which land. It had been in the fridge's neutral zone for an eternity. Its sell-by date was historic and no one had dared claim it as their own, but Gill didn't care. She ripped it open, poured water in and plonked it into the microwave; waited for the ping, which felt like the longest wait of her life.

After slurping, drinking, guzzling, forking, spooning, gobbling and lapping, she exited the storeroom, calmed and fortified. Blue-Eyed Pete had left and her world suddenly felt empty.

By Sunday evening, late at night, in the sanctity of her own bed, her thoughts turned morbid. She tried not to picture the worst but failed. Roadside car carrion or construction site disaster? Paraplegia or coma? Decapitation or dismemberment? By the end of Monday, she wanted to cry. By the end of Tuesday, she wanted to vomit. By the end of Wednesday, she wanted to commit suicide. By the end of Thursday, she decided suicide was a bit drastic and maybe getting blind drunk was preferable. By the end of Friday, she wanted to eat a cow. But five minutes before closing, Blue-Eyed Pete appeared. He was covered in fluster. She was covered in disbelief. 'Alright, luv?' She was now. Especially as Gay Keith had sloped off early and Potatohead and Dagmara were having a cheeky beer in the storeroom.

'Alright, mate!?'

'Sorry I couldn't stop 'n' chat last time. Had to rush off. And this last week's been a complete nightmare. Burst mains at one of me jobs. Had to paint the whole ground floor again. Dry it out, then put damp seal on it, then paint it. Still, not a bad result as it wasn't our fault an' we ended up on overtime for three days.'

'Oh. That's good. Don't spend it all at once.'

'I probably will, actually, but look, I can't stick around. Parked on a single red and the wardens are proper ayatollahs around here, but didn't want you to think I'd forgotten you so I got you something.' From a paper bag, a posh one, he pulled out a box of doughnuts. Her soul pole-vaulted. The smog of her inner turmoil cleared.

'Oh! Thank you.'

'Anyway, can't stick around, as I said, but thought you might like what's inside.' He winked, clicked his teeth and vanished. Except for the doughnuts weighing down her trembling hand, Gill might have thought him an apparition. She opened the lid but it wasn't the dozen glistening, multicoloured doughnuts that tickled her fancy, it was the small ripped notepaper folded in half. Her hand still trembled as she picked it up and unfolded it. Carefully orchestrated ovular letters sloped backwards, as if written by a fusty child. A phone number accompanied the words.

'Fancy going out for a drink next week?'

Well, of course she bloody did!

CHAPTER 16

'Two double gin and tonics, please!' Gill said as politely as possible to the barmaid, who seemed to be suffocating in the schoolgirl tightness of her own fashion.

'Is that two double gins and two bottles of tonic water? Or two double gins and one tonic water?' The barmaid's Australian drawl defied her stoic but minuscule forehead. Her lips looked like deflated bicycle tyres. Her deliberate antagonism seemed unnecessary.

'Actually, I suppose I meant a quadruple gin with one tonic.'

'That's what I suspected.'

'And ten packs of cheese and onion crisps.'

'Ten packets of cheese and onion crisps?!'

'That's right.'

'We don't have any cheese and onion.'

'What do you have?'

The barmaid breathed patronisingly, looked aside, almost shook her head in disdain but dropped to the floor. She conferred with the boxes of self-professed potato snacks and popped up again.

'Serrano ham and truffle mustard, wasabi and ginger prawn cocktail, beetroot and cloves and . . .' She hesitated, as if she knew the next flavour was the petard that would hoist her. 'Blue Stilton with chives and thyme.'

'Oh ... Erm ...' The gift horse neighed. Gill couldn't help herself. 'I think I'll have the cheese and onion then, please!'

The barmaid's upper lip twitched as if a bicycle pump had finally blown some air into it.

'You mean the blue Stilton with chives and thyme?'

'Yeah, the cheese and onion.'

'Well, it's not cheese and onion though, is it, babe? Chives aren't onions and the addition of thyme, I'm guessing, adds a minty and lemony overtone at complete odds with your common or garden cheese and onion variety.'

'You taking the piss? No one can ever taste the fancy bits and not only are chives in the onion family but they taste like onions so, you know, I think for our purposes we can call them onions.'

'I'm not taking the piss, and if your taste buds are functioning properly then the subtleties are perfectly noticeable. Or they certainly should be after ten packets! Besides, cucumbers are part of the gourd family, and you wouldn't call a cucumber a gourd, let alone want to eat a gourd sandwich.'

'Wouldn't want to eat a cucumber sandwich either, thanks very much, mate!'

The barmaid suddenly faltered. A feigned neediness reshaped her. A fluttering of the eyelashes, a swipe of lint off her breast. Her contrariness dissipated. Her demeanour lilted. A softness crept in.

'Alright, Sheila!?' That delicious rasp. As welcome as a bouquet of flowers on a grey day. The appellation confused Gill but Blue-Eyed Pete grabbed his favourite buttock and squeezed it. Her thought process exploded, her vagina contracted, her nipples expanded.

'Alright, sexy, what ya having?'

The subterranean location fulfilled all of Gill's demands: it was near Harry's Hardware but not in London Bridge, Elephant and Castle, or the Walworth Road area; the seating was suitably sturdy and allowed easy in and out access; and it had toilets for the disabled. The booth they sat in was on the left, at the top of the vertical part of the bar's L-shape, so apart from a couple of other imbibers, no one could see them, which suited both participants well. Gill sat with her back towards the entrance, at Blue-Eyed Pete's insistence, and he snuggled into the opposite corner.

Their conversation flowed bountifully. Gill was as good a conversationalist as most and where Blue-Eyed Pete led, she followed. She basked in his aura, glowed in his dark. Was ecstatic to have the man, the myth, the legend all to herself, to not have to share him with the hardware hoi polloi. Their rendezvous, illicit as it was, contradicted everything she ever stood for, believed in and constructed her life around, so she relegated Brolly to the basement of her subconscious. Tied him up, gagged him and threw away the key. The deceit gnawed at her but so did thoughts of contact with her Black Magician, whether he'd brush his fingers against hers again, scrape her knee, chafe her lips or play footsie. No, it seemed. He would not. He didn't even mention the Lemon Zest moment, which grew conspicuous by its absence. He kept his words impersonal and never once revealed anything about his past, his present or his anticipated future. His emotions or his feelings. His family or his friends. Or his job. He kept everything relaxed and lowbrow, like a Mazda convertible, but Gill didn't care, she liked being putty in his hands. She flushed warmly every time he looked at her and hotly every time his eyes tripped into her cleavage.

Three quadruple G&Ts later and Gill hoped she wasn't falling in love as Blue-Eyed Pete pulled his phone off the table. 'Ahh . . . Yeah . . . Sorry to say, I have to leave soon.'

'Oh.' Gill thought they were savaging the night together, exploring its dark folds and sticky crevices. She stared sadly at the condensation rings left by her glass on the table, tried to read them briefly like leaves from a teacup. 'You sure?'

''Fraid so.'

'One for the road?' She didn't want to sound like a damsel in distress, although that's exactly how she felt. He looked at his phone again. Bit his lips. Pretended to agonise over his response, although he knew exactly what it would be. He knew he had Gill where he wanted her. Well, not exactly where he wanted her, but on the way to where he wanted her.

'I'd love to. I really would. I've had a great time, but I can't. But . . .' From his black biker jacket, he revealed a Wispa. Held it aloft like the beguiling talisman it had become. Gill wanted to ask why he had to go but chuckled instead. Knew the Wispa was a message. For her and her alone.

'What's this?' she asked coquettishly, knowing exactly what it was.

'I like you, Gill, and I'd like to get to know you better . . .' Gill was about to return the compliment, but Blue-Eyed Pete hadn't finished. 'Much better.' The fudge that melts in Heaven's sweet chocolate factory.

'I . . . like . . . you too . . .' she stammered. 'And I'd like to get to know you much better, too . . .'

'So we're agreed?' Her droopy eyes, her compliant nod, her complicit smile agreed. 'Good, 'cos I want you to take this but I don't want you to eat it. I want you to keep it. To cherish it. Think of me every time you want to put it in your mouth. And then next week, I want to meet you here again. Same time, same day. Can you do that?'

'I can.'

'But before you come here, I want you to hide it.'

'Hide it where?'

'Somewhere I can find it. Somewhere on your person.'

'On my person?'

'On your body.'

'My body . . . ?'

'Yeah. Not under your tits or up your pussy but anywhere else on your body.'

CHAPTER 17

'Do you, Peter Smith, take this woman, Jol Oknonkwo, to be your lawfully wedded wife?' A cooing, a flapping from above, interrupted the ceremony. Pete looked. Jelly looked. The vicar looked. Everyone jumped to the same conclusion: even though the dove was trapped, its presence was a positive sign. Much better than, say, that of a raven. Or a magpie. Or a pigeon. Pete smiled at Jelly; she giggled back.

'I do,' he said as she shimmied like the model she'd been for almost a decade. After being plucked from their comprehensive as the next Naomi Campbell, THE NEXT BIG THING, she hadn't quite become that, but she'd definitely become a SURE THING, which, in her eyes, was preferable. Her teeth blinded like diamonds. Her grin described a U-turn no sane man would choose. Pete stared into her eyes, which were slick like oil wells. He didn't see her, though, just an impoverished reflection of himself.

The vicar said Pete could kiss the bride. The Nigerians ululated and whistled with playful deference. The English whooped and hollered with thirsty stolidness. Pete wrapped his arm around Jelly's waist and was surprised at how much his body quivered and his heart pounded. He pulled her effortlessly towards him and pecked her fulsome lips as the congregation egged them on. 'You can do better than that, can't ya!?' she teased.

He knew what he had to do. He tilted his head obliquely. French-kissed her as if he'd been born in Paris. The dove hovered closer to validate the romance. The crowd marvelled and the nascent photographer in everyone rushed to capture the moment. She pulled away, licked her lips, beamed more life into him. 'Very passionate, Mr Smith!'

'Thank you, Mrs Smith, I aim to please!' They blinded even the sun that day, charmed the clouds, eviscerated the threat of April showers. Their reception took place in a country house twenty minutes from the Croydon suburb church. They were chauffeured there in a white Rolls-Royce. The guests followed in old-fashioned double-deckers. The grounds were trim, the library literate, the lighting subdued. Cromwell once lived in the country house. Or Churchill did. Or Charles. One of that lot. Pete was dreading his best man's speech because Darren could be a complete tosser at times, was known to skewer a cruel sense of humour through his mates' hearts. For a good few years he'd ribbed Pete mercilessly for dating a fat girl, had called Pete Oinker, Mr Oink, Pete the Pig Farmer, Pete the Pork Pounder and Peter Porker. For a while it had made Pete suicidal. But thankfully, Darren – marginally more mature than he'd been at school – rose to the task and the porcine nicknames remained in the musty changing rooms, the concrete playgrounds of their adolescence, and a pleasant day was had by all.

An owl sent its goodwill through the star-pricked sky. The moon gurned at them like a toothless and inebriated simpleton. Pete unlocked the heavy oak door to their wedding suite – a secret location for closer access to Heathrow Airport, they'd told anyone who asked. It smelled of Latin petals, obscure citrus fruits and privilege. The four-poster bed looked like it had been designed by a vestal virgin. After they played hunt-the-minibar, Jelly ran a bubble bath and Pete poured three vodka and tonics in the en suite living room. He made his double the strength of the other two. He slugged a quick shot from the bottle and carried two glasses to the bathroom. Jelly was crouched in her underwear, whipping the steaming water with her hand. The bubbles had already turned into mini-mountains. She stood up as his eyes quickly evaluated her expensive anatomy.

'Well . . . Cheers again, and here's to a happy life together,' he said as he handed over a glass.

'Cheers. Here's to a happy life together. It's definitely gonna be an interesting one.' Their clink sounded like an expensive doorbell. The bubbles tickled their throats, the vodka cleansed their palate. 'Thank you. For this,' she said. Pete shrugged. Jelly smiled and wrapped her arms around him. 'I really mean it. Thank you.'

'Helps us both out, dunnit?' Pete replied as he returned the gesture and clung to another life, another world. A knock interrupted them and the moment evaporated.

Pete opened the door. Jelly's girlfriend glimmered like an angel. She looked like the yin to Jelly's yang. Long blonde hair sprouted and curled around her chest. Her legs stretched like the sides of an isosceles triangle and her eyes glimmered like emeralds. After bubblegum pleasantries, Pete handed Tessa the remaining vodka and tonic and showed her to the bathroom, where he brushed his teeth, bade his wife and her girlfriend good night, and shut the door on his honeymoon bedroom. Pete shivered. The three of them were honeymooning in Havana but the living room felt like a Siberian concentration camp; at least they'd have separate rooms when they were in Cuba, he consoled himself.

'Angie?' He wasn't sure if she was going to pick up. Initially, she didn't. He had to call twice and sat on the sofa for the second call.

'Hello, Pete.'

'How ya doing?'

'I'm doing OK, thanks.' She didn't ask him how he was doing, he noticed. Not that he would've told her. Not the truth, anyway.

'What you up to?'

'It's Saturday night and I'm just about to go to bed. What d'you want?'

'Don't be like that . . .' He'd never met anyone who liked opera before. He could hear an aria playing in the background. He could also hear her thinking.

'What d'you want?'

'I just wanted to talk. Feeling a bit lonely.'

'I've got nothing to say to you.'

'I love you, Angie.'

'I'm gonna hang up, Pete.'

'Please don't . . . I'm not fucking around, you know . . .'

'So stop telling me and start showing me. Introduce me to your mum and your dad and your sister. Introduce me to your mates. Take me to a restaurant. Doesn't have to be expensive. Can be McDonald's for all I care. Walk with me in the park. Take me to a concert. Hold my hand in public, put your arm around me, kiss me. We've already been through this, and I don't want to go through it again.' Pete loved Angie. Thought she was the most beautiful woman he'd ever seen. Certainly the largest one, which was almost the same. Or the largest he'd ever felt, at any rate. And had intercourse with. He really wanted to introduce her to his family. And to his mates. And take her to a restaurant, which most certainly wouldn't be McDonald's. But he knew he'd never do any of the things she wanted. 'You still there?' she asked.

'Yeah . . .'

'So whaddya say?'

'I dunno if you've seen 'em but garages've started selling Kingsize Twix. They're almost twice as long as the normal ones. I'm away next week but I thought when I'm back, I could bring a packet round, you know, an' we could have a bit of a laugh again . . .'

Angie hung up. Pete called back.

'You're a sad fuck, Peter Smith. Don't ever call me again!' Angie hung up for the second time. Pete didn't call back.

Screams of laughter from the bathroom chipped away at his frozen heart. He downed the rest of his vodka and flicked through his phone's contacts. He needed someone who wasn't as opinionated as Angie. Or as confident. Or self-sufficient. There was Caroline and Deirdre . . . But Caroline lived in a flat-share and Deirdre was part manic depressive, for emergencies only . . . Or Melanie. He liked Melanie but she was too far away . . . Sue . . . Sue would've been perfect, but she kept going on diets . . . And Tracey . . . Well . . . Yes, Tracey would do. She wasn't as pretty as Angie or as large, but she was fun. Not as earnest. Although admittedly, they'd only been seeing each other for a few months, not a few years. She seemed happy with the attention. And the company. And loved his peccadillo with the Mars bars. Yeah, she'd do nicely. He found a Mars bar online, took a screenshot, texted it to Tracey, inserted three winking emojis underneath.

He poured a large vodka and picked up the tonic bottle when his phone pinged back. He downed the double vodka. It made him gasp and cough, but it energised him. Made him feel a little more confident, a little more gung-ho. Tracey replied with a blushing emoji, an emoji with its tongue hanging out and an emoji with two hearts for its eyes. The room was starting to heat up again. Pete wished he could go on a honeymoon with Tracey.

CHAPTER 18

'Alright.' Gill took the Wispa. She'd never been given anything edible before and asked not to eat it. She'd never been given anything edible before and asked to look after it for someone else, either. For a week. And then hide it under her clothes. In the crevices of her fat. For them to do something unmentioned and quite possibly unmentionable with it. For the first time, she challenged Blue-Eyed Pete's stare. He accepted the challenge. She didn't drown in his eyes but swam in them. He swam in hers. And for a few magical moments, they floated, together. Not in a second-rate dive bar in the City, but in infinity.

She wasn't brave enough to make the decision herself so decided to pass the buck. To let fate resolve her dilemma. It was a cop-out, but it allayed her anxiety, which, along with her guilt, had started to lay siege to her conscience. The next morning, after the cursory grunts that defined their typical greetings, Gill snuck past Potatohead and Gay Keith and lumbered to the scene of the fumble. A new Lemon Zest tin had magically appeared overnight. The ladder leaned in exactly the same position. Its ridged steps cooled her fingertips as she grabbed them, but the coolness evoked a warmth; they understood. They had aided and abetted Blue-Eyed Pete. She grinned at the Lemon Zest tin, stroked it. There was a dent on its left rim. She ran her forefinger over it, knocked it with her knuckles. It interrupted the room's quiescence. She fondled the Wispa in her hoodie pocket. The chocolate crumbled. The bubbles flattened. She didn't want to ruin its form so she pulled it out and kissed its tip. The triangular perforations scuffed her lips and prevented satisfactory contact so she kissed the main body, better, a good-luck charm, an exhortation to stay safe. She placed it on top of the tin, tried not to imagine a life without Brolly. Dared not imagine a life without him. Exorcised him from her thoughts. Swooned at the Wispa, its purple sheath that blended with the back wall's dimness. The glow from the solitary naked bulb just about reached it, dramatised it, rendered it clandestine, made it a mystery, a still life waiting to be painted.

If it was there the following Wednesday after clocking off from work, Gill would meet Blue-Eyed Pete. It wasn't, she wouldn't.

It was.

'Oh bloody 'ell!' Gill said to herself. 'Oh Bloody Hell!'

The city schemed about Christmas. What it was going to buy, for whom and from where, which parties to go to, whether to have one itself and where to spend Christmas Day. The rain's gossamer pinheads greased Gill's face and cajoled a damp dog smell from her jacket as she left Borough High Street. Festive lights infused the Thames with magical ripples. At the north end of London Bridge, someone had tied a red ribbon around a large office building, which titillated Gill as she speculated how a Flake or a Twirl or a Ripple might disintegrate under her flesh. Whether their crumbles would melt better than the Wispa's bubbles. She considered how an Aero Mint might complement her body's tang better than that of an Aero Orange. She contemplated how a Crunchie would prickle or a Picnic itch. If a Bounty would fall or a Double Decker fail. She wondered if her sweat would render the chocolate rancid or maybe, like a stew, would improve the taste? Maybe that's what Blue-Eyed Pete wanted. She knew some men liked smelling women's soiled knickers, so why not? It was like slim women wearing expensive lingerie to make themselves feel sexy. It was her little kink. Her little secret. Her little kick. For the first time, she speculated not about the power Blue-Eyed Pete held over her but that which she held over him.

A wreath of mistletoe hung over the bar's entrance and, inside, monochromatic photos of blues' old-timers had been dragged up with garish scarves of tinsel. The bar wasn't yet busy but to Gill's surprise, Blue-Eyed Pete was already seated in their booth. His eyes danced and his teeth twinkled when he saw her. Hers did the same. A harmonica ululated in a middle eight as she navigated the quicksand from the entrance to their table and his eyes popped open her buttons, lowered her zips and grappled with her garments.

'Alright!?'

'Alright?' she returned. 'You're keen.'

'You're right. I am.'

'That for me?' Ten packets of crisps and what Gill assumed to be a quadruple G&T glittered on the table. Blue-Eyed Pete was a smooth bastard, alright.

'Figured you'd be thirsty an' peckish.'

'You know me well!'

'Hoping to get to know you better.' Straight in there, that Blue-Eyed Pete, one-track mind. Gill wanted to laugh with implicit agreement but cackled with explicit innuendo. Like a dirty old man. With raincoat. She didn't sit down, picked up the G&T to distract from her self-consciousness. He must have been there for a while. The ice cubes had almost melted. The top of the drink tasted like water. She angled the glass too acutely and spilt some over her chin. Her face reddened. She downed the rest of the drink more strategically but still thirstily, as if she'd crawled across a desert to meet her lover. She clunked the hollow glass on the table and hoped he'd offer her another one, which would give her valuable time to cram into the booth.

He did.

Gill crammed. And then snacked. Blue-Eyed Pete purchased. And returned. He handed her the drink and smoothed himself into the banquette opposite. A rabid smile smouldered across his face. Gill was glad she was seated because her knees weakened. He held out his drink and they clinked glasses. 'Cheers, luv.'

'Cheers, luv.'

'So d'you do what I asked?' he said quickly, straight after his first gulp, straight after sitting down. Gill was expecting a bit of *How's your father? Does your mother know you're out?* at least.

'I did.'

'How's it feel?'

Gill paused. But not for long. 'Good.'

A ravenous smirk ravaged his face. If she'd been watching a film, she'd have predicted his imminent transformation into a monster, but all of a sudden he collapsed. Her instinct was to scream but that was what little girls did. She prayed his heart hadn't given out, but his drop had been so neat, like a building expertly demolished, that her fear, as instinctive as it was, seemed wrong.

He reappeared under the table, a slobbering Labrador affectionately nuzzling her left knee, but suddenly shot up and ricocheted around the cramped space between her and the booth's corner. Not as erotically as she would have liked, he slapped his hands on her belly, investigated her with all the charm of a backstreet surgeon. Gill tensed. Held her breath. Wanted to hold his too. It wasn't the tender caressing she'd dreamed of. He kneaded her dough repetitively, like he might suffer a strain injury from it. She hoped he didn't bruise her. She definitely didn't want to be bruised. Would have some explaining to do to Brolly. His hands remained in sight and she worried he hadn't even started the search but his gestures became more blood-thinning, more hypnotic, and she started to calm.

Her back rolls' fondling made her shoulders heave upwards and her breasts outwards. Her side rolls' squeezing had the reverse effect and made her body deflate, her stomach suck inwards. Her tummy's teasing made her smile like the beginning of the world and tremor like the end of it. She smelled toothpaste and gin on his breath and tried to sup it in, take what was his into her like she'd done in the storeroom. He sprawled over her, laid his head on her breast. His curlicues tickled her cheeks. She dared not move for fear of disturbing their union, luxuriated in his warmth, his intimacy.

The entrance doors swung open, reminded Gill of the world's existence. They both froze in unholy matrimony. Until male boomboxes distanced themselves, ventured towards the invitation of alcohol. Blue-Eyed Pete was a master of ceremony and felt the timing was right to extend his spatial invasion. He knew Gill was enjoying herself because she breathed onto his forehead. Her breath was fishy. He guessed she'd eaten tuna for lunch. He ignored the smell. Wanted to understand, rather, her real smell. Her essence. Reach deep into her, climb up inside her, be consumed by her, become her, become his own fantasy of her so that all the ridicule he'd suffered at school, all the lies he'd lived, all the deceit he'd encouraged, would vanish. For ever. He wanted to live in a parallel universe where all the pig noises and dismal failures of intimate moments with skinny girls never existed. But he knew that would never happen and this was the second-best thing. He stuck his hand under Gill's top. Her skin welcomed him for the first time and he fantasised about how she'd started to lubricate. She gasped. So did he. And in that synchronicity, each encouraged the other.

To find the Wispa.

He slid his hands, delicate for a man let alone a builder, under her trophy weight. His fingers opened up her paths of resistance, her unexplored land, her mutable concavity. His tickle of her panties' upper rim sent him dizzy. It sent her shivering. The chocolate wasn't there, not under the bottom rung of her stomach. He slid his hands back and forth more than was strictly necessary as the boomboxes returned but parked themselves in a booth or two down. The thrill of capture by inebriated City masturbators, lonely vibrators, heightened the thrill of the game. They'd make the couple pay. The ribbing would be sharp. Vicious like the tip of a sadist's stud. Blue-Eyed Pete moaned. Gill replied to his moan. His nose lay against her neck. It was a dreamy nest. He wanted to kiss it, run his tongue up and down it. Up and down her whole body. Kiss her everywhere. But that would come. Soon. Hopefully, soon. Not in the next few minutes or hours. But in the next few weeks. She was a cautious beast. Needed to be coaxed, enticed, tamed. But then again, they all did, those women of girth. She was definitely coaxed and enticed, he thought, as she stroked her hand through his hair, pressured his scalp and moulded her fingers around his taut neck. Her proactivity was conquering her passivity. He rubbed his tumescence and was proud of its size and its rock-like quality. He wanted to grab Gill's wrist, rub it across his pride, but didn't want to scare her. Not yet. The doors pushed open again. Gentler voices, women's, followed the obligatory route to the bar.

'Oh God!' Gill muttered as Blue-Eyed Pete bit her cheek and kissed it. She pulled away. Stared at him. Swam again. Pulled his mouth to hers. Their tongues writhed like electric eels. Their togetherness knew no bounds. With the force of a sword being thrust into a legendary scabbard, Gill's suitor rammed his hand under the second roll of her stomach's flesh, on her right. He hit upon his prize. It was no longer oblong and phallic but amorphous and sticky. 'Yes!' laughed Gill. 'Yes! Yes! Yes!'

'Yeah!' Blue-Eyed Pete mirrored gruffly. He clawed as much of the melted, messy mass as he could and surprised Gill, not by offering his chocolate fingers into her mouth but cramming them in. She groaned as she clamped them, giggled approvingly. Her whole body giggled too. His smile cut his face in half as she sucked and licked and swirled her tongue over his fingertips, each and every digit, over the hairy knuckles and in between his smooth interstices, back and forth over the love line on his palm and up and down his life line. After she'd ravaged every last hint of chocolate, he stuck his hand under her fold and did exactly the same again. As did she. Until there was nothing more to ravage. He pulled away from her as far as he could, which was only a few inches. They questioned each other, thrilled and scared, emboldened but cautious. Both panted and just as she smiled at him, he slipped back under the table and popped up the other side.

When he returned with another round, Gill's expression crashed through the floor, into the foundations. She pinched her legs. Made sure she hurt herself, that she wasn't dreaming, having a nightmare.

'You're not leaving again, are ya?' He'd only brought back one G&T.

'Sorry, luv. It's been mind-blowing but I gotta get up early for work. Always gotta get up early for work, but I'd love to see you again if you'd like?' Gill felt like a child whose parents had split up and knew her father had to leave but didn't understand why. 'Here? Same day next week? Same time?' She wanted to beg him to stay but that wasn't her style. She wanted to ask him where he was going but didn't want to hear the answer. She wanted to tell him to fuck off because he was taking the piss. Because she had a boyfriend whom she loved dearly. Because she shouldn't even be there in the first place, so the least he could do was honour her deceit and spend the rest of the fucking evening with her. She wanted to tell him never to bother her again and end it all.

'OK,' she said as he pulled out of his jacket not one Wispa, but two.

CHAPTER 19

Gill placed the Wispas on the same paint tin and left the same decision to fate. As if the extra chocolate bar was an emotional amplifier, her conflicted thoughts, pangs of guilt and carnal yearnings were all heightened that following week. Her presence both at home and work was more distant, her focus less sharp and her desire to partake less immediate. Her conversations were less spiky, her observations less abrasive and her energy more sluggish. With Dagmara, she shared partial truths and with Brolly, no truths. Not about her night out, at least. She ate more and drank more but retired to bed earlier, as early as she felt she could get away with, blaming the intensity of her work days for her evening's torpor.

Under her duvet, she luxuriated in self-indulgent solace. She stared longingly into a darkness that was uniquely her own. She listened to the urban soundscape as it was her sole companion. She dreamed of Blue-Eyed Pete ambiguously, abstractedly, often in close-up, against a blurred and colourless background. She wondered where he was, what he was doing, how he was doing it and if he thought about her as much as she did about him. She often replayed the moment in the storeroom and the kiss and the fumble at the bar. All the while, until she drifted off to not always innocent sleep, she massaged her right hand over the spot where he'd found the Wispa, a kind of masturbation with no promise of orgasm.

Fate smiled mischievously upon Gill and the scene of their reunion felt like an eidetic memory. The same steep and mocking stairs, the same enticing mistletoe, the same finely scuffed metallic double doors. Even the same harmonica ululated the same and made her realise the blues, which had seemed so magical the weeks previously, were just another lying corporate algorithm. Blue-Eyed Pete sprawled in the same clothes, with the same left leg angled out of the same booth, with the same chocolate-box smile and the same self-satisfied mien. The same two G&Ts, filled with the same ice and decorated with the same lemon, dripped the same rings of condensation and the same twenty packets of blue Stilton with chives and thyme crisps provided the space with the same mottle. The only difference was a triangular sign that rested on the table like an eight-letter word on a Scrabble rack.

'Reserved!?' Gill noted immediately. 'That's a bit posh, innit? That for us?'

'That is for us, my luv!' Never had the use of the possessive adjective made Gill come over so gooey.

'Oh. Very nice!'

'Yeah, I thought it'd allow us more freedom, if you know what I mean . . .' Gill didn't know what he meant but he revealed it after their second G&T.

'Well, I thought we could retire to the toilets . . .'

'To the toilets?'

'Well, the disabled, to be more precise.'

'The disabled toilets?'

'You know. More space, more privacy, more time . . .'

'Oh . . . OK . . .' Gill said, not sure if it was OK.

'Yeah. To do more things. We can leave our stuff 'ere and not worry that someone's nicked the booth when we're gone. Or our

139

stuff.' He sensed Gill's uncertainty fester. 'Come back when we want, have another drink, not worry about anythink. You know, get to know each other a bit better afterwards. . . .'

'Well . . . If you put it like that . . . I suppose . . .' She knew she was being used, didn't mind being used, in fact liked being used, but wanted some emotional currency for the use, wanted to understand better the man who was using her. Wanted to find out more about him, learn about his life outside their life, about his past, his present, his anticipated future. What made his clock tick, his paint brush swipe. 'If you do come back and do have another drink . . . I s'pose that's a good idea, then.'

The blocked-up mains smelled worse than a pigsty. The grab rails were too greedy and the juttings too earnest. The fan's bellow was off-putting and blocked out the blues. The soiled paper on the floor, a poorly judged missive that had somehow missed its mark, didn't help either. The disabled toilet was smaller than Gill remembered, and sadder. Blue-Eyed Pete closed the door as she leaned her stick against the corner of the basin and the wall. She stole a glance at her reflection as he locked the door. The lines down the side of her nose and chin, dissected by her lips, made her face look like an anarchy sign, a message from her rebelling body. Her foot scuffed against a poorly positioned sanitary bin as she slumped against the wall next to the toilet and stood there, no longer sure how to present herself or what she was doing. Blue-Eyed Pete turned. She twisted, as if making a peace offering of her neck. He accepted, grabbed her tummy and sucked.

A melancholy swept over Gill like a white sheet over a murder victim. She felt curiously detached from the gropes and the slurps, wished she was at home with Brolly, agonising over which takeaway to order, arguing about what film to watch. She prayed her affair didn't give her a love bite but as he squeezed her drooping flanks with neanderthal abandon, her body, like it

140

always did, started to approve. Soppy moans and inarticulate nothings escaped her lips. She didn't mean them to. She was under his spell again and her burgeoning discomfort dissolved like rice paper in rain. She clamped one hand on his brooding, muscular shoulders and the other around his ludicrously slim waist. It felt unusual to hold a whole person in her arms.

Blue-Eyed Pete wiped his face across her smooth breasts, plunged his face into them, inhaled and exhaled deeply and stuck his tongue as far as he could into their inviting nook and licked sweat from them. As a signal of approbation, she stroked his manhood as if it were a starving piranha in treacherous waters. It didn't bite but it jumped. It scared her but she stroked it again. It was hard and large and wanted to be tamed.

There was a focus to Blue-Eyed Pete's passion this time, almost a clinicalness, a self-defeating urgency. When he slipped both hands as deep as they would go, under each side of her belly, she sang out elliptic scales. When he tickled her ribs and found both Wispas near her ovaries, she screamed with laughter.

'Oh Jesus! There they are!' he guffawed.

'Yeah! There they are! They're yours, baby, all yours.'

'Can I take 'em?'

'Take them, baby, yeah, take 'em, right now.'

He genuflected. Stroked her thighs. Stared up at her, looked like Christ beseeching God to allow him to die, to allow him to return home, to Heaven, to save the world. She was his god. His goddess. His everything. His nirvana. He lifted Gill's left flank and stuck his head underneath it. Her flesh flopped over his face, engulfed it. He delineated her uniqueness, ventured where no man had ever ventured before, where the biggest fold hung over the biggest fold. He rejoiced. Moaned like a girl. Nibbled and nicked and lashed and lapped and tongued and sucked and sometimes gasped for air, cleaning the melted chocolate from the pores under her fold, neutralising the soapy aftertaste, the moisturiser's creaminess, all the while grasping hold of her tremendous buttocks.

The City skirts were back at their favourite table, less strung out, more relaxed, with a bottle of bubbly to prove it. Gill's knees wobbled as she barged her way through the bar. Gill could feel her wetness. Regretted not bringing a change of pants. The blues men on the walls winked as she passed. Wished she could blow their harmonica. One of them hoarsely crooned to a lost love. Blue-Eyed Pete returned with two more G&Ts. The skirts stole glances at him. He feigned ignorance at their attention. Gill felt proud, Gill felt like a woman. 'You alright?' he asked as she beamed at him, showered him with stardust.

'Yeah. Good. You?'

'Fantastic. Yeah, that was . . . fantastic . . . Sorry if I'm not such good company right now . . .'

'Oh, no. People think they have to talk all the time 'cos – to – to enjoy themselves, to show they're having a good time, but I don't think that at all. I mean, I like talking. I like talking to you but, you know, sometimes it's good to think and, you know, it shows how comfortable we are in each other's company, just sitting here in silence. I mean, obviously not complete silence 'cos, well, we're talking but . . . You know what I mean . . .'

'Yeah, I do. I know exactly what you mean . . .'

'I think it's sweet you can relax with me an' not have to put on a show . . .'

'Thank you . . . It's nice you understand . . . It was pretty intense back there . . .'

'Yeah, it was . . .'

Gill tried not to monitor Blue-Eyed Pete's drink as it slipped away like sand in an hourglass. She failed. A tristesse clouded their table in an environment otherwise brightened by festive rays. When he tilted the glass upwards for the final sip, she took a deep breath, stuck her umbrella up and prepared a brave face for the inevitable downpour. He took out his phone and considered the time.

'Fuck. Really sorry about this.'

'You gotta go?'

'Yeah. Wish I didn't . . .' He waited for her agreement, but Gill didn't offer one. Thought she'd let him stew. Just a little. He painted a doleful smile and offered his hand across the table. She hesitated. Felt the gesture was too public but couldn't deny the urge. Mimicked his smile, proffered it as the best form of flattery. Relaxed her hand in his palm's warmth. Rejoiced at his grip's tender squeeze. 'I really like ya, Gill. I mean, I know I said it before but I wanted to say it again,' he rasped. 'Make sure you don't forget. Really like you, I do. Think about you all the time. Really wanna see you again but not like this, d'you know what I mean? I think we deserve more than this, with all these City tossers, all these pissheads. Our relationship, our feelings deserve more than this, our . . .' Gill practically choked. Was he going to say the L-word!? 'Well, I don't want to get ahead of meself, don't want to call it that at the moment . . .' Bloody hell. He was. 'Not yet. Not just yet, anyway. But, you know, I feel I have a special bond with you, Gill, and I want to honour that, not abuse it in the disabled toilets again. I mean, don't get me wrong, what we did was ecstasy, but . . . Does what I say make any sense at all? Dunno how good I am with words sometimes . . .'

'It makes complete sense.' At that moment, she was so punch-drunk with love she didn't fully register Blue-Eyed Pete pull out three Wispas and place them on the table as if they were gold ingots. She didn't fully register the business card he laid next to them. And didn't fully hear his words. Which she only recalled after his departure. After he squeezed her hand one last time. After he stood erect. After he turned heads, parted a human ocean with the singularity of his beauty. After the doors swung casually but quickly shut, and after she was left alone with nothing but memories.

She chuckled at the three Wispas; she had to admire his chutzpah. With curiosity, she picked up the business card and stared at it. Lightning struck. Thunder crashed. Rain spat down. Norman Bates stood at the window in the house on the hill. In silhouette. Wearing his mother's clothes. Or wearing Blue-Eyed Pete's clothes. It was hard to tell from such a distance.

The business card was for a hotel.

'Same time next week? I'll leave a key for you at reception. Oh, and put the Wispas anywhere you want . . .' he'd said. 'And I mean anywhere.'

Gill knew he wouldn't inspect the barcodes of the designated Wispas so tore each open and devoured all three in as many seconds. She poured the packets of crisps down her throat as if they were crunchy life supplements and she was terminally ill. Against her better judgement, she asked the Champagne Charlottes if they'd mind watching her booth and its contents. They didn't. Even though the quadruple G&Ts hadn't affected Gill's composure, she stumbled back to the disabled toilet as if they had.

The door was locked. She banged on it impatiently. No response so she banged again. 'Police! Open up!' She needed to be back inside that toilet. Back where he did what he did. 'Not warning you again! This is the police! We will break this door down if you don't open up immediately!' The latch wiggled sheepishly. The door slid open. Gill worried her juices were poisoning her mind; the space was empty.

'Thought you said you was the police?' Gill looked down. A small Black woman nestled in a wheelchair stared at her accusingly.

'Oh . . . Yeah . . . Sorry . . . Thought you was my mate.'

'Is your mate disabled?'

'Erm . . . Yeah . . .'

'What's wrong with her. Or him?'

'Erm . . . .'

'You're talking shit, aren't you?'

'Sorry. I just really needed to go.'

'Use the normal toilets. These are here for a very good reason.'

'I am disabled, you know.' Gill waved her stick in the air as if to prove a point.

'You're not disabled. You're just fucking fat.'

'Fuck off!'

'You fuck off! It's not like I'm telling you something you don't already know. Anyway, what you gonna do? Squash me?!'

'Please. I really need to go.'

'Yeah, you do really need to go. To WeightWatchers, mate. Hope you fucking fall off the toilet an' piss yourself!'

Gill locked the door behind her and shuffled over to the toilet. She wanted to vomit but couldn't. She coughed loudly, squeezed her stomach in time with the cough. She blew her nose. Threw the crumpled ball down the toilet. Wished she had her grab-and-grip device so she could pick up the soiled toilet paper and chuck that down the toilet too. She didn't flush but shuffled back to the basin and stared in the mirror, clamped her sweaty hands onto the cool porcelain. She wanted to cry but couldn't. Wanted to laugh but couldn't. Wanted to purr like an insouciant pussycat but couldn't. Wink like an alluring tigress but couldn't. She twisted the taps. It was the only thing she could do. She hobbled back to flush the toilet. The senselessness and banality of her actions soothed her. So did the familiarity of the sounds. She took a deep breath and honked like a reindeer. She washed her hands as if she'd just contracted a disease. She noticed a chocolate smudge on the anaemic wall to her left. Her chocolate smudge. Blue-Eyed Pete's chocolate smudge. Their chocolate smudge. But then she wondered if it was a shit smear and her mood deflated. She put down the toilet lid, gripped the grab rails and started to ease herself down. The first tear escaped before she sat down; the rest, the torrent, after.

CHAPTER 20

'I thought I'd order four Christmas puddings for after the Carvery,' Gill said as cloves charmed the air, customers muddled together like meat and veg on a Christmas platter and Brolly laid their customary tray of alcohol and crisps on their customary table.

'They are pretty good,' Brolly admitted. 'I remember one of the chefs telling me the secret was not to use currants, sultanas *or* raisins but currants, sultanas *and* raisins. As fresh as possible, too.'

'Well, if they were all as fresh as possible, they'd be grapes.'

'Yeah, well, I don't suppose that'd work.'

'D'you know what the difference is between currants, sultanas and raisins?'

'No. Do you?'

'No idea.'

Half a rugby team entered the premises, caused a natural pause in the conversation. All wore the same white-and-green hooped shirts, the same square jaws, the same depraved glints in their eyes. Brolly inhaled a breath as if he was about to dive deep underwater.

'So there's something I wanted to talk to you about, actually,' he said, more ominously than he'd meant to.

'OK . . .' Emotional upheaval hovered nearby like a mosquito about to draw blood. Gill wanted to splatter it but froze instead, having already done her best to ignore Taxi Rob's comment the previous day about Brolly's weight loss.

'Sorry . . . I, erm . . . I don't know how to say this so I guess I should just come out with it so . . . Well, I'm retiring from the All You Can Eat Carvery Competition.'

'What!?' Gill's face fell into her lap.

'Sorry . . . I know it's a bit of a shock but . . .'

'What d'you mean?'

'I just can't do it any more . . .'

'Brolly!? Why not . . . ?'

'I'm not sure I enjoy it any more.'

'You always look like you enjoy it.'

'It just makes me feel really . . . ill. Every time.'

'But . . . you're the in-house co-reigning champion. You're in the Carpenter's Arms Hall of Fame. You're Brolly "The fucking Bear" and I'm Gill "Don't Give a Fork" Monteith. We're a team! You can't retire! You have a responsibility! To your fans! To our fans!'

'We don't have any fans, Gill, and the only responsibility we have is to ourselves and our bodies. I've already spoken to Landlady Kim about it and . . .'

'You told her before you told me?!'

'I wanted to test the waters . . .'

The hackles of Gill's indignation rose. 'You went behind my back?!'

'No. I wanted to gauge her reaction, 'cos you know, it is a job . . . kind of. And we are part of the draw and I didn't want to risk your position either 'cos . . . you know . . . we are a team.'

'What did she say?'

'She said it'd be the end of an era but she thought it was a good idea. Didn't want me going the same way as her dad or Tiny Tim.'

'What is she now? A fucking doctor?'

'No, but . . . you know . . . we're both overweight and . . .'

'Who's overweight!? Did she say that!? I'll fucking smash the bitch!'

Brolly knew he'd made a mistake as soon as the letter 'o' left his lips. He tried to cower but hadn't lost enough weight. Gill grabbed his pint. His eyebrows recoiled. She scowled. A couple of tables questioned Gill's Christmas spirit. So did Gill. She poured the London Pride down her throat.

'I thought you didn't like London Pride?' said Brolly as she smashed, practically shattered, his empty glass back on the table. He was right; she didn't. It tasted flat. Like someone should throw cigarettes butts in it. She tried to save her face, not wrinkle it up.

'It's alright . . .'

'I'll get you your own pint if you want?'

Gill stared at Brolly like a wet puppy dragged in from the rain. Brolly stared at Gill like a dry puppy about to be kicked out into it.

'Get us a couple and then I suppose I'll head into the arena,' she said dourly.

'That's the spirit. You're a gladiator!'

'Exactly!'

Brolly leaned forward, stuck his hands on the table, about to stand up, but Gill laid her hands on his. Her fingers were distended, like an alcoholic's face. She squeezed his hands, found solace in his muggy skin. 'Will you do the competition today or was last week your final one?'

'Last week was the final one . . .' She nodded with maturity. It wasn't how Brolly'd planned it; it felt wrong. Like a precursor to their splitting up. A trial separation. The beginning of the end. And he hadn't eaten that morning. Never did on Sundays. He already missed the Carvery smell, missed his position at the head of the table, missed the gazes of admiration and wonder from the audience, missed pitting his skills against Gill's. Wasn't prepared for her doleful demeanour and uncharacteristic introversion, wasn't ready for such self-pity oozing from her usually fiery eyes, her combative soul.

'Would you like me to do it today?'

Gill looked away from Brolly, up at the ceiling, stretched her eyelids wide open and shut them tightly. She didn't want to cry. 'Yeah, I'd like that.'

'In that case, I will.'

'Will you? Really?'

'Yeah. If you want me to. Why not?'

'Thank you.'

'No, thank you.'

'What for?'

'For being you.'

'I love you, Brolly.'

'I love you too, baby.'

She sniffled, bit her lips. He flipped his hands upside down, invited hers into his. She smiled sadly and took them. Her eyes moistened. So did his. Neither said another word. Elvis filled the silence. He was having a Blue Christmas, too.

The next morning, fried bacon and sausages wafted upstairs and mollycoddled Gill's taste buds, teased her stomach. She trounced Christmas cheer as she changed into her 'I Hate People' T-shirt and her 'Fuck You' socks. Blue-Eyed Pete swashbuckled into her mind. She froze. He was noisy. She listened to Brolly interact with the kitchen below; he was less noisy. She grabbed her bag. Her hands mocked her morality as she pulled out her purse. Her self-respect chided her morality as she opened it. Her demeanour sided with her self-respect. Her heart thumped like a punk-rock drummer. Two ten-pound notes moaned as she slid her fingers between them. As she found it. What she was looking for. What she hadn't looked at in the cold light of day. Sober. The business card he'd slipped her with the three Wispas. The card was cool

149

and unfussy but elegant and smart. The kind you'd introduce your parents to. The hotel's name and SE1 postcode suggested it was close to Harry's Hardware.

Gill grabbed her phone and typed in its website. Screen grabs faded up and down. To anyone who could afford to buy it, the website sold a dream. A lifestyle. A social media post. A future. Her future. A silhouette of the Shard towered over the London skyline; its dark, mysterious masculinity was revered by the kowtowing sun.

'Breakfast's ready!' Brolly shouted from the kitchen.

Two exotic women, almost but not quite sisters, dark-haired and svelte, stared diligently at the same sleek computer. Their clothes flattered them, their desk flattered them, their reception flattered them. They, in turn, flattered their guests who stood opposite.

'Coming!' Gill shouted back, not quite accurately. Gill itched the card before replacing it in her purse. The itch felt dangerous. Forbidden. She dawdled along the landing.

Funky antique furniture lazed in the en suite foreground as a low-slung bed with high reaching and padded leather headrest dominated plump, inviting, pliable cream pillows on ivory sheets.

The hotel wasn't the kind of place she frequented. In fact, she'd never been anywhere like it. In her life. It was a bit too je ne sais quoi. A bit too pleased with itself. A bit too previous. Not enough fluff around its midriff, not enough dirt under its nails. The anxiety it induced made her want to eat Curly Wurlys all day. Eating Curly Wurlys all day made her happy.

'You alright!?' Brolly shouted.

'Getting into the chairlift!'

Perfect bubbles joyfully raced each other to the rims of two crystal flutes and caressed two perfectly floating strawberries. At the glasses' feet, two chocolate truffles hunkered like proud dogs beside their moneyed owners.

Gill practically swooned into the kitchen. She'd been invited to a posh hotel where everyone was thin and expensively dressed and drank champagne all day and snacked on mouth-watering truffles. It was everything Gill wanted it to be and more. It was her fantasy. Her daydream. Her indulgence. But that's all it would be. She wouldn't betray Brolly.

'Smells great!'

She picked up a sausage and bit a chunk off as she sat down. It was piping hot. She pursed her lips and hyperventilated, circulated the kitchen air to cool it as she opened the Coke bottle. It fizzed and she poured it into her glass. It bubbled overexcitedly. She drank it. The bubbles jumped up her nose. Tingled. She giggled before she coughed. She cut off a slice of toast covered in baked beans. She shovelled it into her mouth. Chewed. It felt comforting. She stared at Brolly and smiled. He smiled back, but not as effusively. She grabbed the ketchup and squeezed a dollop next to the bacon. She did the same with the HP. Tried not to mix the sauces but failed. Forked a handful of chips and dipped them in both. Stuffed them into her mouth, chewed casually and looked up at Brolly. The chips dissolved into crinkly mashed potato before she swallowed them. She looked down at her plate, contemplated what to eat next. Maybe some fried egg on toast. Or bacon. She cut some bacon and dunked it in more ketchup. Inserted it into her mouth. She looked back at Brolly as she started chewing. Something wasn't quite right. He looked at her. A sheep in wolf's clothing. A wolf in sheep's clothing. She looked back down, only saw it on the periphery of her vision, wondered if she'd made a mistake. She tilted her head to his plate. Stopped chewing.

No. She hadn't. Made a mistake.

There were no sausages. Or bacon. Or chips. Or mushrooms. Or fried bread. Not even any bloody tomatoes. And no suggestion there ever had been. Just baked beans and scrambled egg on toast. 'Don't tell me you've gone all veggie!?' she asked with a strain of disbelief.

'No.'

'So what's going on?'

'What d'you think's going on?'

'I don't know.'

'I'm on a diet, aren't I?'

Gill's head hurt like someone had used it as a pin cushion. She floated up into space. It resembled the bottom of the ocean, glittering, dark, cavernous. Planet Earth was a distant pinprick below. She was alone. Lacked oxygen to last much longer, was having trouble breathing, wondered if NASA made space suits for supersize astronauts. She wondered if she bought a ticket for Richard Branson's flight into the unknown whether she'd sit next to Elton John. She liked Elton. He was a rocket man. He liked champagne. And truffles. He'd like her. But he didn't like her because she was sitting on him. Or on part of him. On most of him. In Richard's spaceship. He'd bought two seats, for him and his husband, but his husband was nowhere to be seen because she was sitting on him, too. Elton screamed at her to get off. She became flustered and knocked his wig off by mistake. And his glasses. And he couldn't find his bottle of champagne, accused her of stealing it. Elton was pissed off. He pulled a badge from his rainbow-coloured space suit and pricked Gill with it. She popped and burst, flew off the seat. Elton was happy again; he'd found his husband and his bottle of champagne. Gill fell back to earth with a bang, a burst and a bump.

'What d'you know about dieting?'

'I'm learning.'

'Why?'

'Lots of reasons, but mainly I don't want to end up like Tiny Tim.'

'What? With diabetes?'

'No, Gill. Dead!'

Gill hated Brolly and tucked back into her breakfast, shovelled the food into her mouth as quickly as she could.

'I thought we could discuss it . . .'

'We already have.'

'Not really. Not properly.'

'Yeah, whatever. Whenever you want.'

Brolly knew exactly what that meant and held his tongue, let her finish her breakfast in peace as he started cleaning up around her.

CHAPTER 21

Before retiring to bed, Gill opened her underwear drawer. Her knickers flapped and flounced over each other like a fever of dying stingrays. She picked up a black pair; they had a finger-sized hole in the backside. She picked up another black pair; they were diseased with bobbles. She picked up a third pair, also black; the stained gusset hung by a thread. Although she knew she'd never bought anything of the like, she rummaged optimistically, softly, hoping to happen across something lacy, something frilly, something sheer, something racy. All she found was more of the same. Uninspired function, world-weary and not very wise, over coquettish form.

In bed, she surfed on her phone, looked for plus-size lingerie for plus-size women. Saw wide women, curvaceous women, big-breasted women, supersize women, pear-shaped women. Every woman had a mane of carefully curled hair, a mouth full of expertly polished teeth. Ready to jump, ready to be jumped on, they oozed so much confidence, it spilt on the floor. But none of the women, not even the largest, were even half Gill's size or had any kind of belly to speak of. Not really. No quadruple chins, no dripping flesh, no stretch marks, not even any cellulite. Gill felt cheated, let down, and after three websites, gave up, forced herself out of bed, returned to the drawer where she painstakingly searched through every pair of knickers again, every bra, until she chose what she thought were the least offensive ones. The knickers looked like a window cleaner's spare rag or a dish-washer's best friend. The bra looked more salubrious, was decorated in a barely discernible floral pattern and did at least have a small ribbon at the bottom, where the cups met. The ribbon, she thought, implied tying and untying, coupling and uncoupling, bondage and belonging.

The next day, from Borough Market, she bought cinnamon sticks and star anise and sprinkled them in equal amounts over her chosen underwear. It was a medieval love potion and she was conducting a ceremony, so her bedroom door was jammed shut. The action felt magical. Made her feel more feminine. Beautified her essence. Her aura. She wrapped the underwear into parcels as delicate as she could manage, massaged them, kissed them, prayed to them. Her destiny felt preordained and the underwear smelled more alluring, less Persil Professional.

On the morning of the rendezvous, her skin cringed as Brolly cleaned it in the shower, rubbed it dry in her bedroom, moisturised it on her bed. She ate breakfast as if in a race with the Devil and during the drive to work chided the sun for trying to blind her rather than praise it for trying to soothe her. She noticed two turkeys wearing elf hats near the Elephant and Castle Tube station but remained tight-lipped at the sight. She bought six Wispas from a newsagent's near Harry's and ate them all on the street outside before buying another six. And then another three to replace the ones Blue-Eyed Pete had given her for that evening. And a medium bottle of vodka, which she fitted into her handbag. And a mini one for emergencies, which she slipped into her jacket.

At work, she devoured saccharine snacks and chocolate treats as if they were about to be rationed. Potatohead snuck out to buy four medium tins of Red Bull for her to mix the vodka with. She ordered three Deliveroo drop-offs, one in the morning, straight after she arrived, one for lunch and one in the afternoon. In the storeroom, she undid the replacement Wispas. She hid one under each breast like he wanted her to and seriously contemplated sticking the other up 'there' but felt demeaned by the act, not to mention uncertain of its health implications. She wasn't his sex slave, after all. He wasn't in control, she was in control. She had the power to do what she wanted, whenever she wanted. She stuck it as far under her belly as she could and wondered if there was something wrong with her and if she really was in control.

The sun had just dropped and the streets glowed beatifically, but Gill thought they were flickering. The Red Bull had been a bad idea. Her heart pounded against her ribcage like a champion boxer against an amateur. She hoped she didn't drop dead of a heart attack, needed to calm her nerves, needed a couple of pints. Or one. Or a half. But with all the Christmas footfall, everywhere was packed and she didn't fancy the aggravation, the attention that sometimes she thrived on.

She glided past the hotel without stopping. A bald Quasimodo bellboy slouched outside. People milled inside. What did she expect? It was the season to be jolly and to mill. She pulled down a dead-end side street, the kind Jack the Ripper might have liked if he hadn't preferred the East End. She listened. Police sirens screamed behind her. Church bells chimed in front. She knocked her fist against her forehead as if testing the entrance to her sanity. It was hollow. No one answered. She filled her lungs with pints of air. Air was cheap. Air made her light. She was a boat and Blue-Eyed Pete was about to float her. She held her breath for as long as she could, which wasn't very long. Practised a small orgasm noise as she exhaled. Just in case. She stuck her hands under her polo neck and under her bra. The space under her breasts was a sludgy, chocolatey, Wispa-y delight. She tasted the delight. Wasn't sure how delightful it tasted. She pulled out her emergency vodka, poured it down her throat and threw the bottle behind her.

She avoided eye contact with Quasimodo. Feared he might think she was an undesirable, move her and her mobility scooter on. But he didn't. Despite his aching posture, his face exuded affability, understanding. His thin lips and buck teeth and kind eyes communicated with Gill as he smiled at her, told her everything would work out. The communication relaxed her and she realised she was freezing. She shivered. Wanted to put her scarf and hat and gloves on, but it was too late; he opened the door.

The foyer blended effortlessly into a relaxation area and then a bar. Gold glimmered. Fire flickered in the distance. Christmas music lounged. Gill marvelled at the self-congratulatory suits and self-promoting haircuts. Everyone acted like they owned the place. Standing. Sitting. Mingling. Gill felt like an impostor. She wished she was an interloper so she could hear the conversations. At least she was wearing all black, which was the same colour everyone else wore. She scanned the crowd for her leading man but couldn't see him. She turned to the desk. Muttered greetings to herself to check she could still talk.

'Can I help you?' The receptionist sounded Spanish but looked like she hated paella. Gill wanted to ask if the receptionist was the one from the website.

'Yeah. I'm, er . . .' What was she doing? 'Someone's left a room key for me.'

'Wha's the name?'

'Pete.'

'Your name.'

'Oh . . . er . . .' The receptionist posed like a mannequin, grinned like an automaton. Gill struggled. 'Erm . . . Sorry . . .' Cleared her throat. It really wasn't a hard question. She did know the answer.

'Tha's OK. Take your time.' Gill did take her time. To the watchmaker's and back. Tried to imagine herself featured on the website with the receptionist. Couldn't imagine it at all.

'Gill. Gill Monteith.' Gill was relieved she could remember her own name. The receptionist turned to scan the granite background, a sleek cubby-hole unit for guest communications. She returned with a smile and a white envelope, which she handed to Gill. It had her name on it.

'The lift is just after the stairs on the right. Third floor. You use the key to activate the lift. Enjoy!'

The corridor was still, like a mausoleum. It was lit like one, too, but smelled of the Three Wise Men before they'd undertaken a long journey on a herd of dirty donkeys. She wasn't sure whether to knock, to barge in or run for her life. Or at least hobble. With her walking stick. She knew it wasn't too late. Knew she could turn around. Head home. The prospect welcomed her with open arms, an open-hearth fireplace, mince pies and sparkling English wine. She'd be the prodigal daughter who was prodigiously relieved. But then again, she didn't want all her agonising to be in vain. Didn't want to be one of those dead souls who regretted a life of inaction. A life of timidity. Of fear. A life of what-ifs. And what-could-have-beens. She slipped the key into its slot. The door clicked. A green light encouraged her to go forth but not necessarily to multiply.

The room was smaller than on the website and lacked a suite. Blue-Eyed Pete sat with his back to her in what looked like a bathrobe but might just have been an ill-fitting jacket. He swivelled around and bounced up. 'Alright, darling!?' She was really doing this and so was he. He was a bluster of bonhomie. He was also naked underneath. As far as Gill could see. Which was far enough, but not that far; the bathrobe was tied just below his belly button. His smooth chest glistened. Gill wondered if he was wearing pants.

'Alright, Pete?'

'Happy Christmas, darlin'!'

'Happy Christmas, luv!'

He wrapped his arms as far around Gill as he could. For a brief moment, he looked like he was telling a porky about an unfeasibly large fish he'd just caught. His lips gravitated to hers, smacked hers. His brick chest pressed against her softness, changed her shape, flattened her momentarily, pushed it all up. His breath smelled of alcohol.

'I know you're a G&T woman, but I bought us some champagne. You like that, don't ya?'

'Naturellement!' she returned, remembering a smidgen of French from her GCSE days but feeling more like a cockney character from a cheap TV comedy. He turned to a bottle that was already popped, from which he'd already poured himself a glass. She wasn't sure how chivalrous that was. The strawberries and truffles were noticeable only by their absence. She wondered if he'd eaten them. Wouldn't have blamed him. Didn't want to ask. But felt slightly let down. But then again, the Shard was noticeable by its absence too, and she knew he hadn't eaten that. He handed her an impressively fizzy glass. She knocked it back. He laughed. He poured more. Stared right into her eyes. She swam briefly. She was definitely getting better at this swimming lark. But she started to sink. Batted her eyelids as if they were her arms smacking against the water and he was a dangerous current. She averted her stare. Looked down. Dropped her mouth. Widened her eyes, saucer wide. Wasn't expecting that. Pete's thing. Pete's things. He definitely wasn't wearing pants. It was a bold manoeuvre. Some would say too bold. She looked up at him. Wasn't sure what he wanted her to do. With that. With them. With him. 'Just had a bath. Nice relax after work. Was feeling a bit hot. You don't mind, do you?'

'Erm . . .' She wondered if anyone had ever died of Red Bull and flaccid cock. Thought it sounded like an untimely cocktail. For middle-aged men and their long-suffering spouses. Banned from all gay bars and hen parties.

'Touch it if you want . . .'

'Erm . . .'

'Don't be shy!'

This was happening more quickly than Gill had anticipated. She wasn't sure what she'd expected but it was definitely happening more quickly. Way more quickly. She looked down again. It was growing. From shrimp to sea snake. She felt caught between a cock and a semi-hard place. She'd wanted him to charm the knickers off her but all he'd done was charm them off himself. He took her hand. Led her to it. She let him. He brushed it up and down a few times. She let him. He let go. Let her take the plunge, grab his plunger, but she grabbed the champagne and sucked on that instead. Blue-Eyed Pete wasn't sure if it was Dutch courage or French ennui but took it with English insouciance; he had all night. 'Like the champers, then?'

'Yeah. Got any chocolate?'

'Eh?!'

'Chocolate.'

'Thought that's what you was bringing me?'

'Doesn't mean to say you can't bring me some, too. Or give me some.'

'I'll give you some,' he said with a smirk.

'Truffles or anything?'

'Let's 'ave a look.' He stroked Gill's belly as he brushed past her. 'Nice,' he said. 'It's getting bigger, innit?'

Gill looked at his cock. She wasn't sure if it was getting bigger. 'Sorry?'

'Christmas an' everything . . . You. Your belly. Must get bigger over Christmas. Parties an' all that. Everyone's does. Mine does. I think yours is.'

'Oh, thank you!'

Blue-Eyed Pete crouched down by the minibar and opened the door. He grabbed a bijou tin box of chocolate pretension, of daylight robbery, and handed it to Gill. 'Very fancy.'

She ate every chocolate as he watched on in admiration and lust, a kind of foreplay, as his dressing gown continued to expose his excitement. Moments later, Gill was back to square one as the tin barked emptily at her. Blue-Eyed Pete eased the tin from her hands, discarded it. Their silence, the inescapable chomping of her teeth, had been beautiful while it lasted. He returned to Gill and rubbed his hands over both her breasts, testing her waters, testing her nipples. She could still say no. It wasn't too late to turn and run. Or stagger. It was never too late. Get the hell out of there. 'Bloody 'ell!' she moaned.

'Like that, do ya?'

'Yeah.'

'So what about your chocolate for me, then?' he asked as if it was the perfect segue.

'What about it?' she asked more confidently.

'So d'you hide the Wispas, then?'

'Of course.' The room was hotting up.

'I wonder where they are?'

'I think you want to find out, don't you?'

'I do . . .'

'I'm naughty, aren't I?'

'Very naughty. Did ya think of me when you hid them?'

'I did, an' I thought of you when I didn't hide 'em, too.'

'And how did that make you feel?'

'It made me feel like a naughty schoolgirl. You want 'em, don't you?'

'Yeah.'

'D'you want 'em now?'

'Yeah.'

'All of 'em?'

'I wanna lick 'em off you an' stuff 'em in your mouth and lick it all clean, lick you all clean . . .'

'And then . . .'

'And then I wanna fuck you silly with my big hard cock . . .' He grabbed Gill's lower tummy and pushed as if trying to squeeze it into a corset before sending it off into space. Gill groaned as if he'd penetrated her already.

'Take your shoes off . . .' he commanded. She did as instructed. 'And your socks.'

'Bear wi' me. That's harder than it sounds.'

She leaned on her walking stick with one hand and on Blue-Eyed Pete with the other. With the big and second toe of her opposite foot, she clawed at the fabric, dragged it over her ankles, over her skin as he exercised his hands on her breasts. She'd never taken her socks off while someone was fondling her breasts. It was disconcerting. Like arriving in Scunthorpe when you thought you'd reached New York. He slunk down her body, a snake down its totem pole, and aggressively traced her curves and contours with his fingers. He raised his hands to her waist, unbuttoned her trousers, unzipped them and yanked them off. He bounced back up, nabbed the hem of her polo neck as he went. It tickled her stomach and breasts and arms and hands and chin and nose and disappeared in a puff of smoke as he grabbed her head and stuck his tongue as far down her throat as he could. Their teeth clashed and their lips squashed.

Gill's hormones raged against her dwindling virtue and stomped it into the ground as she slid Blue-Eyed Pete's bathrobe off, ran her hands down his silken skin, played every bone in the xylophone of his back until her hands grabbed his perfect, smooth, pert peach. She groaned like a cheap river cruiser. He moaned like an expensive car. Riding and driving together, they fell backwards onto the bed.

The earth moved. Thunder cracked. Lightning snapped. Gill screamed. Blue-Eyed Pete shouted. The bed collapsed. He sank, not unpleasantly, into her breasts and noticed a dark birthmark. She moulded into the bed's depression and noticed a yellow wire protruding from the ceiling. Blue-Eyed Pete ignored the calamity. It was his dream come true. Lying on a cloud of human flesh. Gill's flesh. He cupped her left breast in both hands and started eating her nipple.

'What the fuck are you doing!?'

'What d'you think I'm doing!?'

'Pete! We just fucking broke the bed!'

'I know. You're alright, aren't you?'

'No, I'm not alright! We just broke the fucking bed!' Gill flapped and flailed, sought something secure but managed no more than handfuls of duvet. Her counter-productive lashing pushed her spine further to the floor, further towards a dead armadillo pose. 'And I think I'm fucking stuck!'

'Course you're not!'

'Well, get the fuck off me and help me up!' Pete ignored Gill's plea, lifted her breast instead. Cackled deliriously upon finding the first Wispa, which, he thought, looked surprisingly like her birthmark. He lapped the treasure up. 'Get the fuck off me!' Gill felt his cock poking into her thigh, didn't want him there any more, pushed him away. He wiggled out of her grip and slipped back to the underside of her breast, thought it was all fun and japes until she thwacked him on the side of the head.

'What the fuck!?' The fun soured. Blue-Eyed Pete watched every pore of Gill's skin close up, every muscle tense, the flower of her womb dry. He'd never seen anything like it before. Never seen anyone look like that before. Intimidated but intimidating. Scared but scary. 'Calm down!'

'Well, get the fuck off me!' Her sickly Red Bull breath, her female whingeing, putrefied the air, but he didn't care. He had her exactly where he wanted her. Where he'd always wanted her. He kissed her. On the lips. Tried to entice her back into his lair. Tried to make the gesture affectionate. Cosy. Alluring. Soothing. Comforting. She smacked him over the head again.

'OW!! Fuckin' 'ell, Gill!' What Blue-Eyed Pete thought of as the curvaceous sexuality of their predicament, the blunt humour of it, dissipated.

'Next time I'll fuckin' punch you. Just get the fuck off me!'

'OK! OK! OK!' He tried to extricate himself from her.

'What you doing?'

'Trying to get out.' He clawed and crawled, pulled and pulled the mattress, kneed Gill in the stomach and ignored her pained grunts, finally dragged himself out of the cocoon where he would have blissfully spent the rest of the evening. The rest of his life. He flexed his crumpled limbs and rose from the floor, had to hold himself back from diving in again, from drowning in her folds again, eating from her orifices. Gill watched with increasing panic as a glazed expression prettified his face more than ever and he grabbed his manhood again.

'Get me the fuck outta here!' She stretched her hand out. He looked at it. Looked at her. Looked around the room. Tried to build a three-dimensional representation of the situation in his mind because he knew he'd return to it. Forever. In his fantasies. Until he died. This would be his favourite. He'd contemplate it with many different bodies, with many different women, in many different rooms, but it would always be the same realistic fantasy, the same fantastical actuality: a naked woman, who he seduced, so bloody heavy she broke the bloody bed.

'FUCKING HELP!'

He pulled her hand. Clenched his teeth. Burst blood vessels. Rippled his six-pack. Felt the veins in his arms pop up like earthworms in a treacherous sand. But no. No way. He was a blackberry muffin compared to her 24-ounce sirloin steak. He suddenly felt naked. Not that anyone was looking any more. He relinquished his grip, picked up his bathrobe, tied it around his waist. More cracking noises followed. More bed slats broke. More of Gill fell to more of the floor. Her feet popped over the bed's edge and her neck stuck out unnaturally, perpendicular to her spine, now like a marooned turtle. Blue-Eyed Pete wanted to shout 'Cowabunga, dude!' but didn't because Gill burst into tears.

'Hey, hey, hey . . .' He kneeled down and took her hand. Stroked it. 'It's OK. We'll sort this out. No one's hurt. You're not hurt, are you?'

Gill shook her head as she wiped the tears from her face.

'Alright. So no one's hurt. No one's died. We just need a bit of help, that's all. We'll sort this out together, OK?'

'OK . . .' Gill's face was crumpled like a sheet of paper with unexpectedly bad news. Blue-Eyed Pete had never loved anyone as much as he loved her at that moment. He headed towards the room's cupboard and pulled out a checked quilt.

'Thank you,' she said as he flopped it over her. She shivered again as he retreated towards the minibar. He crouched down and pulled out all the exotic snacks and dropped them over Gill so that she became her own picnic table.

'Should keep you busy.' He grabbed his clothes from the chaise longue.

'What you doing?' she asked as he pulled on his pants.

'What's it look like? Dressing.'

'Where you going?' she asked as he pulled his trousers over his pants.

'Front desk. Need to get help.'

'Don't leave me!' she said as he pulled on his V-neck sweater.

'You need help.'

'Use the phone!' she said as he slipped into his socks.

'Better to explain it in person. Delicate, you know . . .'

Gill furrowed her brow. He slipped into his trainers. Her chest tightened. He retreated to the bathroom. She wanted to scream. To vomit. No longer blamed the Red Bull but herself. She opened the whisky- and ginger-infused dark chocolate bars and gobbled them down in seconds as Blue-Eyed Pete's bathroom silence cajoled her nerves and her stomach sank further. She thrashed around until the effort hurt. She poured the chocolate vodka balls into her mouth. Crunched the vodka out of them and wondered if there was any vodka in the minibar.

'You're going, aren't you?' Gill asked, trying not to regurgitate her emotions as Blue-Eyed Pete exited the bathroom, back in black, jacketed up.

'I told you. I have to get help. I can't pull you up myself. We need help.'

'Call room service.'

'I need to explain in person.'

'No you don't.'

Blue-Eyed Pete gulped and rued his leading-man looks. They were a double-edged sword. If he hadn't been so bloody good-looking, no one would've batted an eyelid at his sexual peccadillo. He would've just been an average-looking bloke going out with a fat bird. But he wasn't average-looking and he didn't like himself. His eyes flitted over the room. It was a nice room. Not cheap either. He wondered if he'd have to pay for the broken bed. Or if it was insured. His mouth was dry. He was thirsty. He walked over to the desk. Pocketed his phone. Grabbed the bottle of champagne. Took a swig. Spluttered. Handed it to Gill. She took it. He crouched down, took her other hand. Kissed it before she realised what he was doing, before she could rip it away. He stared deep into her eyes, which no longer looked beguiling but like those of a trapped animal. She didn't look away because she no longer saw what she once saw. She saw betrayal, deceit, weakness, insult. He smiled but she didn't smile back. She spat in his face. The spittle was stringy and dark from the chocolate. He wiped it away.

'I'm sorry.'

'You're an arsehole, you know that!?'

Blue-Eyed Pete stood up. Couldn't disagree. His grin wavered but he held it until he turned, whereupon it dropped into a frown.

'You're a sad fucking arsehole! I feel sorry for you! You're a weak-willed worm! You're embarrassing.' He continued to the door. 'You're a fucking embarrassment to your family, your species and your sex. And you're an embarrassment to me. You've got the smallest cock I've ever seen and if I ever see you again, I'll tell everyone you like fat birds but aren't man enough to admit it.'

Blue-Eyed Pete closed the door as gently as he could behind him.

'You coward . . . YOU FUCKING COWARD!'

CHAPTER 22

Gill listened for signs of life beyond her sarcophagus but heard none; no raucous corridor squeals, no bombastic electrical appliances, no awkward grunts of dissembled passion. She was hermetically sealed. The seal calmed her. Made her feel like a baby in the room's womb. She swigged from the champagne and relaxed into the mattress as best she could. She stroked the quilt and stared at the ceiling as if it was a complicated text but within her grasp.

She didn't have to wait as long as she'd expected, which momentarily irked her. They were so soft that at first she thought she'd imagined them. Two enquiries. She held her breath and listened. But there they were again. Slightly less apologetic. Three.

'Hello?' Gill just about projected.

'Is everything OK . . . ?' It was a woman's voice.

'Erm . . . Not really . . .'

'Can I come in?'

'I suppose so.'

The door opened with a click and closed with a thud. A dark mop jerked shyly around the corner, an enquiring nose and a familiar face.

'Ah . . . I see . . . He wasn't kidding.' It was the receptionist. Gill wanted to ask what HE wasn't kidding about. But never wanted to utter HIS name again. 'Are you OK, Mrs Monteith?'

Gill was impressed that the woman remembered her name but not so impressed that she thought of her as married.

'You can call me Gill, but yeah, I'm fine . . . I mean, yeah, nothing broken. Just my pride. And your bed. So . . . Yeah . . .'

The receptionist sidled into the room, crouched onto her haunches and took Gill's hand.

'Well, that's the main thing. My name's Patricia and don't worry. I'll get you out of this mess. Are you comfortable?'

'Given that I'm stuck an' can't move, very.'

'And you're warm enough?'

'Yes, thanks.'

'Good. I might have to bring my manager before we proceed. Is that OK?'

'That's fine.'

'I shouldn't be long, but can I get anything while you wait?'

Gill stole a glance over the room. 'Yeah, you could get us another bottle of champagne.'

Patricia caught her eyes widening moments before they revealed her reaction. She liked Gill's style and knew this was going to be a great story for her friends and family back home. Didn't have the heart to ask for a credit card. Returned less than ten minutes later with chilled champagne in a silver bucket and a camp man with exceedingly thick-rimmed glasses, who rolled in somewhere between a rugby ball and a football.

When the eight firemen arrived, they took a gander around the room as if assessing its suitability for their own romantic trysts. All in black but underlined with dayglow strips, they asked Gill various questions before hunkering down. She adopted a surprisingly upbeat tone, didn't want them to share her embarrassment so didn't act embarrassed. Chucked in a few jokes, self-deprecating ones at first and then teasing ones after. Men's locker room stuff. A couple of sexual innuendos. They loved it. It was almost as if she was one of them. One of the lads. With a small rotating saw, they severed the wooden bed frame into three. The hotel manager watched as if his poodles were having their teeth extracted. The firemen pulled the bottom of the bed away from the mattress and Gill's legs puckered to the floor, allowed her more dignity and a healthier flow of blood.

Two firemen tried pulling her up but practically wrenched her arms from their sockets and she screamed, almost burst back into tears. Patricia rushed to her side, took her hand again and suggested everyone took a quick break, but Gill suggested someone grab her a beer and the whole crew cheered. Two of the firemen opened a large tarpaulin with an endless number of straps around it. They encouraged it under her. Gill leaned on her left side first, which reminded her of struggling out of bed every morning. She wondered what Brolly was doing. She wanted to share everything with him but knew she could share nothing. She tried to rock and roll but her position was too compromising, so she wriggled and wrangled as they toiled and tugged and bit by bit, rough plastic ridges scratched her flesh and finally appeared on her other side. Two firemen looped a rope around a handle either side of her head. The other six firemen crouched beside her, three on each side, and on the count of three, everyone pulled. The ropes tautened and Gill slowly lifted upwards until her body slid down the tarpaulin and her feet sank into the carpet. She stretched her arms outwards to balance herself and finally stood erect.

The moment seemed anticlimactic and Gill thought the firemen seemed embarrassed by their success, in a hurry to leave, but then she realised the quilt had fallen to the floor and she was standing stark naked. Patricia was a step ahead, picked the quilt up and wrapped it around Gill's shoulders. To no one in particular, the hotel manager shouted, 'Bravo! Bravo!' Gill hoped he didn't beg for an encore. He started clapping. Gill joined in and so did Patricia and the firemen and everyone clapped each other and the miracle that was, sometimes, the human race.

After the firemen and manager left, Gill convinced Patricia to share a medium bottle of white wine that was still chilling in the minibar. Gill was unable to reach any of her clothes and was only able to slip on her polo neck. Patricia pulled Gill's trousers up and tugged her little socks over her bloated feet, and decided she wouldn't tell anyone the story. Not for the time being anyway. After they hugged and Gill left, Patricia stayed in the bedroom and surprised herself by calling her parents and telling them how much she loved them.

London's haughtiness, its cut-throat darkness, its unfair lashings of vertically challenged rain confronted Gill as she exited the hotel. The evening's reality inveigled its way into her flesh and bones, made her want to vomit, and although she'd arrived unprepared for the pathetic fallacy that presented itself, she was ready to wallow in it, to drown in it. What she wasn't ready for was what defiled her scooter seat.

'You're fuckin' kidding me!?' Gill felt like the next victim in a Hollywood thriller. She shuffled around in a circular motion. All the way around. Traffic lights beautified glistening bitumen with primary colours. Taxis blended with the watery landscape. Buildings towered malevolently. The killer would be watching her every move. He always watched his victim's every move. Dribbled over their anxiety, salivated over their isolation, masturbated over their imminent demise.

Gill grabbed the Wispa, stepped from under the hotel's concrete protection, held it up for the world to see, for Blue-Eyed Pete to see, wherever he was. 'You fucking arsehole WANKER!!!' She threw the Wispa onto the sodden road and stamped on it. It popped like a damp squib. She destroyed the chocolate. Crushed it. Pulverised it. Until the rain washed it into oblivion and she kicked Blue-Eyed Pete's perversion, his affliction, into the gutter.

She fled the scene, but once satisfied he wasn't following, stopped outside a Nisa. It was on the way to Waterloo Station. Rain bedraggled her make-up, trickled down her phone's screen like someone else's counterfeit tears. She scrolled through her address book but was confronted by an overwhelming loneliness. The world's last surviving dodo. She wanted to spill her ample beans to Dagmara but she was at the theatre. Tiny Tim was still in her contacts but he was dead. Potatohead would be trying to stick his hand up some fluff's skirt and Gay Keith would be sticking his down some bloke's bum. She considered the Samaritans but that felt too wrist-cutting. Taxi Rob would no doubt rush to her rescue but he was too close to home, and as for home itself, she imagined Brolly cutting a pea in half, snacking on a lettuce leaf, canoodling with a carrot. It was just gone nine. She switched her imagination off, retreated into Nisa, bought a hamper of comfort and resolved, after its consumption, to stop at every takeaway on her journey home and eat herself silly.

CHAPTER 23

t would have been a temporal impossibility for Gill to eat at every takeaway, but she completed a heroic eight before London closed for the night. Still buzzing from her indignity and her vodka and Red Bull, she confounded common sense by purchasing more vodka and some ice cream, Häagen-Dazs this time, from a convenience store opposite King Kebab.

Brolly's snoring shook the house's otherwise inert interior as she overegged her cautious parking and comic-book tiptoeing into the kitchen. She snatched two Ben & Jerry's and forced them into bed with the Häagen-Dazs, an exercise in dairy miscegenation, aided and abetted by her Svengali vodka. After digging out small, uneven scoops with her incisors, she poured the alcohol into the holes so that the tubs became edible shot glasses. When the ice cream began to soften, she ripped the sides apart and devoured it like a cannibal eking out marrow from a decaying body. She found sleep impossible but was close to conquering it when the bottle slipped from her hand and wet her lap. She chucked the remaining cream, no longer ice, down her throat and washed the stickiness from her face with the vodka, which stung. What remained, nothing more than an after-hours tipple, she slugged down her throat. It felt like watering brambles with paraffin during a heatwave. She swiped the detritus onto her carpet and willed the patterns on her curtains to send her into a deep coma. They didn't. Brolly's alarm convinced her, however, to finally close her eyes and play dead.

Her bedroom stank like a petrol station's forecourt. Brolly started to suffocate but drew the curtains and ripped open a window. Outside, rain rejoiced. Droplets conspired to rot the window sills, added sparkle to the curtains, infiltrated the carpet. Brolly shivered, slammed the window shut and interrupted Gill from her sham stupor. 'Good night?' he asked after she mumbled incoherently, deliberate nonsense, still in pain.

In the shower, the relentless pelting of water and the incessant rummaging of his hands, still unwelcome, half-baked insinuations, accusations of the night before, made her sway dizzily.

Back in her bedroom, her clothes fought her tyranny and her lungs became their closest allies, pummelled her self-worth and threatened her stability.

In the bathroom again, she saw a misunderstood monster, humane but inhuman, battered and beaten not so much by life but its own self-destructive tendencies, its tongue, tied with a string of newly born ulcers.

In the kitchen, she almost turned her back on her breakfast. But she had nowhere to hide, nowhere to run, no one to talk to, nothing else to trust. She didn't regret her decision. It arrived toasty, hearty and ribaldrous, and she realised nothing would ever take its place. It would always be her oldest, most trusted ally, unlike Brolly, who presided over her like a self-righteous preacher, with nothing more than a toasted mushroom sandwich as his elegiac bullwhip, his poetic loudspeaker.

Outside McDonald's on the Walworth Road, just before the Elephant and Castle roundabout, a multicoloured swap shop of hoodies and tracksuits barged past as she entered. She wanted to trip the reprobates up, bash 'em in, teach them to speak the

Queen's English, bury them back in the dirty, deep hole from whence they came, but instead she tutted, huffed and puffed like an amateur actor with no stage presence. Visiting McDonald's was like meeting an old friend who never satisfied her needs but one she continued to meet anyway. For old times' sake. A trip down memory lane. A quick gander at old processed holiday snaps that hadn't been converted into JPEGs.

Except for the menu and the bespectacled manager, who was wearing a Santa Claus hat, it showed little deference to festivities, which suited Gill just fine. She purchased one of everything from the breakfast menu except porridge and plain bagels. Diagonally opposite, a jumble sale of a man with an unhealthy predilection for tattered and plastic bags reimagined his own story, made corrections in his life's margins. Sheets spilled from the bags as if pilfered from a well of unwanted knowledge. He sipped from a hot cup of something and stared into nothing as Gill devoured everything. She ordered more of the double sausage and egg McMuffin and the bacon and egg cheese snack wrap but Ronald decreed it was past breakfast time and refused to serve her. Umbrage flowered into opportunity.

'Oi! Mate!? Want a Big Mac?' she shouted from a self-ordering kiosk that resembled a passport controller to an austere and foreign land. The man's head jerked around and gurned as if human kindness was the final insult to the injury of his life. A man after Gill's own heart, he revered silence, tried to stare right through her but failed. His gurning grew more creative, mixed it up with a subtle nod.

He clutched his bags tightly as she approached. She handed him two Big Macs. He fought the extremities of his lips from rising to a smile, but his eyes betrayed his delight. Gill watched out of the corner of her eye as he demolished the burgers quicker than she did. They both picked out their gherkins. 'Oi, mate!?' He seemed better oiled as he turned again, more smoothly, to

Gill. She threw him a third Big Mac. He snagged it with one hand. Gill felt like her rose's petals were starting to reopen after a long and tempestuous night when her phone surprised her. 'Harry's Hardware' lit up the screen. She was late. She prayed the ringing would stop. It did. She carried on eating, grabbed the fries, stuffed them into her mouth, but the phone vibrated and rang again. She resented it. Breathed anxious fumes of burger-infused gasoline at it. Wanted to turn herself into a flame-thrower. Melt the phone. Melt her life. She wished the phone would stop ringing but it didn't. But then it did. But then it started again. 'Hello?'

'Where are you?'

'Who's this?'

'Jimmy Savile. Who d'you think?' It was Potatohead.

'What d'you want?'

'You're late, where are you?'

'Yeah, I'm the boss an' I can be as late as I want.'

'Mr Carmichael's the boss and you can't be as late as you want.'

'Yeah, well, I'm still your boss.'

'Gay Keith's running late and so's Dagz. It's just me, it's a fuckin' nightmare.'

'Consider it character-building.'

'Where are you?'

'My scooter just got a flat tyre. Ran over some smashed glass on the Walworth Road.'

'What you doing? Waiting in McDonald's for the AA?'

'Yeah, I am actually.'

'Why am I not surprised? Well . . . Make sure you haven't blocked the road.'

'Yeah, an' you make sure you don't fuck any kids.'

'Fuck off.'

The call gave her more time to procrastinate. And to avoid work. And to eat. She didn't travel her usual way to Harry's but retraced her route from the previous night, up towards Waterloo. Her eyelids drooped. Her vision blurred. She stopped at an off-licence and bought a medium vodka and two large Red Bulls. She poured half the first Red Bull into the gutter, filled the space with vodka and took a massive slug.

She drove the rest of the way up the road, past anonymous offices that refused to announce their clients' professions and past hotels that weren't ambitious enough to party with the West End big boys. She stopped at Morley's Fried Chicken, where she ordered a large bucket of spicy wings, two large fries and a chicken burger. While waiting, she popped next door to Tasty House, the logo for which gambolled like a Chinese Pac-Man. She ordered a meal for four and gave them the Harry's Hardware address for delivery an hour later. On the way to Yummies, her morning snack shop, she temporarily lost her bearings but dropped into a pub that had just opened. It had a glowing electric fireplace and a Mexican metalhead barman. She drank a quadruple G&T, a double shot of tequila and two pints of IPA in under fifteen minutes. The barman couldn't believe his eyes and couldn't help with directions. Outside, she tipped half of the other Red Bull tin into the gutter, filled it with more vodka and supped from it as she googled the directions to Yummies, where she doubled her regular order of two chicken, bacon and mayonnaise baps.

At the hardware store, Gill answered Potatohead's questions about the AA with such acute detail and unerring earnestness that he found it hard not to believe her story, no matter how cynical he'd been. Not that he really cared either way. Gill was desperate for more alcohol but didn't want to hide her truth in yet another tin of Red Bull or an addled housewife's flagon of tea. There were only two customers in the shop, a self-congratulatory millennial couple who wore cheap clothes at expensive prices and usually went home to buy goods online for minimally better deals. 'Oi! Oi! Everyone! Over here, please!'

The gang huddled around Gill like a sports team for terminally unfit turnips and did its best not to flinch at Gill's breath, which smelled like a sweet factory worker's vomit. 'Alright, boys an' girls. It's the Thursday before Christmas and not even the paint stirrers seem to be stirring so I'm taking an executive decision. I'm not much of a speech giver but it's been a busy year and I think everyone's pulled through with flying colours and I'm proud to call you lot not only my colleagues but my mates and, you know, it's a good gang, innit? And I think we work well together and I know we play well together. So, I don't suppose anyone's forgotten it's our Christmas party tomorrow with Mr Carmichael but I'm thinking fuck it, let's start early. We've worked our arses off this year and I think we deserve a bit of a break. An alcoholic break!'

The gang cheered like nuts in a crazy vegetarian roast. Everyone pitched £15 into the kitty and Tasty House delivered at the exact moment Potatohead and Dagmara returned with plastic bags brimming with lukewarm wine and second-rate spirits. Her colleagues knew better than to covet Gill's delivery, but particles of monosodium glutamate insinuated themselves into every nook, cranny and nasal cavity in the store. Cheeky drinks trolled empty stomachs and the gang ordered a collection of pizzas, which Gill doubled in amount and upgraded to large.

After the Chinese and the pizzas, Gill snacked on the sundries and confectionery she'd brought from home. The boys started re-enacting *Star Wars* scenes using broom handles as makeshift lightsabers and Dagmara sidled up to Gill to finally ask her about Blue-Eyed Pete. Gill told her more half-truths and entirely omitted the hotel visit. By the time they finished, the store was shy of closing time but not that shy. Dagmara nipped out and bought forty chicken wings and ten large fries, which were demolished immediately on her return. After they closed the store, the gang staggered through the other staggerers, inhaled damp air and exhaled miniature miracles of mist. Gill drove by their side to the Southwark Tavern, which sweated Christmas cheer. It was the wrong day of the wrong week for Gill's regular table to be reserved so she stood uncomfortably with everyone around a smaller, chest-high table. She felt like a brittle plate being spun by a master juggler who was about to take his eye off the game. She almost ordered a burger and fries to distract her system from its alcoholic flooding but instead ordered two, knowing herself well enough that by the time the first one arrived, she'd be yearning for a second.

She welcomed the drizzle and the chill as refreshing alternatives to the stale claustrophobia inside. The slow-churning traffic, punctuated with indignant honks and precocious hoots, reminded her of a life beyond menus, beyond ingestion. She slumped on her mobility scooter and worried it might tip over. A sore had started to grow on her palm, near her thumb. She tried to burst it with her teeth but it was too hard. She yelped at its sensitivity.

As she slid and slipped and cracked and crannied into the Tesco on Borough High Street, she wondered if someone had stuck Blu-tack on her heels, bubblegum on her walking stick's tip. She wondered why she hadn't brought sunglasses to protect her eyes from the blistering brightness overhead. She hoped it didn't snow because she couldn't ski, even though she knew it never snowed inside and she wasn't carrying any skis. She bought a four-pack of Snickers, a four-pack of Mars, three packs of two large sausage rolls, three of the cheapest IPAs she could find and a bar of plain Galaxy.

She chucked everything in her basket and feasted on the way home, slipping an opened IPA into her coat pocket as she passed two different police cars that had stopped two different Black men. She wanted to blindfold the policemen and the Black men, make them choose between a Mars bar and a Snickers, but thought better of it. She wanted to ask the policemen why they were wearing ski boots and goggles when it wasn't snowing and why they weren't stopping any white men, but also thought better of it.

She stopped at a Jamaican jerk chicken parlour, the awning of which was striped in Rastafari colours. She'd driven past it thousands of times but had never ventured inside. The menu was familiar yet foreign, so she erred on the side of caution and ordered a prawn roti and a jerk chicken with rice and peas and oxtail sauce. She loved the food but didn't respond so favourably to the skinned chicken cadavers that squawked around her feet and pecked her toes, politely requested she never swallow any of their relatives again, not their legs, not their wings and not their breasts. She did her best to ignore the cadavers and continued a conversation with the grey-haired man in a three-piece suit who looked like Bob Marley dressed up as Colonel Sanders for Halloween. If everyone licked his fingers, she tried not to think of what the Colonel licked. Carefully, slowly, stretching out her words so they wouldn't fall over, she assured Bob Sanders, Colonel Marley, that he didn't look like a Curly Wurly and that the meal had been lip-smacking but that the chickens should stop harassing his customers. She'd come again but not if the bloody chickens kept harassing her. He agreed but warned her not to take a jacuzzi out back if she didn't like the chickens because that's where the prawns curled and they were less forgiving about their man-made genocide. More prickly, too. They shared shots of rum as he told her the peas were cool. She didn't find that surprising; they were hanging in the freezer.

She stopped outside King Kebab but the Blu-tack bubblegum prankster had taken things one step beyond a joke. He'd superglued her to the seat. She pushed and tugged and pulled and although her flesh wavered, her tummy wobbled and her breasts rolled, her haunches didn't do anything. She tried to pop her sore again and squeeze her ulcers with her fingers. It wasn't a good look. A bloody metal tang mingled with antiseptic serum, and Gill contemplated filling herself with more vodka but couldn't find any. A husky jumped up at her and she wrapped her arms around it. Or maybe it was a rabbit. Or a mini-pig. Whatever it was, it was cuddly and warm. A fox jumped into her arms, too, and she smothered it in her breasts. It gassed her face and fondled her. It needed a shower and had also been downing Red Bull. A Smart car whizzed by as a dwarf surfed on its roof. The dwarf flicked his tongue suggestively and shouted obscenities at Gill. He was being chased by a fire engine. The fire engine was smoking a cigarette; it was from Camberwell. The men inside were smoking carrots and she realised it was the strippagrams who'd saved her the night before. She waved at them. They cheered back. She finally found more vodka. It was where she'd left it all along. In her coat pocket. She wanted to set fire to herself and breathe saffron and tangerine flames so that the strippagrams could rescue her again, but above her head an agitated two-bit crow screamed like a siren and cawed arrhythmically.

Brolly sat beside her looking like a melting snowman who'd drunk a hot cherry liquor and washed it down with a peach melba. Beside him, a lupine creature gnashed his teeth in concern, worried about a feast he had no provision for. From her heart, spindly plastic green stems sprouted. She tried to pull out the stems but Brolly tried to pull her hands from the stems. She was in a plant trough and didn't want to become human fertiliser growing macabre flowers out of her breasts.

CHAPTER 24

Gill didn't remember collapsing at home. Didn't remember Brolly testing her pulse and giving her mouth-to-mouth resuscitation on the stairs. Didn't remember him helping her stand up when the ambulance arrived. Or being strapped into a gurney. Or having electrodes stuck onto her chest. Or an oxygen mask clamped over her mouth and nose. She didn't remember Brolly holding her hand or being rushed down the corridors of St Thomas's. She didn't remember an argument between two doctors as to which hospital would be more suitable and didn't remember being shoved back into the ambulance and rushed to Barts. She didn't remember more nurses doing more tests and giving her more oxygen. She didn't remember the potassium solution she drank or the beta blockers she swallowed or the cannulas she tried to pick out of her arms. And as she was pushed into an emergency ward, she didn't remember desperate pleas for a woman called Mary to hold someone's hand, to stay with them, to not let go and she didn't remember screams of pain and hysteria when Mary did let go.

But Brolly did. Brolly remembered. Brolly remembered Mary's resigned indifference to the fading night and the chorus of appeal that fought against the morning's onslaught. He revealed it all when Gill awoke. He hadn't slept and his tone matched his ashen complexion.

'I'm sorry,' she confided.

'What for?'

'Everything.'

Brolly gritted his teeth. Resisted the urge to shout it was her own stupid fault. That she should have listened to him all along. Learned her lesson from Tiny Tim like he had. 'Let's just concentrate on getting you out of here, shall we?'

Gill squeezed her eyelids together and nodded. Her dry lips drooped downwards and wrinkles dissected her blotchy toadstool face. 'Yes, please . . .' She stretched out her hand. It was full of tubes and dangled listlessly, like a puppet's. Brolly clasped it as breakfast was placed on the over-bed table, tangential to her. It was a lame imitation of Brolly's heartfelt daily offering. A fried egg tremored like a plastic surgery breast disaster. A slice of ham cowered underneath like a botched skin transplant. A bread roll slumped like a tumour. An orange liquid tried to apologise for its companions.

'Call that a proper bloody breakfast. Don't they know Don't Give a Fork's in da house!?' Brolly said with a trot towards a brighter land.

'Ha. Yeah. Not sure I could manage ten of these. D'you want it?'

'Breakfast?'

'If you can call it that.'

'A slightly dubious claim, I agree.'

'Wouldn't hold up in a court of law, m'lud!'

'Why? Don't you want it?'

'I dunno . . .' A light-headedness clouded Gill's conscience. 'I'm just . . .' Like she was about to snitch on someone she loved dearly. 'I mean . . . You know . . .' She gripped her bed rails tightly, prepared for the world's imminent implosion. 'I don't think I'm that hungry . . .'

Brolly followed Gill's lead, grabbed the sides of his chair, but before he could fall off, his inner hyena sprang forth. 'Don't bloody laugh, you arse!' But Gill giggled, too, grabbed the bread roll and threw it at Brolly. It hit him in the face. He threw it back. It snuggled down her breasts, but she whipped it out and threw it again. Missed. Almost knocked over a skeleton with a colostomy bag. He croaked but didn't peg it. Patients turned, not so much disapprovingly but deliberately, to prove life was still on their side. They wondered what could be so amusing about being stuck in an antiseptic death tank with a bunch of cadavers and an incriminating breakfast a few days before Christmas. They would never know. They would die not knowing.

Complicity forced Gill and Brolly's eye contact. They stared lovingly into each other's abyss. Remembered they were on the same journey but hadn't lived in each other's hearts for a while. They shared breakfast together and soon after she finished the slice of ham, she flicked away a toddler tear and hoped Brolly didn't notice. He did but didn't comment.

Gill had a CAT scan, an MRI scan, more blood tests and a few other tests that she didn't understand. Her body was weighed, her height measured and after the first doctor – a well-spoken tennis court whose muddied lawn was in need of strong grass seed – assured her there really was no threat of imminent death, she spoke to two more doctors, both of whom repeated the same mantra, which, as the hours progressed, comforted Gill more than it alarmed her.

There was no threat of imminent death.

All remained cagey about what had induced her collapse.

But.

There was no threat of imminent death.

She snacked on garish pills and humble pie throughout the day and was given blood-thinning injections every night. She never slept well and hoped to be moved to a private room but wasn't.

She drifted through time like a ghost on a cloud. She missed the Harry's Christmas do, Taxi Rob's next squashing session, the Wobble Club's Christmas fancy-dress party and the Carpenter's Arms' final Christmas Carvery Competition. She told everyone she had the flu and Brolly told everyone, too. He didn't like to lie, but on this occasion believed it was for the best. He spent as much time with Gill as he could, brought as many sandwiches and snacks as he dared and was constantly surprised she never pestered him for more.

Sunday afternoon, the ward reeked of leeks and backstreet abortions. It could've been mistaken for Piccadilly Circus but without the buses and the flashing adverts. Visitors nattered with feigned jauntiness. Tried not to let slip their annoyance at their Christmas's ruin. Prayed their loved ones would still be alive on the twenty-fifth. Underplayed the reality that they wouldn't. Seconds after Brolly handed Gill a bag of treats from Marks & Spencer, the tennis court careened into the space clutching a clipboard and looking like she'd just escaped from a tweed convention. She had a healthy glow, as if no one had told her it was Christmas, and pulled a flimsy segregating curtain around Gill's bed before consulting her notes. 'I'm not going to beat about the bush, Miss Monteith. There's good news and bad news.' Gill swallowed the thin, stale air. Brolly swallowed his chicken and avocado sandwich. 'The good news is, your results have all come back negative. You didn't have a heart attack and you didn't have a stroke, so that's a great relief.'

'It is. Thank you.' Gill sighed cautiously.

'Fantastic!' Brolly chimed.

'But that also means we don't really know what caused your collapse. Most probably a perfect storm, different things combining: your heart's bigger than it should be, you have high blood pressure, you have high cholesterol and you're pre-diabetic, which means your blood sugar is also higher than it should be.'

'OK . . .' Gill hoped she wasn't about to be given a jolly-hockey-sticks death sentence.

'We can give you medication for all of that and we will and it will help, but there's something you can do yourself that will be more effective than anything we can ever do for you. And I think you know what that is, don't you?'

Gill shook her head.

'Well, I think you're more intelligent than you're letting on, Miss Monteith. You're 5 foot 7 inches and you weigh 37 and a half stone, which means you have a BMI of 82. Do you know what that means?'

'Not really.'

'It means you're morbidly obese and if you don't lose weight, a lot of weight, you'll die. In the next few years. Before you turn forty.' The tennis court smiled as if she was looking forward to the funeral. Gill smiled back as if she'd invite the tennis court but would put the wrong postcode on the invitation. 'Do you have any questions?'

A bombastic orchestra grated nearby through impoverished speakers. Gill's blood boiled. It scalded her body. She hoped her large heart wasn't tumescing. She wanted to scream. She wanted to explode. She wanted to hide. To regress. To a time before she hated her mother. Before she bawled because she was a baby. To the labour room in the hospital. But she didn't want to be smacked on the back, didn't want her umbilical cord severed. Wanted to regress to before that. To be sucked up into her mother's vagina, into the uterus, to float in the balloon of amniotic fluid, mysteriously, for eternity, with her thumb in her mouth, with no language to communicate and no thoughts to fret over.

'Er . . .' Gill had several questions but couldn't think of any. She hoped Brolly would help her out, but he was taking an autistic interest in his trainers.

'Knock-knock!' a nasal voice interrupted from behind the curtain.

'Who's there?' chirped the tennis court, as if in on the ill-timed gag.

'Doctor.'

'Doctor who?'

Gill and Brolly stared at each other disbelievingly.

'Doctor Khan!'

'Come in, Doctor Khan!' Without a punchline, Doctor Khan struggled to find the gap in the curtain and flustered around like a fumbling wraith, too lazy to scare itself, let alone anyone else. He eventually grabbed a clump of plastic from the bottom, bent down, snuck under it and snapped back up into the space. One eyebrow hovered above the other, as if lightning had struck when he was impersonating Sean Connery. He and the tennis court ignored their patients and acted as if they'd once been lovers and were toying with their own illicit rekindling.

The tennis court finally excused herself without any further pearls of wisdom and Doctor Khan turned to Gill and introduced himself as her bariatric doctor. No beanpole himself, he looked like he'd been enjoying more of his wife's home cuisine than the NHS might recommend. Either that or he was trying extra hard to share empathy with his patients. He talked about weight-loss surgery and explained the difference between a gastric band and a gastric bypass. He explained that if Gill went down this route, she'd be left with excess folds of hanging skin that would need additional surgery, the operation for which wasn't available on the NHS. He explained she'd have to take vitamin pills and supplements for the rest of her life and he explained the dangers of deep vein thrombosis and pulmonary embolism, wound infection, leakage into the gut and silicone bands slipping out of place, causing heartburn and vomiting.

'But here's the Catch-22,' he teased, as if saving the best for last. 'I'm afraid to say, you're too heavy for bariatric surgery. So even to undergo an operation to lose weight, you still need to lose weight!'

Screams and shouts and deep vein rat-a-tat-tats exploded from the nearby speaker. The apocalypse was nigh and Doctor Khan and the tennis court were two of its unlikely horsemen. Gill stared at Brolly, wondered if he was a third, but knew he couldn't mount a horse, let alone ride one. She guffawed. 'Is something funny?' Doctor Khan demanded from high up on his, as if he was offended that a patient was challenging his monopoly of inappropriateness.

'No. Sorry. Not at all.'

'This is no laughing matter. You could die and very soon. You need to lose weight immediately, Miss Monteith.'

Gill grabbed her stomach as if she half expected it to flee for its life. She sunk her nails into it. Wanted a reaction. It was the chief architect of her downfall, after all. She wanted to hear its side of the story before taking a kitchen knife to it, cutting off all her flesh and sending it to them, to everyone, everyone she knew, bloody and dripping, in the post, in festive wrapping paper. Who'd be laughing then? Not the bloody tennis court or Doctor Khan, that's for bloody sure. It was her party and she'd maim herself if she wanted to. Her funeral and she'd laugh if she wanted to.

'What we recommend is a considered diet and regular exercise,' he continued unoriginally. 'Fruit and vegetables, home cooking, no snacking, no sweets, no cakes. That kind of thing. I'm going to give you my card and when you leave I want you to book an appointment at reception for February and we'll see how you're doing. If you manage to lose weight by then, maybe you want to carry on losing it naturally. Hospitals are dirty places and the less time you spend in them, the better. If you think you'd like intervention, we can discuss the options in more detail. How does that sound?'

'Sounds great,' Gill lied. Doctor Khan regarded her with a degree of scepticism before rummaging through his wallet.

'Seem to have run out of cards.' He scribbled his details on a Costcutter's receipt and handed it to Gill. 'Here.'

'Cheers, Doc.' She wanted to rip it up and throw it back in his face but after inspecting the scraggly piece of paper, a begrudging admiration seeped over her like syrup over ice cream; the doctor had bought a garlic naan bread, two pizzas, two Yorkies, two Frazzles, some lychee juice and a Cadbury's Creme Egg.

'Good luck with everything and I'll see you in the New Year.'

'How much longer will I have to stay here, d'you think?'

'We're all done. You're free to go.'

'Oh wow, great, thanks, Doc!'

The house reminded Gill of a skull without a soul, its eyes dead, its lights off. The front wall leaned precariously. A barrowful of weeds defaced brickage. Paint curled around window frames like mouldy pasta. Inside, stale sauces and soured polystyrene degraded the hallway air. Insect silhouettes posed for an orgy of death through the lampshade. Three damaged balusters loitered against the wall opposite the stairs. Two were long, the other split in half. The ends of each were jagged. Gill frowned as she stared at them. Turned to the staircase and noted the gap their absence had caused.

'Did I do that?'

'When you collapsed.'

Gill nodded wistfully, sighed mournfully. 'Lucky the whole thing didn't break.'

'Might've been a different story . . .'

'Yeah . . .' Her heart palpitated as she entered the kitchen, flicked the light on, prayed she wasn't about to have another episode. She waddled to the cutlery drawer, pulled it open. Wheezed noisily. Wondered if the advent of electric razors had had any impact on suicide rates. Wondered which knife she'd use to cut her wrists if she ever chose to do the deed. The bread knife seemed too unwieldy, too messy, like it would leave too many serrations, not enough questions. The dining knives were too blunt. The small cutting knife that looked like a secret weapon a cruel seductress would hide in her garter might do the trick. Its handle was wooden, its blade thin for less painful incision. There was another knife, too, with an obsidian handle; sleek, violent, masculine. Small Japanese letters communicated on its triangular blade, the cutting side of which stretched further than Gill's hand.

'What you doing?'

'Huh?'

'What you doing?' Brolly repeated.

'Oh . . . nothing . . . Just wondering about dinner . . .'

'Well, I guess the question is, when d'you want to start the diet?'

Gill's eyes shot the knives at Brolly. She looked at a bottle of port, which cast judgement over a stack of unopened mail. Gill approached the port, picked it up, unscrewed its top. 'I don't think alcohol's such a good idea. Give it a rest for a few days. Till Christmas at least?' Brolly suggested.

'There's something I need to tell you.'

He bit his tongue as she drank the sweet stickiness, medicine more insipid than anything she'd had in hospital. It gushed down her throat like a poisoned river down a rotting valley. She coughed, stoked her heartburn, repeated the gesture as her breasts wobbled in disapprobation.

'Gill!?'

'I told you – there's something I need to tell you.'

'Yeah, I know, but . . .'

'Just shut up, will you? D'you want some?'

'I think it's Auntie Violet's, which means it's about ten years old! Probably older. We should throw it away, really.'

'Just sit down, will you?'

Brolly shot the knives back at Gill, gnashed his teeth, but did as he was told. Gill offered him the port again.

'No thanks.'

'Just take it.'

'I don't want any!'

Gill took another slug before quickly upending the kitchen table and a waterfall of household crap crashed to the floor. Food solids stuck to the wooden surface. Abstract stains decorated it. The bottle echoed tersely as she banged it down and shuffled to the sink. She wanted a sponge but there wasn't one. She scoured the room and grabbed a crumpled tea towel, which she wetted and swiped across the table. She threw the towel to the floor and shuffled back to the confectionery cupboard, which she emptied. Onto the table. Methodically. Until not a sweet, a crisp packet, a chocolate bar remained. The contents formed a careless but seductive and eye-watering hillock.

'What you doing!?' Brolly asked, upset, unhappy, as Gill devastated a Lindor bar, arranged herself around the chair.

'Help yourself.'

'I've given up,' Brolly snapped back.

'If you say so.' Gill shoved a Mars bar into her mouth. Chewed and taunted Brolly with her death wish. He tried not to rise to her bait as Double Deckers, Ripples, Crunchies, Twix, Snickers and Rolos followed. His disbelief was dumbstruck, his indignation hurt. A little red Skittle snuck out of Gill's mouth, bounced onto the table and dropped to the floor, where she squashed it.

'Gill, what the fuck are you doing!? Didn't you listen to anything the doctors said? Didn't you learn anything from the last five days!?'

'I was raped.'

'Sorry?!'

Gill poured the rest of the Skittles into her mouth and released the rainbow of flavours.

'I was raped . . .'

191

CHAPTER 25

Gill ripped a Terry's Chocolate Orange from its box and smashed it against the table before ripping off the wrapper and shovelling chunk after chunk into her mouth. A solitary tear dawdled down her left cheek. She let the honesty shine. Brolly grabbed the remainder of the orange and did the same. Gentle sobs escaped her lips as tears followed down her face. She closed her eyes as if she wanted to disassociate herself from the world, clenched her fists as if she wanted to punch it. Brolly tried to spare her the solemnity of his gaze as she crumpled into a quivering wreck of shame and self-hate.

He failed. But asserted his masculinity and went to his partner. Wrapped her protectively in his love, rested his nose on the flat of her head. Her breath smelled of rotting vegetables and blocked digestion. Her hair was greasy like a newspaper that had recently wrapped chips. Dandruff illuminated her centre parting like a badly applied line on an asphalt tennis court. He kissed it. She clawed at his biceps as if they were the only thing that made sense in such a nasty world. Brolly stood there, arched, until the physical effort forced him to renege.

'If you don't want to talk about it, I understand,' Brolly offered in typically English fashion after he'd just spent the previous thirty minutes buying a treasure trove of alcoholic and edible comfort to prepare for Gill's revelation, to ease her pain, to ease his pain. Raindrops tapped balefully against the kitchen windows. It was the kind of weather that usually incited them to order double cheeseburgers with bacon. Blue cheese if they were feeling adventurous. The irregular beat made Gill feel at one with a greater force. So did the sweets. And the wine. And the ice cream. And Brolly. And the squashed Skittle that shone out from the floor like a beacon from her darkness. She unscrewed the first bottle of wine and discarded the top over her shoulder. She filled their glasses to the brim and reminded herself she wasn't a victim but a survivor.

'I've never told anyone else about this 'cos . . . you know . . .' Gill took a gargantuan breath. Brolly forced a smile even though he wasn't quite sure if he did know. He nodded, downed some wine. 'Well, apart from my mum and she . . . We were in the kitchen, at home, and she asked if I wanted a cheese sandwich. I wasn't sure if she'd heard me or not, but I said yes anyway and waited for her to cut the bread before telling her again. She didn't ask who it was or how it happened so I told her and all she said was, "Oh, don't be silly, darling, Mr Gavestan would never do anything like that!" She asked if I wanted Branston or mustard or both, so I said both. She sliced up half a tomato and kind of threw the plate at me, not violently but dismissively, like she was pissed off but couldn't be arsed to tell me. "Don't worry about washing-up, darling, just put the plate in the sink and I'll do it later . . ." And off she walked, out of the kitchen and . . . Yeah . . . We never spoke about it again.'

'Jeez . . .'

'Yeah, but that's just the beginning . . .' Gill poured a small bag of Maltesers into her mouth, sucked the air out of them as she crushed them. They whittled into a reassuring paste, which she rinsed around her mouth before swallowing it with a gulp of wine.

'Have you ever been to a gymkhana?' Brolly shook his head. 'So just down the road from our house . . . My dad worked in the City. Don't even know what he did, to be honest – something to do with foreign investments – but we had tons of land, most of which he rented out to a local farmer who used to hold a gymkhana every year, just, like, half a mile down the road. Horsey stuff mainly, but also competitions for dog-walking and courgette-growing and jam-making, all that Miss Marple kind of stuff, so it was a pretty big deal, something the whole area looked forward to. I think I told you we had stables . . .'

'Yeah.'

'Yeah, so . . . I mean, I was thirteen . . .'

'Thirteen!!?' Brolly asked as his heart sank and Gill nodded. 'I'm so sorry . . .'

'Shit happens. I didn't die.' Brolly reached for a large bar of Aero Mint. Finished it in seconds. Didn't taste the mint or the chocolate. Just the melancholy. 'I mean, I was turning into a woman but I was still a kid, more into ice cream and lollies than boys, but that was the summer my tits ballooned and I had my first period. I was embarrassed but kind of proud, too, you know? And I was pretty. Skinny, too. I think I still had braces at the time and freckles on my cheeks. And I was wearing jodhpurs and a crisp white shirt Mummy had ironed that morning and a black competition jacket. Oh yeah, and Mum'd also spent like half an hour braiding my hair into a pigtail, so although I was still a kid it was one of the first times I really felt like a grown-up. I had black riding boots, too – the works. I was so excited. Proud of myself and my horse, Barnaby, and this is the weird thing, I remember at the gymkhana, I could just feel these invisible eyes . . . leching over me . . . I guess I didn't quite know what they were doing back then but I could feel them, all those eyes, male eyes, wherever I looked, I never quite caught them but I knew they were there, just out of sight but always there, looking . . . And . . . And I always felt . . .

well . . . feel . . . I always feel bad 'cos I liked that feeling, you know? Someone looking at me like that. It felt dangerous . . . thrilling . . . Made me feel . . . well . . . made me feel important, like I meant something, like I had something people wanted, like I was a woman, I suppose . . .'

Gill opened the sharing bags of Minstrels, M&Ms and Smarties and poured them onto the table. They crackled like ice pellets against glass. She corralled them away from the looming cliff edge, blurred their identity, mixed their race, traced her finger through the middle, constructed an invisible wall. She dragged her share close to her chest like a poker player pulling in her winning chips. Brolly did the same. She targeted a clump of Minstrels. He relapsed and targeted everything.

'So I was standing in the middle of this kind of yellowy field and it was boiling hot and I was sweating. I was feeling a bit light-headed and nervous about my first event when I spotted this girl from school, Lucy Thomas. She was a couple of years ahead of me so we never spoke, but I had a crush on her. And people used to say we looked like sisters, which I liked 'cos she was gorgeous. And she was in competition, too, but in a different one to me and when I saw her in the paddock, guess what? She was wearing exactly the same outfit. I mean, most people were, most of the competitors, because that's what you wore at gymkhanas: jodhpurs, white shirt, jacket. But even her hair, it was in pigtails, was the same and . . . I dunno, she looked like someone out of a Jilly Cooper novel. And this is the thing. She was wearing lipstick. I wanted to be like her so I was like, of course! Why didn't I think of that!? I was just at that age where my mum'd allowed me to start wearing make-up, lipstick – well, more like lip gloss but to me, at that age, that was sophistication. I wanted to look nice for the competition and for the judges and I wanted to be like Lucy and, you know, I lived across the road. I mean, it was half a mile but back then, that was nothing, so I nipped home and at some point a voice called out to me . . .'

'Mr Gavestan.'

'Exactly.'

The rain stopped to listen. The central heating warmed up. She confronted the rumbling silence and her dry mouth.

'You OK?'

The whole glass of wine she drank suggested she wasn't. So did her glistening brow, but her meek nod contradicted both.

'And he was my riding instructor so, you know, I'd known him since I was nine, so no biggie.'

'Since you were nine?'

Gill hid her lips, sucked in her cheeks as she nodded.

'That's disgusting.'

Gill's soul deflated like a balloon. Her sense of self-worth withered. 'Yep. He told me he'd left something in his car and, er, 'cos we had a long driveway my dad allowed some of our friends to park there, so the first thing he said to me was – and I remember this like it was yesterday – we were walking past a silver Mercedes convertible. He said, "I was admiring your outfit earlier, but you must be boiling. Why don't you take your jacket off?" And . . . I was like, oh yeah, now you come to mention it, I am boiling. So I took my jacket off and, you know, then he made some comment that I didn't get at the time about my shirt being too small and just as we were approaching his car, he said I was sweating, my back was sweating and he rubbed his hand down my back, like, to show me where the sweat was coming from, but then he slipped his hand over my bum and I remember wondering what he was doing. And he just . . . groped it. Squeezed it. Asked if I liked it and I said . . . I mean, I didn't not like it. I thought it was a bit weird but it stirred something within me, too, and I didn't want to upset him 'cos I liked him and so did my parents and he was my riding instructor so I just said yes, I liked it. I don't know why but . . . I didn't know what he was doing but I liked it and d'you know what he said?'

Brolly shook his head.

'"I thought you would."'

'Jesus. How old was he?'

'I dunno . . . My mum's age. Late thirties probably . . .' Goose bumps rippled over Gill's body. She hid her lips again as she shivered. Wiped the sweat from her forehead. Grabbed the remaining Maltesers. 'He asked me to wait while he looked for whatever he was looking for so I did and when he couldn't find it, which I guess must have all been bullshit, he said he thought he might have left it in the stables and would I mind taking him there . . .'

Brolly's interstices clasped his hands together. He chafed his palms with his thumbs, as if trying to cheat death or at least massage it into a meaningful delay.

'So we went there and . . . that's where it happened . . . And . . . Suddenly I was on the floor . . . face down and . . . he was on top of me and I couldn't move and, you know, his weight, and he was so strong, I was just stuck there with this stale cigarette breath blowing down on me . . . and . . . and . . . it really hurt, like a poker ripping up my inside, really fucking hurt and the straw was really uncomfortable, itchy, and apart from hoping it would end quickly, I hoped, in spite of the pain, I hoped I didn't get any horse shit on me 'cos there's no way I'd win my event if my sparkling white shirt wasn't sparkling white any more . . .'

Brolly unclasped his hands and held them out, a bridge over the diminished lake of confectionery comfort. Gill took them.

'I'm so sorry.'

Gill didn't bathe in Brolly's sympathy for long. She broke the bridge, clawed at her hair. Confronted her own history, her own obliteration, her own dismantling, her own nothingness. The something before the nothing. She chewed the slug inside her cheek. Blood trickled like rust in her own rain. Until she drowned it with a new bottle of wine. She stared at the crushed Skittle.

Picked out a lime one. Dropped it on the floor and watched it bounce towards the fridge. She dropped another lime one and stopped it bouncing away with her foot. Tried to flatten it with her sole but she'd taken her shoes off and it poked into her like a concrete pea, an exoskeletal insect.

'Fucking thirteen . . .' Gill stuck her thumb up her right nostril. 'After that, he threatened me with various shit, told me never to tell anyone and left . . . I just wanted to lock myself in my room, pass out and wake up like it'd been a nightmare but . . . But you know, I didn't want to get into trouble for missing my event so I rushed into the house, rushed upstairs to clean myself and I thought I'd just get through the day and, and actually, I still thought I could win my event so I tried to concentrate on that but . . . The house had six bedrooms, even though there was only three of us, and it was kind of spooky, like sometimes I thought it might be haunted, one of those crooked old farmhouses with tons of wooden beams, and as I was walking up the stairs I heard this noise that I thought was a trapped bird. I never thought it might be a ghost 'cos it was daytime and, you know, ghosts only come out at night, so I tiptoed down the corridor, to the end, to the guest room, and there was my dad, kneeling on the floor in his jockstrap, giving his long-term tennis partner a blow job . . .'

'Jesus Christ!'

'Yeah.'

'So now I finally know why you never talk about your parents.'

'That was the day my childhood fell – well, was ripped apart and my family exploded into little pieces. I locked myself in my room, didn't have a fucking clue what was going on. Didn't understand what'd just happened. What Daddy was doing. I mean, he tried to explain but fucked it up. Badly. My mum came home at some point 'cos I'd missed my event and . . . I was in hysterics. Daddy thought it was 'cos of him so he confessed, they had a massive argument, and he left that evening. Mr Knight wasn't married so Dad moved in with him – quite the scandal that was, in the village – and I hardly ever saw him after that. I mean, a few times but . . . he never made much of an effort and I guess was happy to be rid of Mum and no longer living a lie and I . . . Well, about a week later I told her about Mr Gavestan and . . . I think she always blamed me for catching Dad and ruining her marriage . . .'

'I'm so sorry . . .'

'Well . . . And the reason I never speak to my mum is . . .' Gill wanted to leap out of her seat, tap an ironic dance with a top hat and cane, career up the wall and do a backflip. 'My rapist became my stepdad.'

'WHAT!?

'My mum ended up marrying Mr Gaveston . . . I mean, at least it was after I went to uni but in those weeks after he raped me, as I tried to make sense of it all, wondered if it was my fault or if I should've struggled more to get him off me, to stop him, I vowed to myself I'd never let anything like that happen again and I'd do everything in my power to prevent any man ever leching over me again and wanting to fuck me.'

Brolly nodded austerely, waited for the big reveal, but none came.

'How did you do that?'

'How d'you think?'

CHAPTER 26

Brolly tossed and turned in his sleep as if a war raged outside his window. Pointing fingers exploded nearby, machine-gun accusations fired overhead, psychological devastation weighed heavily on his chest, existential nihilism throbbed deep in his skull. He dreamed he was a eunuch, stripped and tied to a crumbling wall. Itchy firing squads wasted bullets on every prisoner but him. They chose instead to waterboard him, to choke him, but never to kill him. It was the women who kept him alive, their swathes of femininity that flowed in the gasoline wind. They flocked to his side, marvelled at his condition, bemoaned all the soldiers who wanted to skewer and squirm and impregnate them, whispered to each other that if only the other men, the childish warriors, were like him, the world would give birth to the greatest gift of all: peace.

He woke up desperately. Before his alarm. Scrounging pockets of breath. Slapping and scratching the monster that sat tight on his chest as ominous sentiments gnawed at him like ravens in a quagmire of corpses. His heart smacked the pavement of his guilt, the tarmac of his worry, until his irrationality, driving a dictator's limousine, dark with sapping windows that never opened, hit his temporary sanity and ran from it, accelerated from it, sped off from it. He feared the worst. Waved his white duvet like a surrender flag to his troubled thoughts. Threw himself out of his waking nightmares into potentially the biggest nightmare of them all and rushed. He could almost do that now. He rushed across the no-man's land of the hallway. To Gill's room. To her womb. Her tomb. Something just didn't feel right. Was burrowing inside him. Eating him alive. He'd never forgive himself. Wouldn't know how to. He blustered into her space. Prayed he hadn't fucked her up even more. Hadn't let her down further. Hadn't somehow dropped her in her hour of need. Prayed he wouldn't have to push her up a funeral aisle on a flatbed, through a leafy suburban cemetery.

'You practising a fire drill or something?' Her eyes looked like the testicles his nightmare had lost: abducted and tortured.

'I . . . I was worried . . .'

'About me?'

'Yeah.'

'Why?'

'Well . . . You know . . . Mr Gavestan . . .'

'I'm fine . . . Just a bit . . . you know . . . especially with the hospital and everything . . . But I'm glad I'm back home and I'm glad I told you.'

'I'm glad you did, too.'

'Thanks for listening . . .'

'Don't be silly.'

'I'm sorry if I've ever let you down, Brolly . . .'

'What're you talking about? You've never let me down!'

'I dunno . . . Sometimes, I just wonder what I do for you, why you're still with me. I mean, you look after me so much . . . You wake me up in the mornings, you wash me, dry me, moisturise me, cook for me and tidy up after me and . . . well . . . put up with me. I know I can be an awkward bitch sometimes and . . . you never complain, just get on with everything. With life. You're always there for me and I guess I forget, I guess we all do, but, just . . . I appreciate everything you do for me and I appreciate you being there for me all the time and I hope I don't disappoint you.'

'You don't disappoint me at all, but I suppose you can be a bit of an awkward bitch sometimes . . .'

'Don't, Brolly, I'm not in the mood. You don't have to say anything, just hear my words and don't spoil the moment.'

'Sorry.' Brolly heard Gill's words. Nodded. Accepted. Couldn't handle much more sincerity. Turned away. Couldn't handle much more life and death, love and potential loss. Walked to her windows. Parted the curtains. The sky was crammed with cotton buds sullied in octopus ink. A plane's flume dissected the otherwise still life, its body and echo lost forever.

'I was thinking . . .' Gill focused on an invisible presence in the room. Her cheeks wallowed like cheap Chinese dumplings. Her eye bags burst with tacky and unhealthy shopping. She looked like she needed a sunbed. Or a beach holiday. Or a health camp.

'Sorry. I just . . . I know I'm not so good at talking about these things but I wanted you to know that I did take on board what the doctors said and I . . . I will . . .' Brolly froze. His Darth Vader breathing dramatised her silence. He thought he knew what she was going to say but dared not put words into her mouth, dared not influence what she was about to say. She stumbled and struggled. Slipped and slid. Couldn't bring herself to shape the word that bounced around her brain like a square ball in an old-fashioned digital tennis game. 'Sorry . . . I'm sorry . . .'

'No need to apologise,' Brolly comforted as rays of sunshine burst into the room. They were at home, together. On an otherwise negligible Monday morning. Two days before Christmas. After a serious health scare. And other things. Her virtue was still intact. Her moral compass was reset. Each pulled at the other's vision as if it was a tug of war. He was her home and she was his. The window to his soul, the front door to his compassion, gave her the confidence to finish what she'd started. 'I will go on a diet.'

'Are you serious?! That's amazing!'

Although his face lit up, hers didn't. She didn't think it was amazing. She thought her world was turning upside down. She wanted a paper bag to breathe in and out of. Or a crisp bag. A large family-sharing crisp bag, preferably.

'I'm scared, Brolly.' Brolly stepped towards her and did something he'd never done before. Sat down. 'What are you doing!?' she screamed, fearful a bed would upstage her for the second time in a week. But the bed didn't buckle, didn't bend, didn't even tremble. Brolly took her hand. Kissed it. Telepathically sent her a bunch of red roses and plump love hearts.

'Nothing to be scared of. We'll do the diet together,' he said.

'Would you do that for me?' Gill stroked his hand, continued the telepathy, sent him a fluffy teddy bear and some hot-cross buns.

'Why wouldn't I?'

'I don't know . . .'

'Why don't we enjoy Christmas, you know, not go crazy but enjoy ourselves, and then on New Year's Day start how we intend to carry on?'

'You got yourself a deal, buddy,' she said in a half-hearted Western drawl. She tipped her legs over the side of the bed and grabbed hold of Brolly's arm to pull herself up. A cherry blush returned to her cheeks. They shook hands. She threw her arms around his shoulders and held on tightly. The world started spinning again. No one had fallen off. They hugged for an eternity. And kissed. And for the first time in almost five years, made love.

CHAPTER 27

For Christmas, Gill bought Brolly a Premium IPA craft home-brewing kit, a popcorn maker, a large box of cookies, five pairs of Paul Smith socks and a khaki-coloured cooking apron. He bought her an iced doughnut pendant in white gold, a box of Belgian chocolates, a luxury bottle of gin and *It's All Good: Delicious, Easy Recipes that Will Make You Look Good and Feel Great* by Gwyneth Paltrow.

Taxi Rob came for lunch with his mother, who had been diagnosed with Alzheimer's disease over the summer. She clung to his side like a shadow and barely spoke a word unless spoken to. After seeing the love and patience with which he devoted himself to his mother, Gill and Brolly gained a new-found respect for their friend. The Harry's gang came on Boxing Day and partied hard until they passed out. After they stumbled home the following morning, Gill and Brolly didn't shower, didn't change, just slobbed around the house and disengaged from the world at large. They held hands, smiled doughy-eyed at each other and glowed like they were falling freshly in love. They'd bought tickets for the Wobble Club's New Year's Eve party, the theme for which was *Charlie and the Chocolate Factory*, but after breakfast that morning, Taxi Rob phoned. His mother had fallen out of bed and broken her hip. She was freaking out in hospital and barely recognised him. He apologised profusely but couldn't leave his mum alone.

Instead of driving up to Liverpool Street, in the freezing cold, on their mobility scooters, dressed as Violet Beauregarde and an Oompa Loompa, Gill and Brolly chose to extend their romantic streak and watch fireworks by the Thames, but the evening never quite ignited. Tickets for the fireworks could only be purchased in advance, restaurants – the few they dared investigate – were fully booked, and even their local offy had sold out of champagne. They bought two bottles of Prosecco, which remained warmer than room temperature come countdown, and although their freezer's small tray of ice cubes improved the taste marginally, it remained insipid and effectively undrinkable. They went to bed soon after midnight but in unaffected and good spirits.

On New Year's Day, Brolly woke up with a smile. Gill heard his thuds echo along the hallway and relaxed into her mattress, waited for the toast's aroma to waft under her door, to send her into a pre-breakfast stupor. When she heard a click and a metallic scraping, she sharpened her spikiness as if it was a pencil about to give vitriolic copy. Brolly disappeared downstairs but returned moments later as she hid deeper under her duvet and tried to burrow back into the previous day, the previous week, the previous year. She wanted to ask what he was doing but didn't want to confront the answer; she knew exactly what he was doing.

She pulled back her duvet. She rolled out of bed with a woodcutter's groan and pirouetted with fuzzy disdain for her balance before standing tall, standing proud and hoping to stand corrected as she opened her door. An inverse stencil of the toaster and the filing cabinet it once stood on glorified the memory of their former morning ritual. A right-angled indentation confirmed its absence in the carpet. Breadcrumbs testified against it. Only a dry crust, a quarter of its former slice glory, colluded with Gill's sense of nostalgia. The crust beckoned with a Fagin-like finger. She used her grab-and-grip device to snag the crust. She clamped it between her teeth. It challenged her gums' hegemony. It was way beyond its sell-by date, tough, crispy, but she wanted it. She entered the bathroom and ran lukewarm water over it so that it turned into a pauper's bread sauce in her hand. Some of it jellied through her fingers. She caught it in her other palm, sucked it into her mouth and wrinkled her nose. It tasted of glue, the kind supermarkets sell three for the price of one. Brolly popped his head around the corner.

'What ya doing?'

'Just brushing my teeth.'

'You should use a toothbrush for that.'

'Yeah, very funny.'

'Don't move, I'll be back! I've got a surprise!'

Gill used to like surprises; now she wasn't so sure. She mangled the toothpaste tube, forced a sludge onto her brush and overpowered the glue, which had just turned into a sodden cardboard, flop-house aftertaste.

Brolly returned like a circus ringmaster, his arms stretched out showily, ready to catch his audience's applause. Something shone in his hand. Twinkled. Practically tweeted. 'Happy New Year!' He beamed as she scrunched her forehead and returned the New Year mantra with less conviction. 'So we can weigh each other!' Brolly continued. 'They're great. Indestructible. I've been using 'em for a while. It's quite gratifying, to be honest. Kind of exciting. I thought we could do it every Monday, make a note of how much weight we've lost. Maybe even give ourselves targets an' stuff.'

The scales challenged Gill to do battle with them, to kick them, jump on them, head-butt them, scratch out their eyes, but she knew she'd never win, not if he'd trampled over them already and they hadn't broken. Instead, she took them and pacified them, marvelled at them, stroked them. She'd never held a set of scales before, wondered if she'd grow maternal towards them. 'They're great. What a great idea! Happy New Year, lover! I'll look forward to weighing myself. Both of us, on Monday.'

'I thought we might as well do it now . . . You know, get a bit of practice in . . . See what we're up against. I've definitely put weight on over Christmas. Not so sure about you, but I'd think so . . .'

'Shall we have breakfast first? I'm a bit hungry . . .'

'Well . . . It's best to weigh yourself before breakfast. That's when you're at your lightest, and after a piss, and from my own experience, I think there's a great psychological advantage in seeing your weight at its lowest. New Year, new resolution. I'm excited about this, you know, how the year's gonna pan out, how we're gonna change. By the end, they'll probably ban us from the Wobble Club!'

'It's not like thin people can't go.'

'I was kidding.'

For breakfast, he cooked her four eggs, three pieces of toast and one tin of baked beans. For himself, he cooked two fried eggs, two pieces of toast and half a tin of baked beans. 'Oh . . . So this is what a diet looks like!?' she said, not entirely unimpressed. 'Not as bad as I thought!'

'Well, you know, can't suddenly go cold turkey, can you? It's the meat that's the real killer, the sausages and bacon. And they're bad for you, processed meats. Can give you cancer if you eat enough, which I suppose we probably do. Or did.'

'I feel . . .' Despite her enthusiasm to tuck in, Gill hadn't picked up her knife and fork. She felt distant. Stared into space. Thought of Mr Gaveston ripping her insides out with his uninvited cock. His barbed arrogance. His abuse of power. His ashtray breath. She remembered the weight of his seniority crushing her child's spine. The stench of horse shit infiltrating her innocent nostrils, the straw scratching her delicate skin, her clenched hands, her clenched buttocks, his fist in her delicate mouth, stifling her innocence, her childhood, her life. She'd bled for almost two months after that. Had freaked out, thought she was pregnant, was pissed off she wasn't because her mother would have had to believe her then. And then everyone would find out. But fuck her mother. Fuck her father. Fuck Mr Gaveston. 'I feel good! A bit scared if I'm being honest; it's a bit weird, but I want to embrace this and I know it's going to be a challenge, but, you know, we're gonna do this together now and you're my inspiration . . . It feels fucking weird to say that, but . . . yeah! I'm officially on a diet! Wish me luck!'

'It's not about luck, it's about discipline: mind over matter. But I'm proud to hear you say it. We're on a diet together!'

Gill didn't officially return to work until 6th January but claimed she had to return on the 3rd for stocktaking. Droplets had just stopped making little circles in puddles. The sky looked like a semi-finished blue canvas and, as if drawn by a child, a half-hearted rainbow curved shakily behind a block of new builds. She pulled up opposite McDonald's. The old friend who offered her quilts of comfort, cardigans of warmth, encyclopaedias of understanding. Who practically invited her to move in under its Golden Arches. Who never undermined her moods or denigrated her foibles but applauded her idiosyncrasies with a standing ovation, never let her leave without an encore. Often two. Occasionally three. Gill pulled the key out of her mobility scooter but didn't budge. The sun shone through her eyes into her soul and exposed a parallel life. A life where she hadn't gone back home to gloss her lips, where Mr Gavestan hadn't followed her, hadn't raped her.

One thing he'd never destroyed was her education. Although she'd studied Urban Planning at uni and was good at it, graduated with a 2:1, she always fancied being a journalist. Books. Theatre.

Film. Film reviews, ideally. How cushy would that be? How hard could it be to write a few paragraphs about a film? Glamorous, too; interview some famous people, go to Cannes, nibble canapés and drink complimentary rosé. Maybe she would've lived abroad for a while before that. Spain or Greece. Nowhere too challenging. Maybe worked as a travel rep. Got a tan. Had some uncomplicated sex. Been a bit of a slut for a while because, well, why not? She would've liked to be a mum so best get the casual sex out of her system beforehand. She never really enjoyed being an only child, always wanted someone to play with, especially with such self-obsessed parents. Two kids, therefore. Maybe three. Which meant she would've been married. Or at least had a long-term partner. Or maybe not. She admired single mums. She didn't really care about marriage but supposed it showed a certain commitment, a certain attitude towards plumbing and car maintenance. Her partner would've been casually good-looking. Boyish and fashionable. Presentable but not showy. The least good-looking member of a boy band. Maybe an entertainment lawyer. Or something in the media, but not creative; creatives rarely earned money. Certainly not as much as lawyers or accountants. Not usually, anyway. And the creatives were more fickle, too. And more unstable. They would've lived somewhere central for a while, somewhere cool. Hackney or Brixton. And then moved out when they started a family. Richmond, if they could afford it. Or somewhere a bit further out, Kent or even Dorset, by the sea. She'd have kept her hair long and blonde. She was always so proud of her hair. Loved to sit in her bedroom and brush it, stare at her Jason Donovan posters, imagine it was him combing his hands through it. Her black bob was kind of depressing, if she was being honest. And made her face look like something she should hide behind curtains. She would've been thin, too. She had a good figure growing up. All the right curves in all the right places. Well, up until she was thirteen . . .

Goose bumps festered on Gill's pallid hands, made her veins

look like stems on exotic but deadly plants. Her throat constricted. Witch-like noises gurgled from her dry mouth, plumbed to the depths of her chest and then her stomach. Vomit gushed forth like a celebration of all the bile her subconscious had brewed over the years. She wondered if she should go to therapy before she narrowly avoided her mobility scooter with a baked-bean rush, a poor companion to the sun's pure love.

Inside, she was interrupted from a trance-like reverie by a member of staff asking if she needed any help. She didn't remember entering McDonald's. Wasn't sure how long she'd stood in front of the touch-screen kiosk. She didn't need any help. Of course not. She knew exactly what she wanted and how to order it. Everything from the breakfast menu except porridge and plain bagels. And then maybe some Big Macs for dessert. And some McFlurries. She loved McFlurries and they loved her. Maybe she'd spend the day there. It was good to be alone again; she rarely had time for herself.

She tapped her order on the screen. It felt like systemic abuse. She felt subversionary. Visionary. A fat-busting terrorist. A freedom-fighting McNugget. A rebel with a morbidly obese cause. If everyone acted like her, the fast-food chain would collapse. The dollar and the pound would collapse. The world might collapse. She was giving the finger to the man. Ronald McDonald. It saddened her because she loved Ronald, loved his swollen feet for which he could only ever find one pair of shoes, loved his culturally inappropriate afro, loved his banana onesie, loved his jaundiced skin, his unerring love of minors, his winning way with animals. She swayed back and forth as if she was a Christian cult devotee, smiling uncritically at her leader's musical inappropriateness. She glanced at the customers either side, a housing-estate fashion victim, a family in need of a new family, wondered if she might convert them to her cult. Her cause. Her subversion. They were all thinner than her but none of them were beanpoles. Not even the kids, who must have been under ten. Her number flashed up on the screen. She smirked. Laughed at herself. Her life. Her order. Took a zeppelin of breath and shuffled to the counter. 'Alright?' She handed her receipt over to the infantile McZit, who oozed sardonicism and superiority.

'Would you like ketchup with that?' He spoke slowly, lazily, as if the only reason he was working there was that his father had forced him to build character before locking him into the family vault.

'With my bottle of water?'

'Yeah.'

'Yeah, alright. Two ketchups an' two BBQ sauce.'

The McZit wasn't sure if his joke was a joke any more, if his sarcasm was sarcasm, his time-wasting, time-wasting. If it was all on Gill any more or all on him. His acne cringed. His glasses steamed up. He grabbed the sauces, tossed them at Gill and flicked his wedge. She picked up the sachets, turned and threw them in front her, one at a time. Stepped on each one, left a sticky, tasteful, colourful, sloppy trail of truculence in her wake.

Outside, she swilled the water around her mouth, diminished, dissolved and destroyed her vomit's acid tang. She spat the water out as a pride welled up inside. She'd never visited McDonald's before and only ordered one item. A water. She wished someone had witnessed the occasion. Could have celebrated it with her. Abstemiously. She ripped out her phone, took a selfie of herself in front of the Golden Arches, holding nothing but the water. She sent the picture to Brolly with the text: *On a diet, innit!* He replied with three clapping hands. It felt good, she had to admit, like she was in control of her life again. Her stomach squawked but she told it to shut up.

She googled what had been an otherworldly joke, a dirty word. Gym. 'Bloody hell!' she murmured, slightly overwhelmed by the results. Even there, in the pits of South London, there were almost as many gyms as there were kebab shops. And so close as well.

Almost on every corner, it seemed. Lurking. Ready to catch you off guard, shake you up, pat you down, assault you with protein powder, stuff your sweaty betties with Lycra. She knitted her eyebrows and sewed her forehead. Wanted to say the forbidden word out loud. Needed to say it out loud. As if doing so would make the ritualistic sacrifices that happened inside less scary.

'Gym . . .' A shapeless effort, under her breath.

'Gym!' A cursory ejaculation with a small radius.

'GYM!' A proper holler, ripples extending, as if in an unpopulated mountain range, far and wide. A hunched old man with a stick, a flat cap and a ferret-down-his-trousers demeanour stopped in his tracks. He was about 20 metres away. Twisted creakily towards her. She wondered if he was called Jim. A souped-up boy-racer car sped around the corner. The old man stood in the middle of the road but not for long. The car knocked into him. He flew over it. Smashed onto the tarmac. Didn't move. 'Fuckin' 'ell!' There were other witnesses. Gill didn't have to pretend to be busy because she was busy; she threw herself on her scooter and sped off.

The gym, second closest to Harry's but the best looking, concealed its identity well. It hid close to the Mayor's office on the South Bank and looked like a sleek architects' practice, designed to blend in with toffee-noses and full-bodied bouquets. In one direction, the Shard presided like a headmaster over schoolboy buildings; in the opposite, Tower Bridge and the Tower of London held court with the sophistication of elder statesmen. Gill pulled up against the limestone wall that protected the walkway from the Thames. She wanted to know what these people looked like. These people who went to the gym. Of their own free will. On 3rd January. And if she could ever be one of them.

She didn't have to wait long. A trench coat exited as a couple of seagulls floated in the air, squealed to some friends. The trench coat looked expensive. It was wearing a barely visible stick insect with a cob of blonde hair. Its feet were chunky and fluorescent, its freckles punctilious. The insect flashed a snatch of teeth. It glowed healthily. Exuded contentment. Gill gasped, was reminded of her teenage self. An invisible force snapped a corset around her waist. Another trench coat exited, wearing another stick insect with different coloured hair. Clementine. Pale skin. It could have lit up the darkest alleyway like a will-o'-the-wisp lantern. Gill wondered if you had to have a trench coat to belong to the gym or just be a stick insect. The force pulled on her corset strings again. Her back straightened, her breasts jutted, her shoulders squared. An insect couple demanded her attention. The female resembled the other insects. The male was heavier set. With facial hair. They looked like they shared a secret, knew something others didn't. A smugness spilled from their pores and sizzled into the pavement as they strolled away.

The tourists started to notice Gill, gape at her, point at her, take photos of her. The force yanked again. Uncomfortable and aggressive. Fisted her innards halfway up her throat. She retched drily, salivated without spittle. The corset strained her liver, squashed her kidneys. Now wasn't the time. She wanted to be in control when people took photos. Cheerful. Playful. Projecting. Positive. Although, to be fair, they better get on with it because she wasn't going to be this size for much longer. She was on a diet! A high-pitched beep sounded from behind. Gill twisted around. The tourists weren't taking photos of her at all, they were taking photos of Tower Bridge. It was opening behind her. The Tower was working with her. It was her subterfuge. She didn't need to see it open. Her resolve stiffened. It was now or never.

The reception area smelled of Scandinavian forests and corporate membership. Lighting shone like a permanent sunrise or an eternal sunset. A takeaway food counter surprised Gill to her left, endeared the space to her immediately. But the green and purple and sandy foodstuffs, unnatural in their naturalness, made her squirm. To her right, more stick insects flicked through

213

lifestyle magazines, read about how to sit straight and masturbate properly. Gill wondered if everyone went to the Southbank Hotel for evening cocktails. She wondered why eyes flickered towards her but darted away before she could make contact with them. Her corset tightened again. Her breathing deepened. She snapped around to confront another stick insect, its eyes the size of saucers, its sclera as white as snow. It stared at Gill as it glided past. Encouraged Gill to leave with it. Gill's instinct wanted to follow. Her pride wanted to stay. Her sweat told her to do whatever she was about to do quickly.

One of the two things at the desk, more stick bugs than insects, suppressed a scantily clad titter. The bugs weren't as skinny as the insects but still shimmied like they were top of the pops, queens of the catwalk, darlings of the theatre. It was too late for Gill to turn back without losing face. She wanted to keep her face, maintain her position in front of the stick bugs. They stared at Gill. Gill stared back. The non-titterer cleared its throat. The noise sounded like the discarding of an unruly and hairy shrub. Gill cleared her throat in return, mimicry as subconscious greeting in alien communication but with a less hairy and smaller shrub. Her smile betrayed her. Neither stick bug smiled back. Gill suspected they charged extra for that. 'Can I help you?' The stick bug had an Eastern European twang.

'Erm . . .' Gill wondered how many times she could clear her throat without chafing it into oblivion but cleared it again anyway. She wanted to compliment the stick bug on its silken hair, its porcelain skin, its beguiling eyes, its tidy breasts. How much she wanted to be like the insects or the bugs. To flit in and out of life regally, like it belonged to you, not you to it. 'I like your name badge . . . Christina . . .'

'Erm . . .' Her admiration hadn't crystallised quite as she'd intended but it stumped Christina; no one had ever complimented her on her name badge before. 'Oh . . . I'm sorry . . .' Christina's desk wasn't as tidy as her body. She cleared some paperwork. Gill rubbed her sweater. She wasn't sure if their duologue had been curtailed. Christina nodded. Encouraged no one but herself. Picked up a notice. Skimmed it. Stared at her watch. Returned to Gill and for the first time looked, almost, like a human being. 'I'm sorry. Have you come for the cleaning job?'

'Er . . . Yeah, that's right . . .'

'Great! If you take a seat in the lounge, please, I'll let Charlotte know you're here . . .' Christina retreated to the back room. Gill spun around and rushed towards the exit, ploughed through two insects and knocked one to the ground. Unnaturally green coagulant flew everywhere.

Unwilling to confront more slimline propaganda, Gill became a rolling stone, with no direction home. She drove not deliberately, but aimlessly. She crossed Tower Bridge, took a left along the Embankment and a right just after Hungerford Bridge, which brought her up to Trafalgar Square. She couldn't remember the last time she'd visited the West End. A glaze dazzled her face as she marvelled at attractions like a tourist, enjoyed the change of scenery and breathed a freedom that only travel affords, no matter how close to home. The traffic was light and the threat of rain trifling. Trafalgar Square's infrastructure was tricky so she flaunted the Highway Code, careened onto and off pavements, opposed the inconvenient flow of traffic at her whim. Charing Cross Road was a blast. The spectacle of colourful theatres enthralled her and the fast-food joints made her drool. But she didn't break, didn't falter, didn't buckle, didn't brake. She was on a diet!

She felt the pull even though she didn't know what it was, where it came from, where exactly it was pulling her to. The further north she drove, the more intensely she felt it. The air seemed increasingly sweet, in a toffee-apple-at-a-fairground way. Oxford Street was more funnel-necked than she remembered, its entry from Charing Cross Road more perpendicular. It was cleaner too, less grimy. And she had no idea there was such a smart Tube station on its corner. Shoppers scurried like ants from an underground colony. Bargains dripped bountifully around her. It was a free-for-all. Steely countenances, determined gaits and off-putting singularities of purpose elbowed their way towards skilfully marketed dreams. Noise hummed everywhere, white, grey, black. People spoke but no one listened. Drivers understood the collective hypnosis and inched forward carefully. Gill couldn't remember if the pull was the problem or the solution, the virus or the vaccine, but she wanted it, couldn't resist it, went with it.

A building to her left glowed incandescent like a spaceship. Practically hovered above the ground, its windows right-angled on Oxford Street and another street towards Soho. 'SALE' repeated itself in bold and bloody letters along all panes, a clarion call to any passer-by who dared not heed its message. Mannequin stick insects like those from the gym stood in carefree poses but Gill was heartened to see shoppers of all shapes and sizes drawn inside.

Gill's nightmare became her dream. She could practically touch the dream. Taste it. It tasted like Skittles. Not the Fruits flavour she usually bought but the more exotic Tropical ones. With sunhats and cocktail parasols. She could exercise at the gym during lunch and clothes-shop after Harry's closed. And then she could meet Brolly at a swanky hotel. Just for cocktails. Wearing a new dress or top, heels or jacket. All four for special occasions. All black. All sartorial. Fashion at its fastest, at its finest.

An industrial siren stretched to infinity, a plastic drum machine bemoaned its fake lot, a warbler inhaled laughing gas, huffed on amyl nitrite, slung her vocals carelessly. The dream was Gill's future. Her future was bright. The brightness was an atomic bomb. Gill halted to make sure she wasn't having another turn. Sweat sullied her reputation but at least it didn't reek of Red Bull and vodka. Escalators beckoned. Floors begged. Clothes jived. Around her. Everywhere. Like multicoloured sex workers waiting to be chosen for a quick in and out. Gill's fingers tingled with anticipation. She scratched her flank, sharpened her senses, readied herself to cop a feel, to stroke a hem, caress a sleeve.

'Can I help you?' Gill heard the question but didn't immediately register it. 'Can I help you?' Gill turned around. A tanned assistant who looked like Gill's old horse blinked at her. She even had the same yellow mane. It was a sign. Gill's eyes twinkled. Her hand brushed through her hair. Her smile communicated positive vibrations.

'Yes! You can! I was wondering if you had anything my size?'

The assistant stopped blinking and neighed as if Gill was about to go for a ride on her. 'Er . . . No . . . Sorry . . .'

'What? Nothing?'

'I'm afraid not.'

'Oh.' Gill nodded. The assistant nodded back. Gill nodded back at the assistant. They stared at each other like long-lost time travellers who hadn't bumped into anyone for aeons but knew they couldn't stop to chat. 'Do you think you might get something in?'

'Unfortunately not.'

'I see . . .' Gill nodded again. The assistant nodded back. They continued to stare at each other, neither quite willing to make the first leap back into their lonely time continuum.

'You know, you'd be really pretty if you lost some weight . . .' the horse said before neighing, crackling and popping off into astral oblivion. As she waddled out of the store, Gill's smile crumbled slowly but collapsed the moment she stepped outside, cracked into little pieces on the concrete below.

CHAPTER 28

A wooden clipboard hung above the scales, a white sheet of paper from the clipboard. A neat line divided the page in half. On the left was Gill's name, on the right, Brolly's. Underneath, tell-tale numbers revealed scraggly truths. A sharpened pencil dangled from the clipboard, ready to tell more. Gill's eyelids drooped. Her ankles hid. Her dressing gown threatened to resign. She clung on to herself as if she was going out of fashion and yawned. Her yawn sounded like a worried foghorn, a dying pterodactyl. Brolly led by example, slipped off his dressing gown. It was the fourth Monday of their mutual weigh-in. He handed the dressing gown to Gill, but she was picking her nose.

'Gill!?'

'Sorry.' She took his gown as he fussed over his face, stretched his mouth into a nervous turn, a competitive grind, tried to empty his mind but failed. His heart pounded like he'd just drunk a cup of coffee. He stepped onto the machine. Hoped for the best. Inhaled expertly. Bowed his head. Concentrated on the square digits.

'YES!!' He clenched his fists and shook them in the air before opening his hand and exposing his palm to Gill. With little enthusiasm, she did the same and they high-fived. The champion stepped off his podium and stuck his hands back into his sleeves, pulled the gown back on, recorded his victory and handed the gauntlet to Gill, whose grasp was weak. Her heart stuttered. Her eyes worried. Her feet shuffled onto the cold metallic plate. She looked everywhere apart from down. Brolly did that for her. Nodded like a gangster finally convinced his partner was diddling him. Or diddling his wife.

'Anything you want to tell me?' he growled.

'Like what?' she growled back. Their emotions circled each other with fanged teeth, tails erect and claws sharpened. She refused to bow to his pressure. To feel like a failure. To be intimidated. In her own home. In her own bathroom. Which was bariatric for a very good reason.

'I dunno. That's what I'm asking you.'

'Don't think so.'

'You sure?'

'Well, I just asked you to tell me what you wanted me to tell you so I dunno either.'

Brolly's silence spoke louder than Gill's obfuscation. He didn't even nod his head hammily or disbelievingly, just wrote down, very deliberately, very legibly, four numbers that screamed out one word: FAIL.

'Don't you remember what the doctors said?'

'Yeah . . .'

'And . . . I mean . . . don't you like the stuff I'm cooking?'

'Yeah, I do . . .'

'So . . . Well . . . But, Gill! You're supposed to lose weight, not put it on!'

'Are you sure they're not broken?'

'Unless you broke them when I wasn't watching, yeah.'

'Which I didn't.'

'Alright. So no, the scales are not broken.'

The same thing happened the following Monday; Gill had put

on more weight. But instead of challenging her, Brolly made no comment and wrote her number down like an impartial judge. As soon as she left home, however, he stomped back upstairs, ripped the chart off the bathroom wall, grabbed the scales and returned both to his office. He Blu-tacked the slip of paper and its incriminating evidence to his atrocity exhibition, sat down and attempted to work. But the numbers freaked him out, displaced him from his own mind, his own space, his own sense of decorum, his life.

He reversed outside as an ice-cream van drove past. The van's atonal ringing taunted the weather and the inner child in him. He drove down the Walworth Road and felt like a second-rate Jesus carrying his invisible cross along the Way of Sorrows. Potholes jumped at him, exhausts coughed, traffic crowded, pedestrians leered. After the Elephant and Castle roundabout, he eschewed Borough High Street and opted for the less oppressive but still unwelcoming streets where the trees turned their backs on him, the animals caterwauled, the houses slammed their doors. A pub caught his attention. He'd never visited it but parked outside. Dawdled. Weighed up his odds. Envied an expensive couple who passed him, hand in hand. The world was their oyster. With lemon juice and Tabasco. He entered. One for Dutch courage or one for the road, he hadn't decided. The door wasn't as heavy as it looked. It announced his arrival with a debt collector's disregard for other people's property. An intimidated barman looked up from a book and stood up.

'Morning.'

'Morning. What can I get you?'

Brolly investigated the premises. Saw Tiny Tim in a dim corner, knocking down a short and then a pint.

'Er . . . Actually, I'm OK, thanks,' Brolly said and turned around. He was done with crutches. Done with daytime drinking. Done with fuzzy ducks.

Brolly didn't like what he was doing but it had to be done. He left his mobility scooter outside and walked the rest of the way. He'd become quite adept at walking. Two minivans were parked in the loading bay outside Harry's and obscured its entrance. Three metal benches sprawled to its left. A barren but large wooden flower bed slouched in the middle and Gill's mobility scooter drooped out of it like a soggy, half-chewed cigar. On Brolly's side of the road, the pavement opened into a small park surrounded by a waist-high brick wall. A neat row of trees followed the wall but their trunks were no thicker than his forearm. In front of him, a postbox stood like an avant-garde phallus and further on, a gaggle of dustbins entertained a fox. Brolly sauntered up to the postbox. Tried to hide behind it. Failed. But luck was on his side; he didn't have to. Hunched like a jockey on an emaciated metal triangle, a Deliveroo cyclist careened onto the pavement opposite and screeched to a halt.

A double-decker blocked Brolly's vision. He wiped a bead of concern from his forehead. He impounded a handful of tummy. He clattered his teeth. Time travelled slowly. The double-decker lurched forward. The cyclist stomped back out while pawing his phone. He was a pro. Had been inside for less than forty seconds. No messing about. Didn't slouch on his way out, either. Unlocked his bike and inspired Brolly to do something he hadn't done in about a decade: nip and tuck. Across the road, through the traffic. Instinctively. Brainlessly. It was almost a run. Almost fun. He risked life and limb, nipped in front of a black cab and tucked behind an Ocado truck. He stumbled over the pavement, curtsied to the concrete, maintained some dignity and slammed through Harry's doorway, where Potatohead was kneeling on the floor, rummaging through plastic screw bags.

'Hey . . . ! Hi, Brolly!' said Potatohead overenthusiastically. But Brolly didn't fall for it. Knew a ruse when he heard one, to distract, to put him off the scent. He ignored the ploy and tumbled on down the aisle, past the packers and shims on the left, past the hooks and the eyes on the right.

Gill didn't register her appetite's cuckold, his action-packed blur, until it was too late. A convex slice of pizza drooped from her hand as she shoved it into her mouth. In front of her, a large box lay open. Inside lay a half-devastated 14-inch pizza. Below nestled three similar-sized boxes and by their side, two Coke bottles and three small brown bags. One of the bags had been ripped open and its silver lining distorted a remaining slice of garlic bread as if in a funfair's hall of mirrors. 'What you doing here?' she accused, offence as defence, as she wiped an orgy of string and a slop of dough from her mouth and dropped her flaccid slice. 'It's not what it looks like . . .' she said, but Brolly knew it was exactly what it looked like, exactly what it smelled like. Victory. Defeat. A rat. Empirical Pyrrhicism.

Brolly wanted to tell Gill he loved her. Wanted to tell her to order another pizza. To order another three. That they'd eat crap for the rest of the day and all evening, too. For the rest of their lives. That it was their tradition and absolutely no reason to change it. Pizzas, burgers, Chinese and Indian. Chicken and chocolate, too. She should become the fattest woman in the UK. In the world. In the universe. If that's what made her happy. There were intelligent signs of life out there somewhere and maybe she'd be the first one to sight them. The intelligent signs of life. The doctors knew nothing, they were full of shit. She was right. She was different. Her heart was invincible. She was unassailable. A cookie monster, a calorie fiend, a soda junkie. It wasn't what you looked like on the inside, it was the outside that counted. Grow, sweet lady, grow. Grow, grow and grow some more. Eat grapes. Eat Gilbert Grape. Eat Gilbert's mum. Become Gilbert's mum. Become housebound. Become bed bound. Another statistic. A drain on the nation, a TV sensation, a fire brigade conflagration, a tabloid titillation.

'Are you alright? You're scaring me,' Gill said as Brolly tried not to fall into the black hole around which he was teetering, as Dagmara strolled up to the till.

'I'm ready now,' she said disingenuously as she ripped a slice from the pizza box. 'Mmm. This is great. Thanks, Gill. Thanks for getting this, Gill. You're a great friend and so generous with your money! Hi, Brolly, how you doing!?' Gay Keith appeared from behind a row of spades. Potatohead appeared from behind Brolly. All repeated variations on the same lumbering theme, the same feigned soap-opera sincerity, the same wood, the same cardboard, the same slivered sausage and the same tomato paste.

'D'you want a slice?' Gill asked Brolly. Prayed he'd say yes as mandibles halted, cheese congealed, peppers cowered.

'No, thanks.' He turned and headed for the exit without further explanation.

'Brolly?!' Gill cried out as his hubris bullied his twitching body to exit post-haste. 'Brolly!?' she cried again as the gang tried to blend in with the glands and the grommets, the cable connectors and the toilet spares. He retained his dignity, honoured his silence, continued on his way as she spumed upwards, knocked her walking stick to the floor. 'Fuck! Fuck!' she said as Dagmara crouched to pick it up. Gill grabbed her phone, slipped it in her pocket and turned, but knocked her chair to the ground, caught her cardigan on the displays behind her and sent a charity box and a recently returned paint tin crashing to the floor. Gill ignored it all, ripped her cardigan, grabbed some garlic bread and hobbled as quickly as she could after her boyfriend.

'Brolly!?' she pleaded again as his nipping and tucking graduated into weaving. Through the vans and buses and cabs and cars. Onto the pavement opposite, away from Harry's. Gill almost crashed off her mobility scooter the moment she jumped on it. It tipped against the back of the bench and she smacked her knee. Her knee pulsed with pain but she ignored it, searched for her key, which she couldn't find. She ripped out her phone but it flew from her grip, crashed into a nearby puddle. She struggled off her scooter and with her foot nudged the phone out of the dirty water. Didn't try to pick it up. Accepted defeat. Stared it in the face. Shook her head. Laughed a mocking, self-pitying laugh as she saw her romance not as Hollywood but Skegness, the desire to chase after Brolly on her mobility scooter not so much Monte Carlo as Blackpool.

Dagmara picked up the phone, handed it back, joined Gill on the bench. Gill dried her phone and called Brolly. He didn't answer. She didn't leave a message. Dagmara caressed Gill's leg like she'd seen characters on British TV do in times of emotional stress. Dagmara thought it was weird. So did Gill. But neither said anything as the wind ripped up the street like it was trying too hard and an empty cider tin rattled past, encouraged them to bunk off work and become alcoholics for the rest of the day, maybe the rest of their lives.

'Would you mind getting me the pizza?' Gill finally asked.

CHAPTER 29

Gill didn't hear from Brolly for the rest of the day. As darkness waved its magic hand over London, she texted five letters. S.O.R.R.Y. She also texted a yellow emoji with its smile flipped upside down.

She didn't receive a response.

At home, she sat at the kitchen table and pored over Brolly's recently acquired cookbooks. The recipe's gleeful enthusiasm, its smug confidence, its smirking self-worth disconcerted her. Artichoke and aubergine rice. She wanted to vomit. To slam it shut. To throw it in the fire and warm her shivering timbers. But she didn't, she struggled valiantly on even though the text might have been written in double Dutch. Or single Dutch. At least the book had pictures, which she did understand. She hoped to find common eating ground for her and Brolly and succeeded in discovering exotic chicken dishes and quirky lamb dishes and stalwart beef dishes, but what she discovered mainly was a quicksand into which her psyche irrevocably sank.

Minutes before midnight, as the ghost of Aunt Violet's lonely death haunted her and convinced her the house was too big for one person even though two of them still lived there, she swallowed her pride and a handful of Sour Skittles and phoned Brolly again.

He didn't pick up. She wrapped her arms around her chest and accepted no one would comfort her that evening apart from herself.

I'm worried. R U OK? she texted.

He responded almost immediately. *I'm fine. Don't w8 up. I'll wake you 2morrow like usual.*

Gill phoned again but his message soon replaced his ringtone. She imagined him bleeding on an anonymous roadside. Her face wrinkled involuntarily. She wanted to cry but didn't. She texted an emoji with a smiley yellow face and pounding red love hearts as eyes. She counted the seconds as she waited for a response. The wind blew a gale outside and a shrub scraped its leaves against the window. After she reached 139 and hadn't received a response, she gave up. She reread his words a hundred times, tried to gauge hidden subtexts, secret meanings. The 'like usual' marginally warmed her soul and when the front door finally clicked open while she was in bed obsessing over the day's events, the quicksand into which she hadn't stopped sinking slowly loosened.

Next morning, she awoke to the sweet, savoury smell of love. To the aroma of a bygone era. To a shared history. One she'd taken for granted. Which made every morning worth struggling out of bed for. She wondered if she was dreaming. She watched a spider scurry across her ceiling, pinched her tummy, didn't suddenly wake up. 'Baby?' she asked as she tested the water. Her voice wavered more than she expected.

'Morning!'

'You OK?'

He sounded OK but the toast smelled like a trick.

'I'm OK. How you doin'?'

'Yeah, I'm OK . . .'

Brolly pushed the door open and walked in holding a plate. He offered it to Gill like a butler would his queen. She felt regal but bit her lips and pinched her flesh again, her thigh this time.

She still didn't wake up. Not only were all the old favourites on display but new ones, too. Nutella. Honey. White Chocolate. She gasped. Giggled. Snapped her head back as the spider legged it over a curtain rail and disappeared. 'What's all this, then?' Brolly shrugged coyly. She grabbed a slice of toast with white chocolate. 'Bloody hell, this is good!' It tasted how she thought Willy Wonka might have smelled at the Wobble Club. But without the disinfectant and spilt beer. And maybe with a bit more vanilla. 'Why haven't we ever had this before? This is amazing!'

'D'you like it?' Gill nodded as if her head had been tied to a bouncy castle. She offered Brolly her slice. 'I'm alright, thanks.' She tried not to be affronted, tried not to stare at him as if she'd seen something she hadn't wanted to see. Knew this was no time for confrontation. For emotional intervention. Or inveigling. Or home-wrecking. Instead, she acted as if nothing was wrong, fluttered her eyelashes and giggled again because that's what she thought she'd usually do.

'All the more for me, then!'

As well as returning to the Full English, Brolly threw in five pancakes with maple syrup and whipped cream. Gill yahooed like a cowboy at a BBQ pit when she saw them and didn't tease Brolly for his now-regular avocado on toast. The perfect Stepford Husband smiled so unwaveringly throughout that the corners of his mouth started to twitch and ache, but the moment Gill stood up and turned her back, his smile flattened and his eyes deadened. She made it as far as the kitchen door before turning and traipsing back to her love, where she wrapped her arms around his shoulders. 'I wish it could be Christmas again.'

'Me too,' he said with less sincerity.

'That was such a lovely week, wasn't it?'

'It was great.' Gill squeezed the fat around his biceps, kissed his fleshy skull, nuzzled her nose in his bird's nest. His stiff upper lip finally slackened. He placed his hands on top of Gill's and squeezed them. 'Although you might not miss it so much if you knew what was lurking behind you.' Gill weaved her eyebrows together, relinquished her grip on him.

'What you talking about?'

'What d'you think?'

'I don't know. Tell me.'

'The confectionery cupboard . . .'

Gill hobbled to the cupboard, pulled it open. A large fruit and nut Toblerone fell to the floor. So did two tubes of Pringles. Gone were the nuts and the dried fruits, the healthy snacks he'd persuaded her to replace the confectionery with back in early January. She yelped a staccato seal of approval. It was like Rome had never fallen. KitKats and Starbars and Bounties and Snickers and Toffee Crisps and Flakes and Smarties and Skittles and Tangfastics and Rowntree Randoms and Minstrels and M&Ms, and many more besides, prostrated themselves to Gill's admiration, to her delectation.

'Oh my God!' she cackled and plunged her hand into the treasure trove. She pulled out a Mint Aero, ripped it open, devoured it, messed her lips with chocolate. She did the same with a Turkish Delight and the same with a whole box of After Eights. 'I love you so much! Thank you, thank you, thank you!'

Brolly wondered, waited, watched as Gill stuffed her bag full of happiness and heart attack. As she wobbled along the hallway to her mobility scooter. As she packed her arms into her green army jacket, the back seam of which had split. As she wrapped her affection around him one more time. As she opened the door and reversed with full concentration. As he stood outside in the crisp air. As he waved goodbye. As Gill twisted her neck as far as it would go to gaze adoringly at him one final time before driving under the bridge, the graffiti for which had been changed to 'Never Gonna Give You Up'. He stood there for longer than usual. She became a twopenny piece on the horizon. It was the smallest he'd ever seen her.

Brolly wondered when she'd realise. Presumably that evening. He had a sudden urge to return to the pub and check if it was still there, his mobility scooter, that it hadn't been stolen, hadn't been graffitied over, vandalised like Tiny Tim's. The act had been impulsive, felt rebellious, almost wrong. An act too vengeful for its trigger. For Gill's weight gain, for her lack of weight loss. Her lies. Her deception. Her simmering suicide. Her pizzamania. But he'd felt a sense of release in the gesture, too. Another step towards some kind of normality. He had feet, by God, and he was going to use them.

Brolly made a beeline for the bus stop and parked himself behind a Muslim woman with cheap, criss-crossed shopping bags. He took a selfie, filed it in his 'Slim n Tonic' album. He slunk his hands into his pockets and acted as if he was no longer in arrears or threatened with expulsion from the human race, but, finally, a fully paid-up member of it. He turned around to inspect the traffic. Couldn't believe his luck. 'Bus!' It was his bus. The number 35. He idolised it. Worshipped it. Watched it approach with the excitement of a father watching his child take its first baby steps. Its windscreen wipers waved at him. Its indicator winked at him. The queue edged forward. He edged forward, too. The edging gave him much pleasure. He hadn't edged for quite a while. The bus stopped. Brolly grinned from ear to ear. His grin knew no bounds. The queue sleepwalked onto the bus. Brolly leaped onto it with gusto.

'Nice double-decker you got here, mate,' he said without irony, without sarcasm, as if the bus had fallen off the back of a lorry. The driver ignored the comment. Brolly tapped his card against the ticket machine and marvelled at the three-quarters-empty interior. The main colour scheme, not entirely different to his bathroom, was punctuated with dribs and drabs of mustard; definitely more fashion conscious than he remembered public transport.

With a playground jerk, the bus interrupted Brolly's enthusiasm, which was trying to persuade his practicality to venture upstairs. He grabbed another sinewy pole and practically ripped his hand off his arm. He decided upstairs was for the properly fit and trim and his bird's-eye view of South London would have to wait. The nearest seat had a sign instructing passengers to give up their place for those with special needs. Brolly wondered if he had special needs. Icons of a pregnant woman, a mother and baby and someone with a walking stick decorated the instruction. Without a walking stick, he decided he didn't have special needs and lurched past the downcast frowns and choppy brows of his fellow passengers. A sudden and unexpected angling of the bus threw him into a nearby row of empty seats. He straightened himself and settled in, turned around. 'This is great, isn't it?' he said a little too enthusiastically to the woman behind him, who looked like a 1950s tribute to zoo-keeping.

'What is?' she asked.

'The bus. The route. Really efficient.'

'Er . . . Yeah, I suppose so . . .'

'And a lot cleaner than I thought it would be!'

The woman didn't reply, didn't encourage him, covered her consternation with pointed sunglasses and golden rims.

Brolly pulled out his phone. 'You don't mind if I take a selfie, do you?' She shook her head. 'It's just that you're behind me so you'll be in the picture and I just thought it'd be polite to ask.'

'That's OK, I'll hide.' She headed to a spare seat near the driver as Brolly posed with mock po-face and then as if someone had just stuck a finger up his bottom. He filed his photos and settled back to enjoy his first bus journey in living memory.

At London Bridge, rain made the pavement gleam like black spandex. Brolly watched the bus cough and splutter on its journey. He wanted to swap numbers with it, text it, send it silly GIFs and humorous emails, but instead waved it goodbye, knew he hadn't made as much of an impression on it as it had on him.

He walked inside the station. Workers scurried in grey, travellers hurried in black, tourists flurried in colour and with suitcases. He savoured the experience. Worshipped the stadium arena. It impressed him like an expensive haircut. He stared up at the expansive digital noticeboard with a sense of awe. Its yellow letters flickered. Beckoned. Beguiled. A caramel announcement floated through the air. His heart stuttered and his stomach knotted as he located his destination. His journey's reason curled malevolently in his intestines like a snake readying to strike its prey. He sucked on his teeth, clashed their enamel and scoped out the station for a quick fix. A quick snack. A speedy chocolate bar. A racy sausage roll. A fast-moving Cornish pasty. Some beer. Some wine. Some vodka. Anything. Everything. A salubrious selection surrounded him with rainbow colours and easy-to-access counters, but he exercised his willpower. He looked down on such offerings. He didn't need them; they needed him. He disparaged their desperation, cocked his nose, congratulated his resolve and wended his way in between the human slalom posts to his designated platform.

Brolly was pleasantly surprised by the width of the first-class seat to which he'd treated himself. He jammed the left of his body against the carriage's side as his stomach flowed over the arm rest on his right. The discomfort was practically rewarding; he'd actually managed to fit into the seat. A seat. Which he hadn't quite managed on the bus. Air conditioning blew a chill and he huddled deep inside his coat. Hoped he didn't get lost in it. A snack man with a second-rate inventory greeted him. Brolly's heart tremored, his breath deepened, his underarms moistened. He didn't like himself for it, but he knew he couldn't always deny his baser instincts. He bought three G&Ts, a tuna and sweetcorn sandwich and a Yorkie Raisin & Biscuit.

The carriage was empty and the snacks distracted but as oppressive buildings with dirtied souls and weather-beaten clocks gave way to discarded back yards with penniless pockets and sweat-shop knock-offs, Brolly's teeth started to clatter with the commitment of a novelty toy. The iron wheels' whir on the iron tracks did nothing to soothe him. His toes wiggled back and forth to an inaudible beat and he held on to the arm rest as if about to crash off his seat. The snack man returned. Brolly bought another three G&Ts. He didn't want his breath to smell like a distillery, so he also bought another two Yorkies, one to accompany the alcohol and the other when he'd finished.

The station had barely changed since it was built in the mid 1800s. No other passenger descended, and the taxi Brolly had ordered the day before was the only vehicle outside. Brolly knocked on the driver's window. The driver looked back as if one of them was about to break the law but he wasn't sure who. 'Mr Brolly?' he said in a clipped and antique voice that contradicted any criminal leanings and suggested he'd learned to drive on a coach and horse.

'Just Brolly.'

'Hop in, Brolly!'

Brolly wished he could hop in. His head spun from the alcohol more than he expected. A strange semen smell confused the damp air. Giant trees conspired to out-cluster the cloudy grey sky. It was no Viano, that was for sure; the seat was lower than he was accustomed to and its door's gap smaller, but Brolly opened it with aplomb. He grabbed the saloon's roof rail, bent his legs, arched his back and with little thought to style, safety, his driver's mental well-being or the car's suspension, dived in. And screamed out in pain. The dive was a belly flop. He crashed onto the plastic seat as his nose burst against a belt buckle and his shin lost out to the steely door frame.

'You alright, sir?'

'Sorry, mate, yeah, just . . . just slipped.'

'That was quite a slip.'

'I suppose it would sound strange if I said I was a slipper?'

'I think it probably would.'

Brolly spent the short journey, which he could have walked, staring out of the window. He marvelled at the depth of greenery he was surrounded by and held a napkin to his nose in the hope it would stop bleeding before he reached his destination. He was fifteen minutes early but scanned the place as soon as he stepped inside, just in case. The Fox and Hounds hadn't changed in twenty years. It probably hadn't changed ever, except for the flying-saucer fruit machine in the far corner. An older bouquet with a bulbous nose, raspberry but not quite rippled, sat quietly, imperfectly sculpted, in front of the bar and a blonde-maned teenager dreamed idly behind the bar of bikinis and escape. In front of a pint, Badger, from the local production of *The Wind in the Willows*, huffed self-importantly, and a couple of purple-rinsers chatted over a table dangerously close to a dart board.

Brolly rushed past Badger to the toilets and inspected his nose. Blood no longer gushed and no skin had broken, but his philtrum looked like a semi-chewed cherry. He splashed water over it and rubbed away the cherry. He optimistically swept his residue of hair, pulled a grotesque face, pocketed a paper towel and returned to the bar, where he ordered two pints of London Pride, the first of which he finished before the second had been poured. He sat down at a table opposite the entrance.

A couple of younger fructose addicts, mane contenders, barged in with a bark louder than their bite. Brolly sipped regularly from his pint as if it was the air he had to breathe, the only companion he had to while away the time. Mrs Badger strutted in next. Her ears twitched in alarm as she couldn't help but lock eyes with Brolly. The mane distracted both by asking if he was staying for lunch. She handed him a faux-leather-bound menu, which he scrutinised as if it were a tome of international significance.

The heavy oaken door almost refused entry to the next guest.

233

Made her sweat. Made her work. Crevices that even the most seasoned mountaineer would think twice about climbing sank deep down the sides of her face. Her hennaed hair curled wildly around her head like a shrubbery in need of support sticks. The bags under her eyes suggested she'd spent her life doing someone else's shopping and her legs buckled as if she was waiting for someone to score a goal through them. Her eyes slipped over Brolly and went on their way. She stepped into the centre of the room and investigated. Brolly gulped. He turned clockwise and gaped, almost rudely, at the woman, who resisted movement's temptation and who he recognised barely more than she recognised him.

'Mum?'

CHAPTER 30

'You haven't forgotten, have you? About this evening?' an earnest voice asked as the door at number 12 clicked open.

'You haven't bloody let me forget,' a gruff voice replied. Brolly's mum, Audrey, nodded with a genial frailty as her eyes betrayed a dullness, a dying, that against her better instincts and after all those years, for better or for worse, in sickness and in health, she still sought to reverse. Andy had watched the dying but had stopped caring long ago. He stepped into the world again, into his world. A sense of relief massaged his temples. His small-town suit did its small-town best to excuse his hungover stubble, his bald crown and his grieving liver. Early-morning darkness itched the roofs of houses opposite like fake sable on cheap shoulders. An oppressive mist hung over the cul-de-sac and threatened near-death scenarios. Only Andy's Blakeys, with their forthright chirpiness and their cold-shower vigour, contradicted the funereal dirge that enveloped him, his wife and their life.

Goose bumps scurried over Audrey's skin as she stepped onto the mat outside. She braced herself, tried to ignore the air's bite, its denigration, tried to blow rings from her mouth. Failed. They didn't stand a chance. The mist assimilated them as the door to his steel machismo slammed shut. The engine snarled. A muffled pop song wailed. Audrey waved. Andy reversed. Down the steep drive. She wondered if he'd wave back. If he'd even twist his head towards her. His head banged in her direction as he bounced and levelled onto the tarmac. He twisted it back and towards the road as she waved like an uncanny automaton, like a Cyberpunk Sally. He screeched towards the pavement, straightened up, burned more rubber and sped around the corner.

She rested the glass, with ice cubes, on the ugly office desk in her bedroom at the end of the landing, as far away as possible from his bedroom. She knelt beside her bed. Rummaged underneath it as the motorway at the bottom of their garden droned. She grabbed her meek reward, her humble treat, her secret treasure. The plastic bag crackled with excitement as she upended it. Two mini bottles of sparkling wine, a large box of Maltesers and a bottle of expensive bubble bath made her smile for the first time that morning.

The chocolate balanced precariously on the bath's edge as water crashed into the tub. Bubbles blossomed as Audrey twisted the first bottle top. It resonated with a lethargic poof, a second-rate plop, but if the sound, barely a noise, disappointed her, the curt cracking, the pert popping of ice cubes that followed did not. Before taking a sip, and with a confidence that didn't illuminate the rest of her life, she stepped onto the scales. She looked down and smiled again. Like always, the scales complimented her. Gave her pleasure. Rewarded her hard work. Her calorie counting. Her sweet tempering. Her long, solitary walks. She should have married the scales, not him. She only weighed half a stone more than she did when they married. God bless the scales.

'Cheers, Audrey, and bloody well done!' Temporarily blind to the splatters of mouthwash and splashes of toothpaste that besmirched the mirror in front of her, Audrey held out her chipped glass. 'Has it been worth it? I dunno. Have you enjoyed it? Some of it. Are you proud of your life? Well . . . Not sure I'd go that far. What about your kids? Surely you're proud of them? Erm . . . That's a good question . . . But you've survived, at least? Yes, that's right, I don't think I'd ever call myself a winner, but I suppose I'm a survivor and I suppose that's the second-best thing. Well then, congratulations on being a survivor, Audrey! Thanks, Audrey, and cheers! Yeah, cheers back!' A nostalgic quiescence trickled down her gullet and applauded her vague sense of achievement. She slipped into the alpine-smelling, mollycoddling cocoon of minor accomplishment, grabbed some Maltesers and luxuriated.

Town was less busy than she expected. And colder. And wetter. And windier. Umbrella exoskeletons turned pedestrians into lonely travellers and brave explorers, the shopping precinct their concrete fjord. She usually saw someone she knew, someone to say hello to, to while away her boredom, but not that afternoon. No one. Still, she bought everything she needed and that was the main thing.

At the kitchen table, she agonised over how to address the card. 'Darling' seemed factually incorrect. So did 'My Love' and 'Dearest'. She used to call him 'Teddy' as in 'Teddy Bear' but that sounded too desperate, too yearning. 'Hubby' was too frivolous. 'Mr Pearson' was too weird. 'Andrew' was too formal. 'Andy' suggested a casualness, an ease of acquaintance they no longer shared. What she really wanted to write was 'Arsehole', 'Prick' or 'Twat'. In the end, she opted for 'Andrew'; it was his name, after all.

Her hands trembled as she wrote. *Dear Andrew, Thank you for forty years of marriage. Love Aud. XXX* Her hands trembled as she slipped the card inside the envelope. Her hands trembled as she sealed the envelope. Her hands trembled as she wrapped his present in ruby paper. It didn't look much. Was just an A4 sheet of paper that she'd printed out. But it was more than that, of course. It was a voucher to drive around Brands Hatch in a Formula 4 racing car. She thought he'd like that. She thought she might even come along with him. Make a day of it. A day to remember. She doubted he'd buy her a present, so why not? A kind of joint celebration.

Wind raged. Battered, even, the rain. Sent it indignant, no longer in control, begging for mercy, towards the evening's end as morbid clouds brutalised the moon's emaciated crescent. Droplets clamoured against the dining-room windows, wanted to tell Audrey something but dripped in an undecipherable language. She'd called him three times and each time he said he'd be back soon. The rose petals she'd sprinkled into a romantic carpet from front door to dining table flickered like ailing insects gasping for breath. The three-quarters-spent candles, also ruby, in every downstairs room, dripped tears of wax, invented untrustworthy shadows on the walls. Two prawn cocktail salads, room temperature, no longer restaurant chilled, stood idly opposite each other. A red wine breathed in the middle of the table with anything but relief. Audrey yearned to drink. To drown. To self-medicate. To forget. But dared not, because she knew she needed her wits about her more than she needed a warm glow and cheated cheer.

Like napalm over an innocent forest, his headlights scoured the living-room wall. Her hand trembled again as she picked up her phone. Almost 10 p.m. Her heart raced. Would have trounced the Formula 4 racing car. She tried to calm herself. Gorged on the warm air. Grabbed the table to stop herself from collapsing. Sat down as the front door opened. Tried to look as placid as possible as the hall light killed the atmosphere, as he staggered into the doorway with tie unravelled and hair congealed.

'Wha's all this shit on the floor?' he slurred.

'Why don't you sit down? I bought your favourite . . . Prawn cocktail . . .' He swayed. Coughed up phlegm. Caught it with his hand. Tempted confrontation as he snapped on the dining-room light, staggered over the corpse of romance, ripped a serviette from the table, wiped his hands, threw it back, grabbed a couple of prawns from the cocktail and slurped.

'You need to clean all this shit up.'

'I will.'

In the kitchen, she picked up the warm china plates. The mushroom bled black into the jaundiced dauphinoise, the steak slouched, rigid and bloodless. The music she'd planned remained a playlist in her heart but the gale outside smothered their silence. She idly wondered when would be the right time to give him the card and present. Sensed there would never be a right time. Wondered if he'd even be seated as she exited the kitchen. Smiled because he still was. She accepted his stillness as a compliment, even if by default. She laid the plate in front of him, softly, gently. He grunted. Grabbed his cutlery. She returned to her seat. Pulled out her chair as his steak knife grated against his china. She jumped as the glass splattered against her snowy blouse. She hadn't even sat down as he ripped up his chair and threw his plate, her hard work, on the floor.

'Come here!'

'What?'

'Come here!' She knew better than to make him tell her again. Placed her meal on the table and shook, trembled, dreaded, as she stepped towards him. Hops and tobacco lingered in the air like arrogant, uninvited guests. 'Try to have a nice evening an' you call that a meal? The steak tastes like rubber. Aren't you ever gonna learn, you fat fuckin' bitch?' He smacked his entrapment, his trouble, his strife. Firmly in the face. Her shoulders concertinaed. She collapsed to the floor. Her jaw crashed against the carpet. The carpet burned her chin. Her stomach cushioned his size 9s. In front of her lay half a mushroom, a slice of greasy potato and a perfectly sharp steak knife.

The door flapped on its hinges. Banged against the wall. Leaves flew into the hallway, chased after the rose petals, which fled chaotically. Andy genuflected in front of his better half, quivered weakly, stared into the abyss as his ripped stomach stared at him, as his office-white shirt finally celebrated their ruby anniversary. He wiped his hand over his leaking wound, an ineffective little geyser, not spurting but spluttering, as Audrey towered above him, the steak knife in her hand dripping his claret. He couldn't remember how he got there, outside.

'What are you doing, Aud?!'

'Don't you ever call me fat again, you fucking arsehole, prick, twat!'

CHAPTER 31

T he pub's few customers spun around before Audrey did. Sensed a reality-show reunion about to clog the air, corrupt the airwaves. She jerked around like a clock hand that needed oiling. She squinted, hoped her eyes would disabuse her ears of what they'd just heard.

'Brolly?!'

A wave of emotion ravaged her son as he lifted himself off his seat. He felt the seat quiver, the wooden arms wobble. Hoped it didn't all buckle beneath him, denigrate him, demote him to a YouTube clip. To laughing-stock infamy. He tried not to spill the emotion that trickled over his cheek. Hoped his mum didn't deny responsibility, do a runner.

'That's the one . . .' he replied flatly, peeved her greeting wasn't more Hollywood, more award-winning, more tear-jerking. Her vision fluctuated as her eyes tried to make sense of it all. Of him all. She didn't know where to look. Alternated between his beseeching eyes for corroboration and his dripping belly for spectacle.

'Blimey! What happened to you!?'

CHAPTER 32

The playground raged with a riot of hormonal mittens as white flakes floated from above and induced blanket shrieks of approval. The space blurred like an erratic scribble. Mrs Jones rang the lunch bell. Children betrayed their direction, their playmates, their snowmen, rushed for the front of a queue that didn't yet exist. Brolly flicked his right foot upwards but it didn't propel him forward, it left him lurching in mid-air before he crashed to the pallid asphalt. Kneecap first and then little paw. He screamed. He bled. He cried. Mr Bennett escorted him to a classroom that was a first-aid box short of antiseptic and then to another one that was a first-aid box short of plasters.

Like an anarchist barging through a sea of commuters, he slammed and bounced and bungled against his fellow students as they dreamed of snowballs and sledges. The refectory hummed like a cooling oven. Its myriad of council-coloured round tables practically cleaned themselves as the remaining diners gobbled down their dessert and hurried to join the celebratory hubbub outside. Brolly scurried into Mrs Jones's pince-nez eyeline, into her Chelsea-bun authority. She severed her conversation with one of the kitchen staff. 'You're late, boy!'

'Mr Bennett told me to tell you I was with him.' He held out the palm of his hand as if it was a half-hearted peace offering rather than a straightforward declaration of the truth.

'Hmm. Well, hurry up then.' Brolly hurried up. Was given a sludge of steak and kidney pudding, a mash of carrots, a chunk of potato and a yoghurt full of unidentifiable flying fruit. He scurried towards the table nearest both the canteen and the refectory exit. 'Not there. That's already been cleaned. Over there. Next to McManus.' Brolly's heart froze. His eyeballs swirled. His testicles shrivelled. McManus was a little Caligula, a playground Hitler. No one liked him, not even his parents, certainly not his friends. His impish, flat-faced gaze homed in on Brolly, burned his retinas. Brolly suddenly took an unnaturally healthy interest in the ocean creatures that swirled around the refectory walls. He knew the dolphins, the killer whales, the seals, the seahorses and the sea turtles. Didn't know the fish. Wondered what the yellow ones were as he sat down. Wondered what the red ones were as he randomly scooped his fork into his fortification. Wondered what the orange ones were when McManus kicked him in his shin's antiseptic souvenir.

'OW!'

'Shut up!' McManus stole a glance at Mrs Jones, who'd retreated to the canteen, was oblivious to Brolly's further education in pain.

'Eat this and I won't kick you again.' McManus's plate looked like the aftermath of a scuffle on a carrot allotment. He slid it over to Brolly.

'What's wrong with it?'

'Nothing. I just don't like kidneys an' I don't like carrots and the old cow won't let me go until I finished it all.' Brolly mimicked McManus, swivelled his head towards the canteen, from which baritone laughter rang. He shrugged his indifference, scooped up the swill and slurped it down as quickly as he could before sliding the plate back to a toothier-than-usual McManus.

'Thanks, Brolly!' Brolly's muscles tensed. His mouth dried.

He'd never heard McManus thank anyone before. Ever. Somehow, it just didn't sound right and the lunch that he'd been looking forward to somehow didn't seem so appealing.

The sun sent the supervising teachers into careless paroxysms of Mediterranean bliss. Its unexpected heat dulled the rest of the playground, but McManus clasped his hand around Brolly's neck, guided him towards their destination with an indomitable confidence and a vivacious anticipation. The clasp felt strangely comforting, if a little sweaty. A band of merry delinquents fizzed, buzzed and bubbled beside them.

The darkness was disconcerting and the drop in temperature, immediate. Brolly usually held his breath as he sped along the uneven brick floor, its smell of sacrificial baby mice, caged claustrophobia and soiled straw unappealing at the best of times. But today was different. No speeding. No breath-holding. Brolly did his best not to look at the eye-bulging, tongue-flickering creatures that slithered slimily and crawled cruelly and hopped horribly by his side, the mouldy glass besmirched by pond-like water, his only safeguard. McManus gently patted Brolly's shoulder and they ground to a halt. 'Here we are, then!' said McManus as titters of dismay and disgust cartwheeled behind them.

'Is 'e really gonna do this?' questioned a squeaky but sane voice, to no one in particular.

'He can't,' responded a more cynical and lower pitched one as McManus turned around and from his shoulder bag pulled a medium-sized glass. He held it for his mob to marvel at. Like he was a god and it was a platinum chalice full of golden elixir. Gasps and snorts filled the air.

'I almost brought a cup but thought it'd be better if it was see-through.' The mob murmured agreement. Brolly rued the day he tripped over, cursed black ice for an eternity. Since then, he'd eaten more kidneys, carrots, Brussels sprouts than he'd ever anticipated and a bit of grass for a laugh and some leaves and a twopenny piece, too. His throat hurt when he swallowed the twopenny piece but he hadn't been teased or beaten up once since he'd become a human dustbin and he noticed he'd been increasingly treated with a curious awe, a freak-show reverence.

A repetitive croaking, a plea for help, a return to the wild punctuated the increasingly still but sordid atmosphere. A score of beady eyes, still adjusting to the dark, widened as McManus stretched out his hands and grabbed the small aquarium lid. He lifted it deferentially. Metal scratched glass. He replaced it at right angles. Brolly had convinced himself not to look, had been inspecting his Clarks, idly concluded he didn't like laces, preferred slip-ons. But he couldn't help himself, jerked his head upwards with the energy of a child who knew he'd lost.

On the positive side, the water was clean. Sparkling almost. Certainly compared with the grubby hues and discoloured tinctures that slopped around the other tanks, the salamander one especially. The greenery looked fresh enough too, hadn't disintegrated into sloppy sludge. On the negative side, there were way more tadpoles than he'd anticipated. They darted around aimlessly, inconclusively, without a worry in the world. They were larger, too, the tails longer, the heads not so much the size of pins but carpentry nails. He couldn't see if any had sprouted front legs but figured if they had, he really didn't want to know. Didn't want to think about the prospect of the tadpoles growing into frogs, hopping around his stomach.

McManus dipped the glass in the water as ten mouths dropped in unison. He sunk his hand deep into the tank. Wetted the cuffs of his sleeve. Pulled the glass out. Tadpoles swarmed inside. Spilt over its rim. He shook it. Emptied some. Left a two-finger gap at the top and carefully swivelled around, offered the chance of microcosmic infamy to Brolly, not so much a dare as an invitation not to be beaten up. McManus dazzled Brolly with a mischievous incandescence. Brolly wanted to kick him in the shins, stamp on his face and never see him again, but he took the glass instead. Silence strangled the space; even the croaker stopped. Brolly's hand shook but not enough to dislodge his drink. He stared into the darkness, into what had become his darkness, and without further ado, further machination, with surprising grace and dignity, poured it down his throat. He did his best not to gag as a handful of tadpoles tickled his inner cheek, a few fell down his chin, two stuck briefly between his gums and one slipped up his nostril.

The whoops and cheers and whistles and claps unnerved the amphibians and made the snake food scurry and defecate but Brolly glowed with a similar incandescence to McManus as he handed back the empty vessel. He placed a finger over his opposite nostril and pressed before blowing an errant tadpole onto the floor. McManus stamped on it and hugged Brolly. With love, affection and meaning. The gang started to chant his name. 'BROLLY! BROLLY! BROLLY!' His cheeks flushed and, against his better instinct, he started to laugh.

CHAPTER 33

'You should've seen me in September!'

'Why?'

'Well . . .' Brolly faltered. Remembered he'd been a bad son. Hadn't seen his mum for almost a decade. But then again, she'd been a bad mum; the stabbing had punctured more than his dad's stomach, affected more than just his dad's health. 'Well, I was about seven stone heavier then . . .'

'Blimey!' she repeated, as if his spell had sapped her of vocabulary. He smiled apologetically. Nodded dolefully. Edged towards her. She retreated as if he were a wild animal and she a forest trekker. His fractured family identity flickered through his eyes. A hurt and rejection clouded his already troubled face. An insecure sense of belonging radiated through his soul. Audrey's maternal instinct chided her gut reaction. The fruit machine chimed atonal congratulations but not to them. She cackled as a gold rush poured forth. The cackle turned into bemused laughter. One of the mane contenders slapped the money machine. Her laughter turned into stuttering breath. The other mane contender imitated a badly performed Morris dance. Her breath collapsed, crumbled, crashed into an outpouring of dripping emotion. She and Brolly stepped towards each other synchronously, stretched out their love, mixed their tears, grabbed each other and clung, two halves of the same cracked heart.

'So d'you ever see your dad?' Mushy peas blocked her consonants, muddied her vowels. They'd both opted for cod and chips.

'Nah. What about you?'

'Hardly! Well, that's not true. I seen him a coupla times in town, you know, from a distance, but either he runs away or I do. He even tried to put a restraining order on me, too, the arsehole, after the divorce.'

'I didn't know that.'

'Yeah. But failed. D'you remember Katie? From number 26? She told me he'd told Pete, that's her husband, it was the best thing that ever happened to him. Me stabbing him. But 'e never thanked me for it.'

'Well, yeah . . . Probably because he spent a week in intensive care and you spent about six months in custody.'

'That's true.'

'Did you even speak to him afterwards?'

'It was only after I testified that I realised how abusive he'd been, not just physically but emotionally, too, and, er . . . So no, after that, only with solicitors present.'

'You didn't talk to him properly?'

'Nah. Not properly. I didn't have much respect left for your dad by the end and after the judge set me free . . . Oh God, d'we have to talk about this? Makes me sick just thinking about it . . .'

'Not if you don't want to.'

'I'd prefer not to.'

'Alright then . . .'

'What about your brother?'

'What about him?'

'See him?'

'Nah. Don't think he ever forgave me for testifying against Dad. What about you?'

'Tried. A few times. Gave up in the end.' She stared at her cod. Its resemblance to a living, breathing creature, once free, once frolicking, moved her in maudlin ways. 'What a life, eh?'

Brolly beamed particles of empathy at her, sought to smother her with their healing properties. 'I know you don't wanna talk about it but I know Dad wasn't . . . well, wasn't very nice to you . . .'

'You could say that.'

'Yeah, but I wanted you to know I don't blame you for what you did.'

'It's funny how so many people do. Think I stabbed him 'cos I was some mad menopausal bitch, not because I suffered three decades of abuse. Thank you for saying that, though; I thought you did.'

'No, Mum, I didn't.'

'Why didn't you talk to me afterwards, then?'

'I did. I came to see you in custody.'

'No, I mean after the trial. After the judge let me go.'

'Oh . . . I dunno . . .' Brolly's heart weighed heavily. His conscience weighed heavily. Everything weighed heavily. 'I just think the whole thing . . . I think it embarrassed me . . . Made me upset. I just wanted to . . . to pretend it didn't happen, I s'pose. Forget it ever happened.'

'Forget you had parents?'

'Ha. Yeah, I suppose so.'

'You could've called me.'

'You could've called me,' he deflected.

'I thought you didn't wanna talk.'

'Well . . . Yeah . . . I suppose you're right . . .' Her lips quivered. Her chin jutted forward. Her eyes squinted. 'I'm sorry, Mum.' She inhaled as if about to sneeze, but her chest deflated and tears massaged her relief, thawed her heart, no longer cracked but still frozen; cleansed years of dirty thoughts and dark demons, of family flailings and self-blamed failings. Brolly pulled out his napkin, his token of peace, of surrender, and handed it over.

'I'm sorry, too, darling . . .' Her nose blew a hole in the pub's stratosphere. 'But I'm glad you got back in touch. I've missed you, you know. Thought about you a lot. And your brother but . . . Well, I don't think I'll be seeing him again. He's got a family of his own now. Did you know?'

'No, we literally haven't spoken since I testified.'

'Yeah. Married a Malaysian girl a few years back. Had twins. A couple of boys . . .'

'So you're a granny.'

'Yeah.'

'An' never seen 'em . . .'

'No.'

'That's a shame.'

'Yeah.'

'And I'm an uncle . . .'

'Yep . . .'

'Well . . . Congratulations to us both!'

'Congratulations to us both! I love you, Brolly, and I hope I haven't disappointed you.'

'Shut up. Now you're gonna make me cry!' Brolly finished his pint straight after he finished his meal.

'Fancy some dessert?'

'I'm on a diet . . .' Audrey guffawed. Brolly didn't. Felt momentarily aggrieved but overcame his own self-importance and acted up to his mother's sense of humour. She ordered a slice of lemon meringue pie and a glass of sparkling wine. He ordered three slices of banoffee pie and another pint. Their conversation reached a natural and contemplative lull. Brolly stared out of a window, considered the giant trees, their spindly branches, their frail family lines. They seemed to be holding their breath as he puffed out his chest and decided one banoffee pie slice would have sufficed. The biscuit and sticky toffee reminded him of a Twix. The Twix reminded him of his resolve. He soldiered on to the bittersweet end of his dessert, scooped up the final spoonful. 'So . . . there was something I wanted to talk to you about actually . . .'

'Ha! I know you better than you think . . . Even after all this time . . . I wondered if there was something. I've got some money if that's what you need, but not much . . .'

'No, no, no, it's not that. But it's kind of you to suggest it. How much you got?' Audrey stared at him disappointedly. 'I was kidding,' he added quickly.

'Were you? I have got some.'

'Honestly. It was a joke. Forget it.'

'If you're sure.'

'I'm sure. I don't need money.' He stared at his mother. Her crow's feet and furrows and wrinkles and ploughed lines commemorated her life's battle, her shrunk frame and hunched shoulders, more shrunk and more hunched than he remembered, testified to her opponent's brutality. Her eyes, though, faded and dulled but darting and inquisitive, her eyes shone a small victory, a small pride that in turn made him proud. 'Actually, I was wondering if I could come and stay with you . . . ?'

'Oh!' The exclamation bounced off her tongue and danced around the near empty pub like a happy drunkard. 'When . . . When were you thinking?'

'Erm . . . Well . . . I hope this isn't, like, springing it on you a bit but, erm . . .' Brolly revved his throat like he was in a hurry. 'How about tomorrow?!'

CHAPTER 34

The whistling sausages and spitting bacon were a lie. The small crescent that tickled Brolly's chin when Gill joked about her confectionery choices was a lie. His soft footsteps towards the front door were a lie. The reassuring squeeze of her arm was a lie and the lip smack that lingered moments longer than usual was a lie. The only thing that wasn't a lie were the reefs and the half hitches and the figures of eight that chafed his abdomen, the peacocks and the red admirals and the swallowtails that flapped inside it.

'See you later,' Gill said in the hallway, before climbing onto her mobility scooter.

'See you later,' he lied as cascades from their disintegrating relationship dampened his conscience.

'Don't think any of the gang's going out later so I thought maybe we could meet early at Nando's? Or somewhere else if you're getting bored of all that chicken.'

'Never bored of chicken.'

'Or actually – maybe we could try that Indian on the way to Bellybusters? I miss Indian; we haven't had one in ages. And maybe we can watch a film when we get back?'

'If there's time after you've showered me.'

'Yeah.'

'Alright, I'll have a think.'

Gill reversed outside and bounced onto the road. He stepped out as if to deliberately prolong his subterfuge, his guilt. A melancholy wrung the air, dampened the city, stultified the street. A duped bumble bee, solitary and startled but not yet angry, hovered around Brolly's shiny forehead; it was warm for early February. Gill drove under the bridge as the bee buzzed off. Brolly breathed in the melancholy. Practically choked on it. Yearned for a life he hadn't yet left. A girlfriend he still had. A daily routine he still journeyed through. His heart ached. He cupped his mouth and nose in his hands. 'Come on, Brolly, you can do this. You can do this, you can do this,' he repeated like a cut-price mantra as he failed to tear his eyes from his last farewell. As he watched, one last time, Gill's glinting side mirrors, glam-rock Mickey Mouse ears, as they twitched almost imperceptibly along the tarmac's pock-holes. As she pored over her only worry: what to eat for lunch.

The large nylon suitcase, faded but still black, sagged in the middle and was smattered with cobwebs. The crumpled, cheap plastic holdall, also black, honoured historical dalliances with sportive whimsy and was large enough to hide a cricket fetish or a fencing addiction. The damp flannel that he used to rub down both gave them a new lease of life, a veneer of contemporaneity, a reinvigoration to serve their true purpose. The water from the flannel became grimy, quickly. It discoloured the unwashed breakfast utensils, left them with pepper flecks of grit. He cleaned the outsides first and then the insides, where he found a pair of purple socks with turquoise patterns, some orange Y-fronts and three postcards. The postcards were from the Canary Islands, Gill and Brolly's last holiday destination. They had stamps on them and boasted the same crowded beach but lacked missives of holiday cheer. Inside the holdall was a tennis ball, which confused

Brolly because he couldn't remember ever having played tennis. Or ever having wanted to.

He threw everything away and after cleaning up breakfast, he hung one of his Christmas presents from Gill, the cooking apron, on a hook next to the fridge. It felt like he was hanging their love up to dry. And their life. He inspected the fridge contents. Pulled out a beer. Ripped it open. Gulped a mouthful. Regretted his decision. It was barely 9 a.m. Poured the beer down the sink, threw the tin away. Opened the confectionery cupboard. Pulled out a bag of Tangfastics for old times' sake. Ploughed into it. Knew he was creating havoc with his diet. Ate handfuls. Couldn't taste a thing. The sweet, the sour, the fizzy, the tang, the 'fastic; it was all tasteless. The beer, at least, he could taste. He pulled out a four-pack of Picnics. Ripped it open. Deep-throated one like Gill often did. It tasted of self-flagellation, denial and desperation. He tried another. It tasted of confusion, regret and love's loss. Of Gill's egocentricity. Of Gill's obstinacy. Of her inability to communicate, to listen, to adapt. He tried a third. It tasted of nothing. Of chocolate but not of peanuts or raisins or caramel or wafer or even a picnic. He replaced the final Picnic. Grabbed another beer. Forced himself to drink it in one. The first quarter tasted of fear, the second of guilt, the third of indecision, the fourth of resolve.

Light-headed, he threw the bags onto his duvet, checked his phone for messages, texts or missed calls, for signs, for a sign. Knew there wouldn't be any. Signs. He pulled up Gill's contact. Contemplated calling her. His breath deepened, his heart pounded, his nostrils flared, his mouth dried. He wanted to tell her the truth. Beg her to give the diet a chance. More time. Not to cheat. Not to cheat herself. Not to cheat life. Not to cheat their love. But the doctors had already told her the truth, her body had already told her the truth and she'd scorned both, so what chance did he have? A fat chance. A slim chance. No chance at all. He flipped through his other contacts. It was the same old story. He didn't have anyone else to call. He phoned Tiny Tim. A lady with a clipped voice and an attitude to match apologised; the number was no longer in service. His brother's name nestled uncomfortably under Tiny Tim's. They were both dead to him. But maybe not.

He hesitated but finally pressed the call button. 'Hello there, this is Tom. Please leave a message and I'll get back to you as quickly as I can.' Brolly hung up. Was intimidated by his brother's voice and simultaneously enthralled by it. He felt bold, redialled.

'Alright, Tom? It's Brolly. Errmm . . .' His pause was impressive. 'Sorry . . . This is quite hard for me but . . . You know . . . Your long-lost brother and, erm . . . I dunno . . . I saw Mum yesterday for the first time since . . . Well, since she was arrested and, errrr . . . Well, since she was released, and she told me you'd had twins so congratulations. I know things didn't end very well between us but . . . well . . . I miss you, buddy. You're my brother and I've only got one of you . . . And, er . . . well, I'm pretty sure you've only got one of me, too, so I wish we could put everything behind us. I wish I could see my nephews and, er . . . meet my sister-in-law and . . . Yeah . . . I love you . . . Call me back, please. Let's put an end to this nonsense . . .' Brolly hung up. And for the first time that morning, he giggled. 'Bloody 'ell!'

Packing was a novelty, folding a pleasure, double-folding a forgotten skill. The negative space inside the cupboard reminded him of a coffin, the flimsy metal hangers scratches on an eternal void of celluloid. He didn't appreciate the reminder, slammed the cupboard door shut. Did the same with the chest of drawers after he'd finished with them. His office was a trickier beast and for that he was perversely grateful; more signs of life, more possessions, more knick-knacks. More to choose from, more to renege upon. From above, a plane's drone underlined his dilemma. From the road, a speeding motorbike punctuated it with question marks. What to take? What to leave?

He wrapped his laptop in a grey travelling sleeve he'd never used and his scales in padded envelopes that he cut in half for better protection. He grabbed Tiny Tim's leopard-skin suit and before untacking the atrocity exhibition, snapped a photo so he could recreate it at his mum's. He grabbed two full files of paperwork and some jewellery, most of which no longer fitted his puffy fingers and wrists but which he hoped would fit again soon. He grabbed the tissue paper, the stickers and the stationery he used for Suits You, Sir! and stuffed everything into a large army surplus duffel that was his mode of transport for packages to and from Nisa. He patted the mannequin's bony shoulder. The mannequin sniffled, tried not to cry. 'Bye bye, baby,' he said. Behind it, the fridge tried not to vomit its despair. 'Bye bye, fridge, my trusty steed, my faithful friend. We rode well together and I'll never forget you. Keep the chicken for company. And the avocados. And the spinach. You never know, they might come in handy!' The printer vied for his attention, too, tried to be a bit cooler than the fridge. Which was hard. 'Bye bye printer, I'll miss you, too. It's been real. Bye bye desk, bye bye chair.' He skimmed his fingers along his desktop, walked to the door, and with a final flick, an antiquated flourish, bade his office farewell.

He stopped by the toaster, which hurled hurtful invectives at him. To shut it up, he shoved two slices of bread into its mouth and entered Gill's bedroom. Twisted clothes and discarded snack wrappers communed on the floor like exotic creatures on a moulting seabed. Drawers jutted out, posters curled at the sides, a wastebin overflowed with snot-ragged tissues. Brolly snatched a black bra, exhausted and frayed. He buried his nose in the bra. Smelled the soap and the moisturising cream. Smelled Gill, who smelled of him. He slung the bra over his shoulder. Wondered when he'd see another woman's bra. Apart from his mum's, which he didn't want to see. Wondered how Gill would clean herself after he'd gone. How she'd fight off the pustules and cold sores and lesions. The ones he'd valiantly battled for a decade.

Wondered if his neglect would kill her. Wondered if it would kill him.

The toast popped up. It smelled like a trap. It smelled too good to be true. He confronted it. Stared at it. Stuck his middle fingers up at it. 'Fuck you, man!' He turned his back on it. Laughed. Felt the approbation from his stomach's flab, the disapprobation from his appetite's whinge. Walked back down the hallway. Snuck back into his room. His former bedroom. It was dying. On its last legs. Gurgling painfully. Secreting the death rattle. It upset Brolly; he didn't need to torture himself like this, he needed to leave.

Downstairs, he ventured along the hallway for the last time. The duffel bag, the suitcase, the holdall comforted him. They contextualised his morning, his life, his thirty-six years on this planet. The weight on his back felt ironic. The handles in his hands felt adventurous. Gill's bra in his pocket felt pervy. Every step forward felt life-affirming. He was going places. He was going to his mum's.

Five steps away from his exit strategy.

Four steps away.

Three steps.

Two steps.

One step.

He unlatched the front door. An unexpected wind howled boisterous encouragement, slammed the door against the wall. Brolly stood behind the threshold, not quite on it. Stared out at the glittering new world that beckoned, willed his legs to take that final step towards his future.

CHAPTER 35

The fade from grey sky to black, from limp open-heartedness to reluctant claustrophobia, was happening in front of Gill's eyes but as she exited Harry's Hardware, she barely noticed. Her rasping dulled the sound of the late afternoon's traffic, her walking stick gave it a haunted beat. She stuttered towards her mobility scooter, pulled out her phone and called Brolly.

He didn't answer.

'Alright, lover? I'm just leaving work so I should be with you in half an hour. Looking forward to the evening! Byeee!'

It was just after she saw the old man meticulously slice a strip off a dripping elephant leg in King Kebab that finally, later than most, she flicked on her solitary light and soon after, her right indicator. As she pulled across the Walworth Road, a white van spluttered in front of her. A dark cloud of cash-in-hand carbon monoxide enveloped her, clogged her lungs. She wanted to shove the complexities of the London low-emission zone up the white van man's arse, but coughed fitfully and, with an unsteady but quick hand, cut across the break in the oncoming traffic.

The mud on the road outside the luxury flat development had dried. All the apartment facades had windows. Next to a semi-closed gate, two cigarette pinpricks glowed brighter than the fluorescent outfits the smokers wore. The chill air tweaked her skin as the construction workers' priapic curiosity explored her amorphousness. She ignored their gaze. Bumped onto the pavement soon after the dilapidated bridge, grabbed her phone for a second time in half an hour and called Brolly.

He didn't answer.

'Just pulling up now. Feeling a bit peckish so I think I'll come in for a quick snack. I quite fancy a Topic. Haven't had one of those in ages but think we still got some unless you've eaten 'em all. And some Tony's Chocolonely. Been getting into that at work. We should buy a shitload at Asda. I fuckin' love it!' She hung up, contemplated the house. It unnerved her. It was suffering an existential crisis. A nihilistic nightmare. Not one light glowed welcomingly. Not a flicker moved reassuringly. Its interior didn't shiver, even, or tremor or tremble. It had curled up under a blanket, if not ready to die, then at least to temporarily excommunicate itself from life. She pulled up outside and dialled Brolly for the third time.

He still didn't answer.

She didn't leave a message but struggled off her mobility scooter. A pizza box and some crusts dirtied the entrance. She kicked them away and with increasing unease unlocked the door, warily pushed it open. The street's ambient light groped the hallway's periphery. Her lips parted. Her fists clenched. Her eyes darted. 'Brolly?!' The question bounced around the hallway, ventured up the stairs, collapsed into the kitchen. She tried to make sense of what she saw. Of what she didn't see. No mobility scooter, but three interlopers confronted her: the suitcase, the holdall and the duffel bag. She flicked on the light. It polluted the kitchen, outlined a solitary leg, half a seated body. She squinted. Closed the door behind her.

'Brolly?' The figure didn't answer, didn't move, didn't twitch, didn't even breathe. The darkness drowned it. A winter jacket suffocated it. 'Brolly, you're scaring me!' Her voice betrayed a vulnerability. She pulled out her phone again. Coated her paranoia with some surrealism, called Brolly for the fourth time. His ringtone chimed from the kitchen. It should have soothed her but didn't. The phone lay in the middle of the table. It lit up his face with sick jaundice. Gill didn't hang up. Watched his reaction. Waited for him to answer, uncertain if she wanted him to. He didn't, didn't react at all. His listless body seemed disconnected to the moment but hypnotised by the technology. The ringtone repeated itself dispassionately, sounded like a hollow victory for mankind, a pathetic defeat for their relationship. As she hung up, his eyes tried to find hers. They flickered in her direction. The darkness devoured them.

Gill ploughed down the rest of the hall, twisted her hand around the doorway, flicked the light on, sighed with relief that Brolly still looked like Brolly, albeit a paler shade of his former self, a morose remonstration, a ghostly imitation. 'What's wrong, lover?' asked Gill with tremulous foreboding. Brolly twisted his head towards her, hung it with his best stray-dog mimicry, with cigarette stubbed and kicked rib melancholy, with the weight of the lonely and the unloved and the unseen and the unheard.

'I'm sorry,' he said.

'What d'you mean?'

'I'm sorry.'

'What for?'

'I'm so sorry.'

'I don't know what you're talking about?'

'I'm really, really sorry.'

'Brolly, what're you talking about? What've you done?' Gill sank both thumbnails into the flesh of her forefingers.

'I can't do this any longer.'

'Can't do what?'

Brolly threw his eyes around Gill as if searching for a prompt card but closed them as if the words were tattooed on the back of his eyelids. He forced a deep breath, reopened his eyes, prayed his heart didn't explode, his water ducts didn't leak. Stared directly into Gill's soul.

'Us. I can't do us any more.'

'What d'you mean?'

'I'm leaving.'

'What!?' asked Gill softly, scared.

'I'm leaving, Gill. And I'm so sorry.'

'Where are you going?'

'My mum's.'

'But you haven't seen your mum in years.'

'I saw her yesterday.'

'Oh . . . Wow . . . OK!'

'Yeah . . .'

'How is she?'

'She's fine.'

'Well, that's . . . good. How long are you . . . leaving for?'

'I just can't do this any more.'

'How long are you leaving for?'

'Well . . . Forever, I suppose . . .'

'Forever!?' Gill giggled, welcomed her giggle with open arms, cheered its lightness, its inappropriateness, its lack of occasion.

'I don't know why you're laughing. There's nothing funny about this. This is the saddest thing I've had to do, like, ever. I was going to leave this morning and call you when I was on the train but I couldn't . . .'

'Why not?'

'I don't know.'

'Don't leave.'

'I have to.'

'Why?'

'Why d'you think?'

'I don't know.'

'I can't stand by and watch you die.'

'What're you talking about? I'm not dying.'

'You're killing yourself.'

'No, I'm not.'

'You are.'

'Says who?'

'The doctors.'

'Bollocks. They say that to everyone.'

'I'm pretty sure they don't.'

'Those two were weird, I didn't like 'em.'

'Stop making excuses and blaming other people. You're morbidly obese, Gill; it's as simple as that.'

'Yeah, well, so are you.'

'Yeah, but at least I admit it and am doing something about it and am seeing some kind of change.'

'I admit it, too.'

'Yeah, but you're not doing anything about it.'

'Yeah, 'cos I don't want to.'

'Which is why I'm leaving!'

'It's my body and I can do what I want with it.'

'Yeah, you can, which, as I just said, is why I'm leaving. It's your body, do whatever you want with it. I don't want to force you to do anything you don't want to. I love you too much for that, Gill. I love you. You do understand that, don't you?'

Gill's forced levity plummeted, her casual disregard for the truth disintegrated, her disdain for the obvious dwindled, her contrariness curled, her brashness dampened, her thighs trembled and her heart fluttered. Brolly stood up. His chair legs screeched a warning across the kitchen floor. He stepped towards her. Grimaced. Held out his hand. She sensed he was offering a final lifeline. Reminded herself the truth was sacrosanct. Should never be messed with. Never belittled. Was everyone's best friend, no matter how snarky it could be, how unpleasant. She took his lifeline. Appreciated its warmth and tenderness. 'I understand.'

'Good, because that's all you need to understand. I know I don't tell you very much, but I do tell you sometimes and I'm telling you now. Again. I love you, Gill. You're my life. You're my heartbeat. You're my companion. You're my best friend. You're my everything and . . . you know . . . I thought one day you'd be my wife. I watched you collapse once, resuscitated you when I thought you were dying.' Brolly sniffled, wiped his nose. 'It was horrendous. It was absolutely horrendous. Most traumatic thing I've ever been through in my life, watching that happen, waiting for the ambulance, longest fucking fifteen minutes ever, watching them strap you up and . . . I mean, I'm glad I was there and I'm glad I could be of help because, you know, you needed someone to be there for you, to help you. But what I don't want to do is stand by while you carry on ignoring lessons that anyone should've learned. I can't watch you shovel more crap into your mouth, I can't facilitate you, enable you, pretend it isn't upsetting me. And, you know, it might happen next week, or next month, or next year – who knows? Maybe it'll happen in a few years but one day, your body will give up, your organs will collapse, you will have a heart attack, you will have a stroke, you will get diabetes, you will have your leg amputated. One day, one of these things will happen. Maybe a couple of these things will happen at the same time and you know what? I'm just not strong enough. I can't bear to go through it all again. Watch someone I love, die. Which is why I'm really, really, really sorry. I can't watch you do this to yourself, kill yourself slowly. It makes me too sad. It upsets me, it really does. And, you know, fine, maybe I'm being selfish, but I can't do this any more, can't pretend nothing's wrong because it is . . . Really. Fucking. Wrong.' Brolly sniffled again.

Gill wiped a tear from his cheek. 'Please don't go, lover.' She wrapped her arms around him, pulled him as close to her as she could. Scrunched her eyes. Rubbed her nose against his neck. Breathed in his essence, smelled his breath, prayed he'd be by her side forever, that he'd always plug the gap in her that she knew existed, that she knew only he could plug. 'Please, don't do this to me,' she whispered as she stroked his hair.

'I have to.' Brolly unlatched himself from her affection.

'But we haven't even talked about it.'

'We talked about it over Christmas, about a diet at the beginning of this year, but you cheated. I trusted you and you cheated so now I can't trust you any more, and anyway, you don't want to lose weight. You just said so! So it's not even about if I trust you or not, it's about the fact that you don't want to lose weight, which is, you know, fine . . . I suppose . . . I just . . . I wanted to honour you by telling you what I thought, to your face.' Brolly retreated. Gill threw her hand out, grabbed his arm.

'Don't do this to me, lover, please don't do this!'

Brolly shrugged off her concern, took another step back.

'Please don't make this harder than it already is.' He flipped around and grabbed his phone as Gill's countenance bubbled in horror, as her brain processed the racing car of reality that hurtled towards her, as her heart pounded, as the pounding splintered her bones, as the splinters pricked holes through her skin, as the holes oozed with sticky, bloody despair.

'Please don't, Brolly. Please don't leave me.' But he did exactly what she didn't want him to. 'Please don't do this to me, Brolly, please don't,' she repeated. 'You're my life!' She followed him out of the kitchen, as she wiped droplets from her tearing eyes, as she lay her palm on his back, as he stepped past the collapsed banisters, as her heart battered her ribcage, as she pawed at his shoulder, as her stomach muscles rippled, as her face started to melt. 'I'm begging you, Brolly, don't leave me. Please don't . . . I don't want to be without you . . . I don't think I can be without you!'

By the radiator, Brolly bent over and picked up his duffel bag, made the mistake of turning around, saw Gill's panic. He shook his head in distress, anxious he didn't witness further breakdown, sad that he'd made it happen, sadder that she'd made him make it happen. He slipped his right arm through his duffel bag's strap. 'Tell me what to do, baby. Please! Please! Tell me what to do and I'll do it!' she wailed.

'I've already told you and you didn't do it!' He desperately wanted to step outside the discomfort of Gill's emotional genuflection, her self's immolation.

'Tell me again and I'll do it!'

'I want you to lose weight but I don't want you to do it for me, I want you to do it for yourself.'

'I'll do it for myself, I promise! I'll go on a diet! I'll lose as much weight as I can! We'll eat salad every day and drink slimline tonic with our gin! Please baby, I'm begging you, please don't go!' Brolly shook his head. 'I'm going, Gill, I'm sorry!' He grabbed his holdall, slung it over his left shoulder.

'Give me another chance, baby, please!'

'Let's talk when we've both calmed down.' He grabbed his suitcase, almost scuppered her stance as he swung around with it, stepped towards the front door.

Five steps.

'Please don't go!' she cried as she watched him progress with a dawning realisation that her words were nothing more than dirty flies in his planned departure's ointment.

Four steps.

'BROLLY?!'

Three steps.

His determination ignored her. Her determination lunged towards him.

Two steps.

He extended his hand towards the door latch.

One step.

She threw her arms around him. Bear-hugged him as best she could, pulled him towards her, tightened her grip, interrupted his resolution, upset his balance. He tripped. She collapsed. They crashed. Uncomfortably. Awkwardly. Painfully. His forehead cracked against the wall, his nose splattered over it. He screamed. They landed. Heavily. With further outpourings of pain. Two skydivers tied together, their practised landing a limb-jarring failure, a Twister-like disaster. A stillness temporarily congealed the corridor. Brolly's clothes seeped out of his suitcase. His skin seeped out of his clothes. Gill's face throbbed, but for the first time since her return, she relaxed, sighed relief, found solace in the befuddled organism below her that inhaled and exhaled, that inflated and deflated, the organism, her boyfriend, who loved her, who she loved back. She squeezed Brolly's shoulder with all the affection she could muster. 'What the fuck are you doing?' Brolly rasped, his neck twisted, his nose numbed, his blood trickling millimetres from the glossy skirting board and what appeared to be a dirty toenail.

'Did I tell you I love you, too? I know you told me, but I can't remember if I told you?' she asked as she did her best to flatten his girth.

'This is really hurting. Can you just get the fuck off of me!'

Gill wasn't sure if she could. Broken memories of the Southbank Hotel jived in front of her mind's eye. She repressed them, darkened them, concentrated on what was still positive.

'I just want to make sure you understand me, too, baby. I do love you, more than anything. You do understand that, don't you?'

'Yes, Gill, I do understand. Can you get off me, please, I've got a train to catch!' Gill manoeuvred her unwieldiness and with all her might pushed down on her hands, on Brolly. 'AAAAGGGGH!'

'Sorry, lover.'

'What the fuck're you doing!?'

'Trying to help you catch your train.'

'Well, make sure you don't break my bloody bones while you're doing it!'

'Sorry. Do you want to get up first and then pull me up?'

'Given that you're lying on top of me, I think it's easier if you get up first.'

'OK.' Gill repositioned her hands on the flea-bitten carpet and repositioned her legs so they straddled his. With a wrestler's enthusiasm for his arch-rival, Gill grunted and groaned and offered her best imitation of a knee press-up, the only imitation of any press-up she'd ever attempted since school. Her biceps quivered, her patellae pounded, the bottom of her stomach remained unmoved but her voluptuous bottom jiggled backwards and the rest of her body jittered upwards. She managed to kneel on all fours and as her lungs clamoured for oxygen, she caressed the back of Brolly's thigh to communicate the evening could still turn out for the better. He jerked away to communicate it couldn't.

She needed something to claw onto, to aid the next step of her ascent, to help her return to official bipod status. The letterbox was too slight, its width barely sufficient to slip both hands into. The dented copper handle, screwed loosely to the living-room door on her right, was too flimsy. Any of the three-piece suite arm rests next door could do the trick but clambering there on all fours seemed time-wasting. Not to mention humiliating. The cast-iron radiator to her left seemed the best bet. She reversed away from Brolly. Twisted her body towards the heater. Gripped its metal bars.

'OW!' she screamed.

'You OK?'

'Hot, that's all.' Burgundy bands coloured her palms as she tugged her sweatshirt sleeves over her hands and grabbed the bars again. This time they comforted rather than scalded. For a second she had a mental glitch, felt an empty universe flood her. Couldn't remember how to co-ordinate her brain with her body, how to move her limbs. For a millisecond she betrayed her own hubris, wondered if Brolly might have a point, if the doctors were correct, if Tiny Tim had been her personal Jesus, died for her eating sins so that she didn't have to. The thought bubble burst, dripped contempt all over her as she regained control, exerted herself, flexed her stomach muscles, pushed with her legs, pulled with her arms, burst capillaries, groaned like a wild creature mating in a forest.

The radiator wobbled, screws in the wall rattled. Gill stopped, didn't want to flood the hallway so re-strategised. Positioned herself over the radiator, breathing heavily; pushed upwards rather than pulled outwards. The radiator teetered. Concrete dust and dried particles patterned the carpet. Splinters pricked through her knees, lacerated the balls of her feet, flayed her elbows. Her thighs shook, her knees knocked; she wanted to surrender to her physical ineptitude, to embrace her life's dedication to indulgence, to gluttony, but knew she was doing this for love, for her love, for her Brolly. Slowly she arched upwards, straightened her spine. 'Bloody 'ell!' Her pores exuded a subtle smell of startled skunk.

'You up?' Brolly asked, his head still averted.

'Yeah. Shall I help you?'

'I'll be fine.'

'Suit yourself. When's your train, d'you know?' Gill asked calmly.

'There's one every thirty minutes until about sevenish and then one every hour until about eleven.'

'You've got plenty of time.'

'Yeah, but I don't want to get there too late.'

Gill hobbled to the kitchen, stopped in front of the confectionery cupboard, suppressed, for once, her urge for its contents. Looked to the cooker. To the breakfast utensils. To perhaps her favourite utensil of them all: the frying pan. She picked it up. It weighed deliberately, with meaning, with emotion, with complicity. She'd never actually used it before, but it felt good in her clutch. She exited the kitchen. Waxed nostalgic for all the sausages and all the bacon the pan had fried over the years. She caressed her stomach as it rumbled down the hallway, smiled affectionately at Brolly as he used the radiator to pull himself off the floor. Her smile didn't waver as he looked at her, as his brow furrowed, as his confusion doubled, as her outstretched arm scared him, as she smacked the frying pan against his skull.

For the first time ever, the frying pan defied its defining purpose in life. It stuck. Only for a few seconds. But it stuck. To Brolly's forehead. And rang hollowly in the hallway's shocked silence. 'What did you do that for?' he asked as blurred little birds fluttered above him, his vision spun and claret gushed from his pulsating, twopenny-piece gash.

'I'm sorry . . .' Gill responded, aping his words, instinctively understanding them better now than she had moments earlier. 'I'm so, so, sorry . . .'

'What did you do that for!?' he repeated.

'Are you OK?'

'You just hit me with the frying pan!'

'I'm sorry, I really am!' she repeated as blood coloured half his vision, as his eyes blinked stroboscopically and as he started to teeter.

'Are you OK?' Gill asked again, knowing very well he wasn't.

'I don't think so . . .'

'Let's sit you down for a while.' Gill took his hand tenderly.

'I should really catch my train.'

'Just relax for a moment. Make sure you're not concussed.'

'OK.'

Gill worried the kitchen would be too far for him to walk, even the living room a stretch, didn't want him collapsing again. Wasn't sure what she'd do then, who she'd call. She guided Brolly to the stairlift. He slumped into it. Practically fell straight out of it.

'Careful!' she admonished. He stopped his fall, jacked himself back up as she strapped the belt around his waist.

'What're you doing?'

'In case you slip out again; don't want to hurt yourself. I'll get you some water. That should help.'

'OK.'

Brolly had a sense he should scarper, catch his train, reset his life. But he couldn't, couldn't do anything except watch Gill, who took his hand and kissed it. She smiled. He smiled back and wondered why the lights were flickering, why the hallway was darkening.

One step before the kitchen, Gill's life flashed in front of her. She froze and thawed in the time Brolly's phone first pierced the air. She gyrated and attempted the second verb she hadn't attempted since schooldays. To run. It was a physical impossibility, but she did manage to flounder forth with kneecapped alacrity. When she turned the corner, around the banister, she froze again. Brolly's head hung over his sternum as if in a deep slumber and blood dripped onto his trousers with the consistency of time ticking. Gill shook Brolly's nearest shoulder. 'Brolly . . . ?' He didn't respond. 'Brolly!?' she repeated, fearing the worst as she shook him again. She stepped up a couple of stairs and reached over him, pulled the phone from his jacket's pocket. It stopped ringing. She looked at the caller ID. It was his brother, Tom. She emitted a pleasantly surprised whimper, but knew she had to proceed with caution; Brolly hadn't spoken to Tom as long as she'd known him. She sniffed like a bloodhound eking out a promising trail as she unlocked the phone and pulled up the contact list, found Tom. She pressed the 'message' icon. The text bar appeared. She contemplated what to write, what not to write, whether to write anything. She pulled up Brolly's recent calls. He'd called Tom that morning. She flicked through more calls. Days and months away; nothing. A year; nothing. Her internal bloodhound yelped confidently. *Hey Tom, thanks for returning my call*, she typed. *My plans have changed but I'll get back in touch when I'm heading back to Mum's. Looking forward to catching up! Cheers, Broll.* She pressed the send button and typed a similar text to his mum.

Back in the kitchen, Gill placed the frying pan on the table. Her hand was trembling. She didn't know what she'd just done. Knew exactly what she'd just done. She picked the pan back up. Turned it over. The pan was trembling. She noticed a mosquito splash of Brolly's blood on its outer rim. She hobbled to the sink, squirted washing-up liquid over her finger. She smeared her finger in small circles over the pan until the blood was just a memory, an illusion of her compassion. She rinsed it and dried it against her backside. She replaced it on the cooker, wiped the table with a sponge scourer and rinsed that, too.

From the fridge, she grabbed a beer and ripped it open. It hissed at her. The spume around the ring-pull made her happy to be alive. The smell made her thank God for hops. The amber rivulet that cleansed her throat made her thank God for four-packs, off-licences and supermarkets. She was still wearing her jacket. She pulled her phone out and unlocked it. Dialled 999. Took more strength from the beer as the ringtone filled the air. She lowered the phone, placed it in her left hand, hovered her thumb over the call button. Stared at the keypad. Clicked her teeth. Tapped her feet. A man asked her which service she wanted and she hung up.

CHAPTER 36

'Alright, mate, d'you know much about sleeping pills?'

'What d'you wanna know?'

'How many should I take?'

'Depends which ones you're taking.'

'I was hoping you could advise me . . .'

'Depends what you want them for.'

'Well . . . to go to sleep.'

'I think they're just in the aisle down there.' The teenage cyborg with a phone for its hand gestured non-specifically, as if programmed to keep his customers in store for as long as possible. His programming had been a failure; the Walworth Road pharmacy, close to the Jamaican jerk chicken parlour, was empty except for Gill.

'I got these two.' Gill held up both hands, hoped the gesture might inspire the cyborg to offer better informed medical advice. It leaned forward. Squinted at the packages.

'"Night, Night" and "Sleep Well". Yeah, they'll work.'

'Yeah, I know they'll work; they're sleeping pills. Any preference?'

'Not really.'

'And how many should I take?'

'Have you read the packets?'

'Yeah but . . .'

'What do they say?'

'One or two . . .'

'Yeah, so you should take one or two.'

'Yeah but, you know, given that I'm probably, well, I suppose, given that I'm bigger than most people . . .'

'A bit bigger . . .'

'Yeah. Given that I'm a bit bigger, should I take a few more?'

'Yeah, you can if you want.'

'What, like two to four?'

'How many times bigger are you than the average person, d'you think?'

'I dunno . . . Three or four . . .'

'So take three or four times more pills. Like, three to six or four to eight.'

'Is that, like, a medical opinion?'

'What d'you mean?'

'Well, I don't want to wake up and find I've given myself brain damage by taking too many.'

'If you got brain damage, you probably wouldn't even realise.'

'Is there someone else I can talk to?'

'Yeah, hang on.' The cyborg swivelled around to the pharmacy behind the counter. 'DAD!?'

CHAPTER 37

As Gill stood outside her front door, she wasn't sure what to think. Part of her hoped Brolly had already left, part of her hoped he hadn't. Part of her hoped he'd woken up and was resting in the kitchen, part of her hoped he was still slumped in the stairlift. Part of her wondered about calling the ambulance again, part of her wondered about handing herself over to the police. From across the street, jeers and laughter distracted her. She turned around. A clutch of adolescents jumped on top of each other like mating frogs. They turned a corner, their excitement faded, and the street quietened. Gill pulled her keys from her jacket and glanced over both shoulders. She opened the door; Brolly hadn't moved.

Confident that few people managed to commit suicide by taking sleeping pills, Gill finished her Google search. She slipped her phone back into her pocket and ignored the cyborg's dad, who had toed the family line and confirmed she should take no more than the packet's recommendation. Two pills. She popped separate piles of eight onto the work surface next to the cooker.

From above the confectionery cupboard, she grabbed two coffee cups with faded floral patterns and laced them with tap water. She grabbed one of the piles and hobbled back to Brolly.

Like a Guy Fawkes doll, his head still drooped over his chest and his shoulders sagged forward. His deep breathing underplayed the gravity of the situation, falsified its criminality, contradicted its medical imperative. The bandage she'd stuck over his wound had turned soggy, a varicose-vein purple, but it had, at least, stopped the bleeding.

She wedged the cup between his thighs. She pushed his chin upwards and tried to open his mouth but as soon as she did so, his head dropped. It was harder than she expected to keep his jaw open. His forehead was too greasy to grab and his nose too quaint. Pulling his hair seemed too gladiatorial, his ears too comical. She relaxed his head and scratched hers. Sucked her lower lip. Threw the sleeping pills into her mouth, arched her hands over his skull and pulled his jaws open. She leaned in, stuck her lips over his. Some pills dropped but some stuck to her palate and in between her gums. She swirled her tongue to encourage their departure. His tongue was flaccid, his mouth unresponsive, but his spittle strangely appealing. Not that she was trying to French him. Not in that unconscious state. But after one tongue lash too many, just, maybe, a little bit too keen, too inquisitive, too reminiscent of incipient affection for a recently deceased corpse, she broke what had become an unexpectedly amorous embrace and picked up the water. She drank as much as she could without swallowing. She replaced the cup between his thighs, lifted his head again and sealed her mouth over his again, no tongues this time. She spurted the water inside and clamped his mouth shut. She shook his skull as if it was her favourite cocktail mixer. His body tensed. He coughed and spluttered. Spittle splattered her hands. His eyes burst open. She screamed in shock, relinquished her grip, threw herself against the banisters. He shouted in bewilderment, an incomprehensible sludge of panic. She leaned back in, clamped one hand over his mouth and with the other gripped the back of his head, violated him into silent submission.

Wrapping the masking tape around Brolly's mouth was straightforward. Threading it around his body was pernickety and irksome as the gap between the stairlift and the wall was minimal, two or three fingers wide. Nonetheless, she wanted to do it right. Didn't want him to crash to the floor should the seat buckle, somehow give way. She'd never forgive herself if he hurt himself while she was asleep.

After she finished, the silence spoke to her. It was, surely, a masculine silence. Disapproving and judgemental, its enveloping cavernous, its impasse patriarchal and condescending. It intimidated her. Frightened her. But not as much as his eyes. His eyes had scared her more. Not his sclera, flecked with dainty tributaries of burst blood vessels, but his irises. His irises, which hadn't only stared at her but into her. His irises, which hadn't recognised her, which hadn't even seen her.

CHAPTER 38

Gill woke with a psychological start and a disturbed walrus gasp. She had an ephemeral, evanescing recollection that she'd been drowning in her nightmares. Quite possibly in chicken korma. Or maybe chicken masala. Some of her right cheek glistened. Drool dampened her pillow. An unease tightened her body's every tendon. Her eyes focused on the ceiling, her hand clenched the side of the bed and she started to remember, not her nightmare but her reality. 'Oh God . . .' she muttered as if suffering someone else's hangover. 'Oh God,' she repeated as she realised the hangover was hers, as the eight sleeping pills she'd also taken, as a form of solidarity, to gauge their effectiveness, dithered and lurched through her memory. 'Brolly?' she tentatively called. He didn't respond. He never responded these days. 'Brolly?!' she shouted, more loudly. 'BROLLY!?' she finally screamed. She threw her duvet aside and set a new personal record for struggling out of bed. She ripped her door open so forcefully that its doorknob made a small dent in the wall it smashed against. 'BROLLY!!' She extended her arms like horizontal buffers, half expecting the hallway to tilt and unbalance her. Every step pummelled the floor, reverberated through the house. She grabbed the banister. It grounded her anxiety. She ignored the dark womb that used to be Brolly's sunny bedroom and followed the banister's hairpin, darted her eyes downwards. He was still there, still slumped, still buckled, still wrapped in plastic masking tape, still looked like a poorly executed, semi-waterproof mummy.

It was only when she stood next to him, witnessed the soothing sight of his rhythmical breathing, that she started to relax, glad he didn't suddenly lunge at her, try to strangle her. Her teeth's enamel shone through the gap between her lips as her mouth curled and her eyes smiled. She stretched her palm out, held it against his forehead. She didn't know why but it felt like the right thing to do. His forehead was lukewarm, like a recently abandoned cup of tea. She ruffled his hair and inspected his thinning roots.

In the kitchen, she opened the confectionery cupboard and grabbed a handful of Cadbury's Creme Eggs. She peeled off their wrappers and stuffed them down her throat. She shuffled over to the sleeping pills and popped another eight onto the work surface next to the cooker and crushed them.

CHAPTER 39

Gill's work day was a snail with a very heavy weight on its back. It was her and Dagmara's turn to lock up the store, but Dagmara had a date. Gill sent her off early, picked up her biro and chewed its already mangled end. The store grumbled. It felt unloved, under-employed. Without any kind of human interaction to occupy it, it took on a sinister overtone. All those knives and hammers and ropes and chains. Legal tools for illegal deeds. Gill needed to concentrate but needed distraction. She switched on the radio. Cheerful ululations, flared jeans, flower power grooved through the store. She racked her brain, drew diagrams, scribbled down swear words, shouted some out, served an ostrich of an old lady, crossed out most of the diagrams and crushed the biro's end so that plastic splinters dropped to the floor. Just before 6 p.m., she came up with a succinct shopping list and two diagrams that remained intact. On the dot of 6 p.m., she flipped the 'open' sign to 'closed' and hobbled towards the shield-anchor eyebolts hanging from the back wall, on the left. She was grateful the ones she wanted, the largest ones, 150mm in length, weren't in the bottom two trays but the middle one, which, at a stretch, she could just about reach. She needed seven but decided to round the number up to ten.

CHAPTER 40

After drilling the first hole to the right of Brolly's bed around her upper abdomen level, Gill returned the power drill to the duvet, on which she'd laid the rest of her pilfering. She picked up an anchor eyebolt and unscrewed the anchor from the eyebolt. She slipped it into the wall, pleased with the size of drill bit she'd chosen; its fit was snug. She grabbed the long set tool, which looked like a glorified nail but without a sharp point, introduced it into the anchor, and smacked it with the hammer. Three times. And a fourth, for luck. The action was satisfying, the sound, like an industrial pop of the weasel, rewarding. With her fingers, she screwed the eyebolt as far as it would go. She tightened it with flat-nose pliers. She grabbed a single wheel pulley, which was shiny, zinc-plated and 100mm in diameter, and clipped its hook through the eyebolt. She hesitated and took a deep breath before tugging. Neither the anchor nor the eyebolt moved a millimetre.

She undid a jute rope, 20 metres in length, and slipped it through the pulley wheel. She held both ends and tugged again. The pulley didn't budge. She tugged it twice and then a third time, more violently. She tied a makeshift knot around her waist and slipped her right foot backwards as if anchoring a tug-of-war team. She leaned her body against the rope, gently at first and then with more confidence. The more she leaned, the more her thigh quivered. The rope cut into the flesh around her back. The tautness stung but also gratified; the eyebolt and the pulley held firm.

She drilled another hole and installed the second pulley next to the long window hidden by the curtains on the left of the bed. She pushed Brolly's chest of drawers away from the wall on the right and installed the third pulley. The fourth she installed in between the door and Brolly's wardrobe, on the left.

At the top of the stairs, she pressed the stairlift's remote control. The chair jerked minimally, did its job stoically, without asking questions. She hadn't realised how sweaty she was, how quickly her heart had been beating, until she stood still. She monitored Brolly's progress as she dried her hands on her trousers, wiped as much sweat as she could from her body. The stairlift jolted to a halt and she waited for Brolly to do something unexpected, something funny, something clever, something silly. But he didn't do anything, so she took his right hand. Sought his pulse, measured it.

She grabbed the folding platform trolley, locked its wheels, unfolded it, dropped it next to Brolly. 'Baby?' she whispered as she stepped closer to him again. 'Baby!' she demanded with more authority. He looked haunted. Like his soul had taken a holiday, was considering a fully blown, self-imposed, irreversible exile. She slapped his cheek. Softly, then harder. His face whiplashed, his chin wobbled. She teased open his eyelids. His irises contracted but she was distracted by a back-alley smell. She looked down. A damp patch that hadn't been there moments earlier besmirched his groin. She moaned. Fancied a beer. Fancied getting shit-faced, turning back time. She slit the masking tape with her Stanley knife, threaded the middle of the rope behind his back and under his arms. Three times. She rested half the rope on his lap and returned to the bedroom with the other half, which she threaded through the pulley system so that the rope zigzagged through the space. She took the rope from Brolly's lap and unbuckled the safety belt, prayed he didn't slip from his precarious perch.

Two steps from the bottom of the stairs, she turned around and wrapped both ends of the rope around her waist, twice. She tied it into a half knot and pulled the remote control out of her pocket. She turned to face Brolly, felt like a trapeze artist about to jump backwards from a dizzying height. She wiped beads of fear from her forehead, breathed in her body's apprehension. She reached for the banister with her left hand and with her right, grabbed the rope. She prayed everything she'd ever learned at Harry's didn't let her down, didn't give her brain damage, didn't snap her spine. Didn't give him brain damage either, snap his spine, break his neck. She pressed the remote control.

The stairlift's inner cogs sounded like a machine indignant at its own failure. Its wheels strained, attempted to grate cheese from a block of granite as she teetered, played a game of trust with herself. Leaned further backwards and was thankful she'd never cheated at solitaire. She pushed against the third step with a controlled force. Her heart jumped with panic as Brolly budged. Minimally but then suddenly. Not so much with a jerk as an irrevocable surge, a man-made wave, a roll of the dice between the safety of the landing and a tumble-down death from the stairs. The rope tightened against Gill's ribs, contracted her lungs, cut into her organs. She dropped one step and then another, relinquished her grip on the banister, swayed over the hallway, gyrated, held firm, thudded onto the floor as he crashed with almost psychic obedience onto the trolley. 'Yay!'

Brolly's puppet-like limbs answered to no one. His unwieldy girth answered specifically to Gill, truculently, insolently, with attitude. Coercing him through his bedroom door proved trickier than she anticipated but she didn't give up. Couldn't give up. She pushed and pulled and huffed and puffed and once she forced his upper torso across the threshold, his lower torso followed easily. She pulled the trolley as close to the bed as she could. She screwed one pulley directly behind Brolly's headboard, which she didn't use immediately, and another three into the walls parallel to the length of his bed, which she did use immediately. Using five pulleys in total, the rope criss-crossed the room twice.

'Ready, Freddy?' she asked as she tied the rope ends around her backside again. 'Ready, Freddy!' she responded to herself cheerily and wrapped her right hand around the rope again. It gave her more purchase, cut into her wrist, but she ignored the pain, leaned back and tugged. The rope slid under her buttocks and she stopped. She lifted the rope over her waist and tugged again. Aggressively. The pressure felt like it might sever her in half. She stopped, needed to re-strategise.

In the kitchen, she guzzled two beers and gobbled down a sharing pack of Rolos, a large bar of Caramel and four Milky Ways as she searched for one of Auntie Violet's sturdy dinner trays. The one she had in mind was made of dark oak and had stainless steel handles. She found it in the middle of a pile of giveaway journals under a kitchen chair no one ever sat on.

She tied the rope to the tray's handles, grabbed a pillow from Brolly's bed, slipped the pillow between her back and the tray and tested her idea, tugged for her country. The rope burned skid marks across her hand. She strained like she was trying to relieve her constipation. The burns around her hands turned purple. The dinner tray warped, cracked, snapped in half. Her muscles quivered, but Brolly began to rise.

CHAPTER 41

The next morning, Brolly sounded as if he was on a life-support machine. Gill took his closest hand. It was limp. A dead fish. It communicated nothing but her own worst imaginings. She pinched the side of his neck. A little girl's teasing at first but quickly a mischievous pinch and finally a cruel and callous one, a bloody nip seeking a rise from her victim, a shudder, a twitch at least.

None was forthcoming.

She grabbed the rope, which she'd tidied onto his chest of drawers along with the rest of her paraphernalia. She raised his arms above his head as if his favourite football team had scored a goal. She lifted her right knee onto the mattress. Pain stabbed through her leg, smashed against her patella with the subtlety of an iron hammer. She grimaced with an animalistic impression. Wanted to straddle his face, insinuate enforced cunnilingus, a vagina-to-mouth resuscitation, but respected her hips' inflexibility, bemoaned their slowly locking hinges. Instead, she leaned. Used her left arm as the third stick of her tripod, smothered his personality with hers and slipped the rope through the pulley above his bed, the pulley she'd drilled the previous evening but hadn't used. Little knots ravaged her breast like weeds in a summer meadow as she tied the rope around his wrists.

CHAPTER 42

Dagmara sidled up to Gill as she shovelled a mess of egg fried rice and sweet and sour prawns into her mouth. 'You alright, mate?' Dagmara had been nominated by her colleagues to talk to Gill. As a woman and as Gill's confidante. None of them expected their boss to win Slimmer of the Year but that morning they'd all noticed her feeding frenzy, more psychotic than usual, more psychologically disturbed, more self-medicating, more self-abusing.

'Yeah, why d'you ask?'

'Well . . . I mean . . . I don't wanna seem rude, innit, but this is your third Deliveroo this morning and it ain't even lunchtime yet and you're going out with Mr Carmichael in an hour or so.'

'Hungry.'

'Well, yeah, obviously, innit . . .'

'Aren't I always, though?'

'You are, but . . .'

'Didn't have breakfast this morning. Well, I did, but only from Yummies, not from home, so I was hungrier than usual . . . You know . . .'

'Why didn't you have breakfast this morning? Everything OK at home?'

'Oh . . .' Gill's fork froze in mid-air. As if it had a mind of its own. As if the jute ropes at the end of the store, which mingled innocuously enough with all the other ropes, were trying to communicate with it, to tell it the truth. Gill cleared her throat, cleansed her paranoia, dropped her fork into the takeaway box, shielded it from the jute's psychic rays. 'Yeah, yeah, Brolly's got the flu and, er . . .'

'Bloody 'ell! I hope it's not that new thing. You been reading about it in the papers?'

'What new thing?'

'From China. It's the new flu apparently, but more deadly. They locked down a couple of cities or something but it travels really fast an' the first cases have arrived over here already . . .'

'Oh . . . No, don't know anything about that. Doesn't sound very nice.'

'Nah. Coronavirus. Looks like something out of the movies.'

'Corona? Like the beer?'

'Yeah. That's the one . . .'

'I'll check it out . . .'

'Yeah, you should, just in case, but everything's alright then?'

'Yeah, everything's fine.'

'Promise you'll tell me if it isn't? I'm here for you, Gill, we all are. Everyone loves you, you know that, don't you?'

'Thanks, Dagz; that's sweet.'

'You coming out for drinks later? I'm gonna get rat-arsed.'

'Would love to but should get back to Brolly, really.'

CHAPTER 43

Brolly kept his wolves at bay, snored like the bear he was. Gill plonked the second kitchen chair, Sunday-best haughtiness suffering from dining table separation anxiety, next to the first. On it, she put an opened bottle of red wine, a bowl full of Fruit Pastilles, M&Ms and Minstrels and a saucepan full of steaming hot water, over which drooped a flannel. She leaned forward and squeezed Brolly's flaring nostrils together. A mobile disco from outside, maybe on roller-skates, temporarily replaced his noise but quickly bled all over the dance floor and into nothingness. Brolly's stomach twitched. A couple of his fingers remembered how to type. His breath exploded through his mouth, his lips flapped like a horse's, spluttered and sucked in another breath. The breath sounded like an audio recording played backwards. She released her grip and Brolly started to snore again.

The plaster on his forehead had dried. Gill picked at it. It pawed at his pores, snarled at his eyebrows, distorted his face. She stopped picking. She tried to chew her thumbnail but realised she'd already chewed it to death. She opted for her index finger instead. After biting what little nail she had left, she picked at the plaster again, ticked it like an overzealous teacher until the hint of a corner appeared. She tugged it. It tugged him. Nothing would ever change. That was the law of the plaster. She had to be cruel to be kind. She ripped. Its adhesive left a faint white memento, an ethereal kiss, around the wound. Pus blemished the coagulated blood. Gill dabbed it with the flannel. Like Mary Magdalene, but with a greater interest in her snacks. She wrung the flannel into the saucepan and its water turned a rose-petal pink.

She threw the water down the toilet, rinsed the flannel and poured more hot water into the saucepan. She grabbed a hairbrush from her bedroom and returned but found it increasingly hard to move without a walking stick. After sitting down, it took longer to recover than she cared to admit, but she started to massage Brolly's head with her brush, tidy his hair, prepare him for an outing he wouldn't receive. His hair needed a cut, was longer than he usually styled it. She gave him something he'd never given himself: a side parting. A flicker of delight rippled across her face. She fussed over a few stray strands, tucked them behind his ears and leaned back to admire her handiwork; Friday nights weren't what they used to be.

CHAPTER 44

G ill pulled the front door shut. Taxi Rob slammed the door to his Viano. She double-locked. He didn't lock at all. He noticed her securing the house before Brolly's exit. She didn't notice his noticing. 'Alright, lovely?!' he asked.

'Alright, mate!?' she responded as he stepped onto the pavement and noticed the thunderous bags under her eyes; her skin, even more swollen than usual; the eruption of new spots and sores over her pallid forehead; her hair, which looked like it had recently been lacquered with butter.

'You alright?' he asked, not as customary greeting but expression of concern.

'Sorry, I meant to call you but was so exhausted last night, I just passed out. Brolly's not so well and . . .'

'Oh no. Sorry to hear that. What's wrong with 'im?'

'Dunno exactly. I think it's just the flu but 'e's been knocked for six these last couple of days, can't even get out of bed, poor thing.'

'Bloody 'ell! Hope it's not this Covid thing! You been reading up on that?'

'Kind of, yeah, but, er . . . I'm pretty sure it isn't, but . . . I mean, I don't know where he'd get it from an' I feel fine, but you never know, do you!?'

'Bloody 'ell! I 'ope not! It's scary, that is, just like SARS all over again.'

'I'm pretty sure it isn't and I'm so sorry I forgot to call, so I'd understand if you didn't wanna drive me around today, but I feel a bit uncomfortable about you coming in the house for our squashing session, just, you know, just in case it is corona, so I was wondering if we could postpone it until he's better . . .'

'Oh . . .' Taxi Rob's face dropped, his smile flattened, the twinkle in his eyes flatlined. 'Yeah, of course. No worries.'

'I know you was looking forward to it. I mean, I was looking forward to it, too; I do enjoy it . . .'

'Do ya?'

'Yeah, of course!'

'That's nice to hear.'

'Yeah, but I don't wanna risk you getting anything from Brolly, especially when we don't know what's wrong with 'im. Better safe than sorry.'

'Yeah, yeah, no, you're right. You sure you haven't caught anything off 'im, though?'

'Yeah, I'm fine . . . I mean, if you don't wanna risk it, that's fine, too, and, er . . . I understand but, yeah, I was thinking when he's better we can do a double session or maybe you can come round on a weekday and we can do it one evening. Order in a takeaway afterwards, make an evening out of it an' who knows? Maybe we can discuss making two sessions a week the norm.'

Gill regretted her overcompensation immediately, but Taxi Rob started to applaud Brolly's mystery illness.

'That'd be amazing!'

'Well, that's settled then!'

'Yeah, no problemo. Be nice to spend the day together just the two of us, actually.'

'I was thinking that,' she lied.

'I was thinking, an' don't take this the wrong way, but I was just wondering, I think you've put on more weight recently?'

'You think so?'

'Yeah, I do.'

'Oh . . .'

'Suits you though, suits you really well.'

Gill blushed. Her eyelashes fluttered. Dimples sprouted from her dumplings.

'Cheers, mate!'

CHAPTER 45

Brolly was vaguely aware of voices. Downstairs. No more than two. Their syllables, consonants and intonations were indistinct and indecipherable. They scratched at his consciousness like a fly on a starving child's face. He tried to shoo them away, preferred his liminal stupor, a pleasant drowsiness, to what he sensed would be the gut-wrench of his new reality. It was the slam of the front door, however, the preciseness of its jar, not aggressive but firm, that did the trick. His eyelids weighed heavily but his eyes opened. They tempted him to regress but he fought their temptation. His head hurt. He investigated his surroundings. Recognised them through a dim haze. Thought he'd already left them behind, was confused as to why they still lingered. His arms ached. They stretched above his head. He pulled them. They jolted and stuck. He pulled them aggressively. His wrists wrenched, his skin around them burned. He saw the rope. The carbuncles of restraint. He tilted his head backwards, saw the pulley clipped into the bolt in the wall. His brain convulsed. His outrage bristled. His scream jostled. Something was stuck in his mouth. His scream fell flat on its face, on his chin. He tried to spit the thing out but couldn't. Something was stuck over it. He twisted his head, stretched his neck as far as it would go, started rubbing his mouth against his shoulder, tried to loosen what appeared to be some kind of tape.

A pink envelope with his name written in charismatic, swirling letters distracted him. The undulating petals of a solitary red rose, svelte and graceful, elegant in an inelegant pint glass, confused him. The heart-shaped box of what he assumed were chocolates disturbed him. They'd been placed on two kitchen chairs opposite. The rose stood on the left chair, the chocolates and card on the right. His brain worked overtime, tried to make sense of his waking nightmare, but a metallic gurn disrupted the process. He looked towards the door just in time to see Gill's eyeballs burst out of their sockets and her mouth elongate with unbridled and heartfelt delight.

'BABY!' she screamed. 'You're awake! Bloody hell! You're awake! That's amazing!' She waddled over to the side of his bed, deposited her family pack of Cool Doritos and large beer on the second chair next to the rose, bent over, pulled the tape off, took the sock out of his mouth.

'What the fuck's going on!?' he asked as she wiped away tears of relief, droplets of joy, and tried to kiss him as if he'd just returned from a trip around the world, or at least from her favourite sweet shop. He shunned her affection, fed her his prickly stubble instead.

'I've missed you so much! I'm so happy to see you! How are you!?'

'Why am I tied up?!'

Gill ignored the question, raised three fingers.

'How many fingers am I holding?'

'Can you untie me.'

'How many fingers am I holding?'

'Can you just undo my fucking hands!'

'Language, Timothy!'

'Why am I tied up!?'

'I just want to make sure you're not concussed. How many, baby? This is important!' Gill held her fingers firmly.

'Are you serious?!'

'See if your vision's OK.'

'Fuck off!'

'Why're you being so aggressive!'

'I have no idea what's going on, but can you just untie me, please!'

'Not if I think you're ill. Please, baby, this is important. How many fingers am I holding up?'

'Three!'

'What a relief! Well done!'

'Oh my God!'

'What?'

'Oh my God!'

'What's wrong?!'

'Oh my fucking God!'

'Brolly, what's wrong!? You're scaring me!'

'You hit me with a frying pan!'

'Oh, that . . . It's not how it seems.'

'It's exactly how it seems! You jumped on me and then as I was getting up, you hit me with a fucking frying pan!'

'The frying pan was a bit of a mistake.'

'You don't hit people with a frying pan by mistake, Gill!'

'I just wanted to have a grown-up conversation with you before you actually . . .'

'HEEEEEEEELLLLLLLLL—!'

Gill exerted her weight onto Brolly, clamped her hand over his mouth. His jaw locked, his head sank into the pillows, he continued screaming as best he could. He sounded like the drone from a remote-control toy aeroplane. He ripped his head back and forth, up and down, but failed to dislodge her grip, damaged the inside of his lips as her pressure bloodied them against his teeth. The scream burned his throat, ripped it. He started coughing and Gill released her grip. She picked up the pink card and fanned it over his face as if cooling him would stop his discomfort. His cough slowly decreased to a splutter.

'Happy Valentine's, lover!' she proffered genuinely enough.

'What!?'

'Happy Valentine's, darling!'

'Are you kidding!?'

'Not at all! It was yesterday but, you know, you were still unconscious then and what's a day between lovers. Happy belated Valentine's, baby!' She ripped the card open with an excitement that suggested it was given to her, not by her. 'Ahhhhh! Isn't that sweet!? Look! That's so cute!' She grinned with a little girl's delectation for the sentimental as she showed him the card.

On a furry white carpet, two kittens, one ginger, one tortoiseshell, leaned romantically against each other, their fur mingling, their stripes conjoining. The ginger's emerald eyes gaped like an enchanted ocean as the tortoiseshell's grey eyes shone like brilliant diamonds in a sludge of tar. Their togetherness was touching, their sense of belonging, of needing nothing but each other, inspiring. 'Let me read what it says inside.' She opened the card. '"I love you, Brolly! Now and furrever" – that's spelt F-U-R-R – you know, like fur. "I love you, Brolly! Now and furrever and hope we'll always be together. Your best friend, your biggest admirer and your heartfelt lover, Gill." I put six kisses at the end and bought you the rose and some chocolates. I thought we could share the chocolates 'cos I'm guessing you haven't bought me anything?'

'Errrrr . . . No . . . I've been all tied up.'

'That's what I love about you, lover, your sense of humour always shines through . . .'

'It wasn't a joke!'

'I suppose it was a double entendre, as they say en France.'

'We need to talk.'

'OK!' Gill sounded like an overenthusiastic gym teacher excited at the prospect of jumping into a cold shower.

'So, erm . . . I can see you've gone to a lot of trouble to . . . look after me . . . But . . . can you undo my hands, please?'

'I will . . .'

'That'd be great,' Brolly responded, not quite believing his release would be so simple. Gill stared at him but didn't lift a finger. Or a hand. Or anything. Brolly stared at her as she shifted her interest to the box of chocolates. 'Can you do it now?'

'I thought I might open the chocolates first.'

'Maybe you could undo my hands first, then the chocolates.'

'Chill out, baby! No hurry!'

'Well, there is, actually. Can you just bloody untie me!'

'No. And if you're going to be like that, I'll eat all the chocolates by myself!'

'I'm on a diet so I don't know why you bought me them in the first place!'

'Fine, I'll eat them all myself.'

'Fine!'

Gill ripped the plastic with her front teeth and opened the box. A cocoa eruption enervated her nostrils as she detached the corrugated protective layer. She swooned. Dribbles of delight moistened the inside of her cheeks. She slobbered over which to choose first. Whether to read the taste guide or go for pot luck. She opted for the latter, closed her eyes and grabbed her first token of affection. It was shaped like a dome but had a coffee bean on its top. She ate it, investigated its texture.

'Mmmmmmm, coffee praline, methinks!!!!' Gill blindly plucked another one, round, with an almond on top.

'Can you untie me now?!'

'These are delicious. Are you sure you don't want one?'

'Gill, please – just untie me!'

'Go on, be a devil! Forget about your diet! Just one. They are yours, after all.'

'Yeah, an' that's so bloody typical of you. Buy me chocolates and eat them all yourself! HEEEEEEELLLLLLLL—'

Gill chucked the chocolate (a dark cherry liqueur) down her throat and grabbed the sock she'd discarded on the bed. Brolly head-banged like a rocker as he resisted her efforts. Her hand muted his noise and her weight defeated him. She stuffed the sock back into his mouth, stuck the tape over it, grabbed everything, including his sweets, and wobbled out of the room with regal haughtiness and self-righteous slight.

Brolly slumped as Gill slammed the door. His hope deflated. His despair soared. His life crashed to the bottom of a deep, dank well, infested with rats preying on rats, tufts of flesh, the softest pillows. He curled the rope around his hands and ripped and tugged and pulled. Harder than before and for longer. Staccato jerks seared his palms, disfigured his wrists, savaged his thumbs. Nothing gave, nothing cracked, nothing split. Nothing except his spirits. He screamed again. Shouted. Cried. His veins popped. Down the side of his head and all around his throat. His eyes bulged, amphibian-like, until they too almost popped. The sock muffled his pleas, made them negligible. He sliced his incisors against the sock, tried to lacerate it, to cut it, wondered if anyone had ever eaten their ex-girlfriend's sock before. His teeth grated against each other, sent shivers of enamelled discomfort through his jaw, down his spine. His jaws started to ache, his ears started to ring, his mouth started to taste unpleasant. He hoped Gill had, at least, washed her sock before she'd gagged him with it.

He ransacked his brain's flightier fancies, remembered all the films he'd seen where secret agents, rugged captives, morally wronged saviours of humanity had escaped maximum-security cells. He mulled over his limited options, figured it couldn't be so hard to escape what was, in essence, his own bedroom. He wished he could somehow make friends with the vermin that surely lived under the same roof as he did. Mice, ideally. Rats, if necessary; he wasn't choosy, he was desperate. The only plan he could come up with, as ridiculous as it sounded, was to gnaw through the rope that bound him.

That evening, a beautiful smell wafted up the stairs. It conjured up fractured sunbeams cascading through Colosseum columns, heart-warming breezes rippling over gondolas and canals, chestnut-haired beauties clattering cappuccino cups over stolen glances. Brolly's stomach growled, voiced its approval, but his conscience roared back; even in this wildcard situation, he was, technically, still on a diet. Not that Gill would necessarily share what she was cooking, but he thought it likely. His common sense and instinct for survival joined the fray, sided with his stomach, which in the end spoke for them all: he could only free his teeth by ingratiating himself with Gill, by mimicking her interests and sharing her passion. By eating, basically. His conscience bowed out gracefully and Brolly waited with bated breath and swooning nostrils until he heard Gill exit the kitchen and slip into the stairlift.

She put both American Hot pizzas, large in size, on the chairs and smiled at Brolly. The smile was almost apologetic. 'Look, I just wanted to say . . . I know this is all a bit weird and I'm sorry about everything, I really am, and I know we didn't get off on the right foot earlier but I wanted to let you know . . . I wanted to let you know I'm not planning on keeping you here forever like a complete psycho . . .' Her words hung in the air like Charles Manson's jockstrap. 'I just need time to get used to your decision, to you not being here . . . I mean, I know that doesn't make much sense 'cos obviously you are here, but . . . I suppose I wanted to spend some more time with you, like we used to, eating together, getting pissed together – I mean, we did have some great times, didn't we?' Brolly couldn't lie, nodded. 'I'll untie you in a minute, but yeah, I just wanted to reassure you that nothing's going to happen to you and I'll look after you and at some point, I'll let you go and we'll pretend this never happened . . . How does that sound?' Brolly nodded again. 'Great.' Gill leaned over and tore off Brolly's gag. Brolly moaned. She pulled the sock out. He took a deep breath.

'Maybe you could just untie me now and I'll stay for a while? However long you want? We can do all the things we used to. I can even come out of retirement for the Carpenter's Arms tomorrow. Imagine that! The place'd go crazy!'

'I dunno . . .'

'Why not?'

'Well, you know all those films we watch when the victim has a heart-to-heart with her kidnapper and she promises never to tell anyone about the kidnap if he lets her go?'

'Yeah.'

'And we always go, duh, yeah right, like the nutcase serial killer's really gonna let you go because you've asked him nicely . . .'

'Yeah . . .'

'Well, yeah . . .'

'But you're not a nutcase serial killer, Gill.'

'Just a serial nutter sometimes. As I said, I just need to do this in my own time.' Gill helped herself to a slice of pizza. 'Mmm! Nice.' She fed Brolly the rest of it. He couldn't deny the pizza's swarthy slickness, its Roman charm.

'Can you at least leave the sock out of my mouth?' he asked as she picked up a second slice.

'Maybe. If I think I can trust you not to shout.'

'If I promise not to shout.'

'If you promise not to shout and when I'm in the house, I suppose so.'

'I promise . . .'

Gill was true to her word and as soon as she exited the room, he clamped his teeth against the rope on his left and started to bite on it, but the technique felt wrong, like trying to push a pumpkin through a doughnut. Instead, he slid his teeth sideways, back and forth, so that his incisors' minuscule ridges became little saws. His jaw's repetitive click, the cartilage rubbing against cartilage, rang through his brain. The rope tasted of building site practicality and chemical suppression and after Brolly's lower lip split from the chafing and stretching, the rope also tasted of red-blooded cunning. Gill went to bed and snored. His stomach gurgled. His saliva stuck. The wind whistled in support. Time clung to him like an old man to fading memories and occasionally he stopped to test the hoped-for indentation with his tongue, the sign that his escape plan was more than a poor man's 007 lunacy. His gnawing made barely a dent in the rope, but the next morning he stuck his teeth back into it and, like a professional naysayer, started to disavow the truth.

His jaw became stiff, his neck crooked, his fatigue groggy, but at some point, one morning when Gill was taking a shower, he slipped the tip of his tongue over the rope and was encouraged to discover a groove. It was a small groove, chicken fry recompense for his Herculean sawing, but a groove nonetheless. As he continued, the boredom started to dull his senses and the rope bully his gums. It drew more blood and chafed more flesh. His mouth became a ravaged and raw mess of virulence. But it didn't stop him, it couldn't stop him; it was his mission, to gnaw. It was his new meaning in life. His discomfort signalled his slow journey towards freedom.

As soon as Gill pushed his bedroom door open, it hit her in the face, right between her nostrils. 'Bloody hell, mate!' She sunk her cheeks under her sweatshirt and made a tent pole out of her nose. 'I thought you'd become constipated again.' She hobbled over to the curtains and peeked behind them. The neighbours' curtains were closed. Their curtains were always closed. They were extremely bad neighbours if you wanted a Prosecco-over-the-fence, BBQ-on-the-lawn relationship, but great if you wanted to tie your boyfriend up and keep him captive for a few weeks. Gill ripped open the curtains, opened the windows, fanned damp air into the bedroom. She pulled the tape off Brolly's face and the sock out of his mouth.

'I thought I could hold it but I couldn't. Sorry,' Brolly said with a soft loo-roll yearning.

'How long've you been lying in it?'

'Most of the day.'

'Oh God. I'm sorry.'

'Can you not just let me go, please!? This is . . . I don't know what we're doing here. This is so humiliating. It's just . . . I just don't understand why you're doing this. The longer you keep me, the harder it'll be to let me go and I promise, with my hand on my heart, I won't tell anyone, I'll just leave.'

'But that's the whole point; I don't want you to leave. Just . . . Just gimme some more time. I just need time to work out what I'm going to do.'

'You're going to let me go and carry on your life without me. It's as simple as that.'

'But I don't want my life to be without you. I just want things to be how they used to be. I want you to be fat again!'

'I don't think anyone's calling me slim just yet. Can you untie me so I can clean myself up at least?'

'Pull the other one, you'll just leave!'

'HEEEEEEELLLLLLLLLPPPPPPP!' HEEEEEELLLLLLLLLPPPPPP! HELLLLLLLLPPPPP! HEEEELLLLLLLLLPPPP!!!' Brolly's throat dried quickly, his scream grew hoarse. The louder he shouted, the more it disintegrated into fractured aural abstractions. Gill pulled back the bottom half of the duvet and whacked Brolly's shin with her walking stick. 'OWWWW!!!!' His body writhed in pain. She closed the windows and the curtains, grabbed his sock and tried to stuff it into his mouth, which he clamped shut. He pulled his face away from her, ripped and yanked and tugged at his ropes, thrashed his body, kicked his legs. His faeces slurped out of his backside, slapped against his thighs. The air from under the duvet escaped, made its way to his nose. He coughed in disgust. She forced the sock over his face, rubbed it into his mouth. It made no impact on his clenched teeth. She pulled at his chin, mauled his forehead. He thrashed his head back and forth. She punched him on the side of the face. His mouth gaped open. Gill shoved the sock in.

She taped his mouth and stepped back. Her breathing was short and desperate, her whole body quivered with indignation. But she noticed something. Homed in on the anomaly as if her vision was a lens and she'd just sharpened its focus. She tasted a pang of nausea as she inspected a semicircular groove around which the rope was flecked with a darker hue. She dug her nails into it and realised what it was.

'You arsehole! You've been trying to escape!'

CHAPTER 46

'GILL! 'NOTHER DELIVERY!' Gay Keith shouted as an Amazon Prime delivery man flatfooted it to the till. The package was the largest she'd ordered, the kind children dream of finding under their Christmas tree. Solid, bold, hearty, with a size to elicit whimpers of delight, although, at just under a metre square, it was, in fact, two orders of the same item.

'On the floor, please, mate . . .' The delivery man did as instructed. Gill wiped a slash of processed ham off her lips. He held out his electronic pad; she signed.

'Bloody 'ell, Gill, how many more presents!?' Potatohead asked, impressed with the size of Gill's unwavering affection for Brolly, her deep pockets, her desire to celebrate their undying love, their eleventh anniversary, a fabricated date no one could refute.

'Just one more. Supposed to be coming this afternoon.'

'Brolly's a lucky man.'

'That's what I keep telling 'im!'

'So what is it?' Gay Keith joined in.

'We been through this before,' Gill teased. 'If I tell you, I'll have to kill you an' I don't wanna do that so I'm not gonna tell ya . . .'

Gay Keith bent down, tried to pick it up, struggled to find

purchase on its side as the smooth cardboard slipped out of his clutch. He tipped the box and grabbed diagonally opposite corners, one at the top, the other at the bottom.

'Not as heavy as I thought,' he said and shook it.

'Don't shake it.'

'Too late,' Potatohead added unhelpfully as Gay Keith stopped, uninspired by the package's tight-lipped secrecy, its obstinacy, its refusal to even hint at what hid inside.

'Yeah, well, don't shake it again.'

Potatohead sidled around to the package and immediately ignored Gill's demand.

'For fuck's sake, Potato, wha'did I just say?'

'Yeah, you said don't shake it. I jiggled it. With love.'

'Sounds like you were wanking it,' Gay Keith observed.

'Yeah, wank yourself, not my bloody presents. Just . . . Just put it down, will ya, an' get back to work!'

Most of the chains resembled obnoxious TV presenters, glistened brightly but were cold-hearted, lacked personality, faked interest. A few hung more anonymously, less shimmying. Gill fondled a couple, rubbed them as if hoping to find a misplaced genie, vaguely wondered if she should cancel the people carrier she'd ordered, return her purchases and set Brolly free. She exercised her thumb. Repeatedly clicked the carabiner she'd opened after Gay Keith and Potatohead had gone home. It clicked like a broken metronome. She fastened it around one of the duller chains with larger links. It fitted perfectly. She tugged. Was pleased but unsurprised when nothing gave. Grabbed the foot-long bolt cutters that hung parallel to the chains on her right. She measured out a length and a half of her arms' stretch. The chain's unravelling sounded like a convict's slow boat to China. Or Australia. Gill clamped a link in the bolt cutter's mouth and squeezed. A C-shaped link clattered to the floor.

Wearing the chain around her neck like a heavy metal feather boa, Gill staggered over to the pulleys and slid the links through one similar to the one that hung above Brolly's bed. Her hands were hot and sticky, like toffee pudding. She gripped the chain to cool them before threading it through the pulley. The fit was tight but she didn't need a larger one and that pleased her.

Gill's recent acquisitions preened and pouted on the kitchen table like prostitutes on parade. Their wrapping paper and boxes littered the floor like easy-to-access garments. She guffawed as she inspected them, still uncertain if she'd really go through with her plan. She grabbed three beers from the fridge and a bar of Cadbury's Big Taste Toffee Wholenut from the confectionery cupboard. She ripped open the chocolate and chomped on it like a beaver chomps on wood. She drank a beer as she crushed twelve pills with a serrated knife. The beer relaxed her and she added a thirteenth pill, unlucky for some, and crushed that, too. With the side of her hand, she swept the powder into a pint glass.

Discomfort muddled her face as she hobbled into Brolly's bedroom. Her steps were practically poodle-like, her gait bent and crooked. She wheezed non-stop and crashed onto the nearest chair. Her relief sounded like a steam train's whistle. It warned its passengers of impending danger, possible doom. She placed the pint glasses next to the Valentine's card and, after regaining her breath, pulled the gag from Brolly's mouth. 'Hey, baby, how you doing? How was your day!?'

'Why are you even asking such a stupid question?'

'Oi! Oi! Bit tetchy! Obviously not so good!' Brolly rolled his eyes, shook his head dismissively. 'But no worries, I thought you'd like a beer?' Brolly wanted to say no. Had to say no. Absolutely, irrevocably no. He didn't want to fraternise with the enemy any longer, he wanted to flex his willpower, lift weights with it, bend metal bars with it. He wanted to parade his single-mindedness in front of Gill like a slim new girlfriend who only ever wore high heels and miniskirts.

'Yeah, alright.'

CHAPTER 47

When Brolly awoke the next morning, he wasn't quite awake. His eyeballs melted out of their sockets, his brain oozed out of his ears. In front of him, the cupboard danced jazzily and a new noise, a chainsaw for children, retched from the depths below. He couldn't remember falling asleep or having more than a couple of beers and apart from the waft of fried bacon and sausage, something felt wrong. His jaw ached and his breathing was more agitated than usual. Everything felt wrong. He cursed aggressively. Or tried to curse. A hollow groan replaced his intended words. His heart thrashed around his ribcage like a vegetarian in a steak restaurant. He worried his tongue had been cut off but he wiggled it. It flickered against something unnatural. A circular ring. The ring tasted of leather. Brolly bit it. Chewed it. Clamped it. Tried to crush it. To spit it out. Inside the leather was metal. It didn't give. It was held in place by harnesses either side of his mouth. Bolts of panic shot through him. He tilted his head to the rose, which had lost a petal overnight. He ripped and tugged his hands. They were clamped in shiny handcuffs, which were locked to a dull metal chain by two carabiners. The metal against his bone cut deeper into his flesh than the rope. He reached for the left carabiner, for its screw that covered the hinge. His heart pounded deliriously, an easy fix, a quick escape. But it didn't unscrew, didn't budge. His fingers slipped around and around the screw's metal plate. He tried the other one, noticed a bauble of glue; it was stuck. He screamed. His scream sounded like a sex doll with a puncture in it. No one heard it. No one cared. The scream hurt and a tidal wave of emotion collapsed over him. Brolly's scream blundered into a cough, the cough careened into a whimper, the whimper collapsed into a sob, the sob burst into a bawl, the bawl plundered his nerves, wracked his bones, wobbled his flesh. And just as he thought his reservoir was lowering, soon to reach empty, he heard Gill collapse into the stairlift. He heard the machine's familiar metallic gurgle as it started to inch towards him and he tried to clear the tears by blinking.

'Morning, lover!' Gill bounced through the door as if she'd just played badminton and won. In each hand she carried what looked like more pints of beer. A long plastic tube curled around her neck and from one end hung a mustard-coloured funnel. 'You probably notice something different about today? Apart from the obvious. Taxi Rob had to take his mum into a care home, poor thing, so for the first time in God knows how long, I won't be going to Bellybusters this morning so, er . . . So, I decided to do a bit of my own culinary experimenting, put some fat back on your bones, especially now we've got a blender!'

In an oxymoronic land, somewhere between Slow Dawning Dread and Lightning Speed Precision, Brolly realised that Gill wasn't brandishing more pints of beer. He growled and ripped his head away as she leaned over him. 'Don't be a spoilsport!' She aimed the tubing into his mouth and he started to thrash his head back and forth. Petulantly. Preventively. Painfully. His neck clicked and clacked. The chains rattled and rollicked. His brain smashed against his skull. Gill blurred in front of him. Doubled in width. Grew extra eyes, eyebrows and nose. Gill didn't engage in his struggle; she had all the time in the world, so finally, before he head-banged himself into an unconventional suicide, he stopped. Gill inserted the tube through the gag and into his mouth so that he resembled a human foie gras experiment. She held the funnel almost a metre above his head and poured her first homemade Full English smoothie, the first of four, down his throat.

The return journey from Asda that afternoon was jerky. Stop and start down the Old Kent Road. Stop and start down Humphrey Street. Stop and start down the Walworth Road. Sitting alone in the Viano with Taxi Rob felt like it had the previous weekend: illicit. Not with thrashings of electricity but certainly with some sparks. And in the dark, too. For the first time ever, Gill regretted not being able to ride shotgun, to sit closer to him, to study his physiognomy from the periphery of her vision, to catch his eyes, to reciprocate his cautious flirtation.

Rather than her usual position behind the passenger seat, she sat in Brolly's regular spot, behind Taxi Rob but to his left. Where she could revere the shine of his spanking new biker jacket, not dissimilar to Blue-Eyed Pete's. Where she could infantilise his pointed pixie ears. Where she could romanticise how he steered the wheel, how he manhandled the gearstick. Where she could respond to his frequent gaze in the rear-view mirror with a vital smile, a chirpy positivity, a ripe femininity.

'So d'you think Brolly's got the virus? It's been a week, now.'

'Over a week. Hard to say, but I don't think so. He seems OK in his own way but he's still in bed, completely wiped out. I mean, he's talking an' everything and eating OK so, you know, it will pass, whatever it is, just seems to be taking longer than if it was just the flu.'

'Don't wanna be rude, but I wonder if it's anything to do with his weight. I've been reading the heavier you are, the more at risk you are. How you feeling? No symptoms?'

'Feeling great.'

''Cos you'd think if he had it, you'd have it by now.'

'Yeah, I know. Still got my appetite, still at work, so . . . No fever or anything, so it doesn't seem like I'm gonna catch whatever it is.'

'Maybe you're immune to it. Some people are, apparently. Has 'e seen the doctors yet?'

'Nah, they're all a bunch of quacks. GPs, too. Don't know fuck all about anything most the time. He's not strong enough to walk just yet and I dunno how we'd get 'im to see one. No way he could drive his mobility scooter. Well, I say that, but actually it was nicked so . . .'

'What!?'

'Yeah . . . Outside a pub a while back.'

'Bloody 'ell! How low can you stoop?'

'Yeah, I know. Imagine if he'd been properly disabled or something . . .'

'State of this country . . . I mean . . . Fuckin' disgrace, that is, but no surprise, sadly. But, well, you know, if 'e needs me, I'm here for 'im. If you want me to drive 'im to the doctors, I will. Brolly's as much a mate as you are.'

'Thanks, Rob, that's sweet.' The Viano stopped at the turn to Gill's street. Taxi Rob flicked on his indicator. Its digital seesawing sliced through the artificial alpine air. A flow of traffic halted their progress. Taxi Rob twisted around. His jacket creaked. He stared at Gill. Flashed his teeth with feeling. She welcomed his stare with open arms. He stretched out his hand and placed it on her knee. Around the flesh that dripped off the bone. Gill wasn't sure whether to squeak, squawk or squeeze back.

'And I'm here for you, too, Gill. I know how it is, you know, how it can get, with my mum, looking after someone you love. It's tough. It's lonely. And, you know, sometimes I wish I had someone I could talk to, someone who understood me. Understood what I was going through. I mean, I got the lads an' everything but, so, yeah, you know, and I mean, don't take this the wrong way but if you ever fancy going out for dinner, letting off a bit of steam, I'm here for you . . .'

Gill did take it the wrong way. Was pretty sure the wrong way was the right way. A double negative that equalled a positive. Two small waves that combined to produce a larger one. Two people who mated to produce a smaller one. Subconscious images revealed themselves, partied through her mind. Sunny walks in the park. Picnics in the countryside. Sitting on pub benches at twilight. Horse-riding. Netball. Rounders. Pimm's. Champagne. Strawberries and cream. Friendly neighbours. Happy families. A little Gill and a little Rob. Laughing and giggling. Screaming and shouting. Gleefully running around a paddock. The fresh-cut grass, an elixir to brotherly love and sisterly respect. A life away from London. A life more ordinary. Like the one she used to dream of, but with less magazine glitz. Like the one she used to have with her parents, but less wealthy. A life away from Brolly. Before Brolly. Before her rape. A life where she wasn't supposed to lose weight because she never had to put it on. A life where she was alive after forty. A life where Taxi Rob, good old reliable Taxi Rob, was by her side. Holding her hand. Caressing it. Kissing it. Hugging her in his arms as a gulp of swallows rejoiced above them, flew past in a beat of their hearts, in the shape of their hearts.

From behind, a car blared out its city disgust, its cigarette-butt pedantry, its dog-shit intolerance. Taxi Rob grunted. Unclasped from Gill and screeched ahead, down Gill's street. She grabbed a large fold of flesh either side of her belly button as if hoping to stabilise herself for the journey ahead, for the journey she'd already embarked upon. She looked into the rear-view mirror, caught his optimistic eyes.

'Yeah, alright.'

'Alright?'

'Yeah. Let's go out to dinner.'

'Great!'

She couldn't see his face but knew he was smiling. She was smiling, too.

CHAPTER 48

Time had become an increasing irrelevance to Brolly, no longer an arrow but a disintegrating dart, the tails of which had dropped off, the point blunted. Weekends were more focused, due to Gill's partial presence, but weekdays tended to blur. He lay in bed like a lazily shaped 'Y' and stared at the ceiling, which diffused like an infinite white plain in a snowstorm, pregnant with occasional undulating mounds, lacerated with partial crevices. From it, the naked light bulb hung like an anomalous ice-age spaceship with clumps of dirt stuck to its curve. His whole bedroom, his shrunken existence, seemed like an uncanny still life taken from someone else's impression of his memory of it.

The two kitchen chairs remained at his side and Brolly grew fond of the kittens' company but, at times, fed up with their singularity of expression, their cutesy-pie grins, which were not furrever, he kept reminding himself. The rose better represented his relationship with Gill, having shed all but one petal, which hung from the prickly stem with a dogged determination. He blinked his eyes and cricked his neck. An aeroplane exercised its metal lung, cried out a hoarse greeting, not specifically to Brolly but to anyone who cared to listen. Another one did the same but headed in the opposite direction, with a deeper, rougher edge.

Brolly imagined their vapour trails crossing in the azure sky directly above the house, sending a signal to the cosmos, to anyone who was worried about him, missing him: X marks the spot.

But that was the problem. Who exactly *was* missing him? If Tiny Tim had been alive, things would have been different. If Bangkok Dave had lived nearer, much nearer, had been called, say, Ipswich Dave, things might also have been different. His inbox was probably full of emails from disgruntled Suits You, Sir! customers but none of them had a personal relationship with Brolly, let alone knew his home address. The Harry's gang were Gill's friends so would have no reason to disbelieve her and she'd obviously spun an intricate web of deceit around Taxi Rob. Even his family, as estranged as they'd been, as close as they'd come to welcoming him back into their bosom, had accepted his disappearance as quickly as they'd accepted his reappearance. Gill had shown him the text messages she'd sent Tom and his mum and the response she'd sent back. Tom's unbridled enthusiasm to meet choked him up and his mum's technological savviness, her ability to communicate through emoticons alone, made him proud.

He yawned for the hundredth time, wondered if his chin would ever properly wag again. Being locked up was a pretty tedious business and he was bored. Bored, bored, bored. As much as he hated to admit it, he'd started looking forward to seeing his captor every evening. He cricked his head towards the wall to his left, wondered about asking her to decorate it so that he could watch the paint dry.

Gill circled her hands around the leather straps, found the buckle, undid the gag, pulled it out of his mouth. Brolly's jaw stuck open as if waiting for Gill to throw rubbish in it. She squeezed his thumb instead. His teeth clinked as he snapped his jaws shut. The cartilage cracked like a shark's tail in a hurricane. Distant bells rang in the back of his mind, black-and-white static flickered in

314

between his ears. He sloshed his tongue around his mouth, moisturising its dryness.

'Bloody 'ell!' Brolly managed before being tripped up by the woolly mammoth of his own yawn.

'How you feeling?'

'Strangely complacent, actually.'

'That's nice!' Gill sniffed the air.

'Yeah, I suppose so.' She pulled Brolly's duvet back. 'What you doing!?'

'Just thought I'd have a look . . .' The three adult nappies she'd joined together with masking tape were holding up remarkably well. His penis, covered by the condom catheter, poked out of a flimsy join. The catheter's tubing snaked down towards an empty Sprite bottle which leant precariously, halfway to the floor. She'd changed it that morning and it was half full again.

'I fuckin' love your tummy; it's amazing!' she said out of the blue with a glint in her eye, a sixth-form desire to explore with her fingers. His stomach bulged like a generous helping of ice cream on an apple pie. She stepped closer, traced his pastiness, tickled his curvaceous sides, poked his belly button, dug out some fluff, riffed over his raggedy hairs, fondled his stomach as if it were a new plaything, squashed the flesh together and let it drop, back over his ribs, onto the bedsheets. He purred. She laughed. 'It's definitely grown, you know!'

'You think so?'

'For sure, I don't think you're back to when you started the diet but you're getting there.'

'Hard to keep the calories off, easy to put 'em back on.'

'Suits you.'

'If you say so!' Gill grabbed Brolly's hand, its sea-sponge flabbiness, its aqueous generosity, squeezed it and held onto his fingers. He grinned goofily.

'You still pissed off with me?'

'I dunno, I suppose everyone has to do what they have to do. I was pissed off to begin with but I don't think I've got the energy to be pissed off any more. I know you've got a good heart and in a weird way, it's quite nice not to have to worry about going to work every day.'

'Jammy sod!'

'Well, I wouldn't go that far . . . I mean, I feel bad about letting my mum down but I like not having any responsibility whatsoever. I got a roof over my head, as much food as I want, don't have to worry about putting more weight on 'cos no one's seeing me, no one's shouting abuse at me on the streets, so . . . I dunno . . . My arms, well, more my shoulders actually, ache, but apart from that, mustn't grumble. I suppose it's a bit like being on a low-budget holiday but without any of the stress of travelling.'

'Fitting into a fucking aeroplane seat!'

'People pointing at us all the time.'

'Jeering when they're pissed.'

'Not being able to climb out of the swimming pool.'

'Breaking the fucking loungers!'

'D'you remember the last holiday we went on?' he asked.

'To the Canaries? Yeah, of course!'

'That was good, wan' it?'

'Yeah, classic, apart from the food portions were too small.'

'Yeah . . . And the sangria was watered down, but . . . Do you remember I used to call you Gilly?'

'You used to call me that all the time and then you stopped. Shame, that, I liked being called Gilly. Reminded me of being a kid, before all the shit kicked off, when I was actually happy. My dad used to call me Gilly.'

'Yeah, I remember you saying. But it's weird 'cos when I'm here, waiting for you to come back, I've started calling you – in my head, thinking of you as Gilly again. I miss you when you're not here, you know.'

316

'That's sweet.'

'Yeah. Can't wait for you to come home. Can't wait for us to eat together.'

'Well, I look forward to coming home, too, feeding you . . . It's like you're my little secret, makes me feel special, like you're my own little Tamagotchi.' Brolly laughed.

'Little Tamagotchi! Maybe that can be my new nickname.'

'Yeah, an' maybe you can start calling me Gilly, again?'

'Alright, Gilly.'

'Alright then, Little Tamagotchi.'

'So, what's for din-dins!?' Gill took a quick look at her phone.

'Ah shit, sorry. Gotta put the gag back on. Won't be for long, though.'

Ten minutes later, Gill re-entered his room with a smile that practically scalped the top of her head. But as she twisted sideways and sidestepped into the room, Brolly stared, instead, at the plastic bags that looked like balancing apparatus for her precariousness. Four in each hand, they were a cloying lime green but conveyed honesty through reliable typography: SIMPLY FOOD. His eyes goggleboxed. He gagged on his gag. His murmur of approval sounded like a giant marshmallow rollicking through the French countryside. 'Thank God for Ocado, eh!?' The delivery had arrived exactly on time. 'Gone a bit upmarket today. Marks an' Spencers! Bloody expensive but we're definitely in for a treat!' She divided the bags between the two chairs and undid his gag again.

'Very posh! What's on the menu, then?'

'This, for a start!'

Gill pulled out a slinky silver bottle, dressed to impress, unscrewed the lid, poured a generous shot of vodka down Brolly's throat and then hers. They both coughed.

'Just gotta bring up a couple more things.'

'Don't be long, I'm hungry!'

'I won't!'

317

She returned with her grab-and-grip device and a blender clamped against her hip. After plugging in the blender, she pulled the four bags from the chairs, placed them on the bed and placed the blender on the nearest chair. 'Alright, alright, let's see what we got, shall we?' From her trousers, she pulled a sharp knife and a couple of tablespoons. From the first bag she withdrew two packets of four Chocolate Honeycomb Ice Cream Cones.

'Oh wow!' Brolly remarked. 'Can't remember the last time I ate chocolate ice cream!'

'That's what I thought. Reckoned you deserved a bit of a treat, given what a good boy you've been!' she said with a Starbar twinkle as she pulled out another eight-pack, this time Milk, Dark and White Belgian Chocolate Ice Cream Cones.

'Bloody hell!'

She pulled out two tubs of Pistachio Ice Cream and two tubs of Percy Pig Ice Cream. She pulled out a tub of Mint Chocolate Chip Ice Cream and two cartons of Double Cream.

'Bloody hell! This is amazing!'

'You ain't seen anything yet, baby!' She pulled out a Chocolate Fudge Cake and a Colombian Coffee and Walnut Cake, two Extremely Chocolatey Party Cakes and two Chocolate and Caramel Millionaire's Cakes. She pulled out two more cartons of Double Cream, two cartons of Chocolate Milk, two tubs of Vanilla Ice Cream and four bars of Marzipan Chocolate. She pulled out two Rainbow Layer Birthday Cakes, a Victoria Sponge Cake, a Bramley Apple Victoria Sponge Cake and two Buttercream and Raspberry Jam Balloon Cakes.

'This is making me dizzy, Miss Lizzie!'

'Wha'did I tell you!? Party central tonight! Part of the fun's gonna be choosing what goes with what.'

'We're gonna be fucked after this!' Brolly said as Gill slugged down more vodka before giving him some.

'So come on, let's start! You do the honours, you choose first.'

'OK . . . Let me think.' Brolly scrutinised the treasure; every purchase sang out to him with the emotional resonance of an aria but together the shopping burst forth like a choir fit for a king. 'OK . . . Think I'm gonna go chocolatey. How about two Belgian cones, some Chocolate and Caramel Millionaire's Cake, some Extremely Chocolatey Party Cake, a couple of rows of Marzipan Chocolate, some Chocolate Milk and a couple of dollops of Double Cream?'

'I love it!'

The temperature had risen, the alcoholic fog descended. Brolly's folds of skin had started to stick together, to squelch, his head to roll, his vision to trip over itself. Apart from his slightly split, loosely conjoined nappies, he lay naked again on the bed. The duvet was pulled back to his feet and the remaining cakes, their crumbs, their creaminess, spread across his sheets. One vodka bottle lay comatose, all used up, in the shadow cast by Gill's chair; the other sparkled still, on the chair next to her, two-thirds empty. Boxes, cake trays and wrappers marked a radius of detritus behind and to her side.

'My turn!' Gill slurred as her limbs flopped, her eyes slid, her smile stumbled.

'Supplies running low, gotta make everything count.'

'Yeah, yeah, let me concentrate a moment.' Gill's eyes bounced over the remaining selection. She settled on the Buttercream and Raspberry Jam Balloon Cake, of which half remained. Brolly watched with a blurry-eyed, snarled-fork glaze as she scooped the cake into the blender, wiped her palm around its edge and licked. She grabbed the remaining slice of Bramley Apple Victoria Sponge and added that. She poured the melted remainder of the Percy Pig Ice Cream on top, followed by a pear-sized portion of Double Cream. She was about to screw on the blender lid when she had another idea and added vodka. Brolly laughed. Gill laughed back. His eyelids drooped but he swallowed pools of delectation and expectation. The blender buzzed. Gill stopped it, unscrewed its top, swigged a slow mouthful. 'Bloody hell, that's heavenly!'

'You got a dribble down your chin.'

'Oh yeah?'

'Yeah.'

'An' what you gonna do about it?' Without warning, Gill stretched out her arm and poured the concoction over Brolly's face. He groaned, moaned, laughed in delirious indecision; delight or disgust, he wasn't sure. His breasts quivered, his stomach rippled. The stodgy sweetness shame-faced his pallidity, submerged his wrinkles, eradicated his blemishes. She heaved herself onto the bed and relaxed onto him. Their mutual weight pillowed her fall and she licked him. Lapped him up. From the corners of his lips to the peaks of his cheeks, from the indentations around his eyes to the tip of his nose, behind his earlobes, around his neck, the inside of his earholes. She slid her tongue into his mouth. They pulsated together in debauched delight, in wobbly unison, but their enjoyment proved too frivolous, their humour too bawdy and they clashed teeth and bumped lips. She pulled away but encouraged by his radiating smile, his grinning eyeballs, she grabbed the blender and splashed more onto his belly.

'Bloody hell!' he giggled as it dribbled over his flesh. She stuck the jar in between his legs and grabbed his sticky, sweet, vodka-flavoured fat and kneaded it as if she needed it. Aggressively. Awestruck. With emotion. And dedication. With roly-poly reverence, with liposuction irreverence. The liquid moistened her imagination as her hands slid over his mounds and her fingers slipped under his folds. She grabbed and squeezed and pushed and pulled as he continued to express his delight. She corralled a puddle of goo into her right hand and stuck it over his face, stuck her fingers into his mouth, so that he could lick and suck the sweetness as she sank her whole being, her present and her past, her mouth, her eyes, her nose, into the unique creation that he'd started but she'd encouraged, that she'd nurtured, that she'd force-fed, that they'd grown together. She tongued his belly button and sucked his flesh, gave him love bites galore. Little pubic tummy hairs stuck between her teeth as she lapped around his mountain, across his ribcage. She swiped the thinning goo and gave more to Brolly. He couldn't get enough, still wanted more, always wanting more these days. 'I fuckin' love your tummy!' she said.

'It's all yours, baby! Do what you want with it! It's all yours!'

She ripped off her polo neck and threw it with erotic abandon to the floor. She ripped off her bra and threw that with salacious audacity. Her nipples winked with *Playboy* collusion, with centrefold allure. Her breasts dropped with glamour model unsubtlety, all the way to the bottom of her ribs. They couldn't decide if they were watermelons, marrows or oversized cantaloupes, prize-winning undoubtedly, all of them, whatever they were.

'Which one d'you want, Little Tammy?'

Brolly's eyebrows jumped off his head.

'I want 'em both, you dirty little bitch!'

'You're the one who's gonna be dirty by the end of this, you naughty motherfucker, you sexy little bastard!' Gill grabbed the jar and poured the rest of the Percy Pig concoction over her breasts. 'Ohhh God!' she giggled as her breasts shivered.

'Come on, come to Daddy!' Brolly ogled as Gill inched closer and closer, leaned in and pushed her left nipple into his already begging, gaping, desperate mouth.

CHAPTER 49

B rolly lay stiff as a corpse, practising for his own death, his stomach more bloated than ever, his breath subdued to avoid quickening the imminent decay. His eyes flickered. He forced them to stay open, contemplated the cornice overhead, but his eyelids were too heavy and he gave up almost immediately, exhausted. His hangover hurt. Very much. He missed Gill already, dreaded to think how she felt, smiled at snatches of memory from the previous night. Guffawed, meditated, floated on a marshmallow bed of oblivion. Listened for life signs from outside his four walls, a rebellious pupil, a glamorous air pilot, a sprightly salesman. He heard nothing, no wind betraying heartfelt secrets, no sirens caterwauling for justice.

But then . . .

But maybe not . . .

But yes . . . .

Once . . .

And twice . . . The chafing was so subtle as to be non-existent, a figment of his own imagination, a fig leaf of denial from his own garden of Eden. But there it was again. Gill had forgotten to close his bedroom door and the sound from the hallway travelled better than usual. He opened his eyes, focused on the light bulb, something more tangible than recovery from his headache. A thud followed. Not a knock, no knuckles, no bones; a soft thud. Twice and thrice, a goal in mind. He refrained from groaning, remained hypnotised by an imagined orgy of takeaway sludge slithering down his throat. A riotous medley of gin, jelly and trifle. But the noise grew stronger, more dominant, more repetitive, and the house started to tremble as if being assaulted by a battering ram. Brolly's brow furrowed. He wondered who it could be. No ordinary delivery man, no cotton-socked, cardigan-wearing Christian desperate to save his soul. The door lock splintered, the wooden frame swung on its hinges, bounced off the wall.

A hissing noise ricocheted through the hallway, snaked through the air. More thuds, slow, deliberate, intimidating. More hissing. Brolly grabbed the chain above his head and ripped violently. Doom-mongering droplets dripped from the tense ceiling, oozed out of anorexic cracks in the walls. An artificial splash of apocalyptic sunburn, rolling Heavens, searing Hell, burst from behind his curtains. The handcuffs thwacked against his wrists. The only thing that gave was his skin. He resisted a scream, held his tongue, swallowed his spittle, continued hurting himself, the flesh around his cuffs more distended than ever, more virulent, the wounds damaged, the damage wounded.

Like a scratch of black ink on his retina, a travelling whip investigated the upper staircase, flicked and retracted. He thought he'd imagined it at first but instinctively, gutturally, knew he hadn't. Incisors dripped, a proboscis sniffed, obsidian marbles for eyes, beady and penetrating, stared. A giant creature looked for its prey, clawed its way meticulously up the final steps, onto the landing. The alligator lizard, the crocodile salamander, satanic in its darkness, criminal in its menace, hissed like a scalding geyser, graffitied the air with its tongue as it slunk towards Brolly. The curtains started to burn, a beguiling sunset of fire-flickering

323

encouraged heatwaves in Brolly's direction, threatened blisters as he punished his whole body, tried to shock it into escape. The creature's talons clawed into his mattress, against the reinforced metal springs, dragged its glistening scales, its knuckled skin, its missing shoulders, up and onto the bed. Brolly tried to bite through his gag, kicked and howled, dripped buckets of vodka sweat, tugged his feet away from the creature's jaws as they burst open with no hinge to prevent an all-encompassing arc. A frilly black ruff burst with malignancy around its neck. Its jaw bit hold of the duvet, its head flicked the duvet to the floor. Tears trickled down Brolly's spongy cheeks as the creature forced its jaws, a gaping chasm of putrid indigestion, around his quivering feet, tore rivets of flesh from his shivering calves and slowly but surely consumed his lower torso.

Its tongue flagellated Brolly's flesh, its digestive tract, toe-curling in its acidity, splashed over his skin. The rank smell, pits and pendulums of sulphurous disdain, overwhelmed Brolly, which was probably for the best. The creature lacerated his buttocks, his back, his shoulders, his elbows, consumed his whole body, snapped its jagged marble teeth. Brolly's protest became nothing. He became nothing. Nothing more than the sum of his hands and wrists, which dropped onto the bedsheets with a ruddy splash.

Brolly awoke with a jolt, a passing attack of the heart. He snorted and convulsed; an overpowering heat baked his abdomen, a trickle tickled his forehead. His shut eyes pulsated with an invigorating clementine canvas, his nose picked up corkscrew wafts of grilled meat. He imagined sizzles but heard steelpan drums, laughing, giggling, flirting in the distance. His hand tumbled off his stomach, landed in something dry, dusty, infinite. He rubbed his fingers together, understood the sand that ground between them, heard baby waves lapping at a nearby shore. His nose twitched. Or more accurately, something twitched his nose. It also scratched at his cheek, lazily, friendlily, like a child trying to wake a parent. He opened his eyes.

'Oh!' His friend from Asda, the cheerful lizard, the rainbow warrior, threw its dainty tongue at Brolly's nose. 'Hello!' He gently scooped the little fella into his hand and sat up with a dissipating anxiety. He recognised the beach, recognised the bay, breathed in its beauty, marvelled at its God-like perfection. 'What are we doing here?' he asked as he stroked the lizard's throat in his cupped hand. The lizard blew its own balloon, puffed out its throat. 'Like that, do you?' As if remembering a vestigial shyness, a familial timidity, the lizard scurried out of Brolly's hand and onto the scorching, dazzling sand below. Brolly watched it go and remembered the woman of his dreams. He stood up and turned around. She was still there, flaunting her shapely but toned buttocks, her dental-floss thong, her elegant thighs, her cascading auburn hair. He still didn't recognise her but knew she was still his and he still hers. To her side, the aphrodisiac of a romantic lunch still beckoned. Brolly took a few steps towards her and cleared his throat. She flipped onto her back with the grace of a Russian gymnast, the elegance of a beauty queen. Brolly's breathing deepened as his cat-burgling eyes massaged her tanned breasts, caressed her groin, fondled her shapely legs.

'Ah, you're awake!' Brolly recognised that voice, he was sure of it, those beaming eyes, passionate and loving. He was sure he recognised those breasts, too, those nipples, that gap between the top of those thighs. 'You don't remember me, do you?' she asked good-naturedly.

'Have we met before?' he asked.

'You could say that.'

'Can't've been at the Wobble Club, you're too thin for that, although I suppose you could like oversized men. Do you like oversized men? It wasn't at the Wobble Club, was it?'

'Dunno what you're talking about.'

'Oh . . . Well, you'll have to give me a bit more of a clue, I'm afraid . . .'

'Let's say the beginning of our relationship was quite labour intensive . . .' Brolly blinked. Stared into the woman's beguiling eyes, was about to dive into them when his jaw dropped into the sand and practically tripped him up.

'Oh bloody 'ell! Mum?!'

'That's the one!'

'Bloody 'ell! You're quite . . . You're quite . . .' Brolly couldn't bring himself to admit he'd been sexually ogling his mother, but he coloured like a lobster.

'Nothing to be embarrassed about, darling, I was quite the looker when I was young.'

'Can you put your top on, please?'

'It's not like you haven't seen them before.'

'Please?'

'I don't know what your problem is, you used to love sucking on these when you were a baby!'

'Mum! Honestly!? Can you just cover up, please?'

'Let's be equal opportunists here. I do find *your* tits a little offensive, if I'm being honest: they're a lot bigger than mine, a lot saggier and a lot hairier. Maybe we both cover up?'

'Fine! Whatever!'

A light dew dulled the neck of the champagne bottle as it chilled in the ice cooler. Trophies from the sea, awards from the land coloured anaemic plates as delectable fruits jostled with shapely vegetables in nearby salad bowls. A tropical kaftan covered her modesties; a crisp T-shirt covered his.

'So what you doing here, Mum? It's lovely to see you again!' Brolly said as he chomped on a crab claw.

'It's lovely to see you again, too, darling, but I'm worried.'

'Worried about what?'

'What d'you think?'

'Because I didn't come an' see you?'

'I suppose if you want to be all English and euphemistic, yes, why you didn't come an' see me. I know you've been trying to persuade yourself what a great time you're having but it's not normal, you know?'

'What isn't?'

'What she's doing to you.'

'Oh, it's not as bad as it seems. She doesn't mean anything by it.'

'Darling, wake up! She smacked you over the head with a frying pan, drugged you with sleeping pills and then chained you to the wall. That's not normal behaviour. That's appalling behaviour. She's a monster! An absolute monster!'

'Takes one to know one,' he retorted defensively.

'What's that supposed to mean?'

'Look who's talking! You almost stabbed Dad to death.'

'Well . . . touché. But he physically abused me. And mentally abused me, too. Throughout our whole relationship. You never did that to Gill, did you?'

'No, of course not.'

'Ever?'

'No, never!'

'Well exactly, you're a gentleman.'

'So what're you saying?'

'I'm saying she's a psychopath and if you think she'll ever let you go, you're in for a shock: she won't. She could go to prison for what she's done and she knows it. You think she'll risk that? Of course not. Why would she? She may say she'll let you go but she's lying. She's got too much to lose and you may think you're having a laugh now, gorging on obscene amounts of food, getting pissed on vodka and cake, but . . . Yeah, I know what you've been up to, but the longer you leave it, the harder it'll be. If you don't act soon, you'll die in that bed. You'll die a morbidly obese death. Lonely, undignified, tragic. And that's not what I want for my son.' Brolly

327

discarded his crab claw and stared at his mum as if she was about to smack him. 'You know what I'm saying's true, don't you?'

'Not sure . . .' he mumbled. She stretched her hands over the table and offered them to him. He took them, felt her life line, her energy, her love.

'Time's running out, darling. The sugar, the MSG, all that rubbish is addling your brain and pretty soon you won't be able to think straight. Same with your body, lying there all day without doing the slightest bit of exercise. It won't be able to take all the abuse. It'll give up, just like Tiny Tim's body gave up.'

'He was a bit further gone than me and he only had one leg.'

'Different strokes for different folks. You need to do something, darling, and you need to do it quickly.'

'But I asked her already! She wouldn't let me go and then I tried to bite through the ropes but she replaced them with chains. No way I can escape even if I wanted to.'

'D'you remember at the Fox and Hounds? I was quite shocked by how big you'd grown and I asked what'd happened?'

'Vaguely.'

'Well, I've been giving it a lot of thought and I think your problem is you've never said "no". Not to that arsehole kid at school, not to your dad, not to Gill, not even to yourself. You've never said "no" and I think you need to be clever here, very clever. I think you need to use that to your advantage for once. Who knows, maybe it was some kind of protective mechanism all along . . .'

'I don't understand . . .'

'Have you looked at Gill recently? Properly looked at her?'

'What d'you mean?'

'Take a proper look this evening. To be honest, I'm amazed she's made it this far. So were those doctors at Christmas. She drinks like a fish, eats like a whale, doesn't exercise and can hardly walk any more, and, perhaps most incredible of all, she's still getting fatter.'

'I don't understand what you're suggesting.'

'She doesn't love you! And if she says she does, she's lying! You're her crutch. That's all. Her smelly, sweaty, slightly broken crutch. She's using you, leaning on you, keeping her demons at bay. She's not even your friend. Friends don't lock their friends up. Friends don't tie each other to the bed. She's your jailer, Brolly, and you're her captive. She's your enemy and you're at war with her. Fact. This is a fight to the death and if you don't want to die first, you bloody well better make sure she does. And quickly.'

A parrot squawked nearby. It sounded surprisingly like a pigeon. Brolly picked up his champagne glass, stared at it quizzically, didn't gulp it down but sipped from it delicately, savoured the lychee quavers of success, the white peach maxims of victory, knew that his mother was right.

CHAPTER 50

As Gill's breasts buffered against his face, Brolly no longer allowed fantasies of fluffed erections and flustered seductions to blindside his incarceration. As soon as she loosened the buckle, he spat it out – the gag, his words. 'Where've you been!? I'm hungry!'

Her vertebrae creaked as she groaned upwards.

'What you talking about!? It's only just gone eight. I went for some burgers and beer with the gang but sloped off early 'cos of you!'

'I haven't eaten for twelve hours! I'm bloody starving!'

'I'll get you something, but I'm knackered, Brolly, I think I need an early night. I don't think we can have another session.'

'I need to eat, Gill, otherwise I'll pass out.'

'Yeah, yeah, alright.'

'Well, don't just stand there. Hurry up!'

Gill's nasal breathing, her lungs, her wispy exhalations hated Brolly.

'Alright. What d'you want?'

'Surprise me for main but I want some blended sweet stuff for dessert.'

'We don't have any cakes left.'

'We need cakes!'

'I'll get some more tomorrow,' Gill said apologetically.

'Got any ice cream left?'

'Just some Ben & Jerry's, I think.'

'It's fine having Ben & Jerry's, but we need vanilla, big tubs of it; we should always have vanilla in the freezer so if we run out of cakes, which hopefully we won't after tomorrow, we can add whatever we want from the confectionery cupboard, make our own McFlurries.'

'Makes sense . . .'

'Yeah, and you're gonna have some as well, aren't you?'

Gill stood on the borders of a new country. The plains of freedom tumbled in front of her. She momentarily understood the wisdom of abnegation. Hesitated. Baulked at the prospect of more.

'I've been eating all day . . .'

'Of course you have, you're Gill "Don't Give a Bloody Fork" Monteith!' Gill giggled. 'You have to join me. It's part of the fun, part of being a couple, eating together!'

'That's true. I'll have some, just feeling a bit tired, that's all,' she said without conviction but with some flair, anything to protect her reputation, her top-of-the-marquee name. As she shuffled to the door, Brolly rebuked his empathy as she stole pockets of air through gritted teeth. He chastised his concern as she growled like an injured animal after stopping to ease a stomach cramp. He suppressed his worry as her buttocks wobbled unnaturally like basketballs. Just as she dropped herself into the stairlift, he shouted out.

'Gill!?'

'What?'

'Come back!'

'What!? I'm going downstairs to prepare your food.'

'Come back. I wanna give you something.'

'I'm too busy.'

'Little Tamagotchi wants to give Gilly something . . . Please?!'

'What is it? I just sat down!'

'It's a surprise!'

'Can't it wait?'

'No.'

'Bloody hell. Alright. Hang on.' Her concentration looked like raspberry ripple ice cream with extra cherry sauce as she heaved herself out of the stairlift and hobbled back. 'What is it?' she wheezed, too tired to grumble.

'Little Tamagotchi wanted to give Gilly a little kiss.' For a moment, Brolly thought Gill was going to cry. For a moment, Gill thought she was going to cry, too, but she didn't; she wrung her flannel internally and lit up her face with melancholic contortion. She offered her hand to Brolly's parched lips. 'Your lips, I want to kiss your lips . . .'

'I'd love to kiss your lips, too, Little Tamagotchi, but I can't.'

'What d'you mean? Don't you find me attractive any more?'

'It's not that. I can't. If I sit down again, I don't think I'll be able to stand up again.'

Apart from a small semicircle that she'd carved out for her own space, the boxes covered the whole kitchen table, stretched ten or eleven deep and fifteen or so high. She'd arranged them so the starters stood closest to the table's edge near the fridge, then the additional dishes and finally the main orders towards its middle. Chinese, Vietnamese, Indian, Italian, Mexican, Thai; in spending most of her evenings at home, Gill had gone to town.

The blender had come in more handy than she'd imagined; feeding Brolly all that food, fork by fork, spoon by spoon, would have been a nightmare, too time-consuming, too exhausting. The main trick was to work out how to liquidise the food that didn't come with a sauce. She grabbed a container and opened it. A soggy aroma sagged out. Inside was a murder of meat samosas. Gill bit her lips, rubbed her cheeks, stared at the contents, snacked on a couple and opened the onion bhajis, hoped to find inspiration in the unexpected. She found confetti-like distractions of coriander instead. Decided she could add lemon juice and maybe some water but didn't have any lemons and certainly wasn't going out to buy any. She twisted around to the fridge, ripped it open. Found comfort in the shelves of beer. Hoped a tin might refresh parts other beers didn't. She grabbed a tin, opened it, took a swig, contemplated liquidising cold beer and hot samosas. Grimaced. Contemplated liquidising hot beer and hot samosas. Grimaced even more. Contemplated liquidising cold beer and cold samosas. Didn't grimace, ejected a murmur of intrigue; not ideal but why not?

She prised open a couple of the mains. Lamb tikka jalfrezi and prawn balti. They were saucy. Very saucy; would liquidise easily, even if she chucked some rice in. She stole a king prawn, took another gulp of beer, shuffled back to the fridge; pulled out a lemon-infused tonic water, had a brainwave.

She poured the bhajis into the blender, then the tonic, then a large splash of gin from the box in the corner. Then flicked the blender switch and watched the liquid dirty into a rusty brown. The blender's buzz assaulted her ears. After about thirty seconds, she unscrewed the lid, smelled the concoction. It smelled of wacky invention. She lifted the jar to her lips and poured. She let the heavy, fizzy texture percolate before she swallowed, nodded happily and patted herself on the back.

'So this is an interesting one . . .' she wheezed. 'The first of two starters and all I'm gonna say is, you ain't never had nothin' like it, baby!'

'You're not gonna tell me what it is?'

'It's a surprise. Guess what it is.'

'Have you tried it?'

'Yeah, of course. It's not bad. Not bad at all, actually, an' I'll give you a little clue. If you have too much, you might get a bit tipsy.'

Brolly laughed. 'How d'ya work that out!?'

'Can't say any more, you gotta guess. Come on, baby, we've got a long evening ahead of us. It's gonna be fun. Just open your honey hole and let the games commence!'

Gill passed out in her own bed without pulling the curtains, going to the toilet, brushing her teeth or changing out of her clothes. She wasn't sure if she'd imagined the first shout but had no doubt about the second one. 'GILL!!??' She tried to ignore it but failed. The interruption riled her.

'WHAT!?'

'I WANT MORE!'

'I WAS ASLEEP!'

'I WANT MORE!!'

'SHUT UP, LET ME GO TO SLEEP!'

'I WANT MORE!!!'

'PLEASE! I'M KNACKERED.'

'I'M STILL HUNGRY!!!!'

'YOU CAN'T BE!'

'I AM!'

'I'LL MAKE YOU A BIG BREAKFAST TOMORROW.'

'NO, I WANT SOMETHING NOW!'

Gill held her tongue. Seconds ticked. She passed out almost immediately.

'GIIIIILLLLLL! I WANT MORE!!!!!'

Gill only had two large blender cups so the next morning Brolly upped his Full English breakfast portion from four to five because it meant she had to do more work, make an extra trip from kitchen to bedroom. He also drank as much liquid as he could so she had to expend more energy emptying his catheter bag. When she replaced it with the largest saucepan in the kitchen, he drank even more. She had to sit on the bed to put it on the floor, sit on the bed to pick it up. None of it was easy for her. He asked for more of everything, all the time. Every evening she joined in his gluttony and ate as much as he did. Every evening he insisted on bucketloads of alcohol. A couple of bottles of wine, a six-pack of beer, a bottle of vodka. The later he kept her up, the better. Sometimes, she fell asleep on her chair. Once she almost fell off her chair. He let her snooze, let her snore, enter into a deep slumber, wait for her breathing to find its natural resting rhythm before waking her to demand more.

Brolly wasn't sure how long a person could survive without eating but knew that without water, it was a matter of days. To ensure he wasn't laid waste by his own connivance, he persuaded Gill to place two bottles of water by the side of his bed so he could help himself during her work hours. Using two bands of masking tape, one closer to the wrist, the other closer to the elbow, Gill attached two plastic tubes to his left arm. One end stuck into each bottle, the other out of his wrist like artificially constructed veins. The tube almost reached the top of his middle fingers. All he had to do was co-ordinate mouth with hand and suck.

She did the same with his other hand and on the other side of the bed placed a small saucepan filled with sweet-toothed sustenance. She was happy it would help fatten him even more and he was happy that, should his plan work, he'd have some food, if you could call it that, to tide him over. The first blend she made was Mars bars, vanilla ice cream, chocolate milkshake, double cream, Maltesers and Reese's Peanut Butter Krispy Kreme doughnuts. It was so lip-smackingly delicious that they finished it together and she immediately went downstairs to blend another helping.

During the day, Brolly no longer wasted energy on trying to escape but snoozed. As soon as Gill returned, he kept her busy. The more he made her do, the better. More trips, more takeaway, more dessert, more alcohol. More everything. More standing, more cooking, more blending, more pouring, more lifting, more hobbling, more sitting down, more reaching, more stretching, more bending, more feeding, more leaning, more panting, more breathing, more everything, more, more, more.

CHAPTER 51

A dense calciferous fog clouded the edge of the store's bathroom mirror. A mottle of soap and water stained its middle. The whites of Gill's eyes were pink and her bags underneath bulged as if a backstreet doctor had injected them with goose fat. A cluster of sherbet-pip-sized spots clustered in the centre of her forehead. She tried to squeeze one. It brooded, throbbed viciously back at her. She pulled at her cheek, but it slid out of her fingers. Her skin looked like someone had rubbed cooking oil over it. She brushed her hands through her hair. Rivets of flesh, small tapeworm-like slithers, serrated her skull. A flurry of dandruff fell onto her shoulders.

'Dagz!' Gill shouted from the edge of the store's floor. Daydreaming in the Safety and Workwear section, Dagmara turned around. 'Come 'ere, will ya?' She dutifully did as asked.

'You alright, Gill?'

'Yeah, I'm alright, but I was just wondering . . . Well, between you an' me, I got another date tonight.'

'What!?'

'Yeah,' Gill smirked.

'Not with Blue-Eyed Pete!?'

'Nah, fuck him! It's with Taxi Rob.'

'Taxi Rob!? Bloody 'ell! You're a sneaky one!'

'Semi-date, I think, but, well, between you an' me, Brolly and me, we're thinking of splitting up . . .'

'What!? Since when?'

'I'll tell you about it later, but I was wondering if you could do me a favour an' go out an' get some make-up. I look like shit.'

'Yeah, no probs. I'll put it on, too, if you want,' she suggested with a skiver's delight, a shirker's foresight. 'I'm good at make-up. Took a course at home, once.'

'Oh yeah, alright, thanks, that'd be nice. Pretend I'm a bit of a celeb!'

'You are a bit of a celeb!'

'You know what? Fuck it. Let's make an afternoon of it. Fancy a bottle of wine?'

'Each!?'

'Why not!?'

Gay Keith and a tipsy Dagmara pretended to work diligently but, from different aisles, snatched glances at Taxi Rob as he stood outside Harry's in the early-evening downpour of artificial light. He held his arms stiffly by his side and flicked thumbs against fingers like a jangly schoolboy. Gill inched her way to the exit, painfully, slowly, as if in deference to the traffic's nearby torpor. 'You're looking very smart!' she complimented as she finally opened the Harry's door. A heart-shaped smile replaced Taxi Rob's rigidity.

'Ah, thanks, yeah, you know, thought I'd dress up a bit. All part of the fun, innit?' He'd purchased a designer sports jacket from eBay especially for the occasion. It wasn't a bad price but had a rip under the arm, which had been repaired before it had been dry-cleaned. It made him feel expensive and suave – two things he didn't usually feel. 'And may I return the compliment? You're looking very . . . fresh . . .'

'Ha. You may! I've been called a few things in my time but

fresh is a new one. Cheers!' Gill felt guilty about not making more of a sartorial effort but felt the skin freshener, the moisturiser, the face primer, the foundation, the concealer, the blush, the highlighter, the eyeliner and the lipstick more than made up for the deficit.

'I'm worried about her, you know . . .' Dagmara confided as the Viano pulled into the traffic's fray. 'But I dunno what to do. She won't listen to shit.'

'Yeah, I know, me too,' Gay Keith agreed. I tried saying something when you were buying all that make-up, fucking eating her . . . what was it? Third delivery of the day? But yeah, you're right, she won't listen.'

'What can we do, d'you think?'

'Dunno . . . Not sure we can do anything, to be honest. From my experience, you can only help people if they want helping and she really doesn't want helping at all.'

'Oh boy,' Dagmara sighed. 'Sometimes I think we encourage 'er and stuff, always join in, but the thing is, if we didn't, it wouldn't make any difference. She'd just drink and eat all that shit by 'erself. It makes me really sad.'

'Yeah, I know, me too.'

Gill grabbed some of her stomach and squeezed it, with difficulty, through the petite door frame of the bohemian-type burger bar, off Kingsland Road, on the way to Stoke Newington. It was small but atmospheric, designer lumberjack cabin on the inside, urban dilapidation on the out. The waiters were corn-fed, the candles educated to degree level and the menu an exercise in pontificating ponciness. Still, the burgers were 100 per cent honest-to-God British beef and the fries were all potato apart from the courgette fries, which were all courgette.

Some customers froze in hypnotic disbelief, others dipped chips in their organic beer, one burst into smothered laughter, but Al, the owner, Taxi Rob's mate, dropped what he was doing and bounced over. He looked like Rob's younger, more handsome brother. '"Don't Give a Fork!"' he chirped as he held out his hand. 'Your reputation precedes you! Rob's told me everything about you an' I can see now he wasn't exaggerating. It's a pleasure to meet such a legend!' The rapturous greeting played up to Gill's sense of self-worth and achievement. She also held out her hand and they shook.

'Likewise. Rob told me a bit about you in the van. Lovely place you got here!'

'Thanks! It's something I'm very proud of an' we're expanding very soon, which is what I wanted to chat about. I'm psyched to meet you, I really am. Have a seat and I'll be over in a minute.'

Sepia prints of final frontiers and old-fashioned explorers, how the West was won, hung along a wooden wall like cherished discoveries from obscure bric-a-brac sales. At Taxi Rob's behest, Al had reserved a six-person table and stuck one wooden bench in front of another for Gill to distribute herself over.

After they'd settled, Al returned with a pint of IPA for Gill and a Diet Coke for Taxi Rob. 'So, look, I'll be honest, I came to see you eat at the Carpenter's Arms before Christmas and was blown away. Had to go to a cocktail party that afternoon so I couldn't stay but, yeah, very impressed and . . . Well, look, I'm an entrepreneur, right? I run a few other businesses, too, but this is my passion an', well, we're opening in Brixton next month an' then Portobello Road soon after that. This's been a runaway success an' if those two go well, we got bigger plans, but here's the thing – we're always looking for new angles and I've been reading more an' more about this competitive food-eating thing . . .'

'OK . . .'

'Yeah, so Rob's been extolling your virtues for a long time now and it suddenly struck me that maybe we could offer some food-challenge angle ourselves.'

'And you want me to be the face of the food challenge?'

'Bingo!'

'You got my attention,' Gill said coolly. 'What you got in mind?'

'Well, we offer eight different quarter-pounder and fries so I thought maybe it could be a speed challenge, however many competitors, pit them against you. They'd all pay for the burgers, of course, you'd get yours for free, and if anyone beat you, we'd give them their money back.'

'An' you'd pay me, too?'

'Yeah. I mean, you know, pocket money, fifty quid per appearance or something, but . . . and obviously you'd eat for free as well . . .'

'I'd need free alcohol, too.'

'Yeah, yeah, no problem.'

'And what about my . . .' Gill froze. Imagined Brolly chained to his bed. To the wall. With the gag over his mouth. She no longer knew what to call him. Improvised. 'Sorry, what about my partner?'

'Brolly "The Bear"? Yeah, I saw him, too, obviously. He was great, but to be honest we only really need one of you and 'cos most of the contestants who do these things are guys, we thought probably just you by yourself'd be better . . .'

'Fair enough.'

'Yeah, so anyway, you know, we'd make a splash about the challenge on social media. Our mailing list's about a couple of thousand right now but it's growing all the time. We're also on Facebook, Twitter and Instagram and have our own in-house PR/ marketing so, you know, you'll get a lot of publicity out of it. I'm assuming you're on all the socials?'

'Nah, don't do any of that stuff.'

'You kidding me?'

'Never kid a restaurateur.'

Al laughed as if Gill meant it.

'Well, we'll have to change that. We can help you set all that stuff up. Probably Instagram's best for this kinda thing. Maybe a bit of Facebook, too. Not sure Twitter's necessary. But yeah, if you played your cards right, I reckon you could become quite a celeb. Definitely an influencer. You've got a pretty face and your – well, I hope you don't mind me saying but your size is . . . is . . . a sight to behold. It's very impressive and it's great you're so, you know, confident about it.'

'It's who I am.'

'Yeah, which I fucking love. Being happy in your own skin, doesn't matter where you're from, who you are, what you look like, how much you weigh, what sexuality you are; if you're happy in your own skin, you're a winner.'

'You've already won!'

'Exactly! And I can see that you're a winner, Gill, a fighter, too, 'cos no one ever wins without fighting and . . . Yeah, I reckon people'd follow you on Insta just like that.' Al clicked his finger and thumb. The click suggested fame and fortune, money for nothing and burgers for free. 'But yeah, you know, we'd want to take photos to begin with, send 'em out to our followers, start creating a buzz, merch as well probably, some kind of T-shirt for the competition, and who knows? If things take off, which I really believe they will, we might try to build you up as a brand. I can see calendars, I can see jigsaws, I can see mugs, you know – I think the future is very bright indeed!'

'Bloody hell!' Gill tried to look into the future, thought she could see it glistening somewhere over Al's muscular shoulders, and started to tingle like a doughnut in a vat of frying oil.

Over the course of the evening, Al brought Gill each of the eight quarter-pounders they served. All on the house. Each burger was named after an American city and differentiated by a gimmick – some, a beer or spirit infusion, others, quirky toppings. Gill had never visited America so couldn't tell how accurate the matchings were and if Al had asked her about the subtle differences between each burger, the conversation would have been short, but she enjoyed each and every one. When Al asked, more in disposable frippery than earnest importuning, if she fancied dessert, he was surprised that she did. In the vein of trying all the burgers on the menu (beef ones, at any rate), she opted to try every dessert as well.

'You've exceeded my wildest fantasies, Gill, I'll tell you that for nothing!' Al said as he brought the final dessert – chocolate brownies, salted caramel ice cream and piping-hot rashers of bacon – to the table.

'Told you, didn't I?' Taxi Rob said.

'You did, mate, you did. My only regret at the moment is it took me so long to meet this lovely lady!'

'Bet you say that to all the girls!' Gill blushed.

'Ha. Well . . . I'd be lying if I said I didn't say it to some of 'em, but one thing I'll let you in on, I don't say it if I don't mean it. Here, this'll blow your mind!' Al plonked the dessert in front of Gill. 'Mind if I join ya?' he asked. They didn't.

'So, correct me if I'm wrong but I kinda think I underestimated your talents a bit . . .'

'What d'ya mean?'

'Well, you wolfed down the burgers like they were snacks and then you had another six desserts, not to mention all the onion rings an' fries an' beer, and I kinda get the impression that you could've carried on if we'd had more to give you.'

'What can I say? I'm a pro!'

'Yeah, evidently. But it got me thinking and, well . . . I mean, how many quarter-pounders d'you think you could eat?'

'Dunno. At McDonald's, the most I've had is twenty-two, but if push came to shove, I could do more.'

'Yeah, alright, so this is something we'd have to work out, but what I'm thinking, right? Let's make one massive burger. I dunno, let's say nine or ten pounds, whatever, but we make one massive burger an' that can be another challenge. Maybe we start off with that, forget the eight smaller burgers. Seems a bit Wimpy, if you'll forgive the pun. We make that the food challenge instead. Not only see if anyone can eat it but if they can beat you eating it . . .'

'Alright.'

'And here's the genius, we name it after you: the "Don't Give a Fork" burger! So it'd be "The 'Don't Give a Fork' Burger Challenge!"'

'You'd name a burger after me?'

'Yeah, the publicity we'd get'd be sick. Go through the roof, it would. The brand, your brand, ours too, it'd explode. I reckon we could get in the *Evening Standard, Metro*, probably some of the tabloids – the *Sun*, the *Mirror*, maybe even on TV, too.'

'I fuckin' love it! I'd love to have a burger named after me!'

The return journey was quicker than the outward journey, the mood jocular and jubilant, the idea of Gill becoming a brand and a beef burger the main focus of attention. As they drove through the city towards Liverpool Street, past sleek towers with mirrored glasses, like a bunch of cocksure lads posing on a perpetual holiday, Gill asked Taxi Rob if they could drive over Tower Bridge.

He obliged and the closer they drove, the more she fantasised about parking nearby, walking to the middle of the bridge, hand in hand, marvelling at the architecture, gazing at the Thames, lapping up the ripples of light, the rainbow prisms of cityscape. But she didn't. She didn't ask him. Couldn't. Knew her fantasy was just that. Could hardly step in and out of the Viano these days, let alone walk halfway across the bridge and back, shuffle from one vantage point to another, bask in the shimmering glamour of the London skyline. Instead, she leaned against the window and stared up in silence at the bridge's arcing braces and its historical intrigue.

Taxi Rob parked outside Harry's and without allowing an awkward silence, he hurried out of the Viano to aid Gill's exit, which was clumsier and more agonising than he ever remembered. The distant half-moon tried its best to throw romantic beams over their goodbye but was diluted by much closer electrical impulses. 'Thanks for the evening . . . And for the introduction . . . It all sounds amazing . . .' Gill said in between snatches of breath.

'Thought you might be up for it . . .'

'Yeah . . .'

'Yeah . . .' And there it was, that awkward silence, the English reserve, the prepubescent stumbling block, coloured clumsily with black strokes and grey, lashings of exhaust and mumblings of motor.

'You do like me, don't you?' Gill finally conjectured.

'Yeah, of course.'

'No, but I mean, you know . . . "Like" like me.'

'Oh. Like that . . .'

'Yeah, like that . . .'

Taxi Rob was inexplicably drawn to the hubcaps of his taxi, carbon monoxide monocles, decided it was about time he should restore their sight. Clean them. Clean the whole vehicle.

'I would've thought it was pretty obvious, really,' he said, not looking at Gill.

'So why haven't you ever done anything about it?'

'I would've thought that was pretty obvious, too. You do have a boyfriend who happens to be a mate, too, so, you know . . . Some blokes might've fucked Brolly over but I'm not like that . . .'

'That's sweet,' she replied as he grunted in agreement, as if he was a dunce and he knew it. She pecked him on the cheek, something she'd never done before. She wrapped him in her arms and relaxed her head against his sinewy but homely neck. He rested his hands on the spill from above her hips and relaxed into her tender warmth and for a few very special seconds, until she broke the spell, imagined he'd died and gone to Heaven.

344

CHAPTER 52

The sun was shining like it was trying to make friends. Gill was sweating like she was trying to lose them. Even after she took her jacket off, rolled her sleeves up, she felt unnaturally warm, radiated a fireplace glow. On the way to work, she decided to grab a quick snack at McDonald's. McDonald's cooled her down; so did the five large Fantas she drank, half full of ice. She ordered the whole breakfast menu, except porridge and plain bagels, like usual. She also ordered three Big Mac meals. The idea of walking from counter to table and back again with the order filled her with dread so she asked the server behind the till for help. He obliged and she demolished her food with customary zeal.

As she drove around the Elephant and Castle roundabout, turned past the Tube station on the left, onto Borough High Street, neither on the road nor in the cycle lane but on the pavement, a siren crept up from behind, a caterwaul from her past, a hook into her subconscious. The traffic didn't immediately respond to the warning, but Gill did. She stopped, dazed. A palpitation in her heart rocked her breast, disturbed her brain. Her pre-Christmas hospital sojourn, a dirty memory in denial, flooded back. She worried the ambulance had been called for her, was chasing her, hurtling towards her. She couldn't think who'd called it or how the driver'd tracked her down, but she was sure it was for her. She twisted back and forth, looked for a cunning means of escape, a glitch in time, a cubby-hole in history, but suddenly felt oppressed by the concrete blocks and pillars and slabs that encroached upon her.

The road elongated like hand-stretched pasta. An illegally parked car melted like Easter eggs in a microwave. The pavement popped and buckled around her, cracked open like honeycomb champagne. She clenched her eyes, prepared for the worst, tried to hide, to will herself out of existence. Her strategy worked. The ambulance screeched past as Gill's breathing reached an irregular zenith. She almost waved her hands to flag it down. She wiped moisture from her face, found some on her neck, grabbed hold of her handlebars and held on for life, dear, dear life, as a dizziness threw her for six.

After parking outside Harry's, her left foot caught in her mobility scooter and she almost crashed to the pavement but saved herself with an instinctive placing of her walking stick. Her temples throbbed in time with her heart. Her tongue withered, her liver puffed and her kidneys kicked. Her pores oozed, her skin retched, her stomach thundered. The walking stick wavered under duress but remained steadfast and loyal. Gill sensed something wasn't quite right as she smashed open the store entrance with a force that suggested cruelty to doors.

The disruption interrupted Gay Keith's half-hearted restocking of nails. He jumped. Looked around with a self-righteous outrage that morphed into genuine worry as he saw Gill. Her face burst with a strawberry intensity, her lungs huffed with the puff of a one-lung, fifty-a-day smoker. He snapped up off his knees. 'You alright, Gill?'

She sweated fear as she shook her head. 'Get my chair, will ya?'

'Your chair?'

'From the till . . .'

Gay Keith scurried over to the till and grabbed Gill's chair.

'What you doing?' Potatohead asked while sipping from a steaming mug.

'Dunno. It's Gill.'

'What about her?'

'I'm not sure . . .' Gay Keith scurried back; Potatohead followed. Gill's raspberry ruddiness, its battlefield violence, had relaxed into a more benign psoriasis-like irritation. Her breathing had relaxed, too, more like a thirty-a-day smoker, albeit still with one lung. Her walking stick handle oozed grease and her trunks trembled. Gay Keith stuffed the chair under as much of Gill's backside as he dared without getting scatological.

'Get us a glass of water, will ya, Potato?' Potatohead rushed back a minute later with a pint of tap water, which Gill guzzled as if it was beer. 'Fuckin' 'ell!'

'What's wrong?' he asked.

'Dunno, just came over all weird. Just a bit hungover, I think.'

'Well, you do look like shit.'

'Do I?' asked Gill with a broken rasp.

'Yeah . . . Sorry . . .'

'D'you want us to call an ambulance?' Gay Keith asked.

'Fuck off!'

'Well . . . Potatohead's right. You do look like shit.'

For the rest of the day, Gill felt like she was sitting on the top of a skyscraper during a hurricane. Her vision racked in and out of focus. Little needles pricked her left arm. Her head rolled from side to side like a watermelon in a sailing boat. Bones scraped bones without lubrication, cartilage ground against cartilage. Sweat poured into her eyes, stung her with saltiness. She could smell her own body odour, increasingly ripe Stilton.

She shoved a chicken wing into her mouth. And another. And some fries. The fries, especially, relaxed her, grounded her. There weren't many left and they were cold but they reassured her that she wasn't about to crash off her stall. She dipped her fingers into the BBQ sauce, smeared it over her chin by mistake as the queue in front of her, three different construction workers, watched agog. A familiar sound brought her back to the present. Words. With meanings. Meanings she couldn't quite decipher, accented words, strange, guttural, London-street sounding but with a foreign twang. 'You alright, Gill?'

'Huh?'

'You alright?'

'Oh . . .' Gill noticed the queue. Wondered where the workmen had come from. 'Sorry . . . Think I spaced out for a moment there . . .'

'Why don't I do these purchases for ya.'

'Yeah, alright. Cheers.'

Dagmara served the construction workers but knew something was amiss because Gill didn't touch the remaining chicken, just stared into a distance only she could see, held on to the desk as if on a roller-coaster ride. Strands of her hair clumped together. Bulges challenged the fabric that constrained them. Moments after the final customer rounded the corner, Gill picked up the bucket of wings and vomited into it. 'Oh bloody 'ell!' said Dagmara as she placed her hand on Gill's shoulder. Gill gurgled and gargled but stopped as quickly as she started, her familiar ketchup-coloured complexion a pale lychee.

Only after Gill drove into the hallway and closed the door behind her did she greet Brolly, deflated, as if she'd left her joie de vivre outside, kicked it into the gutter. 'I'll be up in a minute,' she shouted flatly. He grunted as she hobbled into the kitchen, listened to a nick in the quietness, the hiss of a beer as it opened. He heard the second hiss and the third, too, and nodded his approval.

His handcuffs bit into his bloated wrists like guard dogs with locked jaws. A tramline of gore congealed all the way around the skin, a deathly white, a plague yellow around that. To make the case to Gill for loosening them, to make the spectacle even more convincing, he flexed his wrists, their muscles, pulled them against the metal to worsen the damage, to colour it more vivid. The jagged constraints jammed against his flesh, pressured his bones. The bones didn't give, the flesh did. His determination hurt but at least it hadn't yet turned green. 'Hey!' he said with faux cheer, forcing himself to be Gill's best friend after she unbuckled his gag and retreated. 'What's for dinner, Gilly?'

'There's still some Mexican left. I'll heat that up for you but I think I'm gonna retire early. I know I always say that but I mean it today. Really feeling cream-crackered.'

'You'll join me for dinner though, won't you?'

'Yeah, but we can't have one of our sessions.' Her face looked as if a mischievous kid had squeezed a bag of marbles under her skin and they'd shot off in different directions.

'As long as you undo my cuffs a notch or two.'

'What? To help you escape?'

'Not at all. I thought you'd be pleased!? I must be putting on more weight. They've really started to hurt. Look.' Gill looked at his broken skin, the torn flesh, the bloody smudges on the bedsheet under his hands. 'I'm worried they'll cut off my circulation.'

'If I let you go, would you really not go to the police?' she asked. Brolly stared at her with the duelling contradiction of piqued curiosity and ironic detachment.

'Is this a trick question?'

'No.'

'What? You finally thinking of letting me go?'

'I said I'd let you go sometime, so . . . Oh God . . .' she whispered as she started to swallow strangely, to pit her oesophageal waves against those ebbing from her stomach, to neutralise them, to cancel them out.

'What?' he asked.

'Nothing. Just my stomach.'

Brolly's head bounced up and down in sagacious slow motion. If he could have rested his chin in between his forefinger and thumb with the goal of making himself look intellectual, he would have. He wondered in earnest, for the first time, if his plan was actually working. He stared at Gill with heavy eyebrows and piercing eyes as she made no attempt to hide her discomfort, as she rubbed her left arm. 'I don't really know what happened here in the last month or so but with my hand on my heart, I promise I wouldn't go to the police if you let me go,' he said.

CHAPTER 53

The whole country had been lashed with the rain of pre-apocalyptic dread. It'd happened in China first but that didn't really count. Then Italy became a war zone and the threat became palpable. Spain followed and, shortly after, so did the UK, with a foppish disdain for the facts and a jovial shrug of incompetency. Gill was feeling much refreshed after her long sleep but since she didn't read the papers, her conversation about the country's much-anticipated lockdown was short-lived. Nonetheless, she witnessed the terror, the uncertainty, the ensuing egocentricity on every road, on every street corner, on every pavement. Drivers drove more erratically, dissected more red lights, honked more often. Pedestrians kept their heads down, their elbows out, trusted no one not to cough on them, to bump into them, smear the disease, pass on the infection.

Asda was pandemonium. Staff looked ragged and cross-eyed. Shoppers grunted like cavemen, lurched and ogled, roughed and rummaged, bandied trolleys like primitive weapons. Shelves lay devastated and chaotic, disordered and sprawling. Gill's temperature started to rise again, her heart to palpitate, her stomach to gurgle as she did something she'd never done before, something she'd always assiduously avoided. 'What's going on?'

asked Taxi Rob as she stopped at the fruit and veg section and bristled.

'What you talking about?'

'Well, you're not known for your love of vegetables . . .'

'Fucking hate the things! Completely overrated if you ask me,' she lamented, unable to resist a quick moan, as she spotted what she was looking for and grabbed two avocados.

The only other item that piqued Taxi Rob's curiosity, instilled him with a teenage jealousy, a heart-wrenching fear of missing out, was two bottles of champagne. Gill plucked them from a shelf towards the end of their shop. 'Celebrating?' he asked.

'Maybe . . .' she replied cryptically and without further elucidation.

In the car park, Gill grabbed one of the bottles while Taxi Rob packed the shopping. She stuck it under her stomach and clamped her non-walking-stick hand against her flesh to prevent it from falling out of her. As he returned the trolley, she dawdled around the rear tyre until he came back with a bounce in his step, a smile stretching across his face. She pretended to take a preternatural interest in the jet-black tyre, the sparkling clean hubcap. 'Is that alright?' she asked, nodding downwards. Taxi Rob took the bait, dropped to his knees, inspected the wheel, knocked its inner and outer edges with his knuckles.

'Yeah, I think so, why?'

'Oh, I just thought it looked flat.'

'No, it's fine,' he replied as he stood up and turned towards Gill, who pushed herself against him, practically fell into him and, with the force of her personality, pinned him against the Viano. Taxi Rob had missed his squashing sessions and felt an immediate rush of blood, a horseman's hurrah, to his boxer shorts. He could smell her breath as she could smell his. He concentrated on her eyes as she concentrated on his, nothing else, the whole world, the global pandemic a sudden irrelevance. Her softness excited him. She rummaged under her stomach and pulled out the champagne bottle, waved it under his nose.

'This is for you.'

'Really?!'

'For us . . .' she said cryptically.

'What d'you mean?' he asked optimistically.

'I want you to take it home and put it in the fridge. I need some time to sort everything out with Brolly but when I'm ready, I'll call you an' you can come over.'

'What you talking about?'

'I think we're splitting up.'

'What!? You an' Brolly!?'

'He will've moved out by then so maybe you could stay the night, too.'

'You serious?!' snorted Rob. Before he had time to further question Gill, she pressed her lips against his. He didn't need any encouragement, explored her cavity, grabbed a large ring of her flesh and held on tightly for what he hoped would become the ride of his life. Fireworks exploded above his head and he imagined a train speeding into a dark tunnel.

Maybe they would buy that fantasy house in the country, Gill thought, as their tongues mashed. Maybe she would lose a bit of weight and try for kids. Not too much weight, but enough. One kid, maybe two if the first one went well. She was reaching that age, after all, and she'd had more physical contact with Rob than anyone else in her life, ever, much more than with Brolly. And she enjoyed it. And he was kind. And gentle. And honest. And good-natured. And had a steady job. Maybe he was the love of her life. Not Brolly, but Taxi Rob.

After he dropped her off, Gill couldn't stop smiling, as if a weight she never knew existed had been lifted from her shoulders. He honked jubilantly as he drove away, down her charming and quiet street, along which leaves had started to sprout from trees.

The council had finally cleaned the graffiti off the bridge but someone else had graffitied it with 'Boris is a baboon'. A new-found clarity pumped through her veins, cleansed the last of her worries. Life was for living and, by God, she was going to live it. She took a deep, deliberate breath and encouraged the air's crispness to freshen her lungs. It fortified her resolve. She noticed a purple flower already in bloom, fighting against the wall to her side. She plucked it and smelled it, couldn't decide what it smelled of – self-preservation, optimism or the future. Maybe all three. It smelled good.

'Just putting everything away!' she shouted to Brolly, who didn't groan like usual when she walked through the door. She hoped he was OK. She contemplated taking the stairlift to check but assumed he was asleep. She hobbled to the kitchen and stuffed the champagne into the freezer. From the fridge she opened a beer and, rather than down it in one, savoured a few sips and prayed a lockdown would be announced on Monday. She could kill for a holiday, do with a proper rest, calm down from the madness of the last few months. Maybe even reflect. She'd never really reflected before but knew it's what people should do from time to time. Now she'd arrived at a crossroads, maybe it was that time. Time to work out how to progress with her life, with her body, with her career, without Brolly, with Taxi Rob. The beer made her woozy, glorified her grin, made her appreciative of Auntie Violet's generosity, the roof over her head, the four walls that protected her, the floor that supported her, the silence that engulfed her.

She unpacked the shopping and helped herself to a large box of Maltesers and a plastic tub of Haribo Kiddies. She placed the two avocados, a loaf of bread and a new pack of butter by the side of the cooker, next to the purple flower, and when she finished unpacking, pulled two trays from a cupboard, one cherry red, the other sky blue. She cut the avocados in half and peeled the skin off each segment. The task was more fiddly than she expected and did nothing to ingratiate the fruit with her but it didn't matter, she was doing this for Brolly. No matter what he thought of her, how she'd treated him, he'd been a massive part of her life and always would be, even if he refused to ever see her again, which she thought was likely. Avocado on toast had become one of his favourites in his dieting days and she wanted to surprise him, do right by him. She cut the avocado segments into small chunks and popped four slices of bread into the toaster.

She grabbed two wine glasses and the champagne from the freezer. It wasn't very cold but whatever. She placed the champagne in the middle of the cherry-coloured tray and the glasses on either side but slightly below. Collectively, they formed a pleasing and symmetrical triangle. From the cutlery drawer she took the key to Brolly's handcuffs and placed it below the champagne. She placed the purple flower beneath the key, picked up the cherry-coloured tray and took a few steps towards the door. The champagne teetered, the glasses and the key slipped to one side, the right glass crashed to the floor. 'Bollocks!' said Gill as she returned the tray to the worktop and kicked the broken shards, the shattered curves, to the side. She grabbed another glass from the cupboard and plonked it on the tray. She returned everything to its original position, pressured her thumbs against the base of the glasses, picked up the tray and shuffled, practically inched, her way to the stairlift, where she carefully lowered the tray onto the far side of the chair.

'Brolly!? You alright up there?' she shouted but still didn't receive a reply, didn't even hear the child of a neanderthal groan. 'BROLLY!?' She heard nothing, hobbled back to the kitchen with concern. She placed two plates on the sky-coloured tray as the toast popped up. She buttered the toast, used a fork to squash the avocado into it and cut each slice diagonally in half. Her attention was distracted as a ladybird hovered in front of her.

'Alright, mate!' she said amiably. It rested on her shoulder for a few seconds but disappeared behind her. She wiped her damp forehead with the back of her left hand. Her hand was shaking. She took a deep breath and exhaled slowly. She picked up the tray, turned to her right and shuffled out of the kitchen again. She laid the tray next to the other tray on the stairlift. She pressed the remote-control button and watched the chair slowly ascend the stairs, its indomitable hum as familiar as anything she could think of.

'Almost with you!' she shouted, without letting her worry infiltrate her voice. She waited for a reply, listened only to silence. She crinkled her face but instead of wasting more breath, started to climb the stairs like a recovering hernia patient, left leg first, right leg onto the same stair, left leg again. The journey was pernickety and arduous but she concentrated, channelled all her energy, and on the landing she rested her hands under her ribcage as her diaphragm fought for air. She coughed and her body rippled. She didn't pick up the first tray but hobbled to Brolly's bedroom door, which she opened. 'Brolly?' she asked again. He didn't budge. She listened for his breathing, couldn't hear it. She gulped, feared something terrible had happened. She struggled forward. There were only a few steps between her and the bed but if felt like a marathon. She stared at him. He seemed at peace. A smile semicircled his face. She reached out and grabbed his arm. It was warm. She shook it. He startled. She jumped. He grunted. 'Bloody hell, mate! Scared me!' She squeezed his hand gently. 'Got a surprise for you! Don't move!'

Brolly moaned, tired, inquisitive. She returned with the first tray. The champagne bottle communicated to him a dream, a result, an eventuality he dared not imagine. His heart pounded with positive anticipation and as she put the tray on the chair next to him, he saw it. The key. His eyebrows high-jumped over his head. His eyes burst out of their sockets. His mouth cracked open. He screamed and mumbled and groaned, paroxysms of delight, missives of joy. Completely incomprehensible, all of them, but tonally uplifting, sonorously cherubic. He'd never seen anything so beautiful as the key, the dainty, svelte, shiny metal tubing with a small oblong at one end and a deceptively simplistic ridge at the other.

The key.

The key to the rest of his life.

Gill wobbled out of the room. Her smile could hardly fit through the door. She wasn't entirely sure about eating avocado on toast, but it was the gesture that counted. Her gift, her parting gift to Brolly. She picked up the tray, as a shooting sensation powered through her foot. Up the length of her body, through her arm, to her heart. Enough to register confusion, moments of anxiety, maybe a few seconds of fear. Enough to release a murmur of horror, her own plea for more.

More life.

More love.

More living.

It was a powerful electric shock, a whiplash of negative energy. She didn't grab her heart because she didn't want to drop the tray. The tray was for Brolly. His favourite. A surprise. She wanted him to be happy again. The jolt unbalanced her, caused her to crumble against the banister's hairpin. She had no choice but to release her grip. Right hand first. She grabbed the air for non-existent support as images, thoughts, subliminals, too quick to count, to register, to make sense of, garbled her mind. Still conscious but fading, gravity's demand, nature's cruel turn, took care of her left hand. The tray and the plates made remarkably little sound, poofs, thuds, as they plopped onto the stairs below, didn't tumble, came to rest moments before Gill collapsed and dislodged them, crashed on them, past them, down the rest of the stairs, head over heels, tits over arse, until the hallway halted her momentum and she slammed still, an undignified mess, her limbs broken and bent in directions that no one's limbs should be broken or bent in.

CHAPTER 54

'A lotta people reckon Studio 54 in New York was the best club in the world. It's probably the most famous. I've heard some people say the same about Shoom in London or Pacha in Ibiza, but all I can say is, I bet none of 'em've ever been to the Wobble Club!'

'High praise indeed!' Brolly swayed around the bar as if he was on a cruise ship. The carcinogenic exhaust fumes had gone to his head. So had the six pints on a stomach lined entirely with crisps. At least the Vauxhall fleapit was a stone's throw, a kebab's kick away from his ashtray room in his broken-dishwasher house. He hardly knew anyone in London and the karaoke host was the first friendly person he'd met in the two months he'd been in town.

'Yeah. Come along, we're always looking for new recruits. Gimme a call and I'll introduce you to some of the gang. Oi! Tara!' he shouted at the wizened landlady, who was turning into a chimney next to the till. 'Give us a pen, will ya?' Without interrupting the rhythmic puff on her cigarette, the old-age pensioner threw the host a biro and he scrawled his details on a soggy beer mat. 'There ya go.'

'Cheers. And it's fancy dress, did you say?'

'Optional but encouraged. Mostly everyone makes an effort so better you do than you don't. Next one's punk and I got a great surprise planned for the end of the evening.'

'What's that, then?'

'It's a surprise, innit? You'll have to come an' find out.'

Brolly looked at the beer mat. 'What's that say?'

'Tim. Tiny Tim. Just call me Tiny. Or Tim.'

'Or Tiny Tim?'

'You catch on quickly, my friend!'

'I'm Brolly.' Brolly held out his hand and they shook.

'Well, come along, Brolly. Who knows? It might just change your life!'

The small, insignificant lane in between Liverpool Street and Spitalfields Market was deserted. Its cobbled stones spat back the rain, garbled the pug-nosed pub's reflection in the unprepossessing October night. Brolly's lengthy shadow reeled with indignity below the monochrome cityscape and his feet started to grow cold. Blusters of wind chilled his bones, nipped through the lacerations he'd made in his cheap tartan trousers and white work shirt. He'd stuck safety pins through both for 1970s authenticity. He'd also cut his hair marginally shorter, lacquered it with hairspray before spiking it, and camouflaged his eyes with make-up. He imagined himself as the next victim in a comic book's brutal murder, lured by an implied promise of wanton hedonism, sexual gratification.

The lack of human presence disturbed him. He was on the edge of chickening out when a light slashed his face, blinded his sight. A London cab screeched around the corner. Brolly retreated onto the pavement, almost tripped over, was confronted by the gripping stare of its passenger. Her skin was exhausted by the carriage's blackness, her hair enveloped by it, but her eyes glowed like a lantern in a mine. Made her look like an apparition.

A femme fatale. A Gothic intrigue. She stared at Brolly as if she wanted to recognise him but couldn't. The moment passed and the taxi stopped outside the Georgian pub. Her long jacket fluttered in the wind like an oversized raven as she glided into the venue.

The pub's ground floor looked like it was holding a wake for a misanthrope. The misanthrope was no doubt turning in his grave due to the disturbance from the basement. A cheap office desk perched precariously at the top of the stairs near the front of the pub, where a toffee apple with candy-floss-coloured hair didn't stop helping herself to a large bowl of Twiglets. Brolly's entrance fee was reduced from £10 to £5 because he knew Tiny Tim. On his hand he received a Mr Bump rubber stamp. Mr Bump was doing a star jump. Mr Bump looked panicked, like it was the first time he'd ever exercised.

The stairs were steep, the passage uterine. At the bottom, a buffet trolley blocked a fire exit. The swing doors to the Wobble Club exuded a cheap Moulin Rouge sophistication. Brolly swelled his chest, tousled his hair, swung them open. A singer/sandpaper asked if he'd ever fallen in love with someone, if he'd ever fallen in love with someone he shouldn't have fallen in love with. He hadn't, but said nothing as the hairdryer air, laced with a hand-stitched blanket of cigarettes and alcohol, intoxicated him. The ample breasts that bounced in every direction dumbfounded him. The sea of smiles blinded him. The waves of confident and feminine bulges encouraged him.

One voluptuous lady had wrapped herself in see-through cellophane. Another wore a dustbin bag that stopped just above her outraged buttocks. One looked like an ample Morticia Addams; another, maybe her sister, an overweight Elvira. One had given her runty dog a matching pink mohican; another wore a toy crown and a neon-yellow cape with the words 'God Saves, I don't' stencilled onto a ripped white T-shirt. The men were equally enthusiastic in their attire and bonhomie oozed out of their every pore, their every orifice. A chubby Ramone, a paunchy Sid Vicious, a tubby Clash City Rocker all added colour and character to the unlikely smorgasbord of fat punk iconography.

Brolly weaved his way to the bar, through clusters of balloons and clumps of dancing couples. The club's every undulation, its every squeeze, its every pound of flesh was a demonstration of defiance, of pride, of confidence, a V-sign to the cruel, mocking world, to confused friends and disappointed parents, a V-sign from the flock of overfed black sheep gathered under one roof, for one night only, at London's largest, at London's finest, at London's most exultant. Brolly cheered and clapped as a new song plundered the night. A quick drumbeat and a promising riff; the singer asked if teenage dreams were so hard to beat.

The club wobbled in time, in unison, as Brolly ordered a double vodka for Dutch courage and a beer should the vodka fail. The bar was interspersed with bowls of peanuts, popcorn and Skittles; he helped himself and sought out the only person he knew. The DJ booth was crammed at the back of the makeshift dance floor. Tiny Tim towered over the decks like the Incredible Hulk but without any tinge of jealousy. He pumped his fist in the air, shouted the words that crashed out of the speakers, looked like he was training to go professional. He looked unapproachable. He looked like you wouldn't want to go one round with him.

Brolly sought the lady of the night, of the taxi. Couldn't see her slipping through the shafts of light, hovering among the dry-ice clouds, wondered if she'd already vanished. He racked his brain for a chat-up line. Not that he'd ever used one before but if needs must, in case of emergency. There must be some lexicon of the English language more inspirational than 'Hello, there!', 'D'you come here often?' or 'Have you been here before?'

A Black woman squeezed into the space next to him. With her cropped blonde hair, she looked intimidating but drinkable, like a pint of Guinness. Her thighs rubbed against his. Large golden hoops dangled from her ears. She smelled of talcum powder and vanilla cupcakes. Her breasts floundered on the copper bar as if they demanded a rest and were in control. She grabbed a handful of Skittles at the same time as Brolly did.

'Sorry,' said the Guinness.

'No, after you!' he replied. He wanted to ask if she'd come as Grace Jones but wasn't sure if the question was racist or if Grace Jones was a punk. She grabbed a handful and concentrated on the barman. Brolly crushed the Skittles with military precision, as if to confirm his existence, his very position next to her. He grabbed some peanuts and looked at the woman from the corner of his eye. After she ordered drinks, Brolly's heart pumped itself plump. He jumped into a lake of freezing water, threw himself off a cliff's edge.

'So d'you pogo often?' It hadn't come out quite how he intended. The music was close to deafening. He hoped she hadn't heard.

'Sorry, were you talking to me?' she shouted back.

'Er . . . Yeah . . .'

'What did you say?'

'Have you ever pogo'd here before?'

'What's that?'

'Hello, pogo!'

'I don't know what you're talking about.'

'Pogo. You know?'

'No. I don't know.'

'Pogo. How the punks used to dance. Jump up and down.' The barman plonked the woman's drinks on the bar. She pulled out a card and paid. 'Have a good night,' she said without further engagement. Brolly decided the Guinness was a bitter. He finished the bowl of peanuts and the bowl of popcorn, by which time the bowl of peanuts had been refilled so he finished that, too. After two double vodkas, he drank pints and propped up the bar with an increasingly unsteady but punky aesthetic. He minded his p's and q's and became as drunk on the atmosphere as he did on the alcohol. The music started to turn cheesy, Cheddar, not yet Camembert. He was about to turn and investigate when a hand smacked his shoulder. He turned around. 'Alright, mate! You made it!' Tiny Tim bellowed. Brolly laughed with relief.

'Yeah, been here a few hours now.'

'Here all by yourself? Haven't you met anyone yet?'

'Yeah, yeah, spoken to a few people but, you know, don't know anyone really but I really like it, excellent energy!'

'Come an' let me introduce you to some of the gang . . .'

Brolly bought more alcohol and trailed behind the DJ as far away from the dance floor as the room allowed, to a corner and a booth and a table on which a reserved sign stood bow-legged. With every step, the Wobble Club congratulated Tiny Tim, slapped him on the back, shook his hand, ruffled his hair.

'Bloody 'ell, mate! You're like royalty here!' shouted Brolly as they stood by the reserved table and Tiny Tim gnashed his nicotine-stained teeth with pride.

'Well . . . I did start the club so . . . I mean, I don't know everyone here, but I know a lotta people. A lot of 'em are regulars, it's like a religion to them. Well, to all of us. Come here once and it's hard not to come back. If you're a fatty, that is. Dunno if it's such a big deal for anyone else.'

'You started this yourself!?'

'Yeah, I was just fed up of all the body fascism that permeated the club scene, all the elitism, the snobbery, you know, like, if I'm fat, people don't want me in the club 'cos I don't conform to their ideal of beauty and all that bollocks. Living in a bubble, they are. The world isn't full of beautiful, skinny models, it's full of real people of all shapes an' sizes. I just got fed up with it, mate. Just wanted to go somewhere I knew I wouldn't be insulted or hassled or taken the piss out of. I mean, I don't really give a fuck, to be honest; you know, you just think, "Save your breath, prick." I got a thick skin, you know, it's my choice to be a fat fucker, but sometimes it's nice to relax, not to have to worry about all that stuff. So that's why I started this place. For fat people, their friends and admirers; a worry-free zone to let your hair down, or as the case is tonight, stick it up. Come on, let's sit down, I been standing for the last coupla hours. Knackered.' Tiny Tim collapsed into the booth, Brolly eased himself in. Tiny Tim introduced him to the couple opposite, a Goth girl and a Dennis the Menace, and the person to his left.

'Brolly, this is my friend Gill. Gill, this is my friend Brolly.' Brolly hadn't taken any notice of Gill but when he swivelled his head, he nearly dropped his pint. His mouth predicted a drought. His pupils dilated as if he'd been injected with crack cocaine.

'Oh. Hello!'

'You're the bloke I passed in the street.'

'In the taxi?'

'Yeah.'

'Yeah!' He was glad he'd made some kind of impression.

'I wondered if you were coming here,' she offered as Brolly dried his hand against his tartan trousers and straightened it towards her. He liked the way she took it. Firm but feminine. He liked the way their hands slid together. With compassion, duplicity and cookie dough. He liked the halo that shone from her smile, the fire that conflagrated her furnace.

'I was wondering if I was coming here, too.'

'What d'you mean?'

'Well, I just met Tiny Tim in a pub last week and I guess he spotted me at the bar and invited me along but, you know, I've only been in town a while and don't know many people so it was all a bit . . .'

'Bit shy, are you?'

'Little bit.'

'You don't seem it.'

Brolly supped from his beer. 'Thanks. But, well, I almost turned

364

around but then I saw you and I thought . . . you know, fuck it!'

'Ha! Well, I'm glad I could inspire you!'

'Yeah, me too.'

'So you any good at pogoing?' she asked without irony.

'What!?' Brolly asked, his smile tying knots around his head.

'What?' she responded, her knickers not yet twisted.

'Why d'you ask me that?'

'Just a question. What's so funny?'

Brolly wondered whether to tell her the truth, decided it was the best place to start any kind of relationship, platonic or otherwise. 'Well . . . I don't usually do chat-up lines but 'cos I didn't know anyone I thought it'd be a good idea, you know, an appropriate question to break any ice . . .'

'So now you think I'm chatting you up, do you?' Gill asked with a dumpling of a smile, an impish spring roll of delight.

'Are you?'

'I tell you what. Why don't you leave the table, come back an' pretend we never met. Try the line on me, see how it works . . .'

'Alright.'

Delighted at the idea, Brolly squeezed out of the cubicle, grabbed his pint and staggered a few feet away, noticed the newly ripened music, Stilton, no longer Camembert; it had just rained men while living La Vida Loca. But a regal a cappella kicked in and the smell started to vanish. Almost all the punks who could bend down on one knee, did. Stretched their arms out to the nearest punkette, someone they knew or a complete stranger – it didn't matter – started harmonising. The second arm followed as the punkettes played with their hair, hugged themselves suggestively, caressed their thighs, wiggled their hips, joined the lyrical fray as Freddie told everyone how fat-bottomed girls made the rocking world go around! No one disagreed. Most of the punks stood back up, a few remained kneeling, one needed two friends to help him to his feet but, as if by sorcery, as if a wizard had sprinkled magic into the ventilation system, the Wobble Club sang, swayed, eulogised in union, as if possessed by a greater good, a force for the better, a force that suggested Freddie could take them anywhere he wanted and they'd all follow.

In sync to the beat, Brolly strutted up to the table, winked at his already captivated audience of one. She tried not to smile, to look bored. Failed. He downed his beer, slammed it with ironic machismo on the table. She raised her eyebrows in ironic surprise. He ripped the top buttons off his shirt. He was a punk. Punks didn't care about anything. Gill giggled, Gill clapped. He slid next to her, wrapped his arm around her willing shoulder, rested his other hand on her thigh. She took his hand off her thigh as he stared deep into her emerald eyes. 'So, er, you any good at pogoing, m'lady!?'

'I'm one of the best pogo-ers you ever saw, milord.'

'Well then, maybe you'd like to pogo the night away with me?'

'When the punk stuff kicks back in, I will. With pleasure!'

Gill and Brolly chatted all evening and didn't leave each other's side except to visit the toilet or buy more alcohol. Not even to pogo when Tiny Tim reclaimed the decks.

'Oh shit!' Gill exclaimed a few hours later, their only enemy the tame licensing laws.

'What?' Brolly asked as his head bobbed up and down in a romantic sea of reckless abandon, as Fisher-Price-type toy keyboards bounced off the walls.

'Tiny Tim said we should be on the dance floor for the final tune, which is what this is. Come on!'

Tiny Tim always finished the night spinning one of two versions of the same song: 'Fatty Fatty', an unabashed and uplifting paean to body positivity. Either the Clancy Eccles original ska/reggae recording from 1967 (Jamaica if he smelled romance in the air) or the more upbeat and zanier Bad Manners version from the early 1980s (England if the party vibe had blitzed the love-interest).

The dance floor was a rowdy hive of delight. It split at its seams. And skanked. And twisted. And did the mashed potato. And ran on the spot. Waved its hands in the air. The whole club. Every single person. And those who couldn't fit on the dance floor decorated its edges. A few daring clubbers stood on chairs; one rakish wag gyrated on a table. Everyone sang the lyrics. Everyone loved fatty, fatty, fat! Everyone pointed their fingers at everyone else, as if the song had been specifically written for the Wobble Club. Gill pointed hers at Brolly, he pointed his at her. Their teeth shone like beacons, their eyes dazzled like fireflies, but the song abruptly ended. Lights flickered and shone throughout the club, ruined the mystique. The crowd turned and worshipped at the DJ's altar, wolf-whistled, clapped, shouted for more. Tiny Tim held his hands in the air, accepted the adulation, but indicated it should stop, grabbed his microphone, addressed the sweating, grinning amoeba that undulated in front of him.

'Got a special surprise for you, you lovely, lovely lot! Given that you've made such a spectacular effort, punked yourselves up so well, been such a rambunctious crowd, I got one question for you.' He paused. A silence fell over the club. Tiny Tim exchanged eyeballs with the crowd. 'Who's hungry!?' he bellowed. The floor screamed with glee. 'Nah, naah, naaah. I don't think you heard me right. I said WHO'S HUNGRY!?' The floor turned up its volume to eleven. Screamed and cheered and deafened Tiny Tim. 'Alright, that's better! 'Cos I am! I'm famished! So I called one of me mates who runs a takeaway and he brought the order down here and you know what I'm gonna do? I'm gonna share it with you!!' The club whooped riotously. 'Yeah, 'cos I'm nice like that.'

Tiny Tim cricked his head to the right and nodded. The club followed his nod. A sumo wrestler had appeared from nowhere. In front of him was a large gong. And a mallet. The sumo wrestler smacked the gong aggressively. Liquid gold rippled through the stale

367

air. The entrance doors swung open and an older Chinese couple, both wearing crisp white waiter jackets, manoeuvred a buffet trolley into the club. The bar staff watched with good-humoured incredulity. The crowd started to murmur disbelief, approval. They whistled more, cheered more, laughed more, stuck their fingers into the steaming trays as the buffet passed by.

'No, no, no, not until I say so! Anyone I see eating before I give the say-so gets banned from the Wobble Club for life. And I'm being serious!'

A few affectionate boos pierced the air as the couple pushed the trolley through tables and chairs, towards the dance floor. The crowd parted for the trolley. They panted for it. Wanted to party for it. To party with it. The Chinese couple pushed it to the middle of the floor. It dissected Brolly from Gill, split them down the middle.

'Yeah, yeah, that's good, thank you, Mr and Mrs Fong! A big hand for Mr and Mrs Fong!'

As they exited, the crowd showed its appreciation and edged around the buffet like jackals around a carcass. Another gong trembled through the speakers. A traditional Chinese riff followed as Gill and Brolly locked eyes. Gill winked at Brolly.

'Alright, and it's all yours!' whooped Tiny Tim as a drummer counted to four and his mate shouted he wanted a Chinese takeaway.

A mini stampede ensued. Some grabbed paper plates, some the wooden chopsticks, most lunged at whatever was at hand. Gill grabbed at the crispy won tons, gobbled some, threw a couple at Brolly. She missed. Smudged some make-up on a Martian girl. As Brolly roared with passion and threw his spare rib at Gill, the Martian scooped up some sweet and sour prawn balls and threw them at Gill. A couple hit a Dead Elvis in the forehead. Dead Elvis picked up some spring rolls and threw them at the Martian but hit a buxom Rockabilly Chick. The spring rolls fell down her cleavage.

She warbled in disgust as she pulled them from her bra, stuffed one down her throat and threw the other back at Dead Elvis. She grabbed a fistful of chicken chow mein and lobbed that at Dead Elvis, too. The noodles splattered over an overweight Vivienne Westwood, tangled in her messy hair, dropped over her eyes. Vivienne ripped the noodles from her face and threw them back. As the band continued the same mantra – they wanted a Chinese takeaway – a fully fledged food fight ripped across the Wobble Club, much to Tiny Tim's delight.

Halfway through the chaos, Gill, sporting noodles down her cleavage and plum sauce smeared across her face, grabbed the last of the spring rolls and dodged her way around the buffet. She dodged beef and mushrooms and chicken and cashew nuts but not some duck and pineapple. Brolly met her halfway. Peas and prawns and egg fried rice stuck in his hair; his shirt was splattered with sauces of all colours and flavours. 'I got this for you. Thought you might like it!' Gill waved the last spring roll in his face.

'Oh, that's nice!' he said as a slice of lemon chicken thwacked against the side of his head. Gill stuck half the spring roll in her mouth, pointed the other half in his direction. He placed his hands on her hips, pulled their tummies together and bit the spring roll in half. He chewed it quickly, swallowed uncomfortably and smacked his lips against hers. Gill opened her mouth and as the fast food flew past them and above them and sometimes into them, they started to eat each other.

CHAPTER 55

Brolly's screams, muffled as they were, sounded like an ice cream melting from a broken heart. After a while, his throat charred and he stopped screaming, listened instead. For what seemed like an eternity. He tried to persuade himself he heard a rustle, a creak, a moan, anything from Gill, anything to suggest her survival.

He failed.

He heard the nothingness of an eternal motorway, bleak, broken, overgrown with foliage, without cars and abandoned by animals.

He scrunched his eyes tightly. Squeezed out aqueous regret. He opened his eyes, screamed again. It sounded like an ice-cream factory burning to the ground, knowledgeable of the arsonist's identity; a snowman who hates the cold. He ripped his hands against his cuffs until skin started to unroll, to flap as if it was a glove on his hand. He didn't like pain but he liked this pain. For the time being. It distracted him, reminded him of his goal, of his incarceration. He tunnelled into denial, commandeered his emotions, whipped his guilt, his uncertainty, his hypocritical mourning, his perverted love, whipped them all into a cowering, non-confrontational shape, the shape of a sausage balloon. He shoved the balloon into a drawer at the back of his brain and concentrated on the more immediate matter in hand.

Gill had replenished his water before she went to Asda. He'd had a few sips that morning but no more. One bottle was full, the other three-quarters. Gill had also replaced the saucepan with another crazy concoction. He'd had a couple of slurps of that, too. He couldn't be sure how much there was but figured it would last a week or so if he remained mindful. If he was mindful of the water, that would last longer; two or three times longer.

He was confident of his rescue but planned for the worst. A situation where no one acted upon Gill's absence seemed so unlikely as to be an impossibility. It was a Saturday afternoon and Landlady Kim would be the first to notice but wouldn't extend her concern beyond a couple of phone calls. The Harry's gang would be different. They'd notice on Monday morning and make first contact by midday at the latest. They'd call a couple of times in the afternoon and try all of Tuesday. One or more would pop round that evening or Wednesday morning. They'd knock on the door and maybe even hear his cries if they paid attention; his door was open, after all. If they didn't hear him, they'd peek into the living room and through the letterbox. They'd see Gill and call the police.

Brolly calculated he'd have to wait three or four days. And failing that, for whatever reason, Taxi Rob would head over the following Saturday. Good old reliable Taxi Rob. Brolly would have the maximum of a week to wait for his freedom. It was longer than he'd like but he could see the light at the end of the tunnel. He resolved to take three gulps of sustenance and water a day; breakfast, lunch, dinner. All he had to do was lie back and think of England and, on a positive note, he'd lose more weight in the process.

The Wobble Club Top Six

No. 6

'Waddlin' Around'
The King Khan & BBQ Show

CHAPTER 56

A familiar chime roused Brolly from his slumber, high-fived him, convinced him of his prognostication's accuracy, that he was in control. The outside light, soft and dim, pawed at Brolly's curtains like a pet craving love and attention. The call was from Landlady Kim, he was sure of it. It was Sunday, must have been sometime between 12.30 and 1.30. She was checking on Gill's tardiness, her soon-to-be absence. She left a message and the mobile rang all afternoon. In the early evening, the ghost of its final chime fizzled out, evaporated into a memory, into the hallway. Gill never left her phone uncharged and Brolly hoped it would speed up his rescue.

He drifted in and out of consciousness, uneasily and with lingering trepidation, but woke sometime the next morning with a sigh, a barbed throat and glued eyelids. He fluttered away his mucus, twisted his head towards his left hand and persuaded the plastic tubing into his mouth. His sucking sounded like a cordless vacuum cleaner. The gag made the process more arduous, more extended, more aggressive. Still, he had all the time in the world; he was in no rush, no longer had a train to catch. The rush of air made him dizzy but the gush of water rewarded him, reminded him of walking in the rain, splashing in puddles, swimming in pools, gagging on teacups of chlorine. He resolved to start swimming again when he was free, when he could lift himself out of the pool. He turned to his right and sucked at the concoction, which was more dense than the water and harder to drag into his mouth. He didn't swallow immediately but encouraged the goo to permeate his mouth; chocolate and coconut dominated, with maybe a hint of biscuit, caramel and raisins waving from the sidelines.

The next morning, he growled as he yawned, surprised no one had come the day before but confident someone would come that day. He closed his eyes and listened for the usual signs of life. He concentrated. Heard nothing. Wondered why he heard nothing. Not one noise. Not half of one or a hint of one, a smidgen of one or an iota of one. He listened and listened and listened but always heard the same thing: nothing. The silence sounded more oppressive than he remembered, more inhospitable. For once, perhaps for the first time ever, the silence sounded silent. He couldn't work out why. How was that possible? It made no sense. He always heard something: passing cars, joking children, aeroplanes, sirens. Even the wildlife, such as it was just off the Walworth Road, seemed like it was on strike or kowtowing to a higher order. Something was wrong, very wrong. He worried for the first time that his nightmare had somehow become the city's nightmare, maybe the world's nightmare.

The Wobble Club Top Six

No. 5

'Fat Bottomed Girls'
Queen

CHAPTER 57

The day's luminescence was dimming. The boredom's immutability, its mind-numbing inflexibility, bludgeoned Brolly's self-respect, strangled his sense of identity. He drooled. His lower lip glistened with spittle. He was hungry. He was always hungry. Whatever his feelings towards Gill, he couldn't deny she was the perfect feeder, always kept him fed.

He had twisted his head towards his mid-evening snack, flexed his wrist, stuck the tubes inside his mouth and started sucking when something distracted him.

A noise. Finally.

The noise gave him hope, a moment to celebrate, to fantasise again, to entertain rescue, company, a future, his life, his mother, his brother, his diet, his survival.

It began like a metallic rattle, a letterbox opening. But it turned into a beat, a ragged, disorganised battering, drowned out by cheering and clapping, people, everywhere, from either side of the street, from straight ahead, even from directly behind. A trumpet, too, of all things. Some music, dance music, bled out of cheap speakers. The overall noise sounded like a war cry from untrained soldiers without leaders, a rabble of women and children as well as reluctant men. High-pitched, low-pitched,

pitched all over the pitch. It sounded like an unlikely celebration for a battle that would shed only other people's blood. Brolly didn't care, as long as it wasn't his blood. He joined in. Screamed and shouted and mumbled and groaned until it hurt. When his voice petered out, he heard the silence again. It deafened again and he realised everyone else had stopped, too.

Just like that.

It made no sense. No sense at all.

The Wobble Club Top Six

No. 4

'Fatty Fatty'
Bad Manners/Clancy Eccles

CHAPTER 58

t was harder to coerce the concoction from the saucepan to his mouth than he would have liked. He would have liked not to be handcuffed in his own bed, or what had been his own bed, with his ex-girlfriend's corpse lying at the bottom of the stairs. His tongue pressed the tube against the ball gag. He imagined its trajectory to be like a comet that narrowly missed the earth. His sucking resembled a dentist's tube dehydrating a patient's mouth, temperamentally, stubbornly. Another sound pierced his ears and his heart. An echo-chamber of drought, a definitive step forward in time, a setback to his survival stakes. The atmosphere gurgled. The air writhed. He jiggled his elbow, hoped to happen across a stray dollop, found nothing, sucked stale plasticity into his lungs, the taste of the planet's poisoning.

His chocolate concoction was finished.

An invisible force pressed down on his chest, tightened it, caused his heart to run amok. He screamed with angst. Ripped at his chains. The metal links made a welcome relief from the silence. He flexed his biceps, exercised his shoulders, challenged the pulley, the wedge in the concrete, the stick in the mud. He lost his challenge, hurt himself, crunched the bones on the side of his hands, stretched the skin, tore the flesh, coloured himself claret, smears and clumsy brushstrokes. He calmed down, surprised himself with one more gargantuan tug, cursed himself for such naivety, for such unfounded optimism, such a whiplash of discomfort, such a throbbing of pain.

He tried to rationalise his position but failed. He stared at the ceiling. Prayed an insect might surprise him, a spider, a daddy longlegs, might scurry above him, brighten his day. He waited in vain, contemplated the same storm of indifference, of confusion, of disbelief that he always contemplated, that deprecated his soul, belittled his self, mocked his isolation. He wondered if he'd lost weight. He must have; he'd almost been fasting and now he was fasting. Well and truly. He was curious if he could notice the effects of his imposed fast, ratify it somehow.

His upper limbs were the only visible parts of his body. He looked at both hands. His palms looked like faded maps, full of ravines and tributaries, paths and vanishing roads. His veins popped out like ill-conceived water pipes nestling in between little hairs of roughage. Bracelets of blood marked the change of territory to his arms, which were heavier and hairier, the veins less apparent, practically invisible. Flesh drooped from them, gathered in fatty deposits, hung around aimlessly. Everything looked like it always did. He had no idea how to calibrate his fast and its effect but remembered the handcuffs were one size larger than when Gill first put them on. That must count for something. He'd put on a lot of weight but now he was losing a lot of weight. He must be. It was biology. Science. The law of the famine, the law of the drought.

It was obvious no one was coming for him, so his only hope now was to lose enough weight to slip out of the handcuffs. Or rip himself out. It was a passive approach to escape but the only one he could still think of. He decided not to trash his hands into a bloody pulp every day but to go for gold, go for broke, go only when there was no more water left, when he'd lost as much weight as he could without dying, when everything was blank, black and verging towards blasphemous.

The Wobble Club Top Six

No. 3

'Chinese Takeaway'
The Adicts

CHAPTER 59

Time flexed its muscles, pulled Brolly's legs, tickled his armpits. The days and nights, the hours and minutes, the seconds and seconds and seconds, so many of them, so similar, practically identical, blurred into one like an insane and torturously slow stroboscope conceived of by an artist with too much Arts Council funding. Brolly's life had become an incessant straight line without tabulation, a schoolboy's never-ending ruler.

He stared his own mortality in the face, a damp cigarette butt stepped on by the world's disinterest. He lifted his legs off the bed, as high as they'd go – not Heil Hitler height, just right wing with fascist tendencies. His stomach muscles twitched in graceful recognition of his endeavour, that they were still there for him, that after all those years he'd finally acknowledged their existence. His teeth gritted contemptuously but his flab wobbled in strained approbation, his arms jittered in pain as they pulled the chain behind him.

He did it after every slurp of water. His concentration was shot and his ability to count was dismal so he did it until it hurt, until he couldn't do it any more. It strengthened his muscles, should he need them again, stopped them from withering further away, made him expend more energy. Some energy. Any energy. Made him slimmer. The more he lifted his legs, the slimmer he became. The slimmer he became, the more the chance of slipping his hands through the cuffs. Just one hand, that's all he needed. Just one hand. One slip. He was a good slipper. Then there'd be enough slack for him to reach the key, the beautiful, darling key. He relaxed. His legs crashed to the bed. The bed shook and groaned as if he was cheating on it.

The Wobble Club Top Six

No. 2

'We Built This City on Sausage Rolls'
(To the tune of 'We Built This City'
by Starship)
LadBaby

CHAPTER 60

B rolly's breathing no longer sounded like a poor imitation of a death rattle. The imitation had wrapped itself around his parched organs and had improved; it sounded like the real thing.

The top of his tongue stuck to the roof of his mouth, blocked the passage of air, choked him awake. His head jerked off the pillow, bounced back into it. He opened his eyes. The air sandpapered his throat and time stood very still, much like the wardrobe and the chest of drawers and the chairs. He'd heard the same clapping, cheering noise twice more. Might have been thrice? He didn't know, couldn't remember. Outside it was still light, but inside the purple flower next to the champagne had withered, twisted in on itself, relinquished its vivacious colour for a more sultry bruise.

He couldn't remember how many gulps of water he'd had that day but however many it was, he'd had to fight for it and the bottle had communicated its disillusion. Brolly tilted his head to the side and tugged his left hand closer to his mouth. The chain clanked against the pulley. The tubes pricked against his cracked lips, jarred against the gag inside. He stuck his tongue against the tube, against the gag, and sucked. The noise sounded like an ailing cappuccino machine. The pins in the air jabbed Brolly's gums, tingled his fillings. Brolly wriggled his arm, sucked again. Wriggled his arm a few times, sucked a few times more, always with the same result.

The well was dry.

Words with exclamation marks buzzed through his consciousness like newly hatched mosquitoes. He could see their lava, split open on a wasteland below. The mosquitoes flew into prison bars of electricity, crashed to the ground, twitched with the dying hope that Brolly would understand their meaning, remember his hope, actualise his plan. He couldn't articulate the words or their sounds, shape their vowels, chip away at their consonants, but something, somewhere, clicked.

He twisted his head to the right; his neck cracked. He moved his thumb so it lay diagonally over the palm of his hand and gently pulled. His wounds had scabbed; some of the scabs flaked and bled again. The metal jerked up against his bones, jammed. He tautened the chain with his left hand and tugged his right. Tried to tug it through the cuff. The cuff stuttered further up his hand. It clamped his bones. It ripped at his skin, fondled his hope, enough for him to blank out the pain, the unnatural pressure of bone turning against bone, dislocating from sockets. The cuff burned like a branding iron, his skin sizzled slowly, withered, reshaped as more blood seeped. He tugged. He pulled. He ripped. He beat himself up.

But no matter how hard he tried, he couldn't free himself. He tried with his left hand but that didn't work either and at some point he gave up and prepared to die. He didn't want to die, lonely, afraid, angry, in a smelly bed in a smelly room in a smelly house, but maybe dying wasn't so bad; he was dead already.

The Wobble Club Top Six

No. 1

'Hey, Fatty!'
(To the tune of 'Hey, Mickey!' by Toni Basil)
Tiny Tim

CHAPTER 61

rolly's demise was an abstract plank floating in a lake of dirty sheets and desaturated memories. He wondered if he was floating in Heaven or drowning in Hell. A flicker lit up the right side of his peripheral blindness. He wrestled his eyes open. His eyelids were a formidable opponent. Their mucus stuck stronger than ever. He realised he was still in purgatory, still dying slowly in his room. He remembered what a beacon looked like, a beacon of hope. It looked like his next-door neighbours' bathroom light, seeping through the side of his curtains, oozing like a miracle cure for world famine, global starvation, his incredible fasting.

He dabbed his tongue against the inside of his cheek. They stuck together like Velcro; his saliva had jumped his body's sinking ship. He pulled his tongue away. The cheek followed. He dabbed his tongue against his mouth's roof. Same story. His mouth was dry. Burnt like Death Valley. With less investigation and more deliberateness, he dabbed his tongue again. In short, sharp little bursts. Time and time again. Cajoled his saliva, charmed it, teased it, inveigled it. Welcomed it into his fold, under his tongue, behind his lips, against his teeth. It was a slow process. When he heard his tongue swish rather than stick, he accepted his body hadn't given up on him, was actually relying on him, was egging him on. The swish started to sound like a splash, a fish flapping in a puddle.

He pulled his right hand towards his mouth, tried to avoid the tubes that stuck out from under the handcuffs. Stuck his tongue out of his mouth's corner, past the gag, which prevented its maximum reach. He strained his tongue's tip, licked his right hand, above his wrist and below his knuckles, lubricated as much of his skin as possible. A thin coat at first, then thicker, until it dripped with spittle. He didn't like what it tasted of: Gill's death, his incarceration. He licked the inside of the handcuff, too. He lowered his thumb into his right hand's palm and contorted his bones. He tightened the chain with his left hand and pulled. The cuffs clashed against the bottom of his knuckles. Same sticking point as before, but it felt different this time, not so stinging; the saliva was working, the friction was rewarding, and all of a sudden the cuff gave way, just like that, and his hand slipped through.

Brolly screamed in delight. In awe. In shock. He grabbed his gag's buckle and undid it, threw it to the floor. 'Fuckin' 'ell! FUCKING HELL! Oh my God! Oh my God! Oh my God!' He laughed outrageously, rubbed his hands over his face. Never in a million years would he have thought the action would feel so jubilant, so life-affirming. He grabbed his stomach, smacked it affectionately and slipped his legs over the side of the bed. He sat up with dizzy abandon. 'Oh my fucking God!'

He reached for the key. His hand trembled. He hoped he wouldn't knock the key onto the floor. The key scuffed against the tray as he picked it up and it scuffed against the handcuff as he inserted it into the tiny hole. The key turned without any fuss. The click was celestial. Brolly split the handcuff in half, couldn't stop chuckling. He grabbed the champagne bottle and keyed off the foil. He unscrewed the metal wire and pulled it off the cork. His hands shook. His arms shook. The bottle shook. He shook the bottle. He twisted the cork until it exploded. The champagne burst into flumes of congratulation, arcs of relief. Brolly luxuriated in the shower of champagne, swallowed a mouthful and dry-retched. He poured the champagne over his face instead. It was cold, made him shiver, but he marvelled at its bouquet; it tasted of kiwi fruit and iron. The bubbles burst on his lips. He licked them. They tasted of freedom.

Brolly lowered the bottle to the floor, picked up the desiccated flower. It was delicate and fragile. He marvelled at it. It crumpled in his hand. He grabbed the other chair, turned it around, grabbed its back. He raised himself off the bed. His legs twitched, blood practically burst out of his veins. His mouth dried again and his head spun. He wobbled but he made it, he stood up. 'Now we're talking!' He moved the chair away, took his first step but crashed to the ground. 'COME ON!' he screamed as the pain, the surprise, the burn on his knees stomped over his good cheer. He pushed the chair away, didn't fancy his chances of walking, didn't bother trying; like a mountain rescue dog, plodded towards the door on all fours.

The stairlift looked like an executioner's chair. The banisters looked like prison bars. The house had stagnated like a corpse and stank like one, too. The landing was dark and dingy and cold. The carpet ruffled under his bony fingers. He was happy to reach the bathroom. The light switch dangled in front of his eyes like a bait from a cosmic fisherman. Brolly was tempted to eat it but knew what he had to do. He pulled it. He'd missed that noise, that noise he'd taken for granted for most of the last decade. That innocuous but aggressive click. Brolly liked the change of scenery but the bathroom looked tired and dirty. Two pairs of Gill's knickers lay in the middle of the floor, three socks next to the toilet. He crawled to the sink and lifted himself up, to the height of the tap. He turned it on and slipped his mouth under the water. He irrigated his body with the most precious substance known to man. The waterfall seeped into his every extremity. It nourished him, gave him strength. It was a new religion. A new way of life. It was his future, his present, his saviour. He felt blessed.

He ripped off his nappies, dared not look at them, threw them in a corner, crawled over to the shower, turned it on. Cold water sprang from the shower head, jabbed at his flesh. 'Jesus Christ!' he screamed as his body revolted, trembled all over again. He retreated and waited for the water to heat up. He crawled back under the spray and groaned happily. He explored his body, wanted to reassert his life, found new rivets and new bumps, new scabs and new sores, some under folds of flesh, others on top. He didn't mind. He was alive, that was all that mattered. He drank more water from the shower, imagined it was a particularly weak cup of tea and looked forward to when he could drink a real one, soon.

He ripped a towel from a nearby hook and wrapped it around his waist but its covering was clumsy and confused his knees, slowed his progress. He wrapped it around his shoulders and crawled into Gill's bedroom. Like a second-rate moon, a third-rate sun, the street lights shone through her windows. Brolly nodded with relief as he saw Gill's phone charger where it always was, plugged into the wall by the side of her bed. He pulled it out, clung to it as he crawled back the way he'd come.

He contemplated his descent. Liked the idea of the stairlift but worried about raising himself into it. He turned around so that he stared into his room. He hoped never to set foot in it again. He reversed to the top of the stairs, stopped when his kneecaps brushed against the top step. He lowered himself onto his right thigh and manoeuvred his weight onto his backside so that he sat on the landing and his legs dangled below. He grabbed the balusters as he descended, a cheap life insurance, slipped down the steps one at a time. The movement felt unnatural, each bump hurt his haunches, but he didn't care. He was alive. From the third step, he threw the tray onto the landing. It echoed against the wall as it fell back onto the carpet. From the fourth, he lifted a plate and put it on the step above. He picked up a toasted sandwich, furrowed his brow. Pulled the slices apart, flinched at the mould that contaminated the dark mush. Realised it was avocado. His heart fluttered. His mood wavered. Gill lay mangled at the bottom of the stairs, no more than 4 metres away, but she'd made him an avocado sandwich before she died. She'd never made him an avocado sandwich before, never stopped at the fruit and veg section before. Never. He took a deep breath, made the mistake of looking at the anarchic mound, the malignant lump, the decaying body that lay beneath him. He did his best not to collapse in sobs of regret and anguish.

On the third step from the bottom, he shut his eyes, couldn't face Gill's remains, her rotting, disintegrating flesh. The hall smelled like a failed chemistry experiment. He hoped the lice and the mice and the maggots hadn't moved in. He stretched his right foot out and investigated. Could feel Gill's lifelessness. Her dead weight. Her arm. Her ribcage. If he didn't know better, he would have guessed she was a pile of discarded rubbish. Brolly grabbed the lowest banister and swivelled awkwardly onto the hallway floor.

He turned to face the front door but remained tight-eyed as he crawled past. He grunted with horror as he placed his hand on her thigh. It was a cold slab of meat. He ripped his hand off and cuddled up to the wall opposite. The towel dragged after him like a needy friend. His knees jangled in pain, throbbed in time to his heart. Dried food crumbs in the carpet poked into his hand. He sucked his gums. Tried not to vomit as he ran his hands over Gill. He'd never felt a dead person before. Didn't like it. Her phone was still in her pocket and it didn't take him long to find it. He whipped it out and retreated as quickly as he could.

In the kitchen, he flicked the light on. A jungle of detritus confronted him, trees and mounds and pools. He brushed his way through the sprouting foliage like an epic explorer, pulled himself far enough off the floor to plug the phone into a socket. He crawled over to the sink, where he pulled himself up and turned on the cold tap. He found a glass, which he rinsed before filling. He glugged water, glasses and glasses of it, a few pints' worth, more than he'd had upstairs. With every glug, every gulp, he felt more lubricated, more nourished, could practically hear his organs grind back to life.

He had a confusing conversation about Covid-19 with ambulance services, then a similar one with police services. After he hung up, he slipped back onto the floor and crawled to the nearest kitchen chair, but surprised himself by passing it, by passing all the unpacked Asda bags. At the fridge, he raised himself again, opened the door. The fridge hummed calmly, offered its wares: a contradiction of alcoholic celebration and melancholic sauce bottles. He shut the door and investigated the confectionery cupboard below. It burst with character, teemed with colour, reverberated with vivacity. Marketing ploys, special deals, cut prices, four-packs, five-packs, eight-packs, limited editions, family favourites. They all fought for Brolly's attention. He grunted with a hint of nostalgia, a degree of cynicism. The sight of all that chocolate, all those calories, made him nauseous. He slammed the confectionery cupboard shut. He never wanted to see another chocolate bar in his life.

SPECIAL ACKNOWLEDGEMENT

With big thanks to Britta Rogozinski for living with me, Gill and Brolly for many months, asking sometimes how they were, listening sometimes to how they were, what they'd been up to and what they'd been eating.

ACKNOWLEDGEMENTS

With big thanks to the first readers of *The Wobble Club*, all of whom offered up valuable editorial advice about how to improve the text: Brendan Breseth (the very first reader), Britta Rogozinski, Charlotte Tolhurst, Bradley Greer, John Gooden, Sam Ashurst and Greg Day.

With big thanks to the Wobble Club fund contributors for putting their money where their mouths were and kick-starting the publishing campaign: Lucia Armendariz Guerra, Luisa Victoria Armendariz Guerra, Jon Michael Davis, Katrina Hope Barber, Ant Timpson, Felina Louisa, Tatiana Brepson, Joao Fleck, Chris Collier, Naila Ma, Kevin Kopacka, Tom Sawyer, Jacky Lee Morgan, Tessa Farmer, Larry Meyler, Ricard Moon, Orlando Emmanuel Zuñig Navarrete, Janet Bell, Marcel Sarmiento, Chris O'Neill, Juliana Ross, Josie McCoy, Vince Watts, John Gooden, Adam Dix, Charlie Waterhouse, Martin Phipps, Rupert Mellor, Tim Grohne, Aniko Pall, Chris Tilly, James Jessop, Harold Chapman, Susan Dynner, Adam Goldworm, Marc Senter, Doug Buck, John Rolinson, Andrew Griffin, Jonathan Weeks, Mitch Davis, Karim Hussein, Britta Rogozinski, Dave Carter, Tot Taylor, Chris Jacobs, Stewart Buck, Tim League, Rob Hall, Harvey Fenton, Lindsay Mendes, Dan Clifton, Eduardo Panizzo, Giles Ross, Gaynor Hutton, Hannah Bassett, James Mottram, Hugh

Mendes, Eron Sheean, Ard Vin, Travis Sevens, Ed McGurn, Louise Burford, Antony Owen, Lisa Sofianos, Brian Hoyle, Jo George, Steven Shapiro, Laura Cruickshank, Dean Fisher, Buddy Giovinazzo, Susan York, Paul Knaus, Megan Tremethick, Lawrie Brewster, Brenden Beseth, Nigel Morris, Nigel Planer, Edwina Jackson, Milton Kam, Stephanie Trepanier, Rui Cheung, Grace Carley, Mike Riley, Alex Stone, Nigel Proktor, Paul Mayer, Nick Davey, Thomas Clay, Karen Unger, Phil Mucci, Greg Day, Mark Grundy, Matthew Kiernan, Madeleine Truman, Kevin Fullerton, James Silver and Doug Abbott.

With big thanks to: Phil Mucci, Lisa Sofianos and Lawrie Brewster for their invaluable social media and crowd-funding expertise.

With big thanks to: Jen and Sylvia Soska, Ard Vin, John Baker, Stuart Wright, William Wright, Blake Ethridge, Toby White and Rodrigo Gudiño for their social media shout-outs and/or help.

With big thanks to: Britt Pflüger and Elizabeth Fitzherbert for helping me navigate the literary world.

With big thanks to: Imogen Heath for her social media imagery and design, to Tom Clay for suggesting her and for Eduardo Panizzo for his design advice and help.

With big thanks to: James Silver for introducing me to John Bond and the whitefox publishing team.

* * *

**If you enjoyed reading *The Wobble Club*,
please leave a review on your local retailer's website**